The Battle Over Britain

July - September 1940

A Misfit Squadron Novel

Simon Brading

For the few and everyone else who has ever fought for freedom.

PROLOGUE

It was very peaceful at ten thousand feet, with the clear blue sky above and the patchwork quilt of England below. The only sounds were the rush of the wind past the canopy of the sleek Harridan fighter, the thrumming of the airscrew and the occasional creak of the massive spring beneath the cockpit releasing its tension. It was one of the reasons why Aviator Sergeant Gwen Stone loved flying so much; the freedom she felt was incomparable to anything she had ever felt on the ground.

It was almost enough to make her forget there was a war on, especially since in the month that the squadron had been formed and begun to operate she hadn't seen a single enemy aircraft. There had been scattered reports of enemy machines making incursions over the last couple of days and a few of the other squadrons had seen minor engagements with no losses on either side, but Gwen's squadron, number 145, based out of Didchurch, a small town just north of London, had yet to see any action whatsoever.

It was a situation that had the government and military leaders in Whitehall perplexed; because of the ease with which the forces of Kaiser Wilhelm III had crushed the forces of one country after another, then swept the British Exploration Force into the sea, it had seemed inevitable that the Kingdom of Britain would be next and indeed there were rumours of an invasion force gathering along the coasts of conquered France and Belgium, only twenty miles or so from the south of England. However, the expected and feared all-out assault on the British Isles hadn't materialised and instead Kaiser Bill had been keeping his aircraft at home, seemingly consolidating his forces on the continent. Consequently it had been a very quiet couple of weeks and that, combined with the surprisingly lovely summer weather, was making a lot of people complacent, pilots included.

Everybody agreed that it was only a matter of time before the attack came, though, and many people saw those recent aerial engagements as a sign that perhaps it was finally on its way.

Gwen agreed with that assessment and for her the fight couldn't come soon enough; she had business with the Prussians.

However, it was such a nice day that she was sorely tempted to let herself relax slightly and enjoy the flight for once. Flying in the Royal Aviator Corps wasn't like flying for fun back home on her parents' estate; added to the task of just keeping a finicky fighter in the air was the fact that she was constantly having to remain disciplined in her scan of the sky for enemies that were never there, but which might well be the next time she looked. She also had to worry about a damaged spring as well - the creaking that made her seat vibrate every couple of minutes was not only extremely distracting, it was also very worrying.

She'd been having problems with slippage for a week and under the RAC's own regulations the spring should have been repaired or replaced, but she had been forced to make do; it was impossible to open the case of an "Ozzy", an Ozymandias-type spring, outside of a specially-built facility (unless of course you wanted to have several miles of extremely sharp six inch wide brass uncoiling at high speed in every direction) and all the new ones that were being produced were needed for the fighters that the factories were turning out as quickly as they could.

Dealing with aircraft that weren't quite perfect was par for the course in wartime, though, and wouldn't have interfered with her enjoyment of the sortie too much, but she also had to deal with her flight leader's insistence on a far too tight formation, which meant she was having to keep almost half her attention focussed on her wing just to avoid a collision.

Needing fighter pilots desperately in the face of overwhelming Prussian numbers and after having lost so many in France, the bigwigs in Whitehall had brought dozens of pilots with experience from the First Great War, like Squadron Leader Albert "Berty" Withers, out of retirement when their army had been forced out of France. He insisted on maintaining an extremely tight formation, with wingtips almost overlapping (following regulations that were as out of date as his pilot's qualification) which had been fine in the Great War where airspeeds had been far more sedentary and you could almost have a break for tea while you waited for the enemy to close with you, but the advent of spring-power had revolutionised aircraft and they had become much more aerodynamic and a hell of a lot faster. The sleek spring-powered Harridans and Spitsteams that comprised the majority of the fighters of the Royal Aviator Corps were much different beasts to the old steam-powered Sapworth Dromedaries and such that the "flynosaurs", as they were not so affectionately known by the new breed of pilots, were used to. Even near the end of the war when designs became more efficient after British scientists worked out how to put automatic coal feeders in aircraft without risk of them catching fire, getting rid of the need to have space for an extra man, they were still extremely heavy, making them unwieldy and slow and not much faster than the zeppelin bombers that they had been designed to escort. In this war the enemy could be on you in an instant and every second spent checking your place in the formation was a second less spent scanning the sky, but most of the old pilots didn't seem to understand that and still went with the old theory that it was harder to pick aircraft off if they were bunched up together nice and neatly.

There was another ominous creak from below her seat, but much louder than the others had been, and she snarled as the needle on the tension indicator lurched closer to nought - it looked like her spring was getting worse which meant that today's flying time was going to be seriously curtailed, more so than other days.

With a sigh she keyed her microphone. 'Patin Leader, this is Three.'
'Go ahead, Patin Three.'
'I'm getting more slippage, Leader. Down to one-quarter tension.'
'Roger, Three. Damn that spring! Don't worry, we'll be turning for home in a couple of minutes anyway; there's no trade to be had today.'
'Acknowledged, Leader.'

Not for the first time Gwen cursed the spring; it had taken too much flying time in perfect conditions away from her, and that was something that neither she nor the rest of her squadron could afford - when the enemy, *Die Fliegertruppe* of the Prussian Empire, or the *Fleas* as they were derogatorily known in the British press, came across the channel, she and her colleagues would need as much experience as possible to withstand their superior numbers.

During each of the missions that she'd flown over the last couple of months Gwen had had various reasons to curse: the spring for slipping, her squadron leader for the formation, the war for ruining her life, the bright sun for potentially hiding the enemy, but she never cursed her aircraft; she would never do that. Despite its many shortcomings, the *Hawking Harridan* was a fine machine and, along with the *Supranaval Spitsteam*, it was the best that the Kingdom of Britain could rapidly mass-produce.

Gwen resumed her scan of the sky, moving her eyes along the horizon from one side to the other, then completing the circuit by lifting her head to look overhead, avoiding the sun so as not to blind herself. The movement was not nearly as automatic as it should have been yet, she still had to tell herself to do it, but she knew that it would come, if she survived long enough; the more experienced pilots said as much.

In the middle of a scan she hesitated, blinking, as her mind tried to tell her something. Had she seen something? She retraced her scan, going back the opposite way. There! Was that a dot or just a speck of dust on her canopy?

She was about to slide a magnification lens down over her goggles to take a better look when she was interrupted by a call over the radio.

'Close formation, please, Patin Three.'

A quick glance to the side showed that while she had been searching for the dot in the sky she had let a gap open up between herself and the squadron leader's aircraft, in turn forcing "Patin Four" to move over with her.

A few soft nudges on her rudder pedals was all it took to put her aircraft back into formation and she cursed Berty Withers silently before keying her microphone. 'Apologies, Leader.'

Gwen's attention had been elsewhere for less than ten seconds, but when she lifted her eyes to seek out the dot overhead it had grown into an aircraft and spouted fire.

'Break!' She threw her spring into maximum unwind, simultaneously pulled back on the stick to try to get out from between the two Harridans flanking her.

Her warning came far too late as tracer rounds were already penetrating the small formation.

The effect was instantaneous as the armour piercing ammunition of the Prussians ripped half of the squadron leader's wing off and he spun and went into a dive, narrowly missing Patin Two. Her own aircraft didn't come through unscathed either and it shuddered as at least two rounds struck it, opening up gaping holes in the metal of her left wing and damaging the frame beneath.

She had no idea how the other two aircraft in her flight fared, though, and she had no time to look for them as she threw her machine onto its wing and turned sharply after the Fleas.

There were four of them, *Muhlenberg MU9's*, agile fighters that had accounted for far too many pilots and aircraft over France.

Gwen had a few of seconds before they closed back into range and she used one to glance over her shoulder and look for the rest of her flight - there was no sign of them, but she thought she saw a flash of white far below, possibly from a glidewing.

She had no time to keep searching for them, though, because the MU9's were fast approaching.

Instead of climbing back into the sky they had banked and were coming around to get another shot at their victims, obviously supremely confident in their advantage and intending to turn fight.

Gwen grimaced; the Harridan was a wonderful gun platform, stable and capable of accurately delivering a weight of metal that rivalled the Frigates of the Napoleonic Conflict and was more than enough to take down bombers and heavy fighters. It was also fairly manoeuvrable and could out turn even a Spitsteam under certain conditions, but the MU9's were reportedly far more nimble and under normal circumstances she couldn't possibly hope to take on four of them.

Fortunately, though, she had an ace up her sleeve - she reached under her seat to a hidden panel, feeling the four switches there and flicked the one on the far right, praying that the modifications she had secretly made to the wings in the dead of the night over four long weeks hadn't been damaged by the two hits her machine had taken.

She was relieved to hear a high-pitched whirring sound as the small springs uncoiled, extending panels from the wings and altering their configuration. Now she just had to hope that having the odds in their favour and better machines would make the Fleas so sure of their victory that they would become complacent and make a mistake.

Whether they hadn't been expecting such a quick reaction on her part or they were just as inexperienced as she was, the enemy pilots had already made their first mistake by turning the way they had; instead of banking to come around behind her they had turned the other way and her increased rate of turn meant that she was inside them.

One by one the four aircraft came into range. She was unable to get all of them in her sights because they were at different altitudes, but two of them lazily crossed through her sights and she thumbed the button on her stick, holding it down for almost two seconds.

For the first time ever she fired in combat. The first of her rounds passed harmlessly in front of her intended target because she had overcompensated and led her target too far, but then the Flea obliged her by flying into the stream.

The enemy aircraft disintegrated, literally coming apart in the air.

Stunned, Gwen froze.

She had just killed someone.

The rattle of machine guns that weren't her own brought her crashing back to reality and she realised that she had been flying straight and level for several seconds - far too long.

She threw her machine on its wing and pulled hard back on the stick, stamping on the rudder pedals to stop it from diving straight down, feeling her weight multiply instantly by a factor of at least four, but probably more like six or seven. Black started to crowd in at the edges of her vision and she screamed wordlessly, trying to force some blood back into her brain to keep her awake, to keep her alive.

The forces acting on her lessened as her aircraft slowed and her vision cleared just in time to see of one of the MU9's beginning to slide under her nose. She held her fire, though, barely needing to think back to the lessons in flight school about leading targets under turning condition to know not to fire until she had come completely inside it.

Perhaps warned by one of his comrades, the fighter flipped onto its back and tried to dive out of her path, but that just made it easier for her and she made a quick adjustment, turning into a slight dive herself to intercept its path.

She watched the stream of tracers reaching out for the MU9, intercepting it and passing through it, but then it was gone, diving directly for the ground, now less than eight thousand feet below.

She let it go, knowing that it wouldn't be able to get back into the fight even if she hadn't hit it and swung her wings back to the vertical, returning to her tight turn and searching for the last two enemy machines.

Unable to find them, she frantically swung her head back and forth, positive that they were on her tail and about to open fire, but then, when she swung round on her second turn, she spotted them - they were a couple of thousand feet below her, in a shallow dive, heading for the coastline and home. Either she had scared them badly or, more likely, they were running out of spring tension; their bases were a lot further away than hers was.

She considered following them for a second, but there was another screech from below her seat as the spring slipped again and she blanched when she saw that she was down to less than ten percent tension.

A quick glance at the chalkboard with her notes of the flight's movements attached to her right thigh and a few quick calculations gave her an approximate heading for home and she turned the Harridan onto it.

The dogfight had lasted for less than a minute, but she had felt truly alive for the first time in her life; set free from the absurd constraints of formation flying she had finally been able to use her machine the way it was supposed to be used and it had been exhilarating.

Keeping half an eye on the two fighters in case their retreat was a ruse, she put her left hand on the stick and flexed her right; it was aching from the death grip she had been maintaining and was shaking slightly, which she hoped was more from adrenaline than from fear. She took a deep breath and rolled shoulders that had been up around her ears, then tilted her head back and forth, trying to release some of the tension that she hadn't even noticed had built up.

Only now did she replay the fight in her mind and she was amazed to realise that at no point had she even considered running. Fighting had been the correct decision because the MU's with their superior speed would have chased her down easily, but it hadn't even crossed her mind and she had gone at them like a terrier after rabbits. It had worked for her this time, but next time she might not be so lucky.

She reached out to touch the photo of a handsome young man attached to the top of her brushed brass instrument panel with clips that she had crudely soldered in place. She smiled and stroked his face with her gloved fingertips. 'Not yet, darling. Almost, but not quite.'

The enemy fighters had disappeared completely and there was no sign of anyone else in the sky so Gwen turned her attention downwards to the countryside below, looking for landmarks. She soon found a couple - the railway line which stopped at the town near the airfield, which she had used to go up to London on leave last weekend and the old castle on the top of the hill that she had visited once as a child with her parents not so many years ago.

She was only twenty miles from home. At her current speed of a little under three hundred miles an hour that was less than five minutes of flying.

There was another screech from the spring beneath her seat, but this one was far more prolonged and deathlike and the needle on the tension indicator firmly laid itself to rest against the stop that was marked by a red nought.

The Harridan slowed noticeably as the airscrew stopped creating thrust and Gwen cursed. She immediately put the aircraft into a shallow dive to conserve airspeed while she reached between her legs for the large, yellow and black striped lever on the floor - thankfully the Harridan and Spitsteam were both fitted with auxiliary springs, small units in the base of the pilot's seat. They were very weak, though; designed solely to give a pilot a little bit of control in the case of a complete failure of the main spring and were only capable of keeping an aircraft just above stall speed for three minutes. That on its own wouldn't be enough to get her home, but she had height to spare and was certain she'd be able to trade it for distance and make it all the way to the airfield.

The lever took a fair amount of tugging before it turned; the auxiliary spring had probably never been used before, or at least not since the fighter had been tested at the factory, and she offered a brief prayer to whoever was listening that the fitters had remembered to keep it wound.

The airscrew whirred into life as the new spring kicked in, but it was an incredibly feeble sound compared to the deep thrum of before.

She tentatively pulled back on the stick until the Harridan was level and was gratified to see the airspeed indicator remain stable at two hundred and fifty miles per hour. She throttled back slightly and put the craft back into a shallow dive, wanting to conserve some tension for landing.

Ten miles. Four thousand feet. It was going to be very close.

As she got lower, the landscape below became clearer and she started to recognise more and more of the local landmarks.

There was the country pub that most of the squadron had gone to one night, following rumours of a particularly good local brew that had turned out to be barely drinkable, but hadn't prevented them from draining several casks of it before being turfed out in the early hours of the morning to drunkenly drive home.

Up ahead was the church and the graveyard where they had buried one of their own after he had crashed on landing in high winds.

There was the field where another of her squadron had been forced to land when her spring had broken shortly after takeoff, breaking through its case to drape metal into the trees below. She had survived. Barely. But would never fly again.

And there was RAC Didchurch, just beyond the small town that gave it its name, its grass field browned from use and flanked by row upon row of low red brick buildings.

As if it was mocking her, the moment she spotted the airfield was the moment that the auxiliary spring chose to run out of tension.

She cursed for about the tenth time that flight as she reached down to pump the lever backwards and forwards a couple of times in frustration, but nothing happened - the reserve spring had evidently reached its end; months of not being used had most likely caused it to lose some of its tension and it almost certainly hadn't been checked every week like it should have been.

The airfield was now only a couple of miles away, but her airspeed was dropping fast, along with her altitude. It was not too late to divert and bring the Harridan down in a field, but that was a risky proposition in itself; there would be no way of knowing until she was too close to do anything about it whether the field had drainage channels or tree stumps or furrows from ploughing. Even too-high crops might be enough to catch around her wheels and send her cartwheeling. No, it was better to try for the airfield, so she aimed for it and set the aircraft on its optimal glide angle and speed.

They had practised dead-stick landings at flight school and she had flown gliders before, but she had never had to land under these conditions, with damage to her aircraft and very little altitude to play with.

A quick glance was enough to tell her that she was below the optimal altitude, but she hadn't taken into account the effect that her modifications had on the aircraft - the same principles that had allowed her to turn faster now gave her more lift and she found that she was able to put the aircraft into a shallower glide.

One hundred feet.

Fifty feet.

Twenty feet.

Ten.

She curled her toes and held her breath as she cleared the hedges at the end of the field by about two feet with the controls becoming less responsive and the stick shaking in her hands as the aircraft reached its stall point and began protesting.

The Harridan all but fell out of the sky and bounced heavily, jolting her and making her teeth snap together as her chin hit her chest. It rolled for less than a hundred feet before her gentle application of the brakes brought it to a halt level with the brick building that contained the messes and the ready rooms.

She sighed and pulled her helmet from her head, careful not to damage the integrated goggles with their array of magnification lenses, then plucked the photo from the panel and put it in her flightsuit pocket. She pulled back the canopy and closed her eyes as the late spring breeze cooled her sweaty brow and ruffled her mousy brown hair.

She looked up as voices carried to her; people were wandering out of the mess building, attracted by her unusual method of arrival - officers and men, aircrew and groundcrew, all coming to see what the fuss was about.

She unstrapped herself, releasing herself from both the aircraft and her glidewings, then struggled to her feet. Her legs and arms were shaking and reluctant to obey her control and it took her three attempts before she managed to clamber out of the cockpit. Then, not trusting herself, she sat on the front of the wing and all but slid down to the ground where she leaned heavily against the machine.

Her eye was drawn to a hole in the wing beside her, the first of three in a line, neatly spaced about two feet apart. It was almost four inches wide and went diagonally all the way through the wing. She bent down and peered through it, following the path of the shot backwards - it had missed the canopy, and her head within, by less than a foot.

She swallowed as she realised what a close call she'd had and her legs buckled beneath her.

She was saved from a tumble by the arms of a medical orderly. 'Steady, there, luv! You alright? Anything hurt?'

He was a northerner, his accent placing his origins as somewhere around Newcastle. His grey hair also placed him well beyond the age when he should have retired and been spending the rest of his life at home comfortably with his grandchildren, but people had come from all over and from all walks of life to join in the effort of saving their country and men like him with medical training were sorely needed.

She shook her head mutely, unable to speak and he nodded in sympathy. 'That's alright, luv, you just take your time.'

'Aviator Sergeant Stone! What's this all about? Where are the rest of your flight?'

Gwen gave the orderly a weak smile then forced her legs to straighten so she could stand to attention and face the base commander.

The orderly released her and stepped back, but he remained a presence at her side, ready to catch her if she fell, and she was glad for that as her knees trembled, threatening to pitch her on her face.

'We were jumped by four MU9's, ma'am. Squadron Leader Withers went down in the first pass, I think that Echols and Perkins were hit too, but I saw at least one glidewing deploy. I got one definite and another probable before they disengaged to head home.'

The base commander, Group Captain Dorothy Campbell, a Scottish woman in her early fifties, had been a pilot in the Great War, an ace. She had flown with Berty Withers and the news of his death rendered her silent for a few seconds. She stared off into the distance, perhaps commending his soul to whatever old pilots believed in.

The group captain was fresh from the mess, where she had obviously been dining with guests because she was wearing her full-dress uniform. The gold "scrambled egg" on her tall top hat with its purple silk band was gleaming in the sun and her long coat, the blue of the English summer sky just before sunset, with its built in whalebone corset and double row of gold buttons over flaring skirts, was immaculately pressed. She would have looked extremely impressive, but the effect was spoiled somewhat by the fact that she still had her napkin tucked into her high collar. She was accompanied by a wing commander who Gwen didn't know, but who was equally smartly dressed, although sans napkin and without the egg on her hat, of course.

The wing commander was staring at the wing of the Harridan, but when she felt Gwen's eyes upon her she turned and her slate grey eyes met Gwen's green ones. She raised an eyebrow and tilted her head minutely towards the wing and at first Gwen thought she was silently commenting on the holes, but then the blood drained from her face as she realised that she had forgotten to return the wing to its standard, regulation configuration.

The wing commander saw her expression and gave her a barely perceptible nod, then reached out to take the group captain by the arm. 'Come on, Dot, let's go raise HQ on the radio, see if anyone has reported your pilots coming down. Perhaps Berty bailed out in time.'

She began to drag the base commander away, but the older woman stopped suddenly, frowning, her eyes on Gwen's Harridan. She pulled her arm away from the wing commander's grasp and walked to the fighter, taking in the panels that had extended from the tailing edges and tips of the wings.

She sighed and shook her head, then turned to Gwen. 'Aviator Sergeant Stone.'

'Yes, Ma'am.' Gwen stiffened, knowing what was coming.

The woman checked her pocket watch. 'You have until four to clean yourself up and eat. At that time you are to report to the detention barracks. Is that clear?'

'Yes, Ma'am.'

'Dismissed.'

Gwen drew herself up even more and nodded, then turned and marched towards the building and the non-commissioned officer's mess. The watching throng of people opened up in front of her and she walked through them with as much dignity as she could, praying all the time that her legs wouldn't give in and betray her distress.

CHAPTER 1

"Interfering with one of the King's Flying Machines" was a serious offence, one punishable by a long stretch at His Majesty's pleasure and Gwen spent the next two weeks in a cell in the detention barracks with her flying privileges revoked and only two hours of exercise a day outdoors in the hot July sun.

The base commander had visited her the day after her incarceration to give her the news - the wreckage of two Prussian fighters had been found near where she had reported the fight taking place, but three RAC fighters had also been found. Only one of the pilots in her flight, Aviator Sergeant Echols, had turned up alive - it had been his glidewing she had seen. The bodies of the other two, Squadron Leader Withers and Aerial Officer Perkins, had been found inside the wreckage of their aircraft, each riddled with bullets. They had died instantly in the initial attack.

With the news came guilt and she had gone through the moments preceding the attack over and over in her mind, wondering what would have happened if she'd ignored the order to close the formation and instead had kept her eyes on that high-above dot, using her lenses to resolve it into the fighters with their dull grey camouflage pattern. She might have saved them all if she'd done that, but instead of following the instincts of self-preservation which had been telling her that something wasn't right, she had followed the ones that had been drummed into her in basic training and throughout flight school, the ones which had told her to instantly obey the orders of superior officers, no matter how much she disagreed with them.

She had replayed the following dogfight as well, remembering the way the first MU9 had disintegrated under her guns. Each time the aircraft blew apart in her mind she felt the same things she had felt in the moment; elation that was almost instantly replaced by horror, which she had been forced to put aside in order to fight for her life.

She still wasn't quite sure how she felt about the fact that someone had died at her hands - part of her was horrified, of course, but at least part of her was glad that there was one less enemy to kill her people, her friends, her...

She had blocked out that train of thought before it had even started and tried to find something else to occupy her mind.

During those two weeks the war over Britain had started in earnest. The patrol that had caught Gwen's flight had been only one of many incursions by the Prussian Empire that day and they had proved to be the start of a serious aerial assault on the British Isles. Since then things had gone very badly for the Royal Aviator Corps. Losses had been high and Gwen's squadron wasn't the only one that lost almost half its members in the first week alone. Some had even been reduced so far that they had been merged with others until new pilots could be trained.

Throughout it all she was stuck in her cell.

No matter how much she pleaded with the base commander and the new squadron commander they wouldn't let her out, wouldn't let her get in an aircraft and help, no matter how low their numbers fell - if there was one thing that the Kingdom of Britain's military was known for, it was that discipline was paramount, and she had shown a flagrant disregard for that, which meant she was no longer trustworthy in their eyes.

The two weeks had passed slowly, torturously, but then, one day, around mid-morning, two military guards came for her. She was almost relieved, thinking that she was finally on her way to her court martial, and the way they roughly bundled her into the back of a guard wagon along with her kitbag only seemed to confirm that.

Neither of the MG's answered any of her questions about where they were going and there were no windows in the wagon, so the only thing she could do was close her eyes and listen to the rain pounding on the metal shell of the wagon while she tried to come up with some way to defend herself in front of the tribunal, but try as she might, she couldn't find an acceptable reason for what she had done. No matter her reasons, no matter her success, the truth was that she was guilty and there was no way of getting around it. Pointing out she had gotten two kills using her modifications would do nothing to help her, in fact it was more likely to hurt her case; the British like a braggart even less than they like someone who has broken discipline.

Eventually she came to the conclusion that the only thing she could do was hope that they were lenient and that their need for pilots was greater than their need to making an example of one lowly sergeant.

It was a forlorn hope, but it was all she had.

The ride took two extremely uncomfortable hours, the last five minutes of which were along an extremely bumpy road, which mystified Gwen; she had assumed that they were taking her to London to face a court martial in Whitehall, or at least to a Glasshouse closer to the city, but she doubted that there were roads around the capital as rough as the one they were travelling on.

The mystery deepened when the wagon stopped, the rear doors were flung open and she stepped out of the vehicle and onto what she assumed was an RAC base, but was the strangest one she'd ever seen.

For practical reasons most, if not all air bases, had their buildings grouped on one side of the landing field, except for perhaps the fire control station or the ammunition dump; it was incredibly inconvenient to have to cross an airstrip to get from one building to another, not only for the distance involved, but also because you never knew when you might have to play an impromptu game of British Bulldog with an aircraft. For some reason, though, this one had been laid out with two lines of buildings facing each other across the landing field. The buildings themselves were also quite strange, at least on the side of the airfield that she was on. They were of a design that was, to say the least, *atypical* of RAC bases - they had none of the hastily thrown together but sturdy aspect of the buildings on every other base she'd ever been on, nor had they been constructed cheaply and efficiently with brick and iron, but were made of stone and had a quantity of ornamentation and detailing that spoke of an investment of time that the RAC's engineers never put in because it was completely unnecessary and they couldn't afford it. In fact the buildings gave the base more the aspect of an upmarket holiday camp than a military installation, even though just about everything had been painted green, including the dozen or so deckchairs folded and stacked up in front of the nearest building.

The buildings on the other side of the airfield were much more like what she was used to, though, and if it hadn't been for them she might well have doubted that she was on an RAC base at all. They were simple but elegant structures of corrugated metal over a wrought iron frame, with flat sides and gently sloping roofs that came to an obtuse triangle in the middle - the same type of building that could be found on most of the RAC stations that had been hurriedly founded and populated over the last three or four years since the rumours of war began. There were ten of them in a long line, identically constructed and identically green, but of several different sizes, from the single huge one on the end that seemed like it could have enclosed Buckingham Palace, to the half dozen small ones that were not much bigger than the one she had at home.

The airstrip itself was narrower than usual and the only thing that told her it was used as such was its faded and worn nature, although there was an agricultural truck driving along it with two men in the back dumping great forkfuls of cut grass onto it, obviously in an effort at concealment and it seemed that an immense effort was being made to keep the base hidden, especially from the air. Many of the buildings were not just painted green, but were also draped with netting to camouflage them and there were trees everywhere, not the low variety that were spotted around most bases almost as an afterthought, but tall ones that shaded them and overhung them and undoubtedly caused hazards for the aircraft.

While she was curious about the entire base, it was the largest of the buildings on the far side of the strip to which her attention inexorably returned. Its enormous doors were pulled half-way open and in the shadows of the hangar, made deeper by the bright sunlight outside, she could just about make out several aircraft of designs that she had never seen before - personal aircraft, as individual as their designers, which had no business being on a military base and she felt her feet automatically taking her towards the hangar for a closer look, but a stern voice brought her back before she could do anything that the MG's might use as an excuse to punish her for.

'Aviator Sergeant Stone!'

Gwen turned to find the wing commander who had been there on the day of her shame coming from the building that the wagon had stopped outside - a command post bristling with radar antennae. She wasn't in full dress uniform this time, but rather a normal day uniform like Gwen. It was the exact same blue colour as the dress uniform, but infinitely more practical with trousers instead of voluminous skirts and no corset. The buttons on her short tunic top, forming an elegant V-shape, were gold instead of the brass on Gwen's and her top hat was six inches high and purple-banded, as befitting an officer, instead of the three inches and blue band that Gwen as a non-commissioned officer warranted.

Gwen snapped to attention, her hand coming up to touch the brim of her hat, her palm towards the woman.

The wing commander returned the salute, then smiled warmly. 'As you were, sergeant.'

Gwen relaxed, but only slightly; she was still worried about why she was there - for all she knew this was some kind of strange labour camp, although that was looking less likely by the second.

The woman came to stand in front of her and looked her up and down and Gwen did the same, albeit less overtly.

The woman was much younger than she had thought she was when she'd first seen her - perhaps in her early thirties. She seemed far too young to hold the rank that she did, but there was an air of experience and confidence about her that told Gwen that she had earned it. However, there was also a sorrow in her eyes that spoke of a life lived with too much loss and the lines on her forehead were deeper than they should have been for her age, speaking of intense and constant worry.

The wing commander nodded, apparently satisfied with what she saw and turned to the MG's. 'Thank you, I'll take custody of the prisoner now.'

The MG's came to attention and saluted smartly, then got back into the wagon and drove away, the steam-powered vehicle puffing merrily as it bounced across the airfield and turned into one of the larger buildings a bit further down.

'My name is Abigail Lennox, but everyone calls me Abby. I'm in command of this base and the single squadron that operates from it.'

Hope bloomed in Gwen's heart. 'Does that mean...?'

The woman nodded. 'Yes, you have been released into my custody pending my assessment of your usefulness. However this is only a temporary reprieve. If you prove useful and as good a pilot as you are a mechanic, then I will keep you. If not, then it is straight back to where you came from.'

'How...?'

'I have friends in high places and what I want, I get.'

The wing commander winked, then glanced over Gwen's shoulder in the direction the young woman had been staring when she'd called her name and jerked her chin at the enormous building. 'Let's go take a look, shall we?'

Without waiting for an answer, she walked across the airstrip, seemingly uncaring that the wet grass clippings stuck to her highly polished shoes and Gwen had to hurry to catch up with her.

'Where are we, ma'am?'

The wing commander glanced at Gwen out of the corner of her eye. 'Why do you want to know? Are you a spy?'

'A spy? No! Of course not! I'm not!' She stuttered, protesting her innocence, but then went bright red when she saw the grin on the woman's face.

'Relax, Gwen, and please, call me Abby.' The woman stopped in the middle of the field. 'As you might have guessed this used to be a holiday camp for the well to do and their scions to mix in comfort during the summer months and do things like show off their jewels and find good matches for their children. It closed about five years ago when rumours of war started and the King started his austerity campaign and we got hold of it a year or so ago. The engineer boys put up the hangars and workshops for us, but most of what we inherited were sports and leisure facilities, which have been converted to our purposes - for example: you're standing on what's left of the cricket pitch.' She grinned as she stamped on the grass. 'I think you'll agree we're putting it to much better use.'

Gwen chuckled and nodded enthusiastically. 'Definitely! I hate cricket!'

'Me too! Just don't let Bruce hear you say that.' She returned Gwen's laugh, then turned to face the row of elegant buildings behind them. She pointed at the building at the end furthest from them. 'That was an ice rink, but we didn't really need one of those so it was converted into offices for the admin staff. We barely have any of those, though, so it was mostly open space until some of the people on the base converted it to a roller-skating rink - there's plenty of skates available, if that's something that interests you. There was a Lido beyond it, but unfortunately it had to be drained and filled in; it was a bit too obvious from the air. We kept some of the deckchairs though, as you can see, but painted them; they were red and yellow and using them would have been a bit of a giveaway from the air.'

She pointed to the building next to what was the ice rink, which was of a similar construction and size. 'That one contained the Fives courts, but it's the medical centre now. We found a couple of dozen penny-farthings in a rack round the back of it, but I had to have them taken away when people started to race them around the woods when they were drunk.'

She waved vaguely at the other buildings in the row. 'The building I was in when you arrived used to have a model railway in it, but that got half-inched by the engineers and it now holds the radio and command staff. The rest have been converted to dining halls for officers, NCO's and enlisted men and women. There's another dozen or so buildings behind them which were mostly dormitories and have been kept as such, but there was also a ballroom which has been turned into the briefing hall.'

Abby turned and continued walking towards the hangar. 'And as for where we are, geographically - we're in the middle of nowhere, literally, pretty much slap bang in the middle of the Kent Downs. Maidstone is ten miles almost due west of us and Canterbury is about fifteen miles as good as due east. There are a couple of villages nearby, but there are about ten people in each of them and barely even count as villages. And before you ask, the nearest pub is in Maidstone, but there's no need to worry, the messes are fully stocked!'

'Oh, good.' Gwen refrained from telling the woman that it wasn't just alcohol she looked for in the public houses she frequented; informing her new commander that she craved the company of people who had nothing to do with flying or the RAC might not be the best way of ingratiating herself to her. Although, if Abby were to be believed and Gwen's flying abilities and mechanical talents were all that mattered to her, then she probably wouldn't care.

'We're pretty self-sufficient here, actually. We get fresh provisions brought in every day, of course, but we have a water aquifer, several fields of vegetables and even a few dozen chicken runs in the woods somewhere. We've also got a huge steam-powered generator buried at the edge of the base, accessible by a hidden ramp, which provides power to the whole base off the main hydrogen supply. In an emergency we could hold out for a few months without resupply, although there would be a revolution long before that because the beer stocks probably wouldn't last more than a couple of days.'

The woman grinned again, then lapsed into silence because by this time they were nearing the hangar, which had a large white "1" painted on it.

Gwen was now able to make out more details of the strange aircraft within and her steps faltered, her mouth opening in a mixture of surprise, wonder, fascination and not a little desire.

The wing commander halted just inside the doors, giving Gwen a few seconds to take in the sight.

Twelve aircraft of vastly different designs were scattered around the huge space, not quite filling it, but not failing by much. They were brightly painted in every imaginable colour and every possible pattern in stark contrast to the extreme drabness and camouflage of the rest of the base, and seemed almost to shine with a light of their own in the shade of the hangar. The only thing that they had in common was the roundel of the Royal Aviator Corps, a rampant red lion on a sky blue disk, although she could also see that underneath every single one of the cockpits were painted multiple iron crosses of the Fliegertruppe denoting the enemy aircraft they had shot down.

'The squadron is divided into three flights of four aircraft. I lead A flight.' Abby pointed to three small aircraft grouped to the right of them, two biplanes and a monoplane. They were stubby with fairly thick wings giving them plenty of lift. 'We are the turn fighters, responsible for engaging enemy fighters.' Next she turned to point at the four much larger fighters on the left side of the hangar. 'B flight are our interceptors. They're fast and pack a punch. They go after the enemy bombers.' Lastly she indicated the four remaining aircraft in the centre of the hangar, taking up most of the room. 'C flight is our support wing. The big one at the back with the eye-aching camo pattern is our combination bomber and gun platform, the silver one over there is our high-altitude spotter and spy, the small one next to it is our low-level scout, and the blue one is our radar and command platform.'

'Radar? In an aircraft?' Gwen raised an eyebrow sceptically.

The woman grinned. 'As I said before - what I want, I get.' She walked diagonally across the space to the right, heading for the far corner. They passed under the wing of the gigantic six-engined bomber, giving Gwen a good view of the various gun pods studding its fuselage.

Behind all of the machines was the twelfth aircraft. It had been pushed into the corner and was surrounded by piles and piles of spare parts and things that looked like they had been salvaged from scrapped aircraft. It was black with yellow flashes and as they got closer Gwen was able to make out that it was a wreck.

The wing commander gestured at it, the smile now completely gone from her face. 'This one's going to be yours. The pilot... well, let's just say she didn't make it and her aircraft has been sitting here for a couple of months now, ever since Dunkirk. It's past time it was restored.'

Gwen looked the machine over and frowned; it wasn't the type of aircraft that she would have chosen to build and it was also more damaged than she had first though - there were multiple gaping holes in the mainplane and fuselage, the canopy lying on the floor next to it had a couple of ominous holes in it, it was sitting on supports because the undercarriage was bent and broken, and much of the tailplane was missing. It was a miracle it had been able to land at all.

Lennox saw her sour expression and mirrored it. 'Would you rather be back in your factory-standard Harridan or Spitsteam, outclassed by Muhlenbergs and Hock-Hunds and unable to do anything to your government-approved machine to swing the odds in your favour? Oh, that's right, you did. And you shot down two. And they locked you up for it.' A small smile crossed her lips. 'I won't.'

Gwen bit her lip as she looked at the aircraft. 'It's a wonderful machine...'

'But?'

'I hoped that you were going to let me build my own aircraft, not make me repair someone else's. If you just give me a couple of weeks...'

Abby interrupted her sharply. 'Maybe one day I'll let you do that, but we don't have two weeks, we need someone in a machine now. She's a good craft, designed by a good woman and she's far better than anything any other squadron has got. She's a turn fighter as you can see by her lines and like all of our fighters she's designed to take dual springs for long-range operations.'

'Dual springs?'

'Yes, the second spring is mounted underneath the other one, back to back, and can be jettisoned at any time. It almost doubles the range of our fighters.' She gestured at a pile of round brass boxes, eight inches thick and six feet wide, on the far side of the hangar near the door. 'Don't worry, we have plenty of spare Ozzy's if we need them.'

Gwen stared at the Ozymandias springs. There were at least forty of them in the tall pile, still with the factory sheen on them. She could hardly believe that the squadron had them lying around doing nothing when they were so sorely needed elsewhere and to hear that they just jettisoned them when they were used up seemed like sacrilege - she had spent two weeks fighting with a slipping spring, which had almost killed her on that last flight and she wondered how many other pilots had died after experiencing the same problem, or had a spring fail in the middle of battle. That many Ozzy's could have saved quite a few lives.

She felt like screaming in rage, but she said nothing and the wing commander went on, oblivious to Gwen's seething emotions.

'I'm putting you on my wing so I can keep an eye on you, but I don't expect you to just keep quiet and obey orders; we are losing right now and traditional warfare isn't going to cut it, so if you have any suggestions, any ideas as to how we can turn things around, I want to hear them. Chain of command be damned, you come straight to me. Understood?'

Gwen nodded. 'Understood. And thank you for this chance...'

Abby shook her head, interrupting her again. 'Don't thank me; I needed a pilot and you were the best one available - I don't know if you've noticed, but there aren't many of us alive anymore. Look, I know who you are and I know your pedigree, but that doesn't matter to me one bit. All I care about is what you did to your Harridan and how you handled yourself against those Fleas. Understood?'

Gwen nodded and the woman went on. 'I'm taking a chance with you, Stone, hoping that you will bring something to this squadron, but rest assured, I *will* shoot you down myself if you do *anything* to endanger the rest of my pilots. I have a hell of a lot more experience than you and I expect you to obey my orders in the air, but while we're on the ground discipline is more relaxed and you are to have an opinion. That's an order.'

'Yes, ma'am!' Gwen smiled; it sounded like she had landed in the right place.

The wing commander gave her a curt nod of satisfaction. 'Good. You have three days to get her operational.'

'Three...?'

'Yes. Three.' The woman grinned. 'I hope you don't like to sleep!'

Gwen frowned and looked at the damaged machine. If she stuck to just doing repairs it would just about be possible to get it flying in three days, but she wouldn't have time to make any modifications. Which might have been one of the wing commander's motivations in giving her so little time.

'Do you have somewhere to shape Duralumin panels or do I have to provide specifications for them to be done elsewhere?'

'Hut four is a fully equipped metallurgy shop and the fitters shape all our panels in there. They even have raw materials to create anything special we want - Wendy, our armourer makes good use of that, I can tell you!'

'Good.' Gwen nodded somewhat absentmindedly, her thoughts already racing ahead as she stared at the aircraft; having the panels shaped on the base would make things a lot quicker and easier and she might actually be able to squeeze in a few of her changes in the time available after all.

Abby smiled at Gwen's distraction, correctly reading it for what it was. 'Well, have a quick look at your machine, but only a quick one, mind you, then report to the officer's mess in fifteen minutes; it's nearly lunch time and I want to introduce you to the rest of the pilots. It's the building on the end.'

The woman turned to go, but paused and glanced back over her shoulder. 'Oh, one last thing.' She smiled. 'Welcome to Misfit Squadron.'

CHAPTER 2

Gwen spent the first few minutes of her allotted time standing staring after the wing commander, replaying her last words over and over and trying to get her mind around the implications of them.

Misfit Squadron.

The squadron was a legend, a myth almost, like *Father Winter*, or the *Dark Scythesman*. The stories that circulated about them in hushed tones were of reject pilots who had been thrown out of the regular RAC, carrying out impossible acts of derring-do in aircraft that they had built themselves - deeds of heroism and courage in defence of the Kingdom of Britain, all while finding the time to shoot down more enemy aircraft in France than the rest of the RAC combined, although the fact that they were supposedly so invincible and dominant, yet still hadn't been able to do anything to prevent the British defeat on the continent had always troubled her personally and prevented her from entirely believing the stories.

She had assumed they were just propaganda, invented by Whitehall to raise the morale of troops facing defeat, certainly not real, like the Crimson Barons, the elite Prussian squadron that had rampage absolutely unchecked across the battlefields of Europe and terrorised the RAC in France, yet here she was on their secret base in the wilds of Kent, standing among their incredible machines.

However, not even the prospect of joining the most famous, or infamous, squadron in the RAC was enough to keep her from an aircraft for very long and she quickly turned her attention back to the task ahead. She had just enough time to do a quick assessment of the entire machine before she had to go.

Unlike the Harridan, which was very simply constructed by putting metal plates on a complete skeletal structure, this machine was more like a Spitsteam, more like the last aircraft she had built for herself, with what looked like a semi-monocoque design, which meant that its metal skin formed part of its load-bearing structure and was bolted to twenty or so "formers" or "frames" which were essentially cross-sections of the aircraft. It made the construction and repair process much more laborious and time-consuming, but in return it allowed the aircraft to have a much thinner and more aerodynamic wing, which was the reason why the Spitsteam was so fast and manoeuvrable while the Harridan was more of a workhorse. The frames she could see seemed to be mostly undamaged (except of course for the missing tail, which she would have to find from somewhere) and it looked like it would mostly be a case of shaping new Duralumin panels to replace the ones with holes in or twisted by the rough landing.

After looking at the wings and the fuselage, she reluctantly turned her attention to the cockpit.

When the wing commander had told her that the pilot hadn't survived and she'd seen the state of the canopy she'd been afraid of what she would find, but she was relieved to see that somebody had cleaned away any blood that there might have been. The instrument panel was smashed, but she didn't mind too much about that; she would have changed its configuration to suit her own preferences anyway.

Her mind was still working furiously while she walked back across the airfield and she had to force herself to relax and stop when she got to the door of the officer's mess; it wouldn't do to appear distracted in front of her new wingmates.

She knocked and entered the mess hesitantly; as a non-commissioned officer, an NCO, she wasn't strictly allowed in - NCO's had their own mess, just like the enlisted men had theirs. However, she had been invited by the base commander, so if anybody questioned her she would be able to give that as a reason for her presence.

The room she found herself in was fairly large with a bar along one wall and sofas everywhere. There was no sign of the Wing Commander anywhere, but Gwen barely noticed; she was too engrossed with taking in the trophies hanging on the walls.

Every base that housed RAC squadrons which had seen successful action had their trophies in their various messes. They were pieces of aircraft they had shot down, usually labelled with the date, place and the name of the pilot responsible for the kill, but no mess she had been in had quite so many as this one and the haul was even more incredible considering that the base housed only a single squadron, rather than the three or four that was more usual.

However, it was the sight of the four red-painted vertical stabilisers in various states of disrepair, hanging in pride of place over the bar, that was most shocking to her because they were something she had *never* seen before; only one enemy squadron painted their machines red - the Crimson Barons, the elite Fliegertruppe squadron comprising the best Prussian pilots and flying the best fighters that they could put in the air. To her knowledge nobody had *ever* shot down even a single one of them, yet here were four trophies.

She began to walk towards the nearest one, but was intercepted by a waiter dressed in an evening suit with sergeant's stripes on his arm.

She tore her eyes away from the trophies and blinked at him. 'Uh, I'm here to...'

He smiled at her awkwardness and just gave her a small bow, not much more than a nod. 'This way, Aviator.'

She got a slightly better look at the trophies, but only very briefly in passing, as she followed him along the length of the burnished mahogany bar towards a door on the far side of the room, which he pulled open for her, gesturing for her to go in with another small bow.

She went through the door somewhat tentatively and came to an immediate halt when she found herself in a dining room like no other she'd ever seen.

Intricate wrought iron columns were set around the outside of the large square room. They were formed into tree trunks, as delicate as spun sugar, which divided high overhead, extending twisting metal branches out across the room. Thousands upon thousands of graceful iron deciduous leaves hung from these branches, completely concealing the ceiling, forming a marvellous woodland canopy and in among them were hundreds of tiny lights, animated by some ingenious clockwork mechanism hidden above the leaves, which made them spin and dance in and around the beautiful foliage as if they were fey or fireflies. The effect was truly magical and easily visible in the shadows high up in the eaves, despite the fact that the heavy-looking deep-blue velvet curtains on the windows were drawn back to let in the sunshine, but Gwen wondered how much light they would actually provide when night fell. That doubt was dispelled, though, when she noticed the iron globe resting against the wall to her left; it was attached to a delicate filigree arch that spanned the room from one side to the other and filled with lights that were currently unlit - a lunar orb that would march across a sky formed by a roof of leaves over the course of a night.

The large space underneath the "trees" was mostly filled by two long wooden tables, made to look like they were two rough planks that had been hewn from two fallen trunks. They were surrounded by chairs, which were delicate and asymmetrical, in keeping with the magical air created by the decor. They appeared far too fragile to be sat in, although the way that at least a couple of the pilots were tilting them back showed that they were much stronger than they looked. The tables could have easily sat two dozen or so people each, but there were only eleven people in the room, six men and five women, all sitting around the closest table to her, all wearing RAC day uniforms, all with angel's wings over their hearts.

These were the pilots of Misfit Squadron.

Gwen was surprised to see that they all looked so very *ordinary*, not at all like what she'd expected ace pilots to look like, although every single one of them, even the youngest, a blonde woman who must have been barely out of her teens, had a look about them, a composure and an awareness, that spoke of an experience she knew that she herself sorely lacked. They were obviously a close-knit group as well, though, and they were lounging comfortably in their chairs, completely relaxed and not at all on edge like most of the pilots she knew.

One of the men was speaking to the group in a lilting Welsh voice that was rather fitting to the setting and the other pilots were smiling as they listened, but there was a strangely sorrowful tone to the scene, even as they laughed at his retelling.

Gwen stood quietly by the door, both because she didn't want to interrupt and also because she quite wanted to hear the story the man was telling.

'...eight of them, going around in that circle they like, chasing their tails, and we couldn't get *close* to these blighters! You know how it is, when you get behind one, the one behind him has you in his sights - and you really don't want to be in the sights of an MU10, right?'

There were chuckles and agreements at that, but the man continued on without pause.

'So, anyway, we'd been circling around them for what must have been about five minutes, waiting for something to happen when Cece comes over the radio and says "bugger this for a game of soldiers!" and dives down at them.

'Of course we all thought she was going to go straight at them and get a bellyful of lead, but she keeps going down until she's underneath them, then pulls up sharply and only bloody pops up in the middle of them and starts circling - she's going one way, they're all going the other way and she shoots down three of the buggers before they even realised she was there which was when they panicked and broke in every direction. We bagged another two of them, but the rest got away. Still, five out of eight isn't bad for a day's work and they certainly didn't try that trick again!'

The man finished his story to more laughter and as the pilots sought the next distraction they finally noticed Gwen. The looks they gave her were curious and wary, especially after they had had time to take in the wings sewn to her chest, identical to their own.

The wing commander had her back to Gwen but she saw their curious gazes and turned to smile at her. She stood and came to her side. 'Everyone! This is Gwen Stone, she's Cece's replacement.'

There were uncertain looks from many of the pilots around the table, as if they hadn't been expecting the news or if it weren't entirely welcome, and Gwen shifted uncomfortably as a couple of them even frowned at her.

The man who had been telling the story smiled at her, though. 'Stone... That's a rather inauspicious name for a pilot.'

'It was my husband's name.'

'Was?'

'He was shot down over France in the first weeks of the war.'

The man's smile immediately fell from his face and was replaced by a look of sympathy. He didn't offer anything as trite as an apology, but simply lifted his glass silently, a gesture that was mirrored by the whole squadron.

Once they had all drank and placed their glasses back on the table, Gwen met the man's eyes and deliberately smiled, nodding her thanks. 'It could have been worse; I could have been in the Navy.'

There was a moment's silence as the pilots replayed the conversation in their heads, but then it was broken by guffaws and barks of laughter.

It had been a feeble joke, but it had broken the ice and warmed them to her.

The wing commander patted her on the shoulder and leaned in to speak softly in her ear. 'Nicely done. I apologise for the cool reception, but you have to understand that you are replacing someone who was loved and had been with us for a long time. She was also the first pilot we ever lost, so you can understand that it's not about *who* you are, but rather *what* you represent.'

Gwen nodded. 'I understand.'

'Good.' Abby smiled. 'I think you'll fit in very well here.' She gestured at the gathered pilots who had returned to their conversations and drinks. 'They are all talented pilots and most of them are brilliant engineers, but each has a streak of individuality and a restless mind that doesn't exactly mix well with the rigid discipline of the regular squadrons of the Royal Aviator Corps. Remind you of anyone?'

Gwen blushed slightly and the woman laughed and gave her another hearty pat on the shoulder. 'Come on, let's sit down. We were just about to eat.'

Gwen frowned at her. 'Shouldn't I go to the NCO's mess?'

'No. We're pilots, not officers and NCO's, and in this squadron the pilots eat and drink together.'

The food was extremely good, as befitting an officer's mess on an RAC base, and the company was pleasant, but Gwen found that she couldn't quite relax or enjoy herself and she barely spoke.

She wasn't shy and under normal circumstances she wouldn't have hesitated to join in the conversations, especially as they mostly spoke about flying and mechanics and avoided anything even remotely personal, but she found herself surprisingly reticent in such august company. To make matters worse her thoughts kept drifting back to the wreck in the hangar, to the challenge it represented and the future she would have with it. She was already rebuilding it in her mind, imagining how it would fly with the modifications she would make and she found that she couldn't wait to get started, just as if it were one of her own designs.

The other pilots seemed to notice her mood and once they had asked her the obligatory questions about where she had been based and what she had flown, the kind of things any pilot would immediately want to know about another, they left her mostly alone.

Groups of officers wandered in every so often as their shifts in various sections of the base ended. Invariably they would greet and be greeted in return by the pilots, but would then sit at a respectful distance to have their lunch, leaving the Misfits to their conversations.

When the meal was over, most of the pilots stood and began to troop into the bar area in order to keep drinking, the usual activity for overworked war pilots who found themselves suddenly with a welcome day off due to low cloud and intermittent rain, but Abby pulled Gwen to one side, along with the young blonde that Gwen had noticed earlier.

'Gwen, this is Kitty Wright. She'll show you to the barracks and get you sorted. Unpack your kitbag, wash your face, clean your teeth, whatever you need to do, but head down to the hangar as soon as you can.' She smiled. 'No rest for the wicked! And be assured, I *want* you to be wicked, after all *we* certainly are, aren't we Kitty?'

The tall woman at her side grinned cheekily and winked at Gwen. 'Oh, yes indeed! Very! Work hard, play hard and devil take the consequences!'

The wing commander laughed. 'Quite right!' She jerked her thumb over her shoulder. 'Go on, skedaddle!'

'Come on Gwen.' The blonde slipped her hand under Gwen's arm to pull her away and together they went through the bar and outside, turning to follow the cement path around the outside of the mess.

The woman was long-legged and lithe and a good six inches taller than Gwen's squatter, more curvy, form and she had to hurry to keep up.

'You're American, right?'

'Born and bred! Why, is my accent that bad?'

'No! Not at all! And Kitty. Is that short for Katherine? Kathleen?'

'No, it's just Kitty. I was named after Kitty Hawk. You know, in North Carolina.'

'Oh, right! Where the first...' Gwen blinked and stared at her. 'Wright... Don't tell me you're...'

The American grinned and nodded. 'Orville Wright is my grandfather.'

'Gosh...'

The concrete walkway beside the mess turned into a stone path when it drew level with the back of the building and it passed under an arch, like the entrance into a maze, cut into a long line of tall hedges that divided the main buildings from the accommodation section of the old holiday camp.

The change as they went through it was astonishing; all sign of the main buildings behind them completely disappeared and it was like they had stepped off of the airbase entirely to enter a forest.

The stone path branched off occasionally as it wended its way through thick vegetation, past tall oaks and carefully cultivated bushes, seemingly without a plan or a concrete destination and as they crunched along it Gwen caught glimpses of the barracks blocks, set back from the path and nestling in amongst trees that were tall enough to shade them from the summer sun. The overall effect was to make it feel as if each of the buildings were isolated from the world in the middle of a forest, beautifully continuing the woodland theme that Gwen had encountered in the mess, and she wouldn't have been surprised to find out that the intention had been to make the well-off feel like they were "roughing it".

The buildings themselves turned out to be squat, single-storey buildings that were similar in size and shape to a normal military barracks, but that was where all similarity with the purely functional buildings ended - they had a curious aspect that was something between a Swiss chalet and a Viking Longhouse and had been constructed from a dark brown stone, which apparently hadn't required defacing with green paint, that made them seem almost as if they were made of wood.

The only distinguishing feature that separated one dormitory from another were the names picked out in tall gold letters in the pediment above every door and clearly visible from the path. They passed *Dickens* and *Tennyson* before Kitty turned towards *Wilde*.

'Here we are! Home sweet home!'

She held the door open for Gwen, then followed her through.

They stopped just inside, at the end of a long corridor that bisected the building. Stained glass skylights high overhead illuminated the corridor in patchy greens, as if by sunlight through a forest canopy and it had been furnished to look like a hallway in a townhouse of a stately manor, just much longer. However, the dark wooden panelled walls were bare, apart from the electric lights placed every ten feet and brass hooks showing where numerous paintings should have hung - the first sign Gwen had really seen of the reversal in fortunes that the holiday camp had experienced.

'This is the squadron's barracks. All of us are in here, regardless of rank or gender.' She pointed at the solid-looking wooden doors on either side. 'Abby is on your left and Owen, her second in command, the Welshman who gave you such a wonderful greeting, is in the room on your right which he shares with his wife, Wendy. He pilots Bloodhound, the radar and command aircraft and she pilots Dreadnought, the big bomber, and thankfully the rooms have thick walls.'

She grinned, then started walking down the corridor.

There were more doors on each side and she waved vaguely at them in passing. 'These are individual rooms for the other senior officers.'

Roughly in the middle of the building she stopped and opened the door to her left. 'This is the bathroom. There are toilets, showers, even a bath, although we're not allowed to use it unless it's been raining - water conservation, you know?' She indicated the door opposite. 'Ladies on the left, gentlemen on the right and never the twain shall meet. If you catch my drift.'

Gwen nodded with a smile which the woman returned before closing the bathroom door and continuing down the corridor. There were only two doors beyond the bathrooms, one on each side of the corridor, about twenty-five yards from the end. 'And here, out of sight and out of mind, are the NCO rooms. One each for men and women.' She opened the door to the left and went in. 'You're in here with me.'

The room proved to be much more like what she was used to; it was large with half a dozen metal-framed beds in a neat row, divided by standard issue metal wardrobes and each with a lockbox at the foot. However, while the furniture was standard RAC issue, the rest of the decor certainly wasn't; the room was just as luxuriously appointed as the rest of the base, but in different shades of a very unmilitary pink. The large windows were leaded and hung with dark pink velvet curtains, there were several large brass radiators along the walls, picked out with pink lines, and there were two wash stands at the far end of the room made of pink ceramic and shaped like sea shells. There was a deep pink carpet on the floor which had seen far better days and a large organically shaped mirror near the door, with an ornate brass frame, designed to look like vines spreading across the wall, which had flowers blooming among them. Also pink.

'The two rooms down this end were where the children were all lumped in together so that Mummy and Daddy could have some peace and quiet. The girls were in here, obviously, hence the horrible decoration.'

'I quite like it actually; pink's my favourite colour.'

Kitty looked at Gwen in mock horror before continuing. 'Anyway... I've been on my own since we got here; we're a bit top-heavy as a squadron - too many generals, not enough cooks, but don't get me wrong I'll be glad of the company!'

Only the bed closest to the door was made and Gwen's kitbag was on the bed next to it along with a bed pack - a pile of neatly folded sheets and blankets - and two pillows.

The American woman gestured at it. 'Feel free to choose a bed further away if you want more privacy. I don't know about you, though, but I could do with having someone a bit closer; it can get a bit lonely sometimes.'

'I know what you mean...' Gwen sighed. 'I'll take the bed next to you.'

'Great!' Kitty beamed, seeming to be genuinely happy. 'Well, I guess you'll want to get to the hangar as soon as possible and I don't want to keep you from that, but don't forget - we're in this together. I'm sure you'll get to know everyone much better over the next few days, but in the meantime, if there is anything you want, please don't hesitate to ask me!'

'Thank you.' Gwen returned her smile. Somehow she felt closer to Kitty after only a few minutes than she had to the women in her previous squadron after having gone through basic and flight training with them. Perhaps it was because they were closer in age, the women in her old squadron had tended to be older, or maybe it was because the American was just so open, wearing her heart on her sleeve.

'You're welcome, hon.'

Gwen was surprised when the tall woman folded her into a hug and didn't react in time to return it. Kitty didn't seem to notice, though and she was still beaming when she pulled back a couple of seconds later.

'We'll all be in the bar for a good few more hours if you fancy a drink later - there's nothing else to do on this god-forsaken base! Hope to see you there!'

She turned and all but skipped from the room, closing the door after her, leaving Gwen slightly bemused; her treatment by the squadron so far had been a far cry from usual RAC discipline, but she couldn't say that she wasn't happy about the change.

She didn't have any intention of going to the bar that evening and she suspected that Kitty had known that; she had too much work to do to and she would have plenty of time to worry about socialising and getting to know her fellow pilots when it was done.

As soon as the American woman had gone, Gwen pulled open her kitbag and threw its contents onto her bed. She tore off her uniform and put on her work coveralls, covered her hair with a regulation blue headscarf, then raced out of the room, heading back to the hangar, pausing only to visit the bathroom on her way past.

However, when she got to the hangar she found that the aircraft had gone.

There were clear signs of where it had been - the canopy was still there, as were a few broken Duralumin panels that had been torn off, but the rest of the machine was conspicuous in its absence. Puzzled, she walked back outside, thinking to go over to the mess to ask Abby what was happening, but before she could do that she heard the sounds of heavy work being done somewhere close by. She followed the noise, which quickly resolved into the distinctive chuffing of a steam engine and the whine of pneumatic tools, and found that it was coming from the smaller building next to the hangar.

The doors to the building were rolled back, revealing a workshop with the missing aircraft within. There were six men and women swarming over it, already dismantling it.

'You must be the new girl.'

Gwen looked around for the source of the voice and found a boy, sitting on the floor against one of the doors about ten yards away and eating an apple while he watched the work going on. He pushed himself to his feet and sauntered over to her, finishing off the apple and looking her up and down as he came. He stuffed the core into a pocket of his coveralls, then wiped his hands on his front before offering one of them to her.

'I'm Jimmy, an apprentice mechanic.'

Gwen left the hand handing and eyed his coveralls - there was no sign of insignia on them, beyond the RAC crest on his breast, no sign of rank or assignment. He looked a lot younger than her, perhaps fifteen or sixteen.

'Girl?' She raised an eyebrow. 'Why aren't you in school?'

He grunted and shrugged, but left the hand out. 'Left school last year. Can't say it was doing much for me anyway.'

Gwen finally took his hand, more because it felt awkward not to, than out of any real desire to shake it. It was warm and surprisingly dry for a teenage boy.

The boy grinned and shook her hand enthusiastically. 'As well as being an apprentice I'm kind of the dogsbody around her - if you need it, I'll get it.'

'I'm Gwen - Aviator Sergeant Stone.'

She put emphasis on her rank and surname and looked at him pointedly, but he just grinned at her, oblivious to what she was trying to say.

He jerked his thumb towards the machine. 'I've got your fitters working already; didn't think you'd mind if we made a start on strippin' 'er down without you.'

'No, I don't mind one bit.'

Gwen finally smiled; if the boy had organised a work crew for her and got them to start, then she could forgive him for calling her "girl". This once.

'So, what do you want to do?'

Gwen eyed the work going on. The fitters were having trouble removing a few of the panels because the rivets and bolts had twisted out of shape when they'd been damaged, necessitating careful persuasion if they weren't going to damage the frame underneath. It looked like it was going to be at least a few hours before they got it completely stripped down and ready for her to inspect the monocoque frame.

'Are there any blueprints?'

'Officially, no. But I know that Cece had some that she drew up herself. I'm pretty sure Abby has them. I can go ask her for them, if you want?'

'Abby?'

The boy rolled his eyes and sighed. 'Alright, *Wing Commander Abigail Lennox* has them, *Aviator Sergeant Stone*, ma'am.'

Gwen huffed, amused despite herself and quoted the old maxim. 'Don't call me ma'am; I work for a living.'

The boy grinned. 'Righto, Gwen!'

She sighed and shook her head; there didn't seem to be a happy medium with the boy. 'Just see if you can borrow those plans, please, and I'll need a drawing board somewhere.'

The boy pointed to the back of the building where there was an office with a glass front that she hadn't noticed before. 'There's a whole room full of them over there.'

Gwen nodded, happy; everything was in place and it actually reminded her of her workshop back home, it was comforting. However, she frowned as her eyes took in the machine again. 'Why hasn't anybody done any repairs before?' She looked at the blocks that were under the fuselage, holding it off the ground. 'I mean, someone could have at least repaired the undercarriage.'

'Abby refused to let anyone touch it; she kept it as it was as a reminder of her sister, I guess.'

'Her sister? The pilot was her sister?'

The boy nodded. 'Squadron Leader Cecily Lennox, Cece for short. Abby's younger sister.' He frowned up at her. 'Didn't she tell you? Her sister got shot up bad, but still managed to land before buying the farm.'

'Oh god...' Lennox had brought her in to fly her own sister's aircraft - as if she wasn't under enough pressure to get the machine repaired correctly before...

The boy shrugged again - it seemed to be a gesture that served him for most things, sympathy this time. 'I'll go see about those blueprints.'

The boy ran out, heading across the airstrip towards the mess building.

Gwen watched him go for a second, wondering who he was exactly, but then dismissed him from her mind and looked at the aircraft. *Her* aircraft.

She couldn't help but smile as she looked at it, reacquainting herself with its lines. The fitters clambering over it barely looked up as she wandered over, except to give her a brief nod, so focussed were they on their work. She didn't care; she would rather have them continue to work than break off to give some meaningless signal of acknowledgement of her rank.

She scanned their uniforms quickly, picking out the most senior among them, a sergeant with grey hair poking out from under his hat, and made her way over to him. She watched the men work while she waited patiently for him to finish and notice her - they were efficient and practised and obviously very experienced.

'Grab it, Geoff. You got it? Good.' The sergeant wiped his hands on a cloth then turned to face Gwen. He looked her up and down with a very critical eye and she wasn't sure that he liked what he was seeing. 'Aviator Sergeant Stone?' He didn't wait for her confirmation. 'Abby told me you were taking over Wasp.'

Gwen glanced at the nose of the machine and winced; now that he mentioned it she could just about make out the name of the aircraft there. It was completely understandable that she hadn't seen it before, though; it had been all but obliterated by a cannon round that must have penetrated the cockpit after its small act of vandalism.

'Is that going to be a problem Sergeant...?'

'Jenkins, Aviator. And no, it's not going to be a problem. Not at all.' The man's face softened considerably and he sighed. 'If you ask me it's about bloody time someone did something with her. No disrespect meant to the Wing Commander, or Cece for that matter, but a machine like this has to fly, and the best way for Abby to honour her sister's memory is for Wasp to be up in the sky, like what Cece designed her for. Now, having said that, she's your machine now and what you say goes. If you want to make any modifications you just have to give us the say so - Wasp'll stand it, she's a good girl.'

Gwen nodded in understanding - many of the pilots, mechanics and fitters that she had known over the years, ones that had built their own aircraft or spent a lot of time servicing them, swore that their machines had a personality all of their own. They insisted that they somehow gained a measure of sentience, with their own quirks, foibles and preferences and began calling them *her* instead of *it*. Gwen didn't believe any of that, though; she'd constructed three aircraft while she'd been growing up and couldn't say that any of them had gained *any* kind of character or temperament - they had merely worked how they should have and every time they'd broken or something had gone wrong it had been because *she'd* done something wrong, not because they were showing their disapproval or throwing a tantrum. She hadn't even given her first aircraft a name until her mother had insisted that every aircraft had to have one.

Gwen shivered when she remembered what name she'd given it - *Bumblebee*; that was far too close to Wasp for her liking and a coincidence like that might start making her believing in the superstitions that most pilots subscribed to.

Jenkins saw her gesture and brought himself up in indignation, thinking that she was expressing her disapproval of the aircraft. 'Don't look at her like that, young lady! She's a fine machine and you should be happy to have her.'

'I am! It's just that...'

Before she could explain any further, the boy, Jimmy, came running up to them, out of breath and clutching a few rolls of paper in his arms. 'Got 'em!'

Gwen smiled her thanks. 'Put them in the office please, I'll be right there.' He hurried off and she turned back to Jenkins, who still had a sour look on his face. 'Sergeant, believe me, I am *very* happy to be piloting Wasp and I will do all I can to honour it... her, *and* the memory of her creator.'

She looked at him expectantly and after a few seconds he nodded in acceptance. 'Very well, Aviator. May you have every joy of her.'

'Thank you.' She returned his nod with a smile, then gestured at the aircraft. 'Now, before I go take a look at the plans, is there anything I should know? Any damage that will require special attention?'

He shook his head. 'Aside from the missing tail, the frame appears intact. It should be a simple matter of getting everything sorted. Say, five days' work?'

'We have three, Sergeant Jenkins. Can we do it?'

He frowned. 'Three is cutting it fine...' He nodded reluctantly. 'We'll get it done.'

'Thank you. I'll leave you to it, then.'

'Right you are, Aviator.' He nodded to her, then without any more ceremony he went back to work.

Jimmy already had the blueprints pinned out on the large drawing board nearest the door by the time she joined him in the office.

'Thanks, Jimmy.'

'You're welcome, Gwen!' He gave her a cheeky grin and a wink, then sauntered out to join the fitters.

Gwen shook her head in exasperation, but then put the boy firmly from her mind and turned her full attention to the blueprints. She found that they weren't actually blueprints, but rather rough drawings, not at all like the sleek and uncluttered production designs she was used to working with. However, once she managed to see past the clutter of hand-written notes that covered the page they were easy enough to understand and she found that was impressed; the design was simpler than most self-built aircraft she'd seen, but undoubtedly elegant and definitely efficient. Her initial impression that she could improve on it was still correct, though, but it was easy to see that, even if she left it exactly as it was, it would still be much better than a stock Harridan or a Spitsteam.

There was blank paper on the next drawing board over so she moved across to it and began to draw, starting with the current design of Wasp. She drew it in detail from memory, her draughtsman's pencil moving swiftly across the paper with a precision learnt over many years. She barely needed the protractors, compasses and triangles that were at her disposal; the angles and shapes came naturally to her as she merely put on the page what was already in her mind's eye. In fairly short order she had a proper blueprint drawn out, clean and without any extraneous marks or notes, good enough for a factory to use, although no factory could hope to mass-produce an aircraft like this; it was only possible to make by hand, through hours and hours of painstaking, loving work.

She took a moment to appreciating the design, then covered it with a sheet of tracing paper and started detailing her modifications, limiting herself to what was possible with the current frame and achievable in very little time, knowing that the adjustments she really wanted to make were impossible to implement in only three days. She went through several sheets of tracing paper, changing minute details each time until she had exactly what she wanted, then moved to the desk next to it where a clean sheet of paper was waiting for her and started creating a proper blueprint that the fitters could work from, once again working from the image that had coalesced in her mind without any need to refer to her drawings.

'Excuse me, Aviator.'

Gwen looked up from her almost-completed design to find Jenkins in the doorway, his hat in his hand.

'Yes, Sergeant?'

'Me and the lads was wondering if we could go get a spot of dinner.'

Gwen looked up at the clock over the desk and blinked in shock; it was past seven, she had been working for almost four hours. 'Of course. Please do!'

'Thank you.' He nodded and started backing from the room.

'Sergeant!'

He turned back. 'Yes, Aviator?'

'How's it going? How is Wasp?'

The man smiled. 'She'll be fine, Aviator. She'll be fine.'

With a last nod he walked away and left the shed, taking his men with him.

Gwen put the finishing touches to her design, checked it over quickly, then placed the pencil to one side, satisfied.

Her back had cramped slightly from being hunched over the board for so long and she straightened, groaning as her muscles protested.

'Dinner, Gwen?'

She looked up to find that Jimmy had taken Jenkins' place in the doorway.

'Do you think they'll let me into the mess dressed like this?'

He looked her up and down. When he lingered too long on her breasts, she glared at him, but he just grinned cheekily and shrugged. 'Of course they will; they're Misfit Squadron.'

CHAPTER 3

Nobody in the officer's mess even batted an eyelid at her work coveralls, not even the waiters, who she would have expected it from mostly - it truly was a different squadron that she had joined. However, her own sense of decency wouldn't allow her to have dinner in the more formal dining room, so instead she remained in the lounge area and took a plateful of food at the bar.

She couldn't see the rest of the squadron, but she heard them; they were laughing and talking so loudly in the dining room that she couldn't miss them. She found that she actually really wanted to join them, bask in their company, get to know them and maybe even find out their names, but discipline won out and she remained at the bar on her own.

While she ate she stared at the photos pinned to the wall behind the bar - she hadn't noticed them the last time she'd been in the bar because her attention had been fixed firmly on the red trophies over her head. There were a couple of dozen pictures, mostly of the squadron and the pilots, but there were also a few images of enemy aircraft.

In the centre was a photo of the entire squadron in front of the Eiffel Tower, resplendent in their dress uniforms and accompanied by a few French dignitaries. Another showed them on standby in front of what was obviously a French Chateau, most of them asleep in deck chairs not unlike the ones that were stacked outside the mess. There were pictures of individuals, smiling and laughing, and one of Abby with a woman who was quite obviously her sister from the resemblance between them.

There were also a few curious images, among them a couple of photos taken from gun camera footage - the one of two MU9's coming apart at the same time, hit by the same burst, was particularly impressive, but there was also one that showed a triplane with barely visible tracer bullets reaching out towards it, but not quite intersecting it, and she wondered why it was there and where it was from. The photo that most puzzled her, though, was a single dark picture of some crates with Prussian writing on them and she spent some time trying to decipher it before giving up and going back to the more interesting ones.

However, no matter how fascinated she was by the photos, they couldn't keep her from going back to work after she'd finished her food. She drained the dregs of the single pint of bitter that she'd allowed herself, which went on a tab that she discovered had been started for her, thanked the waiter behind the bar, then left.

She had been quick, but evening was well on its way to night by the time she stepped outside and she could only dimly make out the shapes of the squat buildings around the airfield. None of them had visible lights, of course, because blackout rules were in effect. It wasn't hard to retrace her steps across the airfield, though, and she arrived at the workshop only a couple of minutes later. However, there was a heavy black curtain hung across the doorway, blocking all light from escaping, and it was the work of a good few minutes more before she could find the opening and force her way through to the brightly lit interior. She expected the fitters or Jimmy to be there, but she had eaten so hurriedly that she had beaten them back and instead she was surprised to find Wing Commander Lennox standing staring at the half-stripped Wasp.

Gwen stood beside her and together they took in the sad sight of the machine.

The silence lasted for a long minute until finally the woman sighed. 'I'm glad somebody's repairing her at last. I was wrong to keep her as she was; it was a reminder, yes, but it wasn't what the squadron needed, it wasn't good for us. Hopefully when she's flying again she can be a different kind of reminder - not of death, but of the fact that even with all the madness in the world there is still beauty and life goes on.'

'I hope so too.'

Abby turned and smiled at Gwen. 'So, Aviator Sergeant, what can I do?'

'You're going to help?'

The woman gestured at her work clothes. 'I got all dressed up, I might as well do something.'

'Thank you, ma'am, I could certainly use an extra pair of hands.'

'I know. And it's Abby, remember.'

'Well, then, Abby, how are you with a pneumatic bolt remover?'

They had been working for less than fifteen minutes before Sergeant Jenkins walked in with his five fellow fitters. They nodded to the base commander and silently took up their tools to get back to work.

Shortly after that, Jimmy slunk in, bringing with him packets of biscuits and tea in a large urn on a hand cart which he rolled into the corner by the door, out of the way. He turned a large handle on the cart a few times, starting the clockwork heating element in the urn, then adjusted the thermostat so that the hot liquid inside would gently simmer and not boil, slowing the gentle ticking of the mechanism. He lifted the lid on the big brass urn and peered inside, then, apparently satisfied, he wandered over to where Abby and Gwen were removing some damaged control wiring.

'Alright, mum?'

'James.' She nodded at him. 'Thanks for bringing the tea.'

'That's alright, you know me - always happy to help.'

Jimmy grinned at Gwen and the wing commander rolled her eyes. 'Always happy to help a good-looking woman, you mean?'

Jimmy shrugged but said nothing, just gave Gwen another grin and wandered off to start pouring tea into mugs for the fitters.

Gwen frowned as she replayed the short exchange. 'Did he call you "mum" or "ma'am"?'

'Didn't you know? James is my son.'

Without waiting for an answer Abby ducked back into the fuselage, leaving Gwen staring at the back of her head.

A couple of hours later they took a break and wandered over to Jimmy's cart to get some tea and biscuits. The two of them stood watching the boy, who had attached himself to Sergeant Jenkins and was watching him intently, helping whenever he could without getting in the way.

Gwen didn't even have to ask anything; Abby just started to talk about her son, as if it were something she had been desperate to share with someone, but never had the chance.

'Jimmy loves aircraft, he always has done and he begged me to take him with me when the squadron went to France, but I refused and left him here at boarding school, which was just as well, really, considering how that turned out. Not all our ground crew made it back and Cece...'

Abby sighed and took a deep breath, an expression of pain briefly crossing her face before she continued. 'But when we returned I no longer had an excuse and he didn't leave me much choice in the matter either - the MG's picked him up a couple of villages away, wandering around and asking the way to the "top secret RAC base"...'

She smiled at the lad fondly. 'After that I thought it would be best to keep him close so I could keep an eye on him. He's not enlisted, not yet anyway, because he's still too young, but he makes himself useful. He's already a handy mechanic, but he doesn't actually want to fly, he just wants to be around the machines. He takes after his father like that.'

'If you don't mind me asking, where is his father?'

'He died in an accident shortly after Jimmy was born. I was eighteen at the time. It's just been the two of us since then.'

'I'm sorry.'

Abby waved away Gwen's sympathies with a grin. 'I would have left him anyway; he was more than twice my age. I only fell for him because he was a pilot and he obviously wasn't a very good one!'

Gwen had no idea whether she was supposed to laugh at the woman's joke or not, but she was saved from making a decision when Abby suddenly turned deadly serious and put a hand on her arm.

'Right. Before you start making any changes to Wasp, I need to tell you something.'

Gwen tried to maintain her smile even as she prepared to have her hopes dashed. She was sure that Abby was going to shoot down her plans for Wasp and tell her not to change anything about the machine, tell her that she wanted it restored to exactly how it had been before, when her sister was flying it.

'I know Jimmy told you that Wasp was my sister's aircraft and yes, I wish that I had never had the need to bring you here, because that would mean that she was still alive, and yes, I *will* kick you out on your arse if you disobey my orders in combat or do anything to hurt this squadron or anyone in it.' The words came out in a rush and she gasped for breath before continuing. 'But, having said all that, Wasp is yours now and I want you to know that if you wish to make any modifications then I won't stand in your way, just as long as you have her ready in the three days that I gave you. Although, it would be nice if you kept her name; I think she likes it.'

Relief washed through Gwen and she shook her head. 'I wouldn't change it.'

'Thank you.' Abby nodded, smiling sadly. 'Feel free to paint her as you like, though; we had opposite colour schemes, Cece and I, to commemorate being sisters, or something silly like that, but there's no reason for you to keep Wasp like she was.'

'Thank you.'

Abby sighed. 'Well, I must admit that is a bit of a weight off my chest. There is one last thing I have to say, though - I am still this squadron's commander and I need to see the plans you have for her before you start making your modifications; it's my obligation to make sure that no pilot in my charge takes to the air in something that isn't airworthy. So, whenever you have something drawn up let me know.'

Gwen sipped at her tea, then smiled at her over the mug. 'I already do.'

'Already?' Abby looked at her with her mouth open and eyes wide. 'Can I see them?'

'Of course!'

Gwen led the way to the office and gestured at the three drawing boards in the row underneath the windows looking out on the workshop.

'These are your sister's original plans. On the next desk over are the blueprints I've made from them and those...' She pointed at the last drawing board where the finalised design was pinned. 'Those are mine.'

Abby moved to stand at the first drawing board. She reached out to touch the signature in the bottom right-hand corner and Gwen realised with a start that there were two names there, not just one - she'd been so focused on the aircraft itself that she hadn't noticed that the plans were signed not just by Cece, but by Abby as well.

The woman saw her expression. 'Cece and I designed Wasp and Dragonfly together, at the same time. It was the way we always worked, bouncing ideas off of each other until we had something that was much better than we could come up with individually. Without her I just... I can't...' Words failed her and she just shrugged, showing where Jimmy had gotten the gesture from.

She moved over to the next board and smoothed the tracing paper down so that she could see it better. 'You did this in the few hours you had before dinner? That's... Well, *remarkable* doesn't quite say enough.'

She pulled the tracing paper away to reveal the original design underneath, then replaced it. She frowned and leaned forward to peer more closely at the tail section. 'You've shortened her.'

'Only by three inches. She'll be tighter in turns.'

'But won't she be unstable?'

Gwen shook her head. 'I'm compensating by taking two inches from the wingspan.'

The wing commander nodded slowly and sighed as she traced the lines of the wings, their shapes slightly different to how her sister had made them. 'Well, I can't pretend to understand how this will affect her mood, but I can see what you're doing.'

She pulled the tracing paper away and gazed at the plans underneath. 'Do you think I could have these when you're done with them?'

'Of course. I'll put them with the rest of your sister's drawings.'

'Thank you.'

Abby smiled and nodded in gratitude, then moved across to the last board where Gwen had drawn out the design properly. She scanned them quickly, looking back and forth from them to the tracing paper on the previous board, checking to make sure that they were identical. She nodded her approval after only a few seconds, then walked back to the door. 'Sergeant Jenkins!'

Through the window Gwen saw the man look up from what he was doing. 'Yes, ma'am.'

'When you can, come into the office, please!'

'Right away, ma'am.' Jenkins motioned for Jimmy to take his place then walked towards them, wiping his hands on a rag. 'What can I do for you, ma'am?'

Abby smiled. 'Aviator Sergeant Stone has some plans she would like to show you.'

Around midnight Gwen called it a day and ordered the fitters to go to bed and rest. She was pleased, but not at all surprised, to see that they were reluctant to leave their work, but she knew that the repairs wouldn't take as long as she'd thought they would; they worked so well and efficiently that she had been able to take almost a whole day off her estimates. That meant they wouldn't have to miss much sleep, which in turn meant that there was less possibility of an accident happening, or a mistake being made.

Exhausted, she and Abby made their way to the pilots' barracks. The wing commander bade her goodnight and went into her room, leaving Gwen to continue down the corridor. She sneaked into the long dormitory without turning on the light so as not to disturb her new bunkmate and felt her way to the second bed, finding that it had been made and her kit had been moved. She smiled, resolving to make sure that she did something nice for Kitty as soon as she could, then removed her coveralls and slipped between the sheets.

As soon as her head hit the pillow she was lost to darkness and dreams of ratios and angles and a stinging, buzzing insect that seemed to be trying to tell her something.

CHAPTER 4

When she woke up the next morning it was just after dawn, the curtains on the windows converting the sunlight outside into a soft pink glow that gave her just enough light to see by. Kitty was still sleeping, so Gwen slid silently out of bed and tiptoed to the next bunk along where the American had piled her kit.

She hadn't had a chance to wash the day before and she felt and *was* filthy; there was grease under her short nails and her hair was clammy from sweat, so she grabbed her wash bag and a towel and headed straight for the showers.

The bathroom turned out to be a rainforest fantasy of pipes made to look like creeping vines, shower heads that made it seem that she was showering in a downpour, and sinks that were wide leaves turned to catch the rainwater coming from the end of the "branches" above it.

Apparently the pilots hadn't been called for a dawn patrol and were taking the opportunity to lie in (and probably nurse hangovers) so she had the bathroom all to herself, but that meant there was nobody to show her how everything worked and she wasted a fair amount of time just trying to find out how to turn on the showers - the tap was disguised as a leaf on the wall and had been camouflaged better than most army vehicles she had seen.

Once she got it going, the stream was strong and refreshing, and she was tempted to luxuriate in the first shower she'd had since joining the RAC, but the water wasn't very hot and she was desperate to get back to work so she just washed as quickly as she could then cleaned her furry teeth before heading back to get dressed.

When she padded softly into the dormitory, Kitty rolled over and smiled at her. 'G'mornin'!'

Gwen returned the smile. 'Good morning! Thank you for making my bed last night.'

'Don't mention it; we stick together in this squadron. That includes giving a helping hand to someone who is too distracted to make sure she has a decent place to sleep before going to work!'

Gwen laughed at the gentle chiding. 'Nonetheless. What do you yanks say? I owe you one?'

'You do! And I might get you to pay me back with breakfast in bed one day...' She laughed at Gwen's dismay. 'Not today, silly! When you have nothing better to do!'

'Alright, then!' Gwen chuckled in relief; she would have felt obligated to do as the girl asked. 'Oh, I wanted to ask - do the squadron ever fly? I mean, you were all in the bar most of yesterday and as far as I can see everyone is still in bed. In my old squadron we had sorties most of the day and dawn patrols.'

'Didn't you see the forecast? There was solid cloud from five hundred feet up to pretty high yesterday, and the same is predicted for the next couple of days, so no flying.'

Gwen blushed. 'I haven't been keeping much of an eye on the weather since I was grounded.'

'You were grounded? Why?'

'It's a long story. Do you mind if I tell you some other time?'

'Of course not! Now, if *you* don't mind, I'm going to get some more shuteye; one thing we learnt in France was to get as much rest as we could, wherever and whenever we could and this bed is far too comfortable to let go to waste.'

'Be my guest! I'm just going to get dressed and go.'

'Good.' The blonde girl rolled back to face the wall and her voice was muffled as she buried her face in her pillow. 'Oh, and try to pop into the mess sometime, tell us all how your work is going. We're all dying to get to know you.'

'Will do.'

Gwen smiled as she struggled to get her still-damp legs into her work coveralls, hoping that what Kitty said was true.

When she stepped out of the barracks she found not only the low lying cloud of the day before, but also a constant drizzle and a fog that hid the other blocks from view as she hurried along the path and the trees and bushes were indistinct and hazy around her, which somehow made her surroundings even more magical than they'd seemed the previous day.

The mess was empty apart from two yawning waiters, who had drawn the short straw and got stuck with being on duty so soon after dawn, and she hurriedly washed some toast and scrambled eggs down with tea before leaving again.

She had barely gotten to the workshop before the other fitters arrived as a group and immediately took up where they had left off the night before without her needing to say anything.

By midmorning the last of the panels had been taken off and the frame had been completed from parts of two Spitsteam tails that Jimmy had dug out of the salvage at the back of the main hangar. It was only a couple of hours work for it to be checked and polished and finally Wasp was ready for reassembly.

Satisfied, Gwen sent everybody to lunch and headed to the officer's mess.

While she ate at the bar she revised her estimate of how long the job would take and quickly came to the conclusion that she had gained at least a couple of hours. She decided to celebrate by allowing herself fifteen minutes to have dessert and another half-pint of Bitter, but that plan was immediately put paid to when a powerful-looking woman with strong features and dark brown hair slid onto the stool next to her.

Gwen recognised her as one of the Misfits, the one that she had seen sitting with the Welsh pilot during lunch the day before. She couldn't for the life of her remember the woman's name, though, but she was saved from any embarrassment when the woman introduced herself with a wide smile.

'Gwen, I'm Wendy, Wendy Llewellyn, Dreadnought's pilot, Misfit Squadron's armourer and Owen's wife. In that order. But don't tell him.'

Gwen laughed and took the woman's offered hand. 'Pleased to meet you!'

'I'm glad I caught you before you went back to work; Sergeant Jenkins came looking for Wasp's guns a few minutes ago and I told him that I wasn't going to let him have them until I talked to you.'

Gwen frowned. 'Why? Are they alright? Because, well, you know, I'm going to need them.'

It was Wendy's turn to laugh. 'No, they're fine! I had to repair one and another was destroyed, but we have a few dozen of the same type lying around just in case. No, that's not what I wanted to talk to you about! I was wondering if you'd like to try something a little different...'

Gwen immediately scrapped her plans for a treat and followed Wendy into the woods behind the hangar.

According to the woman, when Whitehall had been drawing up plans to convert the holiday camp into a base for the Misfits, Abby had had them put another of the military buildings among the trees as a workshop for her. It had been deliberately put well out of the way, at least half a mile away, both for safety and because she liked to make a lot of noise.

She took Gwen in through a small door to one side of the main sliding doors and flicked a row of switches on the wall. Ranks of electric spotlights flickered on overhead, illuminating the windowless space within. It was huge, easily four times the size of the workshop that Gwen had Wasp in and it was completely filled with workbench after workbench, which were in turn covered with weapons of all descriptions.

Gwen wandered over to the nearest bench, which was on its own in the corner, and laughed when she saw the large, unpainted metal tubes on it. They were rockets, about six feet long and five or six inches in diameter, unreliable weapons that had been developed during the Great War then quickly discarded after they had killed as many friendlies as they had enemies and consequently not seen much use since. 'Are you stockpiling for bonfire night or planning to send mice to the moon?'

Wendy laughed. 'No! Actually, they're something I've been playing with - I thought it would be quite fun to use them on bombers.'

'Really? To do what? Dazzle the pilots?'

Wendy smiled slyly. 'I developed them for ground attack initially and if my calculations are correct they should penetrate about fifty inches of reinforced concrete, so imagine what they'll do to a bomber.' She chuckled at Gwen's shocked expression. 'Eventually, when I've worked out all the kinks, I want to be able to put them on the turn fighters so they can be more effective against big aircraft.'

She beckoned for Gwen to follow her and led the way towards the back of the room.

As Gwen walked behind the woman she let her eyes roam across the other benches. One row was covered with small machine guns and pistols for infantry use, but of several types that she had never used or even seen before and a couple more held various heavy guns and artillery pieces of large calibre many of which were obviously meant to be mounted on ground vehicles. However, it was the longer, thinner guns on the last two rows of benches that Gwen's eyes lingered on, the ones that were designed for aircraft, but she was disappointed when she saw that they were mostly standard .303 Whiting machine guns that Wendy was servicing or repairing, carrying out the normal upkeep of the squadron's guns.

That disappointment completely disappeared when Wendy reached her destination, though, because the long benches that ran the length of the far wall held far more interesting items.

Eight .303 Whitings, ready to be taken away and fitted to Wasp were laying side by side with two other types of guns, both larger and heavier.

Wendy put her hand on one of the .303's and turned to smile at Gwen. 'These are yours. They are the armament that Wasp was originally designed to take and that are in all of A flight's aircraft. Wasp has eight and there are also eight in Dragonfly and Ballerina. However, Bandicoot has six, plus two of those firing along her nose.' She pointed at the next, slightly larger machine guns sitting next to the .303's. 'These are .5's and these are what are in most of B flight's aircraft. They have a slightly bigger punch, but you still need to concentrate fire to take down a bomber.' She patted the .5 then moved to the next guns, which were much longer and looked far heavier. She grinned and stroked one of them fondly. 'And these beauties are .79 inch Anglo-Helvetia cannon. They only fire seven hundred rounds per minute compared to the thousand five hundred that the machine guns can deliver, but the larger, more powerful shell will punch a hole through even a Hoffman's armour.'

Gwen frowned. 'I thought they didn't work.'

Wendy shook her head without losing her smile. 'Oh no, they work fine, just not for very long before they jam. At least, not until I got my hands on them, anyway!'

The woman winked, but the frown didn't ease from Gwen's face. 'And you want to put them into Wasp? They're far too heavy and they'll never fit in the wings; they're too thin.'

'Call yourself an engineer?' Wendy chuckled. 'I'm sure you'll figure something out if you think about it for a few minutes! And as for the extra weight, that's very easy to solve. I reckon you have two choices - we can get rid of all the .303's and put four of these in Wasp instead, or you can keep four of them and replace the other four with two of these. Both those options come out at about the same weight, give or take a few pounds.'

Gwen went over to the cannons and looked down at them. It would be wonderful to have them in Wasp and the aircraft would then have a sting to rival the nose-mounted cannon in the MU9's, which RAC pilots feared so much.

'Has the wing commander signed off on this?'

Wendy nodded enthusiastically. 'Abby spoke to me about this last night - she only bloody came in and woke me and Owen up just after midnight...' The woman chuckled again, she didn't appear at all upset to have been woken up to talk about what was obviously her favourite thing in the world. 'There's already some of these in a couple of B flight's aircraft, which was easy enough to do because they're big enough, and I've put ten in Dreadnought for fun, but she wants them in all our machines eventually and reckons that if anyone'll be able to work out how to squeeze them into teeny tiny A flight aircraft it's you and your team.'

Gwen looked at the cannon sceptically. It really was so much bigger than the normal Whitings, but if the RAC had been able to put them in Spitsteams, then it shouldn't be too hard to get them in Wasp.

'Before you make up your mind whether you want to make the effort, though, I've prepared a little demonstration.'

'I know what a cannon does...'

'Humour me! Please?'

Gwen smiled. The woman was very enthusiastic about her work and she had to admit it would be good to let off some steam before getting back to work.

She nodded and the woman clapped her large hands together in glee. 'Fantastic! This way, then!'

She started taking Gwen towards the door in the back of the building, but then something occurred to her and she stopped and grinned. 'Hang on a second; might as well have some fun while we're at it.'

She jogged back to the bench by the entrance and picked up one of the rockets, then came jogging back, casually carrying the heavy tube in one of her hands. She smiled at Gwen's concerned look. 'Don't look so worried! They don't blow up unless they're fired. Well, not very often anyway.'

There was a red button by the door with a large sign over it that read "Going to have some fun? Press me or run!" and the woman stopped at it. She laughed at Gwen's puzzled expression. 'The MG's have to respond to any gunfire on the base, just in case it's an enemy attack. One time I forgot to sound the warning beforehand and all hell broke loose. Abby said that if I forgot to do it again she'd chase me round the airfield with a cattle prod.'

She pressed the button and a klaxon sounded above their heads. She did it three times, holding the last one for twice as long as the others, then winked at Gwen and went out the door.

A short way into the woods behind the workshop Wendy had a testing range which looked like a much longer version of the firing ranges that Gwen had spent so much time on during basic training, trying somewhat unsuccessfully to learn how to shoot the .22 popguns left over from the Great War. (It had been quite amusing to Gwen, but not as much to her instructors, that she had never quite been able to reliably hit paper circles from fifty yards with a rifle, but when it came to going up against moving targets, at more than five times the distance, in an aircraft, she had had no problems whatsoever.)

The range had been cleared of vegetation, although the tall oaks lining it almost completely overshadowed it, creating a kind of tunnel, ten or fifteen yards high. It was about twenty yards wide and ended roughly five hundred yards away at a target area which was sturdily constructed of three tall green-painted metal walls, thickly lined with sand bags, which would easily absorb machine gun fire and probably the shells of some of the larger artillery pieces that Wendy had in the workshop.

A large metal worktable was just under half-way down the range. It was covered by a metal roof to protect it from the elements and mounted on a low, steam-powered platform on fat wheels that could easily be moved over the dark grey steel floor with round lightening holes punched through it that had been laid the length of the range. Two guns, a .303 and one of the large cannons, were already set up and waiting for them there, clamped firmly in place on two iron stands that resembled anvils.

Wendy put the rocket on the worktable, then bent over the guns and did a quick check. In seconds she had finished and she grunted in satisfaction, then turned to Gwen, her big grin still in place.

She picked up two pairs of protective goggles from the bench and handed one to Gwen. 'Here, have a better look at what we're going to be shooting at.'

Gwen carefully turned the goggles over in her hands. They were similar to aviation goggles, small panes of glass mounted in a brass frame, completely enclosing the eyes, with magnification lenses on arms that could be slotted into place, but the lenses on these were far simpler and they had been made with glass that was much thicker and durable.

She put them on then started fiddling with the lenses. It took a few tries for her to find the right combination for maximum magnification, but then the brown, grey and green rectangles at the far end of the range sprang into sharp focus. Gwen blinked in surprise when she recognised the camouflage pattern. 'Are those panels from Prussian bombers?'

'Yep! Whitehall give me as many pieces of downed aircraft that I want in return for me sharing my little ideas with them. I've set up a couple of armour plates from HO111's for today because they're the thickest. Keep your eye on the panel on the left.'

Wendy bent over the .303 again. She had attached a long brass telescope to it and she sighted through it now, turning the brass wheels on the side of the stand to finely adjust her aim.

Finally satisfied, she turned her head to grin at Gwen, then pulled the trigger.

The sound of the gun was far louder than the klaxon had been and Gwen winced, but the burst was over almost before it had begun; the woman had only held the trigger for a second.

Gwen peered at the target. The rounds had hit in the centre of the leftmost panel and it was scored with a couple of dozen marks in a short vertical line, showing that the gun had recoiled slightly despite being tightly held on the heavy stand. The paint had been obliterated, showing the silvery metal underneath, but she couldn't tell if the armour had been penetrated or not.

'Let's go take a closer look, shall we?'

As they strolled down the range towards the panels in companionable silence, Gwen stole glances at the woman. The smile hadn't once left Wendy's face since the moment she'd stepped into her workshop and Gwen wondered if she looked the same when she was caught up with an aircraft.

It didn't take them long to get to the armoured panels and the big woman walked up to the one on the left and gave it a heavy slap with the palm of her hand. 'There, you see? More than twenty decent hits, face on as well, and look! Only two rounds actually penetrated! If the panels had been at an angle and it had been more of a glancing blow, then I doubt even those would have gone through.'

Gwen bent to peer at the panel from up close. The woman was right; while it was dented and deeply scored there were only two small holes in it. Two rounds had punched through metal that had already been weakened by the other shots, but they probably wouldn't have had much energy left to do anything once they were inside an aircraft, if they weren't stopped by another bulkhead first.

'That's not unexpected, though, I mean, one of the first things they teach you about going up against bombers is to aim at soft spots like the control surfaces or the cockpit if you can.'

Wendy nodded, her smile still firmly in place. 'True, true. But what if you didn't have to?' She jerked her head back to the guns. 'Come on!'

They went back to the workbench and this time the big woman bent over the cannon.

When she straightened up this time she handed Gwen some ear protectors. 'You're going to need these.'

She waited until Gwen had the padded ear muffs in place, then gave her a thumbs up and bent to the trigger.

Even with the protectors the sound the cannon made was much louder than the machine gun and the effect on the panel at the end of the lane was similarly greater - the target was almost cut in half by a neat row of about a dozen holes that ran from near the base of the panel almost all the way to the top. It looked as if every single round had penetrated and, by the amount of sand pouring from the sandbags behind it, the rounds had had plenty of energy left over to do serious damage afterwards.

Gwen returned the woman's grin. 'Well, I'm convinced. I'll take two, please!'

Wendy laughed and nodded enthusiastically. 'I thought you might! These beauties can even put a hole straight through the armour around a bomber's steam engines! But before I let you get back to work...' She rubbed her hands together in glee as she walked over to the end of the bench and lifted the rocket, slitting it in place on a rack installed on the bench that looked something like the metal trays French baguettes went into the oven on. There were six spaces in the rack and Gwen wondered if the woman often shot off six rockets in a row just for fun.

Aiming the rocket was a simple matter of lining up the rack with the target and in seconds the woman looked up from the rack. 'Ready?'

'No.'

She laughed and bent back down, but then something seemed to occur to her and she straightened up again, her face serious for the first time. 'That fire bucket by your feet has water in it, right? Because we're going to need it...'

Gwen glanced down, but couldn't find any buckets.

She looked back at Wendy to say so, but as soon as she lifted her head the woman grinned and set off the rocket.

The missile streaked down the range, making a high pitched whistling noise that was cut off abruptly as it exploded against the armoured panel that the .303 guns had failed to do much damage to. There was a deafening bang and a white flame that blinded Gwen as if she'd been looking into the sun searching for MU9's.

'Got the bugger!' Wendy whooped and started sprinting down the range. 'Come on!'

Mystified, Gwen started running after her.

'Bring the bucket!'

Gwen was already starting to turn back when her mind caught up with her body and she realised that Wendy was poking fun at her, laughing madly as she ran. She chuckled and slowed to a jog, letting the woman pull ahead.

Almost without breaking stride, Wendy grabbed a fire extinguisher from a row of a dozen sitting ready just outside the target area and started to put out the small fires that had been started in the sand bags. There wasn't any real danger of the fire spreading, especially because of the constant drizzle in the air, but she made sure to extinguish every last one and Gwen wondered idly what Abby had had to threaten the woman with for her to be so careful.

Gwen arrived just as Wendy was putting the extinguisher down and they stood together and stared at the panel, what was left of it anyway - it was barely more than a twisted frame around a gaping hole with a pile of melted metal on the floor underneath it.

'What the hell was in that rocket? That wasn't any explosive I've ever seen.'

'I've got a friend in the Chemists' Guild and she asked me to test a few things for her if I had the chance. She did tell me what was in the various compounds, but I'm not a chemist and didn't really understand, and besides, I don't really care what's in it as long as it makes a nice big bang!'

Gwen laughed. 'I don't care much either! Just make sure I get some of these when they're ready!'

In the end Gwen asked Wendy to bring two of the cannons, but all eight .303's as well, just in case she couldn't get them into the wings.

In her absence, Sergeant Jenkins had had the fitters running the control cables though their channels and fitting the first freshly shaped panels onto the fuselage, but as soon as Wendy and Gwen arrived with the guns on a small steam cart everybody dropped what they were doing and set to work on how to fit the cannons.

They obviously had to go as close to the fuselage as possible, not just because that was where the wing was thickest, but also, and more importantly, so that their weight was as close to the centre of gravity as possible. It was also easier to strengthen the frame around them there so that the increased vibration of the more powerful guns didn't shake the aircraft apart.

The first problem that they came up against when they attached the cannon to the frame was that they were almost twice as long as the Whitings that they were replacing. However, most of that was the barrel and it was just a matter of having it poke out through the front of the wing, instead of being completely enclosed by it, like the Whitings had been. Gwen found she rather liked the look of the barrels sticking out; it added an aggressive look to the smooth lines of the aircraft.

The body of the gun wasn't quite as easy to fit in, though, but Sergeant Jenkins almost immediately provided the solution. Apparently there had been a squadron of Spitsteams based nearby the squadron while they were in France. They had briefly been issued Spitsteams with the failed model of the cannons (before hurriedly being reissued with Whiting equipped models) and he had gone over to take a look at them with some of the other senior fitters one day.

Supranaval had neatly solved the problem of the larger gun bodies by creating large blisters in the wings to accommodate them. Wendy had changed the old drum-fed system to a belt-fed one, though, considerably lowering the guns profile and that, coupled with the fact that Wasp's wings were slightly thicker than the ones on a Spitsteam, meant that the blisters could be quite small and would barely affect the aircraft's aerodynamics.

Wendy stayed through the whole process, watching the engineers work with interest and keeping an eye on her "babies". When Gwen gave the final word that she was going to keep the cannons she helped them install a trigger on the control stick with a selector to fire the different guns individually or all together. She also provided two small, but powerful, clockwork devices to automatically re-cock the cannons in the case of a jam, although she assured Gwen that, unless she tried to empty the guns in one go, she shouldn't ever have a problem.

Four hours later, when new, freshly-shaped panels were finally in place and the guns were protected, Wendy slapped everybody on the back, told Gwen that she couldn't wait to see how many aircraft she shot down, then left to join the rest of the squadron at the bar, her grin, impossibly, wider than before.

Gwen and the fitters worked until just after midnight, with only a short break to wolf down some sandwiches for dinner, and were back in the workshop just after dawn the next day, the last full day that they had, trying desperately to make up the hours that had been lost on the guns.

Jimmy spent most of his time with them, except when Gwen or the fitters sent him on an errand, but the wing commander hadn't come back after that first night, perhaps because she didn't want Gwen to feel like she was keeping an eye on her.

The weather steadily got worse during the day and graduated into a full storm just before lunch, with thunder pealing a couple of times a minute and lightning flashing through the clouds, alternately blinding and deafening them, but it finally broke shortly before midnight, just as they put the finishing touches to the new paintwork and declared the work done.

The next morning dawned clear and fresh, with not a cloud in the sky, almost as if it had been planned, but Gwen didn't see it. Nor did she notice when somebody came to call Kitty for a dawn sortie, or wake up when the squadron took off. She eventually rolled out of bed, bleary-eyed, about an hour later and stumbled to the bathroom, where she stood under the shower for a long time, taking advantage both that the tanks that had been filled by the rain and that the mirrors on the roof were heating the water more than they had the last few days. She was still there when the squadron returned and barely heard the buzzing sound of their airscrews over the water as they landed, but it was enough to rouse her from her lethargy and spur her into action.

She dressed in her day uniform and headed for the mess.

The other pilots were in debriefing or taking care of their machines, so once again she was on her own except for the waiters. That didn't last for very long, though, because the wing commander walked in just after she'd finished a soft-boiled egg and had started working on some toast with honey.

'I thought I'd find you here! I'm glad you got some rest this morning because you're going to need it. Finish your food, then get your flightsuit on and meet me outside the workshop in half an hour - I already know you're a damn fine mechanic, now it's time to see if you can cut it as a pilot as well.'

CHAPTER 5

It felt good to be putting on her flightsuit again. It had been folded at the bottom of her kitbag, all but forgotten, since she'd taken it off after that fateful flight and she'd feared she would never wear it again. It was not much different from her work coveralls, just a plain one piece suit in a lightweight brown fabric, baggy enough to wear thermal clothing underneath, with a small black chalkboard attached to her right thigh, but it had a much deeper significance than her work clothes; she only put it on when she was going to *fly*.

She sat down on the bed to pull on her black leather calf-high boots, then reached under her pillow to grab the photo of her husband. She touched his face with her fingertips and gave him a smile before putting it in her breast pocket.

From separate boxes at the top of her wardrobe she took out her RAC issue compass, which she snapped onto her right arm, and her chronograph, which went on her left.

Lastly, she dug the box with her flight helmet and gloves out of the bottom of the wardrobe. The helmet was as simple as the flightsuit - a fairly stiff padded leather helmet with attached goggles and magnification lenses which could be slid up and down at whim. She put it on; it was easier than carrying it, then tucked her gloves under her arm.

Fully dressed she stood and inspected herself in the mirror.

The woman was the same one that had stared back at her every day for the past few weeks, but in flight gear she just looked so much *more*.

With a smile, she touched her fingers to her helmet in salute and marched out, heading for the airstrip.

Waiting on the airstrip was Wing Commander Lennox and her yellow aircraft, Dragonfly, its elegant lines picked out with black highlights. It looked like the whole of the rest of the squadron were there too - they had dragged the deckchairs into the sunshine in front of the mess building and settled in. They looked like they were expecting a show. They were still in their flightsuits, but she was shocked to see that there was not a single RAC regulation suit among them; they were all wearing custom suits, each a masterpiece and they were displaying a riot of colours to rival those of their machines.

Suddenly finding herself quite nervous and certainly feeling drab and unattractive in her standard issue flightsuit, Gwen stomped over to Abby, who was performing final checks on her machine with a couple of Dragonfly's fitters before takeoff. She looked up as Gwen approached and came round the aircraft to meet her.

Gwen came to a halt and took in the sight of her new commander's custom yellow leather flightsuit, picked out in black to match her aircraft. It was tightly fitting around the legs and lower abdomen where it had bulging pockets holding liquid to help her combat the stress of tight turns. It flared out from her waist to wide lapels that would be folded closed to form a high neck when she was flying, but which she had left open in the mid-morning sun. She had her custom compass on her left arm, and an ornate brass antique chronograph on her right, which told Gwen that she was left-handed.

Her suit was a delight to behold, but it was her helmet which caught Gwen's attention for long seconds. The helmet itself was yellow leather, matching her suit, and was designed much like Gwen's, but, instead of the simple hinges over the temples that held the goggles and lenses on a normal helmet, it had some kind of mechanism to which were attached an extremely complex array of lenses, a few of which were different colours for various light conditions. Wires went from the mechanism through loose gold rings along her collar and down the outside of her left sleeve to her glove where they finally disappeared. Slight bulges on the back of her glove revealed where they had gone and their purpose - they were pressure controls, electric devices that would turn the clockwork mechanism at her temple and slide chosen lenses up and down at a simple press.

'Ready, Aviator Sergeant?'

Gwen was startled out of her inspection and coloured when she realised that she had been staring at the woman for some time. 'Yes, ma'am.'

'Well, then, I suggest you go and get Wasp.'

Gwen nodded and hurried over to the workshop, smiling when she saw that the doors were closed, hiding the machine inside from prying eyes. The six fitters were at attention in front of the workshop waiting for her, Sergeant Jenkins standing a few feet in front of a line formed by the other five. Every single one of them had dark circles under their eyes from lack of sleep, matching the ones she'd seen in the mirror earlier, but they wore their tiredness as a badge of pride. Jimmy was to one side, leaning against the wall and he gave her a grin and thumbs up.

The fitters came to attention at Jenkins' order when she came to a halt in front of him and he saluted her, paying the traditional tribute to the pilot of their aircraft, even though as an NCO she didn't warrant a salute.

She nodded solemnly, acknowledging the salute, but unable to return it by regulations that prevented possible damage to her lenses. 'Sergeant.'

Jenkins nodded to her. 'At your command, Aviator Sergeant.'

'Roll her out, please.'

Jenkins smartly turned to bark at the other fitters. 'Right! You heard the boss! Get those bloody doors open!'

The fitters broke to each side, the movement as well-coordinated as if they had practised it (which she didn't put past them) and Jimmy joined them as they pulled the doors open.

The Sergeant continued giving orders and the men and women raced to positions around the fighter, which was almost invisible in the dark confines of the workshop - Jenkins evidently had a flair for the theatrical and had kept the lights off, not wanting the machine to become visible until it was revealed by the bright sunlight.

Another order had the fitters pushing and Gwen held her breath, straining to hear any reactions or comments from Abby or the gathered pilots as they finally got a good look at Wasp. There were a few as the more mechanically-minded among them began pointing out her modifications to the others and she heard the word "cannon" two or three times, but the murmuring very quickly died away again, which wasn't wholly unexpected; they would reserve their opinions for when they saw how she flew the aircraft and wouldn't be impressed by a fresh coat of paint and some repairs that could have been done by anybody with the help of the expert fitters that Misfit Squadron had to offer.

The fitters rolled Wasp around to Dragonfly's right side before turning her smartly and bringing her exactly level.

Despite Gwen's modifications and the two cannons poking forward from the wings, it was clear that they shared the same original designers. However, the contrasting paint jobs made them look very different - Gwen had kept the bottom side of Wasp a gloss black in homage to the heritage of the machine, but she had had the top half painted a bright pink, the colour of the sky at twilight on her parents' estate in Oxfordshire (she hadn't been lying when she'd told Kitty that it was her favourite colour). It was undoubtedly garish, but it would fit in perfectly with the rest of the machines in the squadron, some of which were much much harder on the eye, as if their pilots had been competing to see who could do most damage to the enemy's eyes. The paintwork on the enormous Dreadnought was especially jarring, for example; it had been painted with a dazzle camouflage, usually reserved for ships, and in clashing colours that certainly didn't serve to camouflage anything.

Abby wandered over to Gwen. 'Well, it looks good, and I see you fit Wendy's guns in, but she needs a couple more coats of paint to really do that colour justice.'

Gwen grimaced; the fitters had obviously been up much earlier that morning because Wasp was buffed to a high shine, but it showed that they had only had time to do the primer and a single coat the night before - the black was fine, obviously, although it could do with being deeper, but the pink was looking decidedly grey and sorry for itself as the primer showed through.

Abby saw her expression. 'Not to worry, it's her airworthiness that matters this morning, you can finish off the paint some other time. Go on, get your pre-flight checks done and let's go have some fun!'

'Yes, ma'am!' Gwen returned the woman's grin and skipped off to carry out her checks.

It didn't take long and soon she was sitting in the cockpit ready to go. She plugged her helmet into the radio and the wing commander's voice immediately came over her headset.

'All set?'

'Yes, ma'am. What are our call signs?'

'The squadron call sign is Badger, you're Badger Two and you're sitting on Badger Base, understood?'

'Roger, Badger Leader.'

'Good. Release springs.'

Abigail pulled the lever that released the hold on her Ozymandias spring and gently moved the throttle forwards.

The airscrew in front of her smoothly and silently started to turn and out of habit she cringed, saying a silent prayer, waiting for a creak or crack to indicate that the spring was starting to slip, but it never came; this squadron didn't have to make do with worn Ozzy's like everyone else.

The airscrew built speed as she slid the throttle forwards, the thrum of it moving through the air swiftly becoming audible and the machine seemed to come alive around Gwen, like a racehorse in the starting gate, or a greyhound sighting the rabbit.

'Chocks away!'

The wing commander gave the signal to the fitters who pulled the wooden blocks from the wheels and the two machines surged forwards, throttles to the stops. Gwen was pushed back into her seat far harder than she had ever been in her Harridan; despite having the same spring, Wasp was so much lighter and better at converting the power provided into thrust. She lightly touched her brakes to allow the leader's machine to draw ahead a few feet, then pushed her nose down, bringing her tailwheel off the ground to better build speed.

She couldn't believe it when she felt the machine come alive around her and almost immediately began clamouring at her to pull back on the stick and set it free. The takeoff run was incredibly short, barely four seconds instead of the six or seven the Harridan took and she rotated at exactly the same time as the wing commander, only just restraining herself from yelling in exhilaration as Wasp came unstuck from the ground with a joyful leap.

The two machines climbed swiftly and were already above the level of the trees as they passed the last of the buildings, only half way down the runway. As soon as they had clear air below them, Gwen adjusted her position and settled behind and slightly below her leader.

'Check in.'

Abby's voice came over the radio loud and clear and Gwen scanned her instruments, quickly seeing that everything was showing perfect readings, as expected. 'Badger Two, Roger.'

'Climbing to angels six on heading three one zero.'

Gwen followed her onto the new heading, still climbing, and found her face was starting to hurt with the huge grin that was plastered onto it. She worked her jaw, hearing it crack, then tried to relax, but found that the smile just kept coming back.

After what seemed like no time at all, they levelled out and Abby dropped back to bring Dragonfly alongside Wasp. Gwen saw her looking the machine over, doing a visual check, but then their eyes met and the woman grinned and gave her a thumbs up.

'Well, she certainly looks good. Let's see how she handles. I'm going to go through some manoeuvres, try to stay with me.'

'Roger, Badger Leader.'

The woman touched her fingers to her helmet and Gwen returned the gesture before dropping back to her original position.

Abby flew straight and level for a few seconds and Gwen was about to ask if something was wrong, when suddenly Dragonfly rotated through ninety degrees, instantly standing on its wing before pulling into a sharp turn. She put Wasp into a similar position, marvelling at how easily and quickly the aircraft rolled, then followed Abby as she put her machine into a series of aerobatic manoeuvres, each more strenuous than the last. Gwen had no problem keeping up with her, though; Wasp was far more agile than both the Harridan and the Spitsteam (she'd had the chance to fly one a couple of times in training). The machine was actually very much like the aircraft she had built specifically to do aerobatics in when she was thirteen, only much more powerful because of the military-grade Ozzy, instead of the Pickering that she'd been limited to - one of the earliest commercially-available springs, at times it had seemed barely capable of getting her off the ground, let alone powering her into a loop.

After a couple of minutes Dragonfly levelled out again. 'Still there, Two?'

'Still here, Leader.' Gwen found she was gently panting for breath; sustained aerobatics were physically demanding and she was slightly out of shape because she hadn't flown in far too long.

'Check in.'

Gwen gave her instrument panel a quick once over, but, as she had expected, all the readings were perfect. 'Badger Two, Roger.'

'I want to see how your modifications have affected Wasp's turn rate. I'm going to fall back about twenty lengths behind you. When I say so I want you to put her into maximum turn and I'm going to follow you round, understood?'

'Understood, Leader.'

Dragonfly decelerated as Abby throttled back, disappearing into the blind spot behind Wasp's tail, then about twenty seconds later the wing commanders voice came over the radio. 'Badger Leader to Two, go when ready.'

'Roger.'

Gwen put Wasp on her wing and pulled back on the stick. Black started to close in around her vision, threatening to overwhelm her, but she continued to bring the stick further, using both hands, until it was almost in her lap, knowing that Wasp could take it and that she herself wasn't yet at her limit.

Her weight increased and her head became so heavy it felt that her neck was going to collapse under the pressure, but she forced herself to look upwards through the canopy, searching out Dragonfly, curious as to how the two machines compared. She immediately found the yellow machine almost directly overhead, on the other side of the circle that the two aircraft were drawing in the sky, but it was only when the yellow machine perceptibly began to move backwards that she realised that Wasp was catching up. She slotted a magnification lens into place, sneaking a closer look at the wing commander's face while she could, and was inordinately pleased to see surprise and shock to match her own evident in the woman's expression.

Even though Wasp was already turning better than Dragonfly, Gwen was positive that it could turn even tighter; there were no signs whatsoever of the wings stalling, no buffeting or looseness in the stick due to the high angle of attack. However, the black encroaching on her vision was a warning that, if she tried, she might fall unconscious, which wasn't exactly desirous in the air, and especially not in the middle of a fight. The story would have been much different if she'd had her own custom flight suit, like the other Misfits, instead of her standard issue RAC one; they were designed to slow the flow of blood from the head and keep pilots awake under much greater force. She just had to hope that the wing commander would allow her to make one or, even better, get her parents to send her own from home.

Wasp continued to gain steadily on Dragonfly and after less than half a minute the tailplane of the Wing Commander's aircraft swam into Gwen's sights. She smiled and made sure that her radio was off before murmuring softly, 'ratatatata.'

'I think that should do.' Abby's voice over the comms betrayed the strain she was feeling from maintaining the turn for so long and her lazy roll out spoke of a tiredness in her arms that matched that of Gwen's.

Gwen followed her out of the turn and neatly slotted back into position behind her right wing and slightly below her.

'Oof, that was hard work!' The wing commander's chuckle carried over the radio. 'I think we'll take a bit of a breather for a couple of minutes. Do something a bit less vigorous. Badger Base is under our left wings, follow me down and we'll give them a bit of a show. Come on to my left wing as we turn, power dive together, pull up and run along the strip at zero altitude, buzz the mess, then into an Immelmann with opposite barrel rolls to finish at the top, you go clockwise so we cross with me in front. Got it?'

Gwen smiled; she loved aerobatics and it looked like she had found a kindred spirit. 'Got it, Leader.'

'Just make sure you're far enough behind me to not chop my tail off on the barrel! Alright, on my mark... Three, two, one, mark!'

They peeled off and Gwen slotted Wasp neatly in behind Dragonfly's wing as they dove towards the air base almost a mile below them.

Even thought they were heading almost directly towards it, Gwen still had to look twice before she was certain that what she was looking at was the airfield and she realised that if she hadn't known it was there she probably wouldn't have noticed it - it looked like nothing more than a clearing among the trees, just like so many others that were visible below, although it was maybe a tad more regular. There was certainly no sign of the well-camouflaged buildings that were tucked under the trees and only with her lenses at full magnification could she make out the colourful dots that betrayed the presence of the pilots in their deckchairs.

The air speed indicator needle crept towards and then past the marker for four hundred miles per hour as they screamed out of the sky at slightly more than a forty-five degree angle and Gwen nervously looked over at her wingman as they went below two thousand, then one thousand five hundred feet - even though what they were doing wasn't anything at all special or dangerous, she wasn't absolutely certain of Wasp's capabilities yet and wanted more time in the air with the aircraft before pushing its limits.

The wing commander seemed to have taken her new pilot's unfamiliarity with her machine into consideration, though, and no sooner had Gwen glanced across at her than she started to come out of the dive, rather more gently than she could have done.

Gwen was too busy flying to have another good look at the air speed indicator, but she thought she saw the needle hovering around the five hundred mark before they started to decelerate, rounding out of the dive and shooting along just above the trees.

Suddenly the trees disappeared from under them and they were above the narrow airstrip.

Gwen swallowed as Abby dipped her machine into the void, taking Dragonfly further down until grass clippings flew up in her wake, but she matched her and even edged Wasp into a closer formation that would have made Berty Withers proud.

The buildings flashed past them on both sides so quickly that they had gone the whole length of them and before Gwen knew it they were level with the officer's mess, the pilots out of their chairs, jumping up and down, cheering and waving, then once again the blackness was closing in as the stick came back into her lap and she followed Abby as Dragonfly shot back up into the sky. The blackout didn't last long, though, because they soon got to the top of their loop, where they remained inverted for a heartbeat before Abby initiated her barrel roll. Gwen followed suit and the two aircraft smartly came out of the inversion and were once again flying straight and level with Wasp tucked back under Dragonfly's right wing.

Gwen couldn't help herself this time and she whooped, adrenaline causing her heart to pump what felt like ten times its normal speed. She glanced across to Dragonfly and found the wing commander watching her, a broad grin on her face.

'Not bad, Badger Two.'

'Thank you, Leader. That was fun.'

'Yes, it was, rather, wasn't it?' Abby chuckled before setting Dragonfly to climb again, turning in a wide circle around the airfield. When they were back up at six thousand feet she levelled out again.

'Alright, last test. You break right, I'll break left. Fly straight for a ten count then turn round. We'll go head to head, then straight into a dogfight. Best of three wins, understood?'

'Roger, Leader.'

'Good! On my mark... Three, two, one, break!'

Gwen pulled into a swift ninety degree turn. Her face was really beginning to hurt now with the stress of maintaining her constant grin and the added strain of the G forces, but she didn't care one bit; this was flying, this was what she had signed up for and she was looking forward to testing herself against her new squadron commander.

There was no trace of her smile when they landed ten minutes later. The wing commander had absolutely thrashed her.

Twice.

Despite Wasp's tighter turning circle she had never been close to getting onto Dragonfly's tail. Every time she'd thought she had the upper hand, Abby had carried out some kind of impossible manoeuvre or other and taken away her advantage in an instant. Even going into the tightest turn she could, skirting the limits of her abilities to remain conscious, did her no good, as the wing commander would always find some way to cut her off and put her in the firing line.

They taxied to the hangar and as soon as they had shut down and jumped out the fitters grabbed the two aircraft and pushed them inside, hiding them from the possibility of chance discovery by passing enemy.

Gwen watched as the men and women wheeled low winding machines under each of the aircraft and jacked up what to Gwen's eyes had always looked like an overgrown screwdriver, slotting it into the round opening on the bottom of both fuselages. The gentle chugging of the steam engines increased slightly in volume and the metal columns started to spin, gently and carefully rewinding the Ozzy's.

Abby came out of the hangar where she had been speaking with her fitters and walked up to stand next to Gwen, beaming widely. 'Excellent job on the repairs, Gwen and I'm really impressed with how you've improved her turn rate. But, as you know, just being able to turn tighter than your opponent won't automatically win you a fight, experience will. Don't worry, though, you'll get that experience soon enough. Just stay on my wing like you did today, watch and learn and above all else, please try to stay alive. Got it?'

'Yes, ma'am.'

'Good.' She looked at the chronograph on her right wrist. 'Right, I'll let Fighter Command know that I'm keeping you when I speak to them, but, as of this moment, you are back on active duty, Aviator Sergeant Stone. You'll join us for the afternoon sortie, so if nobody tells you differently be in the briefing room at twelve-twenty, please. Rest, have a cup of tea and I'll see you then.' She gave Gwen a nod, then walked away, heading towards the mess and the pilots gathered on the other side of the strip.

Gwen barely saw her go; she was too busy staring at Wasp, wondering how she could make the machine better. She felt hurt and humiliated and angry tears of impotence were prickling at her eyes as she thought about the ease with which the wing commander had bested her, but she wiped them away when she heard someone coming up behind her.

She expected it to be Jimmy, coming to say something inappropriate, so she ignored him and continued to stare at Wasp, but after a few seconds there was a high-pitched chuckle and Kitty came around to stand in front of her, blocking her view of her aircraft. The American woman was wearing a dark blue helmet and a striking red flight suit with a single white stripe running vertically down the sides of her limbs and body, the tightness of which just served to highlight her lithe figure. She put her hands on her hips and stared at Gwen, appraising her, obviously seeing the reddened eyes and the pursed lips that Gwen knew were her tells for when she was upset.

'She beat you.'

It was a statement, not a question, but Gwen nodded anyway.

'And you're pretty cut up about it, right?'

Again Gwen just nodded, not trusting her voice to stay steady.

Kitty sighed and shook her head. 'Well, don't be! She beats everyone in the squadron, most of them a hell of a lot easier than she did you.'

'How do you know that?'

Kitty gestured to her helmet, with its array of lenses. 'We were watching - why do you think she did it above the airfield? We run all our practice dogfights in sight, that way the rest of us can watch and learn. Plus it gives anyone who's off duty a good show. And believe me, you gave them a much better show than most of the rest of us ever have.' She pointed to the other side of the airstrip where men and women were folding away deckchairs outside both the NCO and enlisted men and women's messes. Gwen had been so concerned about embarrassing herself in front of the pilots that she hadn't noticed that there had been a whole other audience to worry about.

Kitty smiled as she continued. 'As I said, there's no reason to stress about losing to her, or read too much into it either; she's been flying since she was tall enough to reach rudder pedals and is the best pilot any of us have ever seen, friend or foe. She has twenty-seven confirmed kills and at least double that in probables. So don't let it get you down or make you resentful, just suck it up and learn from her. We all do.'

Gwen forced a smile. 'I'll try.'

'It was very exciting by the way and everybody was damn impressed with how well you did. Oh, and I won the pool! So I have that to thank you for - I'll buy you a drink tonight once we're released!'

'Pool? What pool?'

The American grinned. 'Yeah, we were betting on how long you were going to last in the dogfights and none of us came *close* to guessing you would last as long as you did. So, what does that tell you?'

Kitty raised an eyebrow, but didn't wait for an answer before striding off back to where the other pilots were still sunning themselves.

74

Gwen turned back to Wasp. Kitty's words, especially her last ones, had lifted her mood considerably, but they had also opened her eyes to the fact that it wasn't any fault with the aircraft that had made her lose, it had been a fault with herself - as Abby had said, she lacked experience.

Misfit Squadron had seen a hell of a lot of combat, if the trophies in the officer's mess were anything to go on, whereas she had only been in real combat once and the practice dogfights she'd had at the RAC flight school training were nothing compared to that kind of experience.

She would improve as time went on, though. All she needed to do was follow her wingmate's lead, learn, get to know her machine better... and survive.

She smiled at her garish pink aircraft. 'Sorry I doubted you, girl. I'll do better in the future.'

She gave Sergeant Jenkins and her fitters a wave, then turned on her heels and headed towards the mess; a cup of tea sounded pretty good all of a sudden and maybe they would have some crumpets left over from breakfast.

CHAPTER 6

A helpful airman pointed Gwen towards the briefing hall, which turned out to be a large building, almost the size of the hangar, in the woods a little way past the barracks. It was actually in plain sight of her room, but somehow she hadn't noticed it before, although that was probably because she hadn't been in her room very much during daylight hours.

In contrast to the rest of the holiday camp side of the base, it wasn't built of stone, but was rather an impressive building of cast iron and plate glass, which must have held spectacular balls during the long summer evenings. Its magnificent design, very similar to the Crystal Palace on Sydenham Hill in London, was marred somewhat, though, by the blackout curtains covering every window, many of which were closed despite it being the middle of the day and were probably never opened.

Gwen walked along the small path leading up to the door and stepped inside. Within was a single large room with a small stage at the far end and enough wooden folding chairs to seat perhaps the whole base. The only support for the roof, apart from the walls, was provided by four flimsy-looking iron pillars that sprouted delicate filaments. These met in a spectacular spider's web of silvery beams high overhead, but once again the effect was spoiled by the curtains which were draped over them, completely hiding the glass ceiling from view.

Six large boards were set up at the far end of the room in front of the stage. The two on the left were covered with maps in what looked like a permanent display and Wing Commander Lennox was filling a third. The others were empty.

Gwen made her way down the central aisle of the seats to the front and joined Abby. The woman was pinning photographs to the board around a large scale map of Kent - they were aerial images of the local landmarks, some of which Gwen thought she recognised from the flight that morning.

'Visible references are few and far between out here and I had these photographs taken when the squadron first moved here a couple of months ago so that we could familiarise ourselves with them without having to fly around too much - one of the drawbacks of making it so that the enemy can't see the base is that we can't see it either! But then Jimmy came up with a bit of a brilliant idea.'

She pointed to the four pictures that were pinned at each corner of the map. Puzzlingly they appeared to show empty fields. 'Take a closer look at these.'

Gwen leaned in closer and frowned when she saw nothing in them beyond grass and crops.

Abby smiled. 'You don't notice anything peculiar about the shapes of the fields?'

'Well... I suppose they're shaped a bit like a cross...'

'Very much like a cross, actually! But not enough to appear completely unnatural. There are about a dozen fields set out just like these throughout the Downs. The longer arm of the cross points towards the base, so if you lose your way and can't spot any of the other landmarks, then you should be able to find a field somewhere that will point you home. You should familiarise yourself with the rest of the landmarks as well though, just in case.'

Gwen nodded. 'Will do. By the way, why go to so much trouble to keep the base a secret?'

'Because Whitehall have always known that the Fleas were going to go after RAC bases to try to destroy our air power by denying us ground facilities and this base is a priority target for the Fleas - a lot of the communications that have been intercepted since we got back from France mention "Operation Odd One Out" which is their code for the search for our base. You've been a bit busy recently, so I'm not surprised you haven't heard, but that's exactly what they've been doing. They've bombed out almost all of our airfields in the South in the last week, including your old base, RAC Didchurch and we're one of the last official RAC bases still operating.'

'Before you ask why they didn't try to hide other bases the same way they have ours, it's because it would have been impossible, as well as fruitless - most RAC bases were established well before the war and they're on every map the Prussians have. And besides, Britain just doesn't have enough resources to spare to run more than one base like this.

'The situation's not as serious as it sounds, though; most squadrons have just moved to flying clubs or private airfields and it's apparently become quite fashionable among the aristocracy and well-off to have an RAC squadron operating from one's private airstrip. But it's not enough just to have a flat bit of grass and a place to sleep, though; many RAC squadrons don't have proper repair facilities and as a result they're suffering.'

Abby looked up at the sound of voices and Gwen turned to see the other pilots coming in through the door. They were laughing and joking, making quite a lot of noise and she watched them, soaking in their high spirits.

Despite their jocularity, when they reached the front of the auditorium, they sat down and fell silent, looking at their leader expectantly.

'Aviator Sergeant, take a seat and we'll start.'

'Yes, ma'am.' Gwen wandered towards the pilots, looking for an empty seat.

Kitty waved at her from the second row and pointed to the seat next to her and Gwen nodded in thanks and took it.

Abby waited for Gwen to sit down before starting. 'Right! First of all, I know I've already said it, but after today's display I'm happy to make it official - Aviator Sergeant Stone is joining the squadron...'

She was cut off by the sound of stamping feet and every single one of the pilots turned in their seats to grin at their newest member. Gwen grinned back at them and did her best to meet all of their eyes one by one.

When the noise finally died down, Abby continued, a wide smile on her face. 'As I was saying, before I was *so* rudely interrupted...'

She was interrupted again by laughter, but it didn't last nearly as long. 'With Gwen's arrival we are back up to full strength...'

'About bloody time too!' A young man with shockingly white hair in a plain black flightsuit cupped his hands around his mouth to call out.

'Yes, thank you, Charles. Anyway, this necessitates a bit of a reshuffle. So, Wasp will move onto my wing, which means that

Bandicoot will be moving into the three spot and Bruce will become the leader of the second pair. Got that, Bruce?'

'Right-oh, boss.' Gwen looked across the aisle to where a man in a dusty-looking light brown flightsuit was lounging in one of the seats in the front row. If his accent hadn't already marked him out as Australian, the patch on his shoulder showing the white Southern Cross constellation on deep blue background of the defunct Austral-Zealand Air Force certainly would have.

'Good. At sixteen hundred hours we'll takeoff and head towards Dover, climbing to angels twenty-two. If Fighter Command has any business for us then we'll go after that, if not we'll see if Bloodhound can find us some fun.' She grinned. 'It's been a few days since we had a decent scrap and we don't want the Fleas forgetting who we are, do we?'

Eager, throaty chuckles greeted her question.

'Once more, Vulture and Hummingbird won't be needed for this mission, but your aid has been requested elsewhere. Charles, you'll take Vulture over Belgium, Fighter Command will give you your briefing at fourteen hundred in the radio room.'

'Got it.' The young man with the white hair nodded.

'And Ophelia, Hummingbird is going into France again, I'm afraid, briefing at fourteen thirty hours, also in the radio room.'

The small woman sitting on the other side of Kitty groaned loudly. She was so short her feet only just touched the ground, with white freckled skin and a halo of the brightest red hair that Gwen had ever seen.

Abby looked at her in sympathy. 'I know, but you're the only scout Fighter Command has that can get us clear pictures of the Prussian buildup over the channel and get home safely.'

'Just make sure there's plenty of stout in the bar for when I get back.'

Abby nodded with a smile. 'Drinks are on me, as always.' There was a cheer from the rest of the pilots at that, but the wing commander immediately waved her hands to stop them. 'Only hers! I'm not paying for your drinks, you spongers; I'd go broke in minutes!' She continued speaking over the chuckles. 'Assembly on the flight line at fifteen fifty hours, until then you're free to put your feet up. Dismissed!'

As the rest of the pilots began to stand up and file back towards the exit, Kitty turned to Gwen. 'Scarlet and I are going to get lunch, do you want to join?'

'I'd love to, thank you! Uh, who's Scarlet?'

'That would be me!' The red-haired woman leaned around Kitty to wave. The woman had a beautiful soft voice with a lovely Irish brogue which Gwen had to struggle slightly to understand. She was wearing a green and brown camouflage-patterned flightsuit that was considerably more drab than anything anyone else, apart from Gwen, was sporting. It also didn't have any of the liquid filled pockets around the legs and abdomen which combated G forces like most of the rest of the Misfits had built in to their custom suits. 'The only person in this squadron who calls me Ophelia is Abby, everyone else just calls me Scarlet. You know, because of the hair.'

'Pleased to meet you!'

'Likewise!' Scarlet smiled and the three women stood and followed the stampede towards the doors - none of the pilots wanted to waste precious moments of freedom.

Ten minutes later the three women were sitting in the dining room of the officer's mess, grouped around the end of one of the tables with Gwen at the head, the American on her right hand and the Irishwoman on her left. The rest of the pilots were in the mess as well, either in their own groups around the tables or sitting out at the bar.

While they were waiting for their food to come Gwen was trying to get to know her companions a bit better.

'Do you often have to go on solo missions over France?'

Scarlet shrugged. 'Well, there's not much for a scout to do now that we're stuck in England and Hummingbird isn't much use in a fight, so I tend to get roped into doing things like taking photos of Prussian airfields from close enough to count the aircraft in the hangars, or seeing what the regional commander's dog is having for breakfast.'

Gwen laughed, but immediately stopped when she realised that neither of the other two were even smiling. 'Really? A dog's breakfast?'

The small woman nodded seriously. 'I landed Hummingbird in a forest clearing, hiked five miles through the trees and sneaked into a warehouse to take pictures of crates which were supposed to contain weapon supplies for a possible invasion. We figured out afterwards that it was some kind of mix up with translation of enemy codes, but they ended up being crates of food for a Prussian Army general's pack of hunting dogs.'

'Oh god...'

Scarlet shrugged. 'You can imagine I wasn't best pleased with Fighter Command when I found out. I wanted to fly up to London, park Hummingbird on the roof at Whitehall and give them a good talking to.'

'Why didn't you?'

'Abby convinced me to get drunk instead. And paid for the drinks.' She gave Gwen a lopsided grin. 'Since then it's become a bit of a tradition for her to do that every time I go on a stupid mission, which I think is a more than fair trade!'

The three women looked up as a waiter came over with their food. Gwen had ordered a steak, something she hadn't had since before the war because of shortages and had been shocked to see on the menu, Kitty was something called a vegetarian and had asked for baked potatoes with assorted vegetables and Scarlett had a large slice of shepherd's pie.

They ate in silence for a while; the same as with sleep, eating was something that was done quickly and whenever possible, and, even though they knew that they had some time to spare, it was a hard habit to beat, especially for the two veteran Misfits.

Eventually, though, they slowed down, as much for their digestion as for a desire to continue to enjoy each other's conversation and company.

There was something that Gwen had been itching to ask since the first moment she'd stepped into the mess, but hadn't had the opportunity and she took advantage of the momentary silence to do so. 'The trophies in the bar. There's a few red ones... Are those what I think they are?'

Kitty and Scarlet shared a knowing look.

'We were wondering how long it would take,' said Scarlet. 'Usually a guest to the mess can't take their eyes off them and it's the first thing they ask about.'

Kitty nodded. 'Anyone who knows they're from the Crimson Barons, anyway - there's been quite a few army generals and cabinet ministers who haven't glanced at them twice.'

'We had a few run-ins with the Barons in France and always got the best of them. Over the course of the five engagements we had with them the wing commander shot down one and shared another with Bruce. Cece got one as well and Kitty here got a share of one with Derek.'

'Wow! So how did you get the trophies? Did somebody have to go out and recover bits of the wreckage? Wasn't that a bit dangerous? Did you get sent to do that as well?'

Gwen looked at the Irishwoman, but it was the American who answered.

'Actually, the Barons sent us the souvenirs.'

'Excuse me?' Gwen blinked at her.

Scarlet laughed. 'Yes, it was all very gentlemanly of them. The first time we shot one of them down a courier, one of the pilots, arrived under a white flag on a spring-powered tricycle with the vertical stabiliser wrapped up in white linen. He brought with him a letter detailing the personal history of the pilot whose machine it had been, along with news that he had bailed out and was looking forward to meeting us again.'

Gwen shook her head, bemused. 'How civilised.'

'Well, just because our leaders are like a pack of rabid dogs at each other's necks, doesn't mean we have to be.'

Scarlet spoke with a straight face and Gwen got the impression that it was something that she and Kitty and probably most of the other pilots believed. She, however, couldn't quite bring herself to think that way; she hated the Prussians for the death of her husband and wouldn't be satisfied until they were destroyed utterly.

She said nothing about that, though, and listened as Kitty picked up the story. 'Anyway, when the same thing happened the second time, Abby sent a message back with the courier to Hans Gruber, their leader, and over the course of a few dispatches she agreed that we would pay the same courtesy to them. They also agreed to return the bodies of any pilot who was shot down and killed over enemy territory. The fourth Baron we shot down went into the drink off Calais and didn't survive the crash. The Navy recovered the body and we sent it back to them with full honours.'

'Hans Gruber... I feel like I should know that name.'

Kitty nodded. 'You should, but only if you stepped inside a movie theatre or read a society paper in the early thirties. He was a big thing in Hollywoodland for a while and did a lot of Flyvies, usually playing the chivalrous enemy - "Heroes Over The Poppy Fields" was one, but he was most famous for "The Baron and the Princess," which is reportedly where he got the name for his troupe from.'

'I saw that one four times!' Gwen's mouth dropped open. 'I had such a crush on him when I was ten!'

Scarlet winked, leering slightly. 'Didn't we all, luv!'

Gwen frowned in confusion as she tried to take in the information of who was in charge of the most infamous enemy squadron, responsible for the deaths of so many pilots of so many nations, trying to equate the mild-spoken and gallant Hans Gruber that she'd seen so many times on the silver screen with the image she had built of the enemy being half-crazed, die-hard fanatics. She found she couldn't and forced herself to stop trying, not wanting to humanise an enemy she had sworn to kill. 'So, why haven't we seen the Barons over England?'

Kitty snorted in amusement. 'Apparently they're doing some kind of recruitment drive propaganda thingamajig through Prussia at the moment, celebrating their victory in France and using Gruber's fame to drive up the numbers of young men and women who want to join the Fleas.'

Scarlet smiled wryly. 'Don't worry, they'll be here soon, I'm sure of it. And then the muck will hit the airscrew, believe me.'

After lunch, most of the pilots returned to the deckchairs in front of the mess and Gwen joined them, finding that there was an extra chair already set out for her.

Conversation was kept to a minimum, though, as most of them took naps, catching up on the sleep that they had lost getting up for that morning's dawn patrol and making sure that they were fresh for the afternoon's flight. Gwen found herself nodding off as well and just gave in to the temptation to snooze.

The only time the pilots showed much sign of life was when first Hummingbird, then Vulture took off on their respective missions - the Misfits, woken by the sounds of the airscrews, lifted their feet off of the floor and held them in the air while the aircraft were on their takeoff runs and only put them down when the machines were safely over the trees and into clear sky.

Soon enough, though, it was half past three and waiters came out of the mess to wake the pilots with cups of tea and plates of cakes and biscuits. There was just enough time to eat and drink, then pay a quick visit to the barracks and the ablutions before being back on the flight line at ten to the hour.

Gwen and Kitty crossed the airfield together and went into the hangar.

It was a hive of activity, centred around each of the remaining ten aircraft as teams of fitters carried out last-minute checks before takeoff.

Gwen's eyes automatically went to Wasp, sitting with the other aircraft of A flight to her right. The paintwork still needed a bit of work, but she found she (almost) didn't care; for the first time she was going to go into combat in an aircraft that was *hers*. And besides, Sergeant

Jenkins had said that the fitters would give Wasp another coat of paint after the squadron had been released that night and would do the same every night until they were satisfied that the colour was as deep as it could be.

Kitty was in B flight which meant her machine was on the other side of the hangar to Wasp. Before they split up, though, the American pulled Gwen into a hug. 'Be careful up there, OK, Gwen? Stick with Abby; she'll see you clear.'

'You take care as well.'

'I always do!' Kitty smiled then skipped away to her aircraft, Hawk, a large, twin-boomed monoplane painted in red, white and blue.

Gwen watched the American go with a smile, then walked towards Wasp.

Sergeant Jenkins was waiting for her with the rest of her team of fitters, the five who had worked on the repairs with her. She was about to ask him if everything was ready when something caught her eye and she stopped in her tracks - underneath her cockpit were painted two iron crosses, representing the two kills she had made the day she had been grounded.

She reached out to touch them, but before she could, Sergeant Jenkins spoke from beside her. 'I wouldn't, Aviator, they might still be a bit wet.'

She looked up at him. 'Thank you.'

'No need to thank me; you earned them and it was a pleasure to put them on. And it's something we'll be all too happy to do again, as often as possible! Isn't that right, chaps?'

He addressed his question to the other fitters, who had been listening and were grinning from ear to ear as they nodded eagerly.

Gwen was about to reply, but Jenkins held a hand up to stop her, pointing over her shoulder as a wave of silence and stillness began to spread throughout the hangar. She turned to see the wing commander standing in the gap between the hangar doors, illuminated by the thin ray of bright sunshine coming between the barely open doors.

Abby looked from one aircraft, with its corresponding group of pilots and fitters, to the next as she waited for the hangar to fall completely silent. When she looked towards Wasp her eyes met Gwen's and she nodded almost imperceptibly before continuing her sweep, checking the readiness of the aircraft under her command.

Finally the silence in the cavernous space was complete and she nodded to them. 'Good afternoon, Misfits. Fighter Command says there is plenty of business heading our way this afternoon so everybody stay with their wingman and look out for each other. Stay safe and happy hunting.'

'Happy hunting.' The pilots and fitters echoed her words before going back to their preparations, but Gwen stayed where she was as Abby came directly to her.

'Aviator Sergeant, how are you feeling?'

'Raring to go, ma'am.'

The woman smiled. 'Glad to hear it. Now, just remember what I said - stick to me like glue and do not break off unless I tell you to or you have absolutely no choice. No chasing after targets, no matter how juicy they look, because it might well be a trap. By the way, those orders aren't just because you're new and it's not a comment on your ability, it's just the way we do it - Misfits fight as pairs. Always. It's a hell of a lot safer.'

'Got it.' Gwen nodded. She wasn't too unhappy about the rule; anything that made sure pilots got home safe was a good thing in her books.

'Good. Get your checks done, we takeoff in five minutes.'

The woman gave Gwen a last smile then spun on her heels and went off to see to her own machine.

CHAPTER 7

Less than ten minutes later the squadron was in the air and climbing hard to the south-east.

The takeoff had been a perfectly choreographed ballet with A flight coming out of the hangar first and immediately turning and accelerating, closely followed by B flight. However, it was the takeoff of C flight that had really made Gwen goggle in wonder.

The two aircraft from C flight that were accompanying them on the mission, Bloodhound and Dreadnought, were very large in comparison with the aircraft of A and B flight. The eye-achingly dazzle-camouflaged Dreadnought in particular was the biggest aircraft Gwen had ever seen - the ridged fuselage of the combined bomber and gun platform made it look like a whale with wings and it almost seemed impossible that it could fly at all, let alone takeoff from an airfield that hadn't been designed for machines of its size or extreme weight.

The solution that Wendy had found, or rather taken the inspiration from Charles' Vulture for, was more than a little unusual; a hatch, identical to the bomb bay doors that Dreadnought had on its belly, opened along the top of the aircraft and a huge ribbed balloon, much like a Zeppelin, deployed from it, swiftly filling with hydrogen from the tanks which supplied its six hugely-powerful steam engines. The balloon wasn't enough to lift the monstrous machine on its own, though, but Wendy had come up with a further innovation and Dreadnought's six airscrews rotated on their axes to point directly upwards, black smoke briefly spewing from them as they spun to full power.

The thrust from the engines combined with the lift from the balloon was more than enough to get the machine into the air with plenty of lift left over for it to carry another aircraft, which was what it did - ropes from winches in the wings of Dreadnought had been attached to hard points on the uniformly light-blue Bloodhound and the two machines rose majestically into the air, gaining altitude almost as quickly as the eight, much faster, fighters.

It was certainly a strange sight, but Gwen had seen far stranger; her parents had taken her to the yearly meetings of the *Société Aéronautique* when she had been growing up (month-long trips to the aviation centres of the world like Stockholm, St. Petersburg, Kyoto, Paris and New York, which had doubled as their family holidays) and many of the members, who had come from all over the world, had had far more unconventionally designed aircraft. In fact Gwen still didn't quite know how many of them even managed to fly, let alone transport their owners to meetings.

While she continued to climb with the other aircraft of A and B flights, Gwen snatched as many glances as she could at the two machines, noting how the balloon was deflating gradually over time - apparently the engines fed off the hydrogen in the balloon first, before using what it had in its tanks, so when it no longer needed the extra lift it didn't have to be released and there was nothing wasted.

Disappointingly, she lost sight of the two machines before they had transitioned into a more normal mode of flight, something which she would have liked to see, but she was positive she'd get another chance before too long and she put them out of her mind to concentrate on the job at hand and the, hopefully, coming fight.

The two flights of aircraft, in two finger-four formations, stayed together, despite having differing rates of climb, and reached twenty-two thousand feet in a surprisingly short time.

Once there the wing commander reported in to Fighter Command.

'Sapper, this is Badger Leader, over.'

The reply came quickly. 'Badger Leader, Sapper here. Go ahead, over.'

'Badger Squadron on station and awaiting orders, over.'

'Badger Leader, we have some business for you. Thirty plus aircraft at angels twenty on heading one two zero. Forty miles out and closing fast.'

'Acknowledged, Sapper, and thank you. Out.'

'Happy hunting, Badger Squadron. Sapper out.'

There was a click as Abby switched over to the squadron channel and despite the fact that the Misfits would be heavily outnumbered, Gwen could hear the confidence and glee in her voice. 'Well, you heard that, Badgers. Looks like we're in for some fun today! Turning to heading one two zero.'

A few seconds later, once the aircraft were settled onto their new heading, she called again. 'All Badgers, check in.'

Gwen, as Badger Two, had to answer first and a quick glance at her instruments showed that everything was perfect, as expected. 'Badger Two, Roger.'

One by one, the rest of the squadron reported in. Badgers Three and Four were the other two aircraft in A flight, Badger's Five to Eight were the four aircraft in B flight and they were followed by Bloodhound and Dreadnought, who were Badgers Nine and Ten, who were trailing some miles behind the fighters and still climbing steadily, but ready to render support if needed.

As soon as Wendy had finished reporting in, Abby came back over the radio. 'Right. Same plan as always - A flight will engage the fighters while B flight goes for the bombers. Dreadnought will circle overhead at angels thirty in case we need her while Bloodhound stays back to watch for surprises.'

There was no need to say anything else and the radio fell silent, leaving each of the pilots to prepare themselves for the coming battle in their own way.

'Wish me luck, darling.' Gwen kissed her gloved fingers then reached out to touch the glass of an ornate frame holding the photograph of her husband on the panel in front of her. One of the fitters had kindly made it for her, engraving it with clouds along the top and rolling fields along the bottom, and she had installed it at the same time as she'd replaced the cracked instruments and changed their configuration to better suit her.

'Badger Leader, this is Badger Nine, over.'

'Go ahead Nine, over.'

'I've got the blighters on the scope. Two formations. Ten plus at angels twenty and twenty plus at angels fifteen, over.'

'Thank you, Badger Nine. All Badgers, A flight will climb to angels twenty-five. B flight remain angels twenty-two.'

The pilots acknowledged and Gwen followed Abby as she began climbing again, the colourful shapes of B flight dropping away beneath them.

On the ground it might have been sunny and warm, but up so high it was very cold and Gwen wriggled her toes inside her boots in an effort to keep the life in them. She was wearing thick thermals under her flightsuit and thermal socks, but she sorely missed the custom suit her parents had given her for her sixteenth birthday. Regular RAC squadrons had to wear the ones that were provided, but things were much different in Misfit Squadron and she resolved to send for hers as soon as she could; not only would the heating make life a lot more comfortable at high altitudes, but she also desperately needed the G force protection it offered.

'Badger Leader, this is Badger Three.' Bruce's Australian accent was easy to recognise and Gwen glanced to her right at the brown biplane, Bandicoot, that was bobbing along on Abby's other wing.

'Go ahead, Three.'

'Enemy in sight. Two groups. Nines above one-elevens, right where they should be.'

Gwen reached up to slot lenses into place over her goggles and squinted into the distance. She saw nothing except a smudge, which might have been from the exhausts of the steam-powered HO111 bomber group, but could quite equally have been a cloud. Of the MU9 fighters that she would be engaging in only a few minutes she could see neither hide nor hair and she cursed; she desperately needed her helmet as well as her suit - the lenses on it were Swiss-crafted and far superior to what the RAC supplied to its pilots (which was understandable considering how much they had cost her parents).

'I see them, Three. Badger Five, B flight is yours. Engage as you wish. Happy hunting.'

'Roger, Leader. Happy hunting and see you at home.'

'A flight, check in.'

By the time she and the other two pilots had confirmed their status, the enemy aircraft had entered range of Gwen's lenses. They were coming straight for the Misfits, blissfully unaware of the predators stalking them.

'Badger Three, you and Four take the five on the right, I'll take the five on the left with Badger Two. Dive on my signal.'

'Understood, Leader.'

Gwen smiled in anticipation. It was an ideal attack situation; they would take the enemy by surprise, pass through them with impunity, then turn back to attack them again, just like the MU9's had done to her old flight, but hopefully the Misfits would do far more damage than the Fleas had.

However, that plan went out the window when the profiles of the enemy fighters changed as they tilted their noses up and started to climb.

'Badger Leader, Badger Three here. They've spotted us, boss.'

'Roger, Badger Three.' There was barely a pause before Abby announced what she wanted to do. 'We'll climb a bit more, make sure we stay above them.'

During the next minute and a half, the two opposing forces played a game of cat and mouse, jockeying for position, but it was a game that the Misfits were always going to win; not only did they have the superior aircraft, but they had also started off in a superior position.

When the Fleas saw that they weren't going to be able to get to the same altitude before meeting the Misfits they turned and climbed away. However, this took them away from the bombers that they were supposed to be protecting and they gave up on that tactic quickly, turning back around and levelling off. It seemed they had resigned themselves to starting the fight at a positional disadvantage, an attitude which seemed curious to Gwen, until she realised that she had completely forgotten that the enemy outnumbered the Misfits by more than two to one and it was understandable that they were confident.

With the pieces now set out for the start of the game it was a matter of less than two minutes before the Misfits were over the fighters and Abby gave the signal to dive.

The enemy fighters broke their formation moments before the Misfits got within range, but that was no protection from the guns of Abby and Bruce and two of the Fleas were sent spinning away.

Gwen followed her wingman into a steep climb after passing through the enemy formation and they regained some of the altitude that they had substituted for speed, but they were never going to get back to the same height and when they turned to come back they were a scant thousand feet above the Fleas. It was still a significant advantage, but not nearly as clear a one as they'd had before and the next pass was far more dangerous as a consequence because they weren't approaching nearly as fast or at such a steep angle and the enemy fighters were able to lift their noses and fire back, albeit somewhat awkwardly.

Going head to head with MU9's was a less than idea tactic; the machine guns that most of A flight's aircraft had were enough to take down an enemy fighter if they got in a few solid hits or even a bomber with sustained fire and a hefty amount of luck, but they were no match for the MU9's - their six machine guns were supplemented by a cannon mounted behind the spinner of the airscrew, similar in calibre to the ones that Wendy had provided Gwen with. A single shot from that gun might tear off a wing, or render the body of a pilot completely unrecognisable as having been human.

Thankfully, though, the enemy pilots were more concerned with catching back up with their bombers than trying to get a good shot at the four Misfits and after the pass Gwen saw another Flea going down, destroyed by Abby, and a fourth limping away southwards with the left half of its tailplane missing.

With the height advantage now completely spent, the fight quickly became a melee and Gwen immediately lost sight of Badgers Three and Four as her focus narrowed to Dragonfly ahead of her and the Prussian aircraft threatening them. Her job was to make sure that nothing got onto Abby's tail, but unfortunately there was nobody doing the same for her and her neck muscles were becoming very tired, very quickly, as she swivelled her head back and forth, constantly fighting against the G forces to do so.

However, Abby's manoeuvres were such that none of the enemy ever had a chance to come up behind them.

The wing commander didn't fix on a single enemy for more than a second, like most pilots did, but instead took a few shots before turning and spinning away unpredictably, firing at targets as they presented themselves. It shouldn't have worked, but time after time an enemy somehow conspired to pass through her sights and in short order another two Fleas had to break off too damaged to continue. Gwen's every instinct was to chase them and make sure that the pilots wouldn't be able to return and threaten more British lives, but she gritted her teeth and stayed with Abby, trusting in her wingman to know what was best.

When the enemy had split to focus on the two pairs of Misfits they had done so unevenly and there were still two Fleas left facing them when the wing commander's calm voice came over the radio. 'Badger Two from Badger Leader. You have the lead.'

Gwen swallowed nervously before acknowledging. 'Roger, Leader.'

She knew that the tactics Abby had used didn't really work when there were only two targets; they were designed for fighting when badly outnumbered, which was probably the case most times that the Misfits went up in the air, so she quickly assessed the relative positions of the remaining Fleas and selected the one that would be easiest to engage.

She banked Wasp towards it, feeling rather than seeing Dragonfly slot in behind her and instantly felt safer and more confident than she'd ever felt on a sortie, knowing that she had somebody she could rely on to protect her vulnerable back.

It was far too easy.

Now that the odds were even and they didn't have to worry about someone sneaking up behind them, the superiority of the Misfit machines shone through. Within seconds, Gwen was able to get behind the enemy fighter and stay there, quickly lining up a shot which surgically removed one of the MU9's wings and it spun away.

Gwen looked around for the last fighter and eventually found it diving for the deck in a desperate attempt to get away. She started to turn after it, but Abby's voice came over the radio, the experienced wing commander reading her intentions. 'Leave it, Badger Two. Form back up on my wing and we'll see how B flight are doing.'

The other two fighters from A flight were above them a few miles away and they headed towards them as Gwen slid into position - it looked like they had also finished off their opponents.

'Badger Nine, this is Badger Leader, over.'

'Go ahead, Leader.'

'What's the status of B flight? Over.'

'Bombers have jettisoned their loads and are bugging out back to France. B flight are breaking off over the coast.'

'Roger, Badger Nine. Anything else look interesting in our area?'

'Negative, Leader, the only other raid I have on scopes is too far away to intercept. Sapper confirms.'

'Understood. Return to base with Badger Ten as soon as B flight is clear.'

'Roger, Leader. Badger Nine, out.'

Abby's voice held clear disappointment as she addressed A flight. 'Well, Misfits, looks like there's no more fun to be had today, so let's go home.'

The four machines of A flight landed safely and taxied directly over to the hangar where the fitters were waiting to push them in to join Hummingbird, already back from its mission. With the larger aircraft not there they were placed to the sides out of the way to be rewound; they would be returned to their ready places when Dreadnought, Bloodhound and Vulture, Charles "Chalky" Isaacs's long-winged reconnaissance aircraft, returned.

The four pilots briefly gathered around Monty Fletcher's bright orange biplane, curiously named Ballerina, to inspect the only damage that the machines had taken. A neat row of semicircles marked the end of his right upper wing, which was now a foot shorter than it had been on takeoff - it had been torn off like a cinema ticket stub during the second pass that they had made at the Fleas and fitters were already rushing to remove the damaged panels ready to repair the frame underneath.

Monty had flown in a travelling show, hence the name of his machine, and was reportedly used to flying under "unusual" conditions so, despite the damage, he'd had no trouble staying on Bruce's wing during the fight or landing afterwards.

The sound of aircraft arriving drew the pilots back outside and they looked up to see B flight on final approach.

Abby frowned and Gwen followed the direction of her gaze - an airman was sprinting across the airfield, timing it very finely before the machines landed.

That was the problem with the unconventional design of the base, usually the buildings would all be on one side of the strip, but it had been designed with secrecy in mind rather than practicality, so going from one side to the other could be perilous and it was just as well there weren't more aircraft operating.

The airman came to a halt in front of them and breathlessly saluted the wing commander before presenting her with a piece of paper. He was young, not much older than Jimmy, and he looked at the aircraft on final approach, then at the four pilots in front of the hanger, as if debating which was worse, remaining under the gaze of the officers, one of which was the legendary pilot commanding Misfit squadron, or risking a run back across the airfield.

'At ease, airman,' Abby said with a grin, without looking up from the paper.

The young man nodded, relieved that the decision had been taken out of his hands, but still decidedly uncomfortable. He sidled away to stand about ten metres from them and watched B flight land, anxiously waiting for his chance to get away.

'There's heavy fog rolling in from the coast over France and Belgium and Whitehall don't think it's likely the Fleas will try anything else today, so we've been released.'

'Cobblers! I was hoping we'd get another crack at them; I only bagged two.' The Australian, Bruce, looked genuinely disappointed.

Abby chuckled. 'So it's not working out leading your own pair, then, Bruce? Maybe I should ground you and find a new pilot. Or swap you with Monty? Let him take the kills and the glory...'

'No thanks, boss! On second thoughts, I'm fine with having a bit of a rest; I can catch up on my drinking.'

They laughed and there was a break in the conversation as they watched B flight settle neatly to the airstrip one by one.

The rumble of Dreadnought's steam engines could be heard over the noise of their airscrews now, but the big machine wasn't yet in sight.

Once the interceptors were safely on the ground, Abby turned back to Bruce. 'So, you're happy how things are? Seriously, now, how was it?'

'It was bonza, skipper! Our machines are closely matched, I really don't know why we weren't flying together before. Whoever thought to put me on your wing must have been bonkers!' He grinned at her, not managing to remain serious for a single second.

Abby fought to retain a straight face, but failed and grinned widely. 'I'm glad to hear it.'

The smile immediately dropped from her face, though, and she turned to Gwen with a scowl, snapping at her. 'Aviator Sergeant Stone.'

Suddenly worried, Gwen drew herself up, trying not to frown at the change in mood. 'Yes, ma'am?'

'Go and get cleaned up, put your uniform on and report to the mess in thirty minutes. Dismissed.'

'Yes, ma'am.' Gwen nodded even as her heart broke and hurried away across the airfield, following in the footsteps of the airman, who had made good his escape as soon as B flight had landed.

The aircraft of B flight were being pushed into the hangar behind her, but she barely saw them, so preoccupied was she with trying to work out what she'd done to gain the wing commander's disapproval. She'd thought that her place in the squadron had been confirmed, but she must have done something wrong on the flight and now it looked like she was going to be thrown out.

The barracks were empty when she got to them, obviously, and she was glad that nobody was there to see her misery. She stomped down the corridor to her room, shut the door, then sat on the bed, her head in her hands, fighting back tears that were as much of anger and frustration as sorrow and disappointment.

She'd begun to feel at home in Misfit Squadron. She'd made friends, which was something she hadn't really done in 145 Squadron, and she'd been given a machine that wasn't her own design, but which she had to admit fitted her perfectly and flew like a dream. But now it seemed that was all going to be taken away from her, just because of something she'd done on a single sortie.

And the worse thing was that she couldn't for the life of her figure out what it was.

The door opened and she looked up to see Kitty standing in the doorway. She started to say something, but the American woman just sighed and shook her head, before going to her locker and starting to get changed.

Gwen slowly followed her example, stripping off her flightsuit and thermals before putting on her day uniform. Her hair was a mess, matted with sweat and plastered to her head by the helmet, but she didn't have time to do anything with it so she just brushed it out quickly then pinned it up and stuffed it under her short uniform top hat.

Kitty finished changing and left with another sympathetic look, but without saying a word, which hurt Gwen; she needed someone to talk to and had thought that the American would be there for her, but it seemed that her loyalty to the squadron trumped any friendship that she might have developed over the past few days.

Gwen took her time, using up all of the thirty minutes that she'd been given, savouring her last moments as a pilot. She folded her flightsuit and placed her helmet, chronograph and compass on top of it, ready to be packed away, fully expecting not to have to use any of them again; when she was kicked out of Misfit Squadron she would probably go through the court martial that had been put off and the result of that would most likely be that she wouldn't fly again, at least not until the war was over.

Finally, she could put off facing the music no longer and she made her way outside. The short walk to the mess through the beautiful gardens felt like she was walking to the gallows, but she straightened her back and took deep, regular breaths, telling herself over and over that she wouldn't cry.

The pilots were in the bar area, talking quietly, but when she walked in they fell silent and stared at her.

All eleven Misfits were there - Scarlet had been back from her mission for a while, but Chalky had gotten back from his only a few minutes before and was still wearing his flightsuit.

It appeared that her humiliation was going to be very public.

She walked stiffly to the middle of the room, where the wing commander was waiting for her, and came to attention.

Her arm was just coming up to salute when the woman stopped her with a low, emotionless voice. 'At ease, Aviator Sergeant.'

Gwen flinched. If she wasn't even being allowed to salute then things must be much worse than she had suspected and she wondered if the piece of paper that the wing commander had received had said something else than just releasing the squadron for the day - perhaps it had been an order for her detention. Or immediate expulsion from the RAC.

There was a long silence during which Gwen waited for Abby to say more, but the woman just stared at her, holding her gaze.

A gunshot rang out from behind her.

In shock, she spun in place to find Owen standing behind her, holding two flat pieces of wood and she sighed in relief when she realised that it hadn't been a shot after all. That relief quickly turned to anger, though, and she spun back to face the wing commander, but found that, instead of just her, it was the entirety of Misfit Squadron facing her and now they were all grinning.

'What the hell? What was that?' She couldn't contain herself and bawled at them, her hands curling involuntarily into fists.

'That, Aviator Sergeant Stone,' said Abby, 'was the last time your back will ever be unprotected; from now on we will all be there for you. You've flown a mission with us which means you're one of us now. Welcome to Misfit Squadron.'

CHAPTER 8

When Gwen was shaken awake by Kitty for the dawn patrol the next morning she was hungover and her mouth tasted like she'd eaten the grass clippings they spread on the airfield, but she was happy. Happier than she'd been for a long time, since her husband had died at least.

The celebration had gone on past midnight and there had been a *lot* to drink - Abby hadn't been lying when she'd said that the mess was well-stocked.

When Gwen had gotten over her anger, and wiped away her subsequent tears of relief, she'd been installed on a stool at the bar, then one by one the pilots had come up to introduce themselves properly.

Abby was first and she brought with her half a pint of Best Bitter, Gwen's favourite. 'I'm sorry for the pantomime earlier, but we had to do something special, not just for you, but for the rest of the pilots as well. The squadron has flown together for months and you know what that can do to a group of people, how close they can start to feel.' She sighed sadly. 'As you know, we were very lucky and didn't lose anybody for a long time, but I always knew that it would happen eventually; this is war after all, so I decided to have some kind of ritual ready, so that the new pilot could feel like they were truly becoming one of us and the other Misfits could feel the same.' She shrugged and gave Gwen a half-smile. 'You're the first to experience it. How was it?'

'Annoying.'

Abby laughed, but Gwen wasn't joking; the feelings of rejection were too fresh in her mind and she hadn't had nearly enough to drink yet to forget them. She considered her words carefully, though, not wanting to say something out of anger that she would regret later. 'I seriously thought that you were going to throw me out and I took it very badly because of how I got here and what would happen to me if you did.'

The smile left Abby's face immediately and her hand went up to her mouth as she realised what Gwen was saying. 'Oh god, I hadn't thought of that... I should have said something, it was damn silly of me to treat you like that. It was supposed to be part of the fun, but I can see how you... Oh god.'

Gwen shook her head and sighed. 'Don't worry about it; I'm sure if it had been anyone else it would have been perfect - even though you put me through hell for a while there, I can still appreciate the symbolism and sentiment. And as for the bad feelings... I'm sure they'll disappear after a few more of these!' She raised her glass in salute then tipped it up, not stopping until the bottom was pointing straight at the red trophies over the bar. The last few drops fell into her mouth and she smacked her lips and grinned. 'There. I feel a bit better already!'

Abby laughed again. 'I'm glad! And I really am sorry. Well, having said all that, may I present myself? My name is Wing Commander Abigail Lennox and I am the commander of this little disaster we like to call Misfit Squadron. I'm thirty three years of age and I have a son, Jimmy, who you've already had the dubious pleasure of meeting. I was a civilian until 1937 when I was tasked with putting together this little group of fools by Whitehall and awarded my rank at the same time. More than a few people weren't too happy about that, although I like to think I've earned it since then. I trod on a few more toes while I was putting together the Misfits and one wag at RAC HQ came up with the name "The Abbess" which unfortunately stuck and spread, but anybody who knows me knows I don't like that and don't call me that, at least not to my face, although I'm sure they call me worse things after long missions.'

Abby took a breather to wet her whistle, swigging her own drink, but not swallowing nearly as much of it as Gwen had. 'Anyway, I'm sure you'll find out a lot more about me as we go on, but before I leave you in Bruce's hands I want you to know that, while it's true that you've stepped into my sister's shoes and cockpit, nobody is expecting you to *be* her. Be your own pilot, be your own person and be one of us.'

The woman smiled and nodded then slipped off her stool and went over to pat Bruce on the shoulder.

The Australian sauntered over to Gwen, bringing with him another pint of Best and a huge smile. 'G'day, Gwen!'

The next couple of hours had gone by very quickly and very enjoyably. During the course of the evening each of the pilots had introduced themselves one by one in order of their call signs, even the ones that she already knew well, like Kitty and Scarlet. Each of them had told her some of their story and every one of them had bought her a drink so by the time the last one had finished Gwen had been feeling decidedly unsteady on her feet.

Hence her pounding headache the morning after.

As Gwen rolled out of bed and started to dress, she tried to recall everything that she had been told, wanting to make sure that she remembered the things that her new squadron had wanted her to know about themselves.

Bruce "Walkabout" Walker, Badger Three and pilot of Bandicoot had been a pilot with the Austral-Zealand Air Force until it had been incorporated into the Royal Aviator Corps a couple of years before the start of the war with Prussia, which was when he had come to Abby's attention. He had fought in the Indochine skirmishes against the Nippon-Chinese Alliance, a series of battles that had been brief, but incredibly bloody.

Montgomery "Monty" Fletcher had been part of a flying circus, doing stunts and sometimes playing the bad guy for fake dogfights. He'd had an accident during one show early in his career and his hair had burned off and only grown back in patches, so he kept his head shaved. His aircraft, Ballerina, had been red many years ago, but even before the start of the war that colour had become synonymous with the Crimson Barons and so he had repainted her orange. He was continually tinkering with his aircraft, keeping up to date with the latest innovations, and would have monopolised more of Gwen's time, asking her about the modifications that she had made to her Harridan, if Abby hadn't come over and forcibly dragged him off his stool to make way for the next Misfit.

Lady Penelope Bagshot was the pilot of Cheetah and led B flight. She was married to a racing car driver, Lord Bagshot, twenty years her senior, and had painted her aircraft in homage to that fact - Cheetah's nose and the front of her fuselage was painted in black and white checks while the rest of her was British racing green. Her husband was a colonel in the army, but she had refused to stay at home and wait like a good wife. She was a lifelong friend of Cece's, they had gone to school together, and when she had heard that Abby was putting together a squadron she had pestered the wing commander for a place in the squadron, insisting that she deserved it because she had been constructing her own aircraft for years (using considerable sums of her husband's money).

Badger Six was William "Mad Mac" MacShane, a Scotsman from a small village near Oban. While the other pilots mostly brought her bitter, he gave her a glass of whisky from Argyll, some of his own private stock - something which he jealously guarded and which a few of the pilots standing nearby eyed with open desire when he poured it, then her with envy when she tasted it. If she'd thought she'd had trouble with Scarlet's accent at first, it was nothing compared to the difficulty she had understanding Mac. He was an inventor, obsessed with speed and had used Loch Etive, next to his village, as a runway for successive variants of Swordfish, his aircraft, originally a seaplane. He had screamed up and down the valleys of northwest Scotland for years, refining his machine, making it faster and faster, until Abby had recruited him. As soon as he had joined the RAC he had removed the floats in favour of a proper undercarriage and since then he had concentrated less on making it fast and more on making it a good gun platform. According to Lady Penelope, whose wingman he was, he was ferocious in the air and would often laugh his head off in the middle of a fight, although he had never done anything to endanger either her or the rest of the squadron.

Derek "Twitcher" Niven, led Kitty in the second interceptor pair and couldn't have been more different in character than the bloodthirsty Scotsman, Mac. He was cold and calculated in the air, never taking a fight he wasn't sure he could win or a shot he wasn't sure would hit. Whenever he wasn't flying, he either had his nose in a book or was out in the nearby forest, studying the wildlife; he was a biologist and an ornithologist, as well as a mechanic, and his aircraft, Swift, had many distinctive features borrowed from his subjects, including a distinctive crescent-shaped wing similar to the bird she took her name from.

Badger Eight was Kitty, of course, and she hugged Gwen, gave her some Kentucky Bourbon that was her favourite drink, and told her the story of how she had been in England - she had fought on the Republican side in the Iberian Civil War and had fled to the Kingdom of Britain when that had gone from bad to worse. Spain was where she had first come across the Crimson Barons, an encounter that hadn't gone at all well for the Republicans and she had lost all but one of the six Americans she'd joined up with in a single dogfight.

Badgers Nine and Ten came together, they were Owen and Wendy Llewellyn, husband and wife, "Sheepish" and "Firepower". They had met in the Misfits, immediately fallen in love and had been married while the squadron was in France.

Owen was Welsh, one of the scientists who had originally developed the radar system that protected the British Isles, and when that project had finished he had been recruited by Abby and tasked with creating a system compact enough to go in an aircraft. He was second in command of the squadron, as much because of the role assigned his aircraft than for any question of rank; rank really didn't seem to matter much, if at all, in the Misfits.

Wendy was English and had been recruited separately by Abby. She was a gunsmith as well as a pilot and was responsible for the upkeep of the squadron's weapons as well as the creation and manufacture of new ones. Her aircraft was the biggest in the hangar and she was one of the biggest pilots, the biggest women that Gwen had ever seen in fact.

Badger Eleven, Charles "Chalky" Isaacs wasn't quite an albino, but his hair was so blonde as to be almost white. He had been an astronomer and astrologist before the war and was a believer in alchemy and numerology and quite a few other "ologies" that Gwen had never heard of. His aircraft, Vulture, had been developed as a platform for his telescope to get him above the pollution of the cities and into the cleaner air high in the atmosphere, closer to the stars. It was incredibly stable with long wings for gliding and a balloon system somewhat similar to Dreadnought's, although his used inert helium instead of the more volatile hydrogen that doubled for fuel in Wendy's aircraft. When he joined the Misfits he had removed his telescope and replaced it with cameras that allowed him to take photographs from so high up that the Prussians usually never knew he was watching them.

The last pilot to take the seat next to Gwen had been Scarlet. Her aircraft, Hummingbird, was a kind of gyrodyne that had the ability to takeoff vertically and hover due to its overhead rotor, but it also had normal wings and an airscrew that allowed it to fly normally and gave it more than other rotor-equipped aircraft. She was from County Galway on the west coast of Ireland and had originally developed Hummingbird as a crop sprayer for her family's farm, but it had been a simple matter to remove the tanks and the spraying equipment and increase the power of the small machine to make it a fast, and relatively quiet, low-level scout.

Gwen was relieved to find that she remembered almost everything that the pilots had told her, because events after Scarlet had gotten off the stool became increasingly hazy as the night had gone on as she had been dragged in among the rest of the pilots and plied with more drink.

They had all gathered around the small piano and she had joined them in singing, accompanied by Lady Penelope, who turned out to be quite talented and had a repertoire that extended well into the recent trends in music. Between songs the Misfits had taken it in turns to tell stories and jokes, most of which she didn't recall very well, but she did have a vague impression of telling the tale of the sortie that had given her her first two kills and she seemed to recall that the memory hadn't been quite as painful as it once had - it was still a tragedy to have lost two colleagues, but it had also led to her being where she was, in the place where, according to them, she was meant to be and where she could do most good in the war.

A wave of dizziness hit her, making her feel suddenly quite queasy and her calm walk down the corridor to the bathroom became something of a rush.

She had a murky recollection of staggering to the barracks through the gardens, which had been beautifully illuminated by the light of the full moon, with the aid of Kitty and Scarlet, who had gotten her uniform off her and tucked her in.

She had one final image of Kitty bending over her to kiss her on the forehead, but then nothing else until the American had woken her that morning.

All in all it had been a very good night and, no matter how bad she felt at that moment as she emptied the contents of her stomach in one of the bathroom stalls, she didn't regret it one bit.

She began to regret it a little when she was up in the air half an hour later - she'd drunk plenty of water and forced down a bacon sandwich, her father's favourite cure for a hangover, but that wasn't stopping her from feeling decidedly queasy in the early morning turbulence.

However, even if she couldn't enjoy the sensation of flying as much as she usually did, she could still take in the view of the sun rising over the beautiful countryside below and that was enough to take her mind off of her nausea and stop her from having to use the greaseproof paper bag Abby had given her before takeoff. She had no idea how she would handle the extreme manoeuvres of a dogfight, though, but fortunately there was no sign of enemy aircraft and eventually they were ordered back to base by Sapper without having done anything other than wound down their springs.

On the way home Gwen cracked open her canopy and the fresh air helped to make her feel much better. However, what was waiting for them at the airfield turned her stomach over almost as much as the alcohol had.

'What on earth is that thing on the grass?'

Mad Mac's voice was even harder to understand over the radio, but apparently Abby was more used to it than Gwen. 'It's a dual Harridan, Mac. That's the Hawkings' private aircraft.'

There were faint clicks as most of the pilots slotted lenses in place to get a better look at the machine sitting on the side of Badger Base's airfield.

Gwen didn't need to, though; she knew exactly what they were seeing; she had seen it before. The dual Harridan was a wide aircraft that was essentially two fighters attached at the wingtip and with the twin tails joined by a single long tailplane. It was a bit like Kitty's aircraft, but much wider, and it had two cockpits. It also had twelve guns, the armament of two Harridans.

'The designers? What the hell are they doing here? We don't fly bloody Harridans.'

'Maybe they've come to get some tips?'

Bruce's dry comment got laughs from most of the squadron, but nobody else offered up any explanation for why two of the most important figures in the aircraft industry had turned up on an airbase that they shouldn't have even known about.

Gwen knew exactly why the Hawkings, creators of the Harridan fighter that she had illegally modified, were there, but she just sighed to herself and said nothing as the squadron fell silent and began peeling off to land one by one.

Gwen landed first with Abby and got out after they were pushed into the hangar, but while the wing commander went to greet the guests she lingered in the hangar and watched the other aircraft coming in. Once both A and B flight were inside, the dual Harridan was brought in as well and placed just inside the doors, which she hoped meant that they wouldn't be staying for long. She joined the other pilots as they went to stand next to the machine, alternating between inspecting the curious aircraft and gazing out into the sunlight where the wing commander was talking with the two visitors.

When Abby came back in and called out her name she hung her head and trudged towards the hangar doors; she'd half hoped that the Hawkings hadn't actually known that she was there and she would be able to stay out of sight of them until they left, but that wasn't to be apparently.

She could feel the curious eyes of the rest of the squadron burning into her back as she walked out into the sunshine and knew that they were following her at a discreet distance, but undoubtedly staying close enough to make sure that they could hear everything that was said.

The Hawkings were standing in the bright sunshine in their customary white flightsuits, beaming from ear to ear as they watched her approach. She came to a halt a few steps from them and was about to greet them formally in an effort to maintain her dignity, but they pre-empted her by quickly closing the distance and crushing her in a hug.

The three of them remained like that for long seconds, long enough for Gwen to hear Bruce's stage whisper in the background as he made sure that the whole squadron and all of the fitters who had come to watch knew exactly who she was.

'Gwen... Gwen... Gwenevere! She's only bloody Gwenevere Hawking! Daughter of Harriet and Sheridan Hawking, who built her first aircraft at seven and helped design and test the Harridan! Blimey!'

The Harridans eventually pulled back, but they remained in contact with her as if frightened she would disappear again; she hadn't seen them since her wedding day, more than a year ago and hadn't exactly kept up with her correspondence.

Her parents were in their mid-forties, but looked younger, although there were far more lines on her father's forehead than before - evidence of how hard they had been working for the war effort, trying to improve on their design and bring out new marks of Harridans.

'Mum, Dad, how are you?'

As always it was her mother, Harriet, who answered personal questions. 'We're fine darling, much better now that we've heard you've landed on your feet! We couldn't believe it when we were told you'd ended up here; it's perfect for you! We're so glad Abby has taken you on.'

'Yes, well, it wasn't exactly smooth air getting here.'

Her father, Sheridan, grimaced. 'We heard about that. Why did you do it, Gwen?'

Gwen shrugged. 'Because I knew my ideas would work.'

'We knew they would work too, darling.'

'Then why not incorporate them! The Harridan could be so much better!'

Her mother shook her head. 'Yes, but it could also be a lot more dangerous. Your modification was very good, we had a look at it, but the only problem with something like that is that it might get damaged and you could end up with asymmetrical wings, completely ruining the airworthiness and getting you killed.'

'That was a risk I was willing to take and it ended up saving my life, not getting me killed. Why not let each pilot modify their aircraft how they want? We could save so many lives!'

Sheridan sighed. 'Because it wouldn't and you know it. Not everybody is as talented as you are, Gwenevere and many people would do something that would prove disastrous, simply because they thought it would be a good idea or had seen a similar modification on someone else's machine. And if one thing worked for someone, whether by design or by luck, it would spread like wildfire; you know how superstitious pilots can be.'

Gwen grimaced. 'I suppose.'

'And besides, we did consider something like your modification fairly early on, but discarded it immediately; the Harridan is designed to take a *lot* of punishment, but you've seen what a damaged spring can do and you put four more of them in your aircraft - a hit to any of them would likely have destroyed you. At the very least it would have ripped apart your wing.'

Gwen shuddered - a couple of months into the war, while she'd still been in training, Whitehall had circulated a gun camera video of an enemy fighter suffering catastrophic damage to its spring. The razor-sharp metal had burst out of the top of its case, instantly shredding the cockpit and the pilot.

Her mother spoke softly. 'We know the Harridan is not as fast or manoeuvrable as a Spitsteam, darling, but it was never *meant* to be and you know that; you were in the drawing room with us. Its strength has *always* been that it can be mass-produced quickly and cheaply and repaired easily, which means that it can be put in the air much quicker than the Spitsteam and right now that is what matters - better that we turn out three hundred Harridans a month for the RAC to face the Fliegertruppe with, than forty or fifty Spitsteams, which are grounded for hours or days at the slightest scratch. That means, though, that anything that takes away from the simplicity of the design destroys that function.'

Her father chimed in. 'Later on, when the Kingdom has some breathing room, when Britain can put a thousand, two thousand, *three* thousand aircraft in the air, we can change the design, or even scrap it altogether and start again, but right now the RAC just needs fighters in the air.'

Gwen nodded. What her parents were saying made complete sense and it was the main reason why there was only one squadron like Misfit Squadron - it just wasn't feasible to spend weeks making a handful of the best aircraft possible when the Fleas were sending hundreds of bombers and fighters across the channel every day. There needed to be decent fighters to meet them and while the Harridan wasn't spectacular, at the *very* least it was decent.

There was a long silence as none of them quite knew how to get away from the awkward subject and back to the comfortable family reunion of before.

It was Abby who finally stepped in to ease the tension. 'It's just as well Gwen is here, then, where we can put her genius to work. And she has been busy since she arrived - would you like to see the aircraft she repaired and modified before we go to the mess for tea?'

Sheridan and Harriet looked at each other before beaming widely at Abby. 'We'd love that!'

Gwen knew that the pilots were staring at her, and her cheeks were burning as she walked past them, but she refused to meet their eyes, instead she just concentrated on the heels of her parents as Abby led them into the shade of the hangar.

She felt like she was back home again, a little girl, taking her famous genius mother and father to inspect her latest effort in the hangar they had built for her on their estate. She had sought their approval in everything that she had created and had received it from them both, but while it had been unreserved from her mother, from her father it had always been accompanied by an if or a but, which, in hindsight, had made her a better mechanic, but had definitely hurt, especially when she was younger.

She stood behind them while Abby introduced her parents to Sergeant Jenkins, who had been overseeing Wasp's rewinding and rearming, then followed a few steps behind as she took them on a circuit of the aircraft, pointing out the modifications that Gwen had made and telling them how much better the machine handled. She was gratified to hear her parents expressing their admiration and appreciation, but wondered how much was real and how much was just for Abby's benefit.

The tour didn't take long and then it was off to the mess.

The usually informal and quiet midmorning snacks and second breakfast for the pilots turned into more of a noisy social affair, with the Hawkings surrounded by Misfits, who threw questions at them about the development of the Harridan and the hand Gwen had had in it. Through it all, Gwen sat at the back of the group, maintaining her silence and feeling her cheeks getting hotter and hotter every time something was said about her until they must have rivalled Scarlet's hair.

The torture lasted only about half an hour, though, until her parents stood and began to say their goodbyes; apparently they were expected in Whitehall and their trip to the Kent Downs had been an unannounced detour. Gwen accompanied them as they made their way out onto the airfield and waited with them while fitters hurried to retrieve their Harridan from the hangar.

Finally they had a few moments alone with nobody else in earshot; Abby had tactfully held the rest of the Misfits back to give them some privacy.

'Are you alright, Gwenevere?' Her father had always refused to call her Gwen and she had given up insisting when she was ten.

'I'm fine, Dad. I really like it here.'

'Good.' He nodded, expressionless as ever and she couldn't tell if he was happy she was with the Misfits or not.

'We were sorry to hear about Richard, darling, but why didn't you come home? We would have taken care of you, you could have gone back to work with the company.'

Her mother reached out to push some of the hair away from Gwen's forehead and she reached up to brush away the hand automatically, but regretted doing so almost instantly. 'I couldn't come home; I needed to feel like I was doing something - I went to join up the same day I got the telegram.'

Her father frowned. 'But why aren't you an officer? Surely with your experience...'

'I didn't tell the recruiters about my experience; I wanted to earn my place, Dad.'

Her father's frown deepened; he had never understood her reluctance to use their name and the reputation they had built to get ahead, never understood her insistence on succeeding or failing on her own merit.

Gwen sighed. 'I'm fine not being an officer, especially in the Misfits; Abby treats us all the same.'

'Even so...'

Harriet laid her hand on her husband's arm. 'Leave it, Sheridan. You know her; she's happy being a pilot and it doesn't matter what rank she is. It's not as if she needs a higher wage anyway, or is going to make a career out of the RAC.' She smiled at Gwen. 'As I said, we're glad Abby's taken you on; we know her quite well, actually; she approached us when she was putting together the squadron, asking if you wanted to join. We didn't think it was a good idea at the time, but circumstances change and you're a good fit now.'

'You... She...' Gwen stared at them, looking back and forth from one to the other.'

'You were in the middle of your romance with Richard and you weren't going to go off to join the RAC. Of course then the war broke out and he ended up enlisting, but we weren't to know that, were we?'

Her instinct was to bawl them out for not having asked her what she wanted, just like she had so many times before when they had made decisions for her, but she realised they were right; when she and Richard had been courting they had had no time for anything else apart from each other and she certainly wouldn't have left him, not even to join Misfit Squadron.

She swallowed the lump in her throat along with her angry words and nodded. 'You're right, of course, but I still would have liked to know.'

Her parents nodded, but she knew that they would just keep doing the same thing over and over; they had never seemed to get their heads around the idea that she was an adult - to them she was still the precocious child for whom they had had to make decisions for over a decade because legally she hadn't been old enough to make them herself.

All three looked around as the dual Harridan was wheeled out of the hangar. Their time had had run out, but it was almost a relief; their love of aviation that brought them together and made them close, but they weren't the kind of family that ever really had personal conversations.

'By the way, we had an airman put a few things on your bed for you - we know that the Misfits are allowed to wear their own flightsuits so we thought you might like your old one.'

Gwen's eyes lit up. 'Thanks, Mum! I was going to ask if you could send it, but it completely slipped my mind.'

'There's also a tin of those ginger biscuits you like so much - I made a batch of them yesterday evening.'

Gwen laughed. 'Now *that's* the best news I've had in months!'

Her mother returned the laugh, but her father stepped in quickly, frowning at them and pointedly looking at the chronograph on his wrist. 'I hate to break this up, but we were supposed to be in Whitehall twenty minutes ago.'

Harriet Hawking scowled at her husband. 'The minister can wait for us; he's made us wait enough times.' She sighed even as she scolded him, though, and turned back to Gwen. 'Much as I hate to admit it, your father is right; we should be going.' She reached out and pulled her daughter into a hug. 'Please write a bit more often, darling. We hated not hearing from you.'

'I'll try, Mum.'

Sheridan folded them both into his arms, his lanky six foot two frame towering a head over them. 'We're proud of you, Gwenevere, never forget that.'

All too soon the hug ended and the two Hawkings walked hand in hand to their curious aircraft.

As always it was her mother who climbed into the right-hand fighter, the "driver's seat" as she liked to put it.

Of the two Hawkings, Harriet was the better pilot. Sheridan could fly perfectly well, but he was too mechanically-minded and always tried to impose his own will on an aircraft rather than working with it. That intractability was one of the reasons why he clashed so often with Gwen; they both had a stubborn streak in them that often caused them to refuse to admit when they were wrong or see when someone's idea was better than theirs. However, in Gwen that trait had been tempered with her mother's flair and artistry and, among other things, the mix of the two had made her a much better pilot than both of them, which was why Gwen had been the one to test the early Harridan models.

It was also why they had built their dual Harridan (with Gwen's help) - they had wanted something that they could fly together, but that was more defensible than a normal dual-seat aircraft (like the already-existing Harridan trainer, which suffered in performance as a result of the added weight).

It was a closely-guarded secret that the two aircraft could be separated at the pull of a lever, even in the air, allowing them to fight as wingmen rather than a single aircraft if necessary. Thankfully, the need had never arisen, although if it did, the Fleas would have a very nasty surprise in store because the two Harridans were only similar to normal fighters in appearance - underneath their metal skin they were entirely different machines. Because the Hawkings didn't have to go on long patrols and were never in the air for more than an hour, range was not a consideration for them and they had adjusted their spring to deliver much higher power over less time. The airscrews had been made larger in order to deliver that power and had a third, even coarser pitch than the two ("fine" and "coarse") that were available on a normal Harridan. The wings also had a different aerodynamic profile to the stock machines to make them far faster and far more manoeuvrable.

The overall effect of their modifications was analogous to the difference between a sprinter and a marathon runner - they could outfly any opposition, including the Misfit aircraft, as long as they were quick about it. But they could also run from anything in the air if they had to.

The Harridan taxied the short distance to the end of the runway, then with a deep thrum accelerated away from the watching squadron, almost all of whom, pilots, fitters and support staff alike, had gathered to see off the almost mythical pair.

In a matter of just a few seconds, the Harridan was leaping into the air and there was a gasp that made Gwen smile as it climbed impossibly, pointing its nose almost vertically into the sky, before sliding towards its wing and making the tightest turn that most of them had ever seen. It dived back towards them and Gwen shook her head at her mother's showmanship as it sped past at just over head height, making several of the less experienced fitters duck, before once again climbing into the sky, waggling its wings in farewell as it headed towards London.

Gwen watched the machine until it was out of sight, then turned to go back to the mess, but stumbled to a halt when she found the Misfits lined up, staring at her.

She was glad to see that there were no accusing looks on their faces, but a few did seem hurt, particularly Kitty and Scarlet, which just made her love them more.

'Why didn't you tell us?' Predictably it was Bruce who spoke first; of all the Misfits he seemed to have the most problems with keeping his feelings to himself.

'Because, as the wing commander rightly told me when I first arrived, my "pedigree" doesn't matter; it's what I am and do that does.'

The pilots turned to Abby as they realised what Gwen had just implied and this time the looks *were* mildly accusing.

Abby just shrugged. 'It wasn't my place to say anything. If Gwen wanted you to know, she would have told you and I'm sure she would have done when she was good and ready.' She met the eyes of the pilots one by one then jerked her head in the direction of the mess. 'Right, fun's over - we're on twenty minute standby until further notice, go get the chairs out and rest.' She turned to Gwen. 'You have ten minutes to get changed, then I want you with the rest of the squadron.'

Gwen smiled and nodded then broke into a run for the barracks.

Set out neatly on her bed were a long linen bag holding her flightsuit, the box with her helmet in, the tin with the biscuits and the black-lacquered wooden chest that she had gotten in Japan.

Ignoring the rest of the items for the moment, she took her leather flightsuit out of the bag and laid it on the next bed over to check it. It was in perfect condition, exactly how it had been the day she had last taken it off and hung it up - it hadn't dried or wrinkled and the liquid pockets around the legs and abdomen were still full and firm; obviously her parents had been taking care of it. The same was true of her helmet; the leather was soft and the lenses were clean and unscratched within their protective felt bag.

Abby hadn't given her enough time to properly savour the moment so she stripped quickly and stepped into the flightsuit, but grimaced when she had trouble getting it over her hips; she seemed to have put on a little bit of weight. She loosened the many straps, then pulled it up, putting her arms into the sleeves before folding the front over and fastening the brass clips along one side all the way to her neck. She jumped up and down a couple of times to seat every properly before cinching the suit tight again, smiling as she felt the familiar, almost claustrophobic, but comforting contact on her whole body.

The helmet went on next and then she went to stand in front of the mirror.

If her standard issue flightsuit had been *right*, her custom one was *perfect*, although she wondered what the other Misfits would make of the sheer *pinkness* of it. If there had been a prize for which of the Misfits had the flightsuit that looked least like military issue she would have given Kitty a run for her money. The suit was tight in all the right places, supporting her body against G forces in a way that accentuated her figure like no corset ever had, giving her curves that made her look womanly instead of dumpy, at least to her eyes.

She admired herself for a few precious seconds, then turned to the black chest.

In its many compartments, it held her most personal items, things that she had had to leave behind when she'd joined the RAC, like photographs of happier times, a bottle of her favourite perfume and numerous keepsakes from Richard, her parents and the people she had met around the world.

It wasn't just the contents of the chest that were important to her, though; the chest itself was one of her most treasured possessions - it had been given to her by the Empress of Japan herself when Gwen had been presented at court in Kyoto with her parents. In return she had given a working model aircraft of her own construction to the Empress's young son who had been nine at the time, just like her.

The box was three feet wide, two feet deep and two feet tall, smooth and shiny and decorated on top with golden cogs woven with branches that were heavy with pink and white cherry blossoms. It was so perfectly made that it had no discernible slits, apertures or hinges, but rather it was opened by pressing four concealed buttons, each the size of a fingertip, that were in unpredictable places around the box. Each individual button started a clockwork sequence which opened a single compartment to the sound of three soft, incredibly beautiful chimes. Pressing two or more of them at the same time opened successively larger compartments to more chimes, but it was when all four buttons were pressed at once that the box revealed its true secret - the main compartment of the box slid open to a rendition of "Sakura," a traditional Japanese folk song, played not only using the chimes, but a miniature shamisen hidden in the lid as well, while the four golden cogs turned slowly to represent the passing seasons and the cherry blossoms on the top fell, then bloomed once more.

She would normally take the time to admire the chest and perhaps have it play for her, but today she limited herself to opening a single deep compartment in the side from which she took two small wooden cubes. These boxes contained her two brass instruments - the chronograph that attached to the left arm of her suit and the compass that attached to her right arm, each far more expensive and elaborate versions of the very basic ones that went on her RAC issue suit.

On her way out of the room she briefly paused once more to gaze at herself in the mirror.

The night before, the pilots had welcomed her into their squadron and made her feel like she was one of them. Now, thanks to the thoughtfulness of her parents, she also *looked* like she belonged.

CHAPTER 9

For a while, the war seemed to be going well for the British and they seemed to have put the disaster in France behind them.

After fighter command had gotten over the initial shock of the couple of weeks during which Gwen had been grounded, they had changed tactics and no longer sent out small patrols to be picked off by superior numbers of enemy fighters. The casualties that had been so disastrously one-sided equalled out, then became favourable, and for a while it seemed that the Fleas were losing twice, if not three times as many aircraft as the RAC, especially when the success of the Misfits was taken into consideration.

The Fleas quickly adapted, though, and increased the sizes of their patrols in turn, sending massive formations of fighters and bombers that the RAC just didn't have the resources to match. The British aviators still managed to shoot down slightly more Prussians than they lost, but they had far less to lose in the first place and soon began to feel the strain.

The Misfits were kept very busy during that time trying to fill in the gaps in the southeastern corner of Britain that many of the enemy raids came through, flying up to four or sometimes five sorties each day. They were by no means the only squadron making such a monumental effort, but they were the ones who were able to make the largest dent in the Fleas' numbers.

Abby let Gwen take the lead more often and with her personal flight suit she was finally able to use the full extent of Wasp's capabilities and put to good practice what she had learnt from watching the wing commander. She brought her total of "kills" to ten, making her a "double-ace", and the squadron as a whole accounted for more than a hundred enemy aircraft without a loss, although every aircraft in both A and B flight had had to be grounded at least once for repairs and most twice (except for Mad Mac, who came through completely unscathed and seemed to lead a charmed life). None of the aircraft was ever off the flight line for more than a day, though, with the fitters often working miracles overnight to get their aircraft back in the air. The only exception was Kitty, who lost most of one of Hawk's two tails to the crossfire between two Funkel FU88 bombers and only just managed to limp back to the airfield. Even so Hawk was only out of action for the rest of that day and the whole of the next, as Kitty and her fitters worked solidly, day and night, to repair the aircraft.

The Misfits' efforts served to take some of the pressure off the regular squadrons, allowing them to recover and rebuild their numbers with new pilots and new planes that were hurriedly brought into service and over the next week or so it seemed that the balance was tipping once more in the favour of the British.

However, everybody seemed to know that it wouldn't last; something had to change.

And then, one bright morning in August, it did.

With the gradual recovery of the RAC, some of the workload had been taken from the Misfits - they no longer had to fly dawn patrols, which meant they could have an extra hour or two of sleep and they were also not patrolling at set times. Instead, they were being kept on two-minute standby as a reactionary force for the entire day during two five-hour stretches. This was a whole different kind of exhausting, because they never knew when they were going to be called upon and were constantly on edge, kept waiting by their aircraft for hours on end with springs wound and fitters ready to push them out of the hangar at a moment's notice.

The call came around ten that there was a large enemy raid massing over France and they were immediately sent up to join a Harridan squadron and two Spitsteam squadrons that were already working their way into position to counter it.

The Misfits climbed hard and were directed by Sapper towards Margate, where the other squadrons were rendezvousing and where the raid was predicted to make landing.

They were easily able to make it to angels twenty five by the time they got to their station over the coastal town, which was only thirty miles away from Badger Base, and were in position to intercept the enemy when the call came over the radio that the enemy had been spotted by the Observer Troop and had gone from being one hundred plus aircraft to two hundred plus, all heading straight for them.

That was the kind of numbers that even the Misfits found daunting, but Abby was as calm as ever. 'All Badgers, this is Badger Leader. We've done this before and you know it doesn't matter if it's ten to one or twenty to one; they're not going to be able to attack us more than two or three at a time anyway, otherwise they'll be getting in each other's way. Alright, A flight, we'll go after the fighters as usual, but our priority today is keeping B flight safe so they can get a good crack at the bombers. B flight, keep your speed up and I want you to bug out at the first sign of fighters coming down at you; we might not be able to keep them as busy as we usually do. Any questions?'

In the face of the task ahead, there were none of the usual jokes or facetious comments, not even from Bruce, just a tense silence that lasted a good few seconds before Abby filled it.

'Right then... All Badgers, check in.'

The enemy formation was still some miles off the coast over the sea when the RAC fighters engaged them and right from the start it was sheer chaos.

The wing commander surpassed herself, taking her usual method of not pursuing any single aircraft to an extreme, turning and rolling continuously, following a completely unpredictable path through the mixed enemy fighter group that comprised MU9's, HH190's and heavier MU10's, squeezing off shots when they presented themselves.

It was incredible flying and, despite having gotten to know her various tricks, tactics and traits, Gwen was hard pressed to follow her. But, if she was having problems, the Fleas were having far more, and several times Gwen saw tracer from an enemy flash by, searching out Wasp or Dragonfly, only to miss the intended target, usually by a wide margin, and instead make contact with a fellow Prussian.

The fight was so frenetic that there was no chance to take note of whether any of the enemy fighters were destroyed by Abby's guns (or by the errant friendly fire), but every so often Gwen would catch sight of a broken aircraft spiralling to the ground trailing dark smoke or pieces, although she never had the time to discern what side it had once belonged to, and as the minutes passed it seemed that the number of enemy fighters around were slowly dwindling.

Gwen was just beginning to think that Abby wanted to keep all of the Prussians for herself and wasn't going to let her have a crack at them when the Fleas changed the game.

'Badger Two, this is Badger Leader. There are a group of fighters, nine o'clock low, heading for the bombers. Cut them off, please.'

For a moment Gwen wasn't sure she'd heard correctly; the Misfits fought in pairs for safety and effectiveness and for Abby to tell her to go off on her own went against everything that the wing commander had drummed into her from the moment she had arrived. Her doubt lasted less than a second, though, and she threw Wasp into a hard turn even as she acknowledged the order and dived away.

She immediately spotted the enemy fighters - four HH190's preparing to pounce on B flight, who seemed blissfully unaware of the enemy lurking above them as they came around for another pass through the bomber formation. They had a head start on her, but she was gaining on them rapidly and a few quick calculations told her that she should arrive in plenty of time to cut them off.

She was still a good fifteen or so seconds away from intercepting them, though and she took the time to wonder why she had been sent off - it could only mean one of two things, either Abby trusted her to go on her own, or the fight was going so badly they needed to split up and double their efforts, or both.

Whatever the reason, she was on her own and that meant that she had to look out for herself for the first time as a Misfit and as she dived she kept a close watch around her, especially in the mirror above her head, although she wasn't particularly worried about anyone coming up behind her while she was diving; she was faster than everything in the air except for B flight's machines. However, it paid to know what was around, especially because at some point she was going to have to pull out of the dive and slow down.

The "double-aitches" never saw her coming.

Once in range she throttled back, so as not to overshoot them, and set her sights on the first one. She gave it a full heartbeat of combined cannon and machine gun fire and saw large chunks flying off its tail, turning the aircraft into an unguided missile, before nudging her rudder and lining up on the next machine in line. She gave it the same treatment and saw more than half of its left wing come off. As it went into an uncontrollable spin she gave her rudder pedals another nudge to bring the third Flea, the leader of the flight, into her sights, but he had seen his wingman disintegrate and had panicked, pulling into a sharp turn.

She watched, emotionless, as the wings tore off his aircraft at the extreme stress.

The fourth and final HH190 was smarter, but equally doomed. He pulled slowly out of his dive, measuring it as best he could and then stood his aircraft on his wing in an attempt to turn towards the relative safety of the bomber formation and its massed guns.

His machine was far inferior to Abby's, though, and she easily matched his manoeuvre, turning inside him and pressing her firing stud. The sleek enemy machine turned into the path of her fire and instantly crumpled in on itself as its already stressed frame was tested further and found wanting.

She levelled out and looked down at the broken aircraft spinning away beneath her, searching for any sign that the pilots might have gotten out alive, but saw none; with the speeds they had been going and the violence of their machines' demise they would most likely have died instantly. She was mildly interested to find that she was completely unaffected by the fact that due to her actions four enemy pilots had lost their lives; any feelings of remorse she might have had after that first kill were long gone and now the enemy aircraft were just that, aircraft that had to be destroyed before they could attack her friends and countrymen.

Gwen began a lazy turn, swinging towards the bombers and lining up for a run on them, but a loud thud and a hole opening in her wing put paid to that idea and had her flinging Wasp on her wing in desperate evasion, cursing her stupidity. She whipped her head around, searching for her attackers and found four MU9's on her tail.

They had position advantage, but she still had superior speed and she used it, diving for the deck, spiralling wildly and praying that her wing wasn't so damaged that what had happened to the third double-aitch wouldn't happen to her.

Wasp held together without a single complaint and she saw the Muhlenbergs in her rearview mirror getting smaller and smaller, the long-range shots that they were taking in desperation falling well short. They pursued her for only twenty seconds more, then gave up when they could see that they weren't going to come anywhere near to catching her and turned towards home.

Gwen levelled out at just over four thousand feet, having dropped over three miles from the fight with the Prussian fighter pack. She had gotten so far away from the battle that it wasn't even in sight anymore, despite the numbers of aircraft involved. She could still hear it raging over her radio, though, as a couple of British squadrons joined in the desperate attempt to keep the bombers from reaching their target. It would have been an easy matter to get directions from Sapper or Owen in Bloodhound back to it, but a quick check of her instruments showed her that she was down to just over one third tension on her spring, which wasn't nearly enough to get her up to twenty thousand feet again and still be able to fight, so she decided that it would be best to go home.

She dipped her wing so that she could look down and get her bearings. There was a thin layer of cloud just below her, but through a few gaps she caught glimpses of the coast and the railway line that ran from London to Margate, which meant that Badger Base would be to the southwest of her.

She turned onto her new heading, then scanned the sky. Seeing nothing in her immediate vicinity she lifted her goggles and scrubbed her face with her hands, closing her strained eyes and taking a moment to rest them.

That had been too close. She had almost died and it was all her fault because she had forgotten the most important rule: never fly straight and level whenever there were enemy in the vicinity, not for *any* length of time - she had been so caught up in her success and so focussed on the bombers that she had stopped looking for danger and had barely been manoeuvring.

Still, one good thing would come from it - she had lived through the experience and would never make the same mistake again.

She took a deep breath, gave her face a last rub, then opened her eyes and froze.

There were four aircraft about a thousand feet directly above her, two more right behind her looming large in her rearview mirror and two finger-four formations about five hundred feet off each wing. However, it was the two aircraft that were tucked inside her wings, so close that she couldn't turn, that caught her attention and particularly the one to her right.

It was a triplane and it, like all of the aircraft surrounding her, was painted bright red.

The pilot of the aircraft was frowning as he looked at Wasp and she could see his eyes darting back and forth, taking in her modifications and its new paint job. He obviously recognised the aircraft, but was puzzled by the changes to it.

She took the opportunity to have a good look at his machine as well; curious even in the face of her terror. The three wings were elegantly swept back from just in front of the bubble canopy and mounted one below the fuselage with the spring incorporated into it, one midway up the fuselage and the third level with the pilot's head.

While the bottom two wings formed unbroken lines, there was a kind of indentation in the top wing where it bent downwards a few feet from the fuselage, attaching to it in a V shape which prevented the pilot's vision from being obstructed. The wings looked too thin to take machine guns, but blisters on them, the same solution Jenkins had proposed for Wasp, showed the positioning of twelve machine guns grouped in six pairs close to the fuselage. Overall, the triplane had a curiously outmoded design, but from the stories she'd heard of its encounters with the Misfits, and in particular Abby, she knew that its performance matched and perhaps even surpassed that of Wasp and Dragonfly.

The red paint, solid on all of the other aircraft, was broken by four thick black stripes that diagonally crossed its fuselage and there were too many roundels to count painted under the cockpit, more even than Abby had - a couple of dozen British lions were joined by nine or ten purple and yellow Iberian Republic circles and a similar number of blue and white French squares. If the unique and instantly recognisable aircraft hadn't been so feared already, the sight of that tally would have dismayed the bravest of British pilots, yet Gwen found herself absolutely indifferent.

The enemy pilot finished his inspection of her aircraft and finally met her eyes. His frown deepened slightly when he inevitably didn't recognise her, but then he smiled as he seemed to put two and two together.

It was that smile that told her who he was; she had seen it so many times, but far larger and on a screen - he was Hans Gruber, Hollywoodland star, pilot of *Flamme*, the most advanced aircraft in Die Fliegertruppe.

Commander of the Crimson Barons.

The Barons were hand-picked by Gruber and their aircraft, rather flamboyantly named *Blutsaugers* by the Prussians (loosely translated by the British, usually with a sneer, as *Bloodsuckers*), were the finest the Prussians could fabricate. Gwen knew that individually they weren't as good as the Misfits and their machines and she was certain that she could have survived against one, if not two or three of them, but she was surrounded by all sixteen of the troupe and was already under their guns - any move that she made would be instantly answered with dozens of streams of metal.

She was dead and there was nothing she could do about it

The realisation was terrifying, but she found a strange calm as she resigned herself to it.

Gruber lifted his hand in salute, a gesture which Gwen returned with a smile, then both of the flanking aircraft fell back out of her vision.

Gwen sighed and reached forward to stroke the photo of her husband. 'See you soon, darling.'

She took a deep breath and stared fixedly at Richard's smiling face, steeling herself against the coming storm, wondering if she would hear the bullets coming, wondering if it would hurt, or whether her body would be ripped apart so quickly that she wouldn't feel it.

CHAPTER 10

The shots never came.

When Gwen finally got together enough courage to look around there was no sign of the enemy - they had vanished as rapidly and efficiently as they had appeared.

Suddenly feeling an intense need to get home she pushed her nose sharply forwards and dived below the low cloud, which had been thickening steadily as she headed south. She came out a scant thousand feet above the ground and searched for familiar landmarks, immediately finding Canterbury Cathedral off her right wing, six or seven miles away. That meant she had been heading in the wrong direction; she must have been far closer to Margate than she had realised when she'd lost the MU9's and needed to head almost directly west to get to Badger base. She pushed the throttle to the stop and turned onto her new course, not bothering to check the map on her thigh for a more precise direction.

She flew just below the clouds, needing the illusion of safety that it provided her, hiding under it for comfort like a giant blanket and in minutes she left behind all signs of civilisation to enter the downs. She found one of Jimmy's fields almost immediately and adjusted her heading to follow its directions.

She had her spring at full unwind still, but that wasn't enough for her and she was almost rocking in her seat, willing more speed out her aircraft, so desperate was she to get on the ground.

Less than ten minutes after her fright she was on final approach to Badger base and she recklessly dropped out of the sky, almost in a panic.

It was the roughest landing of her life and she bounced twice before Wasp stuck to the ground, not complaining at Gwen's treatment of her. The aircraft continued to behave well as she taxied far faster than she should have done towards the hangar, then applied far too much brake, bringing the tail wheel briefly off the ground and scattering the fitters who were waiting for her.

Gwen had thrown back the canopy as soon as she had landed, was fumbling with her straps while the fitters grabbed her wings and was clambering out of the cockpit even before Wasp was in place in the hangar. She jumped to the ground, ignoring Sergeant Jenkins' enquiries about her and her aircraft and only just had the presence of mind to scramble to a sand bucket before she emptied her guts.

After a few concerned looks, the fitters left her alone and went to work rewinding Wasp and seeing to the damaged wing.

It was Jimmy who finally knelt down at her side and rubbed her back with his hand.

'Gwen. I brought you some water. Um... why don't you come outside and get some fresh air?'

Gwen gulped down a mugful of water, then let the boy help her up and staggered out into the weak sunlight coming through the clouds. He supported her as she stumbled to one side and sat down against the cold metal of the hangar and wrapped her arms around her legs. She was shaking uncontrollably and something over her head, a latch or a chain, was rattling in time with the chattering of her teeth.

She had no idea how long she sat there for, but it seemed like only seconds before she felt a hand on her shoulder, shaking her gently and she lifted her head to find Abby leaning over her, frowning, the rest of the pilots standing behind her. Somehow they were all there - she hadn't heard them land or seen them taxi past her.

'Gwen? What's wrong? Are you ill?'

The words barely got through to her and she could only stare up at the woman and shake her head mutely.

'Then what is it? Was it the fight? B squadron said you got all four of the double-aitches with no trouble but that you got bounced by some 9's afterwards. I saw the damage to Wasp - is that it? The close shave?'

Again, Gwen could only shake her head and she squeezed her eyes shut, but waiting for her in the darkness was a wide smile on a handsome face and red, so much red that she quickly opened them again.

'What is it, Gwen? Please. Talk to me.'

Gwen wet her lips, swallowing, trying to find her voice. Eventually she managed to force out a single word.

'Barons.'

A shock ran through the pilots and a couple of them took a step back as if the word had a physical force.

'Are you sure?'

The question made Gwen inordinately angry for some reason and brought her roaring out of her stupor. 'Of course I'm bloody sure! Bloody Hans Gruber bloody popped out of nowhere onto my wing with fifteen of his bloody aces and bloody saluted me!'

The vehemence in her voice sent Abby stumbling back and Gwen pushed herself away from the wall and lurched to her feet, glaring at the pilots. 'He was as close to me now as you are. The Barons surrounded me, had me in their sights and I thought that was it, I thought I was going to be with my husband at last, but all he did was take a good look at Wasp, salute me and disappear!'

Gwen's anger vanished as she looked around the pilots and saw the shock and the sympathy on their faces. She fought to relax, hating herself for having lashed out at her friends and colleagues. There was no recrimination on any of their faces, though, just understanding, which just made her feel worse and she turned her head away.

'I'm sorry, I'm just... I'm sorry.' She frowned as she took another look at the group. 'Where's Bruce?'

Abby grimaced. 'He was shot down. After we took care of the fighters we engaged the bombers. He spent too long flying in a straight line trying to take one of them down and got caught in the crossfire from two others. He bailed out alright, though; Monty saw his glidewing deploy, but obviously we're an aircraft down and at exactly the wrong time if the Barons have shown up at last.' She shrugged. 'These things happen, though.' She turned to address the whole group. 'Right, I have to get on the blower, find out if HQ know about the Barons. You lot get to the mess, have some food and write up your reports. I'll meet you there when I know something.' She turned back to Gwen. 'Good job on those double-aitches, by the way.'

Gwen managed to smile. 'Thank you, but I only got three of them; the fourth tore himself apart trying to get away. I didn't get a single shot on him.'

Abby chuckled. 'You could have claimed him anyway, but I'm glad you're honest. Three or four it's still a damn good haul and not a bad morning's work!'

'Just out of curiosity... How many did you get?'

Abby gave her a crooked smile. 'Only eight.'

The mood was fairly solemn in the mess, despite the fact that between them they had shot down more than twenty enemy aircraft that morning. It wasn't so much the loss of Bruce that was weighing on their minds, especially seeing as they had received word that he had been picked up just off the coast, wet and shivering, but unharmed, it was more the prospect of facing the Barons again; they had too many memories of engagements that had only barely gone their way in France.

Gwen was still a bit shaky, in spite of the three cups of heavily-sugared tea she'd drunk, and didn't particularly want to relive her experience, but she knew she had to and she forced herself to tell the assembled pilots about her encounter with them. She expressed her surprise that they had let her live, but the other pilots just nodded, telling her that if the Barons were anything it was that they were chivalrous - they wouldn't have used their superior numbers to kill her, or take her by surprise, especially after they had identified her as one of the Misfits. They also were of the opinion that Gruber had recognised Wasp, but had wanted to investigate her new colouring and modifications - it had been him that had almost killed Cece, but because she had made it back to base then technically he hadn't shot her down so they hadn't notified him of her death or sent him a piece of her aircraft as their mutual tradition dictated, although she had lost her tail somewhere over enemy territory so they probably had it anyway.

When she had finished, the pilots then told her some of the stories of the skirmishes that they'd had with the Barons. There had never been a decisive battle with them; the pilots of both sides were too good to allow themselves to be shot down easily and while the Misfits had been able to claim a few victories, the Barons were always back to full strength by the next time they had encountered them; they seemed to have an unlimited supply of Blutsaugers to replace any losses. Unlike the Misfits the Barons' aircraft were painstakingly hand-crafted to exacting specifications set down by top Prussian scientists and not by each pilot. They were consequently superior to regular RAC aircraft and only slightly inferior to the Misfits' machines, but were so expensive and slow to make that they couldn't possibly be supplied to the entire Fliegertruppe and instead every single one produced was kept in reserve for the Barons.

Eventually, the conversation petered out and the Misfits began to drift away to armchairs around the room to write their reports of the morning's engagement, but Kitty stayed with Gwen. She waited until the last pilot had gone then pulled her to one side of the room, out of earshot of the others and spoke to her quietly, urgently, giving her a stern look. 'I've seen the photo in your cockpit and out on the airfield just now you said that you thought you were going to join your husband... Do you have a death wish, Gwen? Because that's the kind of thing we have to know. As much for our safety as yours.'

Gwen shook her head. 'No, it's not like that. I don't want to die and I'm not doing anything to bring it on any quicker, I just know that pilots don't tend to live long.'

Kitty stared at her for a few seconds then nodded, apparently satisfied. 'Good, because I like you. A lot. And I'd hate to lose you.'

Abby came into the mess fully an hour after the Misfits had landed. She brought with her a bedraggled and downcast Bruce who was greeted with thundering backslaps from the male pilots and hugs from the female ones, which he seemed to enjoy far more. The jubilation at his safe return didn't last long, though, and the pilots quickly subsided back into silence, settling back into their armchairs and looking at their leader expectantly.

'Whitehall confirms. The Barons have been spotted by various squadrons over Southern England. They haven't engaged anyone, though, which has them rather puzzled and Whitehall's thinking is that they were saving their ammunition and waiting for us to appear.'

Owen snorted in amusement. 'Doesn't Gwen's encounter throw that theory out of the window?'

Abby shook her head. 'Not necessarily; you all know there is a big difference between coming across a single damaged aircraft and finding the squadron prepared for a fight - none of us or them would even consider destroying that aircraft, would we?'

There were several nods at this and Gwen wondered just how well the Misfits knew their enemy, after all it was entirely possible that they had met at least a few of them before the war; the aviation community, and especially the one that constructed their own machines, was a select circle and everybody tended to know everybody else, if not in person, then at least by reputation. The same was probably true of the military aviation community in peacetime.

'Having said that, I agree with you lot; I think that something else is going on, but the bigwigs are sticking with their theory for now, so...' She grimaced, knowing what was coming. 'Effective immediately Misfit Squadron are grounded.'

The pilots all but leapt out of their seats, their protests bombarding Abby, coming thick and fast.

The wing commander held her hands up and the pilots gradually subsided into silence, although not a single one of them sat down again. 'None of you can deny that we need a rest; we've been working damn hard the last few weeks. We're tired, we're jittery and it's affecting our flying and our judgement...' She looked pointedly at Bruce, but didn't say anything else about the error which could have gotten both him and his wingman killed; he was already suffering enough with the loss of his beloved aircraft. 'And while we've been flying all day every day the Barons have been swanning around Europe, sleeping in the best hotels and eating the best food. We need to be in tiptop condition when we face them and we're not. Right now they're fresh and rested and would probably wipe the floor with us and Britain can't afford that. We're also an aircraft down and this will give us time to build one.' She looked at Gwen. 'On top of that, this gives us a golden opportunity to put the talents of our newest member to work. I have decided to allow Aviator Sergeant Stone to construct her own aircraft, meaning Wasp will pass into Bruce's hands.'

Bruce brightened up slightly at that. 'Bonza idea, boss! Wasp is a fine machine, I'll take care of her, I promise.'

Gwen's heart leapt at the chance of being able to build her own aircraft, but there was something nagging at the back of her mind, preventing her from leaping immediately to her feet and rushing out to begin the design process. It took only a few seconds to figure out what it was and she sighed and shook her head.

Abby had been watching Gwen, to see her reaction and as soon as she shook her head the woman smiled and nodded her understanding and approval; Gwen had made Wasp her own and she could no more give her up, than she could a machine that she had built herself. The wing commander shrugged and looked at the Australian. 'Sorry, Bruce, it looks like you're going to have to build your own aircraft.'

Gwen saw his face fall and remembered him telling her that he hadn't actually built Bandicoot himself - he had won her in a card game, then completely renovated her. She waved to catch Abby's attention.

'Uh, if you don't mind, even though I'm keeping Wasp, I'd like to offer my services to help Bruce design his new machine. It will do me good to get back to the drawing board for a while.'

Abby opened her mouth to give her approval, but was cut off by a whoop from Bruce, who leapt across the room, lifted Gwen off the ground and jumped up and down with her in his arms.

The pilots laughed and cheered him on.

When Bruce finally put Gwen down, Abby continued. 'We're also going to rotate leave. Starting tomorrow morning one pilot from each flight will get three days. I was going to send our most junior pilots, Gwen, Ophelia and Kitty, away first, but if Gwen is helping Bruce I'll have to change those plans; it would be good to have a design ready before she went away so construction won't be delayed any more than it has to be.'

'Actually, I already have a few good ideas and if we're stood down and I'm free to work, then I'll start right away. I should have the first drafts ready in a couple of hours for you and Bruce to approve, then, once I have that, I should have the blueprints ready by, I don't know... midnight, maybe? That way you won't have to change your plans.'

The pilots went very still and stared at Gwen with open mouths, all except Abby, who just watched their reactions with a grin, having already seen what she was capable of.

'No way! That's impossible!' Mad Mac's thick accent finally broke the silence.

'Wanna bet?' drawled Bruce, who had suddenly become Gwen's staunchest supporter. He stood by her side with his hands on his hips, glaring at the rest of the pilots as if daring them to say anything else.

'As a matter of fact, yes!'

Gwen slipped out of the mess while the pilots were busy furiously placing bets and drawing up odds on whether she could accomplish what they saw as an impossible undertaking, but was just a mild challenge and an interesting exercise to her.

While she walked over the airstrip towards hut two, the workshop where she had repaired Wasp, she thought back to the moment when Abby had told her she could have her own aircraft. She still couldn't quite believe that she had turned her down, but it had felt like the right thing to do at the time and it still did; she had developed a connection with Wasp over the weeks that they had flown together, it felt like they understood each other and it would have been a betrayal to abandon her.

The office hadn't been used since she'd last been in there and everything she needed was in place waiting for her.

It had been several years since she had designed an aircraft from scratch; the last one she'd worked on had actually been the Harridan and that had been mostly her parents' project, she had merely offered suggestions and made adjustments to it after each test flight. However, while she hadn't physically gone through the process since she'd made her last personal aircraft in her teens, she had designed and built hundreds in her mind since then and those designs came pouring from her now.

She started with Bandicoot, sketching it in detail from memory. It had been ahead of its time when it had been built, but that time had been almost ten years ago and it had only really remained as effective as it had thanks to the brilliance of its pilot. Once she had that clear, she began elaborating on its basic design, much as she had with Wasp. However, because there was no already-built machine out in the main workshop area, this time she could start from scratch and she pulled every idea she'd ever had out of where she'd stored them for just such an eventuality. In successive sketches she added a third wing, then reduced it to just one, changed the airscrew position to behind the cockpit, played around with the gun positions to alter weight distribution and concentrate firepower, attached the wings to the back of the fuselage and swept them forwards, then swept them back again. Each design was more unconventional and complex than the next, but she instinctively knew that each and every one of them would work.

In minutes the first large sheet of paper was covered with concept drawings, but instead of changing it she just moved to the next drawing board. Then the next a few minutes later. Then the next.

Once she ran out of basic concepts she returned to some of the best ones and began to refine them, building on them and taking them further.

By the time the other pilots wandered in, having made their bets and finally noticed she was missing, she had covered six sheets with dozens of designs and had begun to slow down. She didn't look up at them, though, she just continued with her work and they remained as quiet as they could while staring in wonder at her designs.

About twenty minutes later, after she had been working for a little over an hour, she put down her pencil, having covered eight sheets of paper and turned to smile at the pilots.

'Well?'

She invited them to comment; interested to see how many of them would agree with her own assessments of them, whether they would be able to differentiate between which were serious contenders and which had just been her letting her imagination run wild.

Predictably, Abby stepped forward, but it was a surprise when the other pilots also looked to Kitty.

The two of them began a discussion of the designs on offer and quickly counted out most of the ones that Gwen had already discarded, but also did the same to a few of the others, citing reasons that Gwen herself hadn't even considered and found that she readily agreed with after only a moment's thought. Some of the more outlandish designs were rejected as well with some reluctance, not because they didn't think they would perform well, but more for the difficulty they would pose for the fitters to service and maintain.

Eventually they narrowed the field until they had two options: a monoplane with swept-forward wings attached to the rear of the fuselage and a biplane with short thin boomerang-shaped wings. Both designs had much greater firepower than Bandicoot with two of Wendy's cannon already incorporated into them.

The two women called on Bruce to make the final decision and he stepped forward to look at the chosen designs.

'Well, I like them both, but I've become quite partial to a nice biplane so I'm going to have to go with this one.' He tapped the biplane design.

It wasn't Gwen's favourite of the designs and, like Wasp, it wasn't what she would have made for herself, but it was a good choice for the Australian and she nodded her approval. 'I'll get to work on some blueprints. I'll have them ready in a couple of hours.'

There were groans from a few of the pilots at the news, but grins from others and she smiled at the clear demonstration of who had bet against her and who had put their belief, and their money, in her.

When Gwen finished her blueprints she rolled them up and took them to the mess where the other pilots were waiting for her. Every eye turned to the clock. It was only just gone eleven.

'Pay up!' Lady Penelope crowed ecstatically.

Mad Mac grumbled in reply. 'Now wait just one god-darned minute! The designs need approval first, she might have to make changes!'

Someone ran for tacks and the blueprints were pinned to the wall in between a photo of the squadron gathered in front of a chateau in France and a piece of an HO111's rudder.

The pilots gathered around, watching expectantly as Abby inspected them, half of them hoping that she found some mistake while the other half prayed that she wouldn't.

The wing commander stood in front of the paper and bent forward to peer almost myopically at the bold pencil strokes.

'Hmmm...'

Her doubtful noise combined with her frown provoked excited comments among the pilots and some concern in Gwen, who immediately went to Abby's side to find out what the woman had seen. She bent forward to peer at the paper with her, but had to fight to keep a straight face when Abby whispered out of the corner of her mouth. 'I'm just teasing them. Play along.'

The wing commander stretched out a hand to point at a section of the fuselage and Gwen nodded vigorously. 'Hmmm!'

'Tone it down! You'll give the game away!'

The two of them ummed and ahhed for a minute or so before they realised that the room had gone completely silent and looked over their shoulders to see the Misfits staring at them, fully aware of what they were doing.

Abby winked at Gwen, then turned around to face her pilots. 'They're perfect! Mac, gimme my money!'

There were cheers and Gwen was glad to see that none of the Misfits was particularly unhappy about losing, especially because the victors immediately set about spending their winnings on drinks for them.

With no flying to be done the day after there was nothing to stop the Misfits from partying the night away and that was what they determined to do. However, because the blueprints had been finished so quickly, Abby had no reason not to grant Gwen, Scarlett and Kitty their leave and the three women decided to get a fairly early start the next morning, so they left the party just before one and staggered to the barracks together.

Despite making a good try of it, Gwen wasn't quite as drunk as she had been the night of her ceremonial acceptance into the squadron, but she was certainly just as happy and she fell asleep with a huge smile on her face, never realising that her distress at her encounter with the Barons had vanished the moment the possibility of designing a new aircraft had arisen and hadn't resurfaced even once.

CHAPTER 11

Since Kitty's family were in America, Scarlet's were in Ireland and Gwen's had visited only recently, the three pilots decided to go up to London for the three days of freedom that they had been given.

They didn't officially go on leave until ten in the morning so the three of them rolled out of bed late and went to breakfast around nine, a bit hungover and sat together to finalise their plans. Things were made slightly difficult by the fact that they were in the middle of nowhere, but in the end they determined that the best thing to do would be to take one of the squadron's automobiles to Maidstone. From there they could catch a train to central London then hop on the Tube to whichever hotel Gwen could book after they'd finished eating.

Their plans were blown to shreds fifteen minutes later, though, when Abby came back into the mess; she had overheard that they had planned to go to London and had rushed off to make a few calls and obtained permission for them to fly into the restricted airspace of London and land at Hyde Airstrip, the main airfield of the capital, used only by the Royal Family, their guards and the most well-heeled of the socialites and nobility, which would cut several hours off their journey.

That wasn't the only thing she'd done for them - she revealed that the manager of The Dorchester owed her several favours and that she had called one of them in and gotten them a room for both nights.

When they thanked her she revealed that she had had an ulterior motive in arranging things for them - their aircraft would be on hand in case they were urgently needed and the hotel was within walking distance of Hyde Airstrip.

At two minutes to ten the three pilots were sitting in their cockpits at the end of the runway with their springs under tension, waiting for the signal that they were free to go. The three aircraft made an unlikely group; the large red, white and blue Hawk clashed painfully with the pink and black Wasp, while the tiny Hummingbird was almost invisible next to them in its highly effective green camouflage.

Abby was standing by, looking at her watch and when she saw that it was precisely ten o'clock she saluted them, then waved them away with a shooing motion. The pilots laughed and took the time to return her salute before opening their throttles.

The watching Misfits, sitting in the sun outside the mess in various states of disrepair after a night of heavy drinking, lifted their feet from the ground and the three women were treated to the sight of Mac, taken by surprise coming back from the bathroom, throwing himself to the floor in order to do the same as Wasp and Hawk raced past them down the airfield. They were neck and neck the whole way, the power of the heavier Hawk competing with the agility of Wasp and the two aircraft lifted into the air at almost the same time and climbed briefly before banking towards London. Wasp turned tighter and was on its new course first, ahead of Hawk, but the interceptor soon caught up again with its superior speed. However, neither of them was in the lead, because Hummingbird, despite being slower, already had a head start because of its vertical takeoff ability.

As Badger Base disappeared behind them, Gwen and Kitty throttled back and formed on Scarlet as she sped just above the treetops, heading directly towards London, less than fifty miles away as fast as Hummingbird could go. The Irishwoman had actually wanted to take advantage of the journey to try out a few tactics that she had come up with and over breakfast she had asked Kitty and Gwen if they would mind spending half an hour or so dogfighting with her. Neither of the other Misfits had anything like the small woman's capacity for alcohol, though, and weren't particularly feeling up to it after the previous night's revelry. She had been disappointed and had tried to persuade them with offers of drinks in the nightclubs of London, but had readily agreed to drop the idea when they pointed out that it would be best to get to the city as quickly as possible so that they could fit in as much fun as they could during their time off.

The trees immediately around the base gave way to fields, which became more and more populated with houses when they left the Kent Downs behind. They stayed at low-level, not only because was

Hummingbird safer closer to the ground, but because they were also far less likely to stumble across any Fleas - just because they were on leave, didn't mean that the Prussians were and, despite the fact that Sapper had said that there were no enemy aircraft in the area, they still kept a good watch.

They caught sight of a squadron of Spitsteams taking off from a country estate near Rochester and adjusted course slightly to buzz them, just for fun, waggling their wings when the fitters and support staff waved at them.

Five minutes later they flew by Dartford, which was covered in a haze of smoke; enemy bombers that were damaged by British fighters invariably jettisoned their loads before turning for home, not caring who or what was below them and the bombers from the previous day's raid had left a trail of destruction along the coast from Margate towards their targets - three airfields south of London - and the town had been the unlucky recipient of at least a few of them.

London's airspace began a couple of miles beyond Dartford and they passed the first of the three lines of anti-aircraft batteries that protected the capital. The first comprised dozens of batteries of guns which guarded the approaches to the city in a semi-circle that went all the way from beside the Crystal Palace in the south, round to Woolwich in the east, before ending just beyond Enfield in the north. The next, a couple of miles closer to the city, began on the hill in the middle of Brockwell Park near Brixton and swept past the Isle of Dogs before ending in Highbury Fields. The last completely encircled the centre of London and comprised more than double the amount of guns as the other two, but if they ever fired that would mean that bombers were almost directly over the city itself.

London's defences had yet to be breached by the enemy, though, and some politicians and newspapers insisted that it was impenetrable, that no enemy would ever overfly the capital of the Kingdom of Britain, but the Misfits knew that was just propaganda; no amount of anti-aircraft batteries could possibly bring down the numbers of bombers that they had seen just the day before. Hopefully, though, the claims would never be tested; the enemy had no real reason to bomb London - aside from the small Royal Guard squadron stationed at Hyde Airstrip and Whitehall itself, there were no military targets in the city and the industry and shipping in the capital were insignificant when compared to that concentrated elsewhere.

Soon enough, the Imperial Observatory on the hill at Greenwich was in sight and the Misfits climbed up over it to a thousand feet to give them a better view of the city.

Even though most homes and power stations had converted to burning the much cleaner Hydrogen in the last decade, London hadn't quite been able to completely shrug off its previous dependence on coal. It was much better than it had been; at least now you could walk outside without your clothing becoming black, but the city was still permanently shrouded in twilight and while some claimed that gave it mystery and romance, most people, especially the ones that actually had to live there, just said it was filth.

Only the tallest buildings could rise above that constant smog and several did so, but only two of those were really worthy of their attention. The first was the dome of St Paul's Cathedral, which seemed to have been guarding the conscience of London forever and had remained unchanged and untouched through revolutions in both industry and beliefs. The second was the graceful form of the glass-paned iron tower of Isombard Kingdom Brunel's extension to Buckingham Palace, the tallest building in the Kingdom of Britain and only rivalled by the monstrous edifices built over the Atlantic. The extension and its tapering tower that had been likened to a "glass shard through the heart of London" by its detractors, had been commissioned from Brunel by Empress Victoria at the turn of the century and had been conceived by the great man as a monument to both her reign and the lofty status of the British Empire at the time. Its usually sleek and elegant silhouette was marred, though, by a dozen antiaircraft guns, perched on specially-built extensions around the upper levels - the King had insisted on "doing his bit", paying for the batteries out of his own pocket and placing them on his own tower for best effect, despite the fact that when they fired they would likely shake his expensive china off the shelves and rattle the artworks.

Their destination, Hyde Airstrip, was less than a mile to the west of the Palace and they turned towards the tower, using it as a reference point. Air traffic control gave them permission to land and they approached the airstrip from the south, swinging wide to give the Palace a wide berth, not wanting to spook the antiaircraft gunners into firing at machines that would undoubtedly be unfamiliar to them.

After landing they were directed to the Royal Guard squadron hangar near the south end of the airfield, positioned so that in an emergency the Spitsteams of the Guards could accelerate from the hangar straight onto the airfield and they taxied back to it past dozens of civilian aircraft of all shapes and sizes, from grand flying yachts and deflated zeppelins, to smaller pleasure cruisers and fast messenger vehicles for the various diplomatic services in the city. They all had a sad look to them and a thin layer of dust, despite a twice-weekly cleaning being covered by the exorbitant fees their owners paid; all civilian traffic had been grounded the past six months by order of the King and the aircraft likely hadn't flown since then.

Fitters were waiting to guide the aircraft inside the hangar, placing them to one side, out of the way of the Royal Guard aircraft before beginning to rewind them. It was the work of only moments to shut them down and then the three pilots climbed out to be met by a contingent of twelve Royal Guards. Their red uniforms initially sent shivers through Gwen, but they quickly subsided, especially when she saw how handsome the young men among them were and how they were admiring the Misfits. The envious looks of the women among them didn't particularly hurt either.

The Guards escorted them to a small but luxuriously appointed dressing room attached to the hangar where they were able to change out of their flightsuits and store them in lockers so that they wouldn't have to carry them around London and risk damaging them. Then, with their day uniforms on, they were once again accompanied by the entire contingent to the entrance opposite Wellington Arch and passed through the security gate.

As they strode away, Scarlet turned to blow a kiss at one of the Guardsmen who blushed, his face the colour of his uniform. The Misfits laughed gaily and linked arms, all thoughts of the war and the danger posed by the Crimson Barons temporarily forgotten in the excitement of being on leave in London.

The Guards had offered to procure them a motorcab, but they had refused; it was only a short walk to The Dorchester up Airfield Lane along the boundary fence of Hyde Airstrip and their overnight bags were extremely light because under regulations they had to wear their uniforms at all times, except when they were sleeping.

They checked in and were taken up to their rooms by a uniformed doorman who all but sneered at the NCO uniforms of Kitty and Gwen and wasn't at all impressed by Scarlet's lowly Aviator Lieutenant's uniform. They didn't let that spoil their mood, though; they were there to enjoy themselves and besides, the sight of the room that Abby had gotten them more than compensated for any snobbery from the staff - the "room" turned out to be a suite with four huge bedrooms with equally huge four-poster beds, a central lounge area with two sofas each, a fully stocked complementary bar with champagne already on ice and a view to the west over the neighbouring airfield that they appreciated far more than a they would have done a view of the city centre.

It was just as well Abby had sorted the bill, though, because it probably would have come to more than a year of their wages. Combined. Each night.

They chose rooms and dropped off their bags, only taking the time to make sure their hair and makeup was alright before heading straight back out.

Stepping onto the London streets was like stepping into another world after the isolation and quiet of the Kent Downs.

Airfield Lane was one of the main thoroughfares of London, part of the ring road that completely encircled the centre of the city. Autocars were everywhere, most of them spring-powered and quiet, but there was also the occasional vintage steam car chugging along noisily, although thankfully they tended to have been converted to Hydrogen, which limited the amount of pollution they emitted.

This close to the airfield there weren't very many people on foot, though, and it was only when the Misfits got to Marble Arch at the end of the road and turned onto the splendour of Oxford Street that they encountered the crowds. It was Saturday, the weather was perfect and it seemed like the whole of the city was out and about enjoying themselves, filling the wide pavements in front of the shops to capacity.

Apart from the large number of men and women in uniform and the occasional glimpse of anti-aircraft guns on building roofs there was barely any sign that there was a war on and life seemed to be going on as usual. The boutiques looked like they were fully stocked and the people wandered around, many of them clutching packages wrapped in the gaily-coloured paper of the various boutiques, as if they didn't have a care in the world, as if young men and women weren't dying to guarantee them the freedom that they were enjoying. Gwen felt like she should be angry with them, should be shouting at them to wake up and do something, but she found that she was strangely comforted to know that, because of the efforts of her squadron and so many others like them, people like these could lead normal lives that weren't filled with fear.

With no need to maintain radio discipline and no other Misfits in transmission range to overhear them they had spent much of the journey discussing what they wanted to do in London. They all agreed that the nights were definitely going to be spent in one or more of the clubs in the centre, but it had been a lot harder to agree on what to do during the days. Kitty had only been to the city a couple of times and had never done the rounds of the museums and art galleries. She was particularly interested in going to the Aeronautics Museum, which had a full-scale model of her grandfather's famous aircraft in the lobby, but she also wanted to visit the Darwin Museum right next door to it with its collection of fossils and dinosaur skeletons. Scarlet and Gwen had visited most of them already, though, and were understandably rather reluctant to do such time-consuming things. They had countered with suggestions of their own, highlights of London that were more appropriate to their interests, or that casual visitors to the city wouldn't necessarily know about. Their first suggestion, which had rather bemused Kitty, was actually to have tea.

They took a pneumatic lift up the outside of Selfridges to the renowned tea rooms on the roof and sat around a table looking out at the view over the rooftops while waiters served them from the gigantic and world famous brass machine, designed, reportedly, by Selfridge himself, that brewed to perfection over fifty different types of tea at the same time in its various gurgling tanks. They ordered one of the more exotic types, but didn't find it to be anything special, although obviously it was better than the mud-like substance, brewed for hours, that had passed for tea on Gwen's first RAC base. The tea was accompanied by scones with clotted cream and strawberry jam as well as a dish of the first strawberries they had seen in months, grown in one of the hothouses of Kew.

Once again, Scarlet managed to hone in on the best-looking company available and once they had finished their tea they were joined by three young men, who doffed their expensive velvet top hats in greeting, then bullied a reluctant waiter into pushing two tables together for the six of them.

Unfortunately, the men's intellect didn't match their looks and the Misfits endured less than ten minutes of banal conversation before making their excuses and leaving. Their lack of interest in the men didn't stop them from accepting their calling cards or allowing them to paying for the teas, though, but the cards did go straight into recycling bins as soon as they stepped out of the lifts and back onto the street.

Their next port of call was Hamleys, a short walk away on Regent's Street, where the latest innovations and technological advances were displayed in model form on its four floors, each of which was a single giant room.

As always the ground floor was filled to capacity with children and adults alike, all gawking at the railway engines that were weaving and chuffing their way around tracks that took them from cities to mountains and from American plains to British countryside. The biggest crowd was gathered around a working quarter-size model of the latest innovation, which had been set in pride of place in the centre of the atrium - the Gallant, the fastest locomotive in the world. It employed the latest in hydrogen compression technology in a uniquely streamlined form that was reminiscent of the fuselage of an aircraft and which allowed it to approach speeds that were previously unheard of.

The three Misfits barely sparing a glance for the locomotive, though, or for any of the other things that were delighting the crowds, although they did spare a moment to appreciate a spring-powered model of a Spitsteam as it buzzed over the British countryside, eternally describing a circle on the end of a long piece of wire. Instead, they headed directly for the stairs to take them upwards to their destination on the fourth floor.

There weren't quite as many people on the second floor, where clockwork road-going machines were displayed in all their varieties and could be sent careening around enclosed racing circuits and where child-sized automobiles could be piloted around diminutive tracks lined with padding by the offspring of whoever had half a crown to spare for five minutes of fun.

The crowds thinned out even more on the third floor where a gigantic brass basin filled with water held ocean-going behemoths and lithe modern naval vessels with belching funnels, alongside elegant clippers and sailing ships of ages past which were blown along by trade winds provided by fans placed around the edges of the tanks, all of which were occasionally persecuted by the submarine boats of the Prussians, which were booed by the children (and quite a few adults) every time they surfaced and jeered when they failed to destroy their targets with tiny clockwork torpedoes.

They climbed the last set of stairs to the fourth floor and were unsurprised to find that it was almost empty.

Aviation, despite having been revolutionised and made much cheaper and accessible by the advent of spring power, was still seen by most as being very much the province of the privileged few, so it attracted far less interest than the other exhibitions, particularly the railway, which the public was very much in love with, seeing it as the method of transport that belonged to the people. Parents looking for a toy for their children, usually looked elsewhere and those people who were merely wandering the store in search of an hour or more's entertainment were largely thinned out by the wonders below and by the necessity of using staircases to ascend. Consequently, the large space immediately under the roof was almost exclusively populated by a more serious sort of individual who had had the fourth floor in mind as their destination all along. They were the enthusiasts and intellectuals, the pilots and inventors, the visionaries and dreamers who saw flight as being the future of mankind.

Hamleys had been Gwen's suggestion of something that the Misfits could do with their time. Her parents had brought her many times while she had been growing up and she had actually been quite surprised that neither of the others had ever visited the aviation floor before; it was *the* unofficial meeting point for the aviation community. Although, now that the borders were closed and most of the British experts were working towards the war effort there were probably far fewer visitors than there had been during peacetime.

The stairs finished in the middle of one wall, giving them a view of the entire floor and they stood and gazed around.

It was just as Gwen remembered. The multitude of aircraft on display had slowly changed and been renewed as designs and fashions evolved, but the way in which they were presented, lovingly recreating the magic of flight, was the same as ever and, despite no longer being a child, the wonder that she felt when she gazed at them hadn't faded.

The display was decidedly patriotic, with flights of mainly Spitsteams and Harridans streaking overhead, suspended with what Gwen knew was fishing line, but Hamleys would never neglect innovation, no matter its source and the Prussian Empire was also well-represented with various Muhlenburgs, Hoffmanns, Funkels and Hock-Hunds. However, while Hamleys showed no discrimination against their inventors, they were not beyond catering to the national feeling and the Fleas were definitely coming off much worse in their confrontation with the RAC. One of the HO111's had even been rigged with a small gas burner and was falling out of the sky in flames in a very convincing manner, which made the three pilots wince; fire was the nightmare of all pilots, but thankfully it had been made much less likely to happen, at least in fighters, by spring power.

The few people that were there were gathered in groups and deep in discussion, probably about the merits of certain aircraft, or some theory that one of them had put forward, but there was one man off on his own to the side, standing on a step ladder and attaching a shiny silver model to a new display advertising the new American-built luxury aircraft. Gwen smiled and immediately went towards him, ignoring the admiring silence that fell in her and the other pilots' wake when the men and women saw their uniforms and more particularly the wings on their chests.

As well as a pilot, John Dunne had been one of the early pioneers of aviation. He had worked as an aircraft designer for the army, but had retired in 1913 with health problems. A year later when the Great War had started and aircraft had taken on a new importance, Hamleys had snapped him up to convert their top floor, previously a storeroom, to a dedicated aviation display. He had worked there ever since and had become something of an institution, often joining in the discussions when he wasn't working and his opinion was respected and sought after by most of the members of the "Top Floor Club" as the regular visitors liked to call themselves. When her parents had brought her to London it had often been because they had meeting in Whitehall or the Palace and rather than have her sitting bored in a waiting room somewhere with nothing to entertain her they had brought her to Hamleys and left her in this man's charge. She had spent hours on end in his workshop, helping him construct models of the latest inventions, some of which had been copied from her parents' designs. He was in his sixties, with a shock of white hair on his head and a bushy moustache, equally white.

She stopped a few feet from him and waited for him to have the silver aircraft safely anchored before speaking. 'Mr Dunne.'

'Yes?' The old man finished what he was doing and stepped off the ladder before turning to her. 'What can I...?' His eyes lit up with recognition and not a little bit of joy. 'Why! Young Miss Hawking, as I live and breathe!' His eyes darted to her left hand. 'Ah, but I see it is no longer Miss! Mrs...?'

'Stone.'

'Stone! And an Aviator Sergeant no less. A pilot!' His incredibly quick mind darted back to her name and he frowned. 'Stone... Not Matthew and Joanne's boy, Richard?'

Gwen nodded, a lump rising in her throat.

'My word! Congratulations! How is he? He hasn't been in in, oh, it must be seven years! And is there a little Stone, a pebble, dare I say, for me to entertain just like I hope I did the delightful parents?' The old man grinned, but when she didn't answer he frowned, his busy gaze scanning her face as if searching for an enemy in a suspiciously clear sky, reading her expression. 'Oh. How insensitive of me. I'm so sorry, my dear.'

Gwen shook her head. 'You weren't to know, Mr Dunne.'

Dunne smiled weakly and spoke quietly, reaching out to put a comforting hand on her arm. 'Please, Gwen, call me John; you're a little too old and grown up for "Mister" and I hope we know each other well enough to be on first-name basis.'

Gwen smiled and nodded. 'I believe we do! John, these are my friends, Ophelia Flynn and Kitty Wright. They're in my squadron.'

'Very pleased to meet you young ladies.' He raised an eyebrow at Kitty. 'Wright? *Kitty* Wright? As in Kitty Hawk? As in Orville and Wilbur?'

She nodded, grinning and he groaned, rolling his eyes theatrically. 'As if being upstaged by Gwen Hawking when she was twelve wasn't enough, she brings a Wright with her...'

They laughed and he smiled at them. 'Would you like a tour of the workshop?'

Gwen was already very familiar with the workshop, but that didn't bother her one bit; the old man was always working on something new, and her nod was just as enthusiastic as those of the other two pilots.

'Wonderful! Come on then, before the gannets descend to feed.' Dunne nodded at the men and women who had started to gravitate around them, trying to listen in on their conversation and obviously desperate for a chance to speak with the aviators. The names "Wright" and "Hawking" were already being repeated in hushed tones and Dunne had to raise his voice to be heard over the increasing volume of noise. 'Don't worry! You'll get your chance at them soon enough!'

He winked at the Misfits, then led the way to the back of the room where there was a small door, hidden behind scenery which represented the rolling hills of the Cotswolds.

The workshop was small compared to the main room and extremely cluttered. To one side there were row after row of wooden drawers, many of which were open to reveal that they were filled with aircraft pieces and spare parts in miniature, but exquisite detail. The three remaining walls were completely obscured behind drawings, prints, sketches, paintings and the occasional blueprint of aircraft of all types, haphazardly pinned up in no apparent order. However, it was the large workbench that occupied most of the space in the centre of the room that caught their attention; on it were the beginnings of several model aircraft, including the beginnings of the frame of a large four-engined bomber and a MU9 with a broken wing, but also an almost-finished triplane that was disturbingly familiar to Gwen.

Kitty and Scarlet saw the direction of Gwen's gaze and looked at her in concern, but she smiled at them; they didn't need to worry about her, not in a place that had made her so welcome and provided her with so many magical memories.

Gwen walked over to the triplane and bent down to get a closer look at it. 'This isn't quite right, John.'

The old man frowned. 'Really? I've got some sketches around here from someone who actually saw her in flight on a recent diplomatic journey to Prussia. Hold on, I'll dig them out...'

He rooted around in the drawers underneath the worktable, pulling out one cardboard tube after another and discarding them again until he found what he was looking for. 'Here we go.' He popped the end off the tube and pulled out a thin sheaf of papers, which he spread on a nearby drawing board.

The three pilots gathered around to inspect them. The original was an overly dramatic depiction of Flamme leading a flight of Crimson Barons, overflying a cheering crowd that was waving Prussian flags. It looked like a preliminary sketch for a later work by someone who wasn't a particularly good artist and who didn't have any idea whatsoever about aircraft.

It had been the only thing that Dunne had had to base his work on, though, and he had used his vast experience to cleverly extrapolate the inner mechanisms of the aircraft from it and create a simple blueprint. It was a remarkable feat and both Kitty and Scarlet were suitably impressed, but Gwen knew that this was how the old man had been forced to create almost all of his models and almost thirty years of experience had given him a lot of practice of doing just that.

She surveyed the blueprint critically, knowing that the man would appreciate advice and corrections far more than he would simple praise of his talent.

'The wings need to be swept back five more degrees and the lowest one has a slightly shorter span than the other two. By about a foot, I'd say. Also the tail is too short by at least eight or ten inches and the cockpit is too far forwards.'

'Ah! Of course, I was wondering why it seemed so unstable in my mind. That would solve a lot of the yawing problems.'

'Also the red isn't quite right, it needs to be more...' Gwen searched quickly through the rainbow of paints that were stacked in the middle of the work table and pulled one out. 'This one.'

Instead of thanking her again, Dunne frowned at her, once again searching her face. 'There's something you're not telling me, isn't there... You've seen this machine, haven't you?'

Gwen nodded. 'Yes. So have Scarlet and Kitty.'

'But we didn't get to see it up as close and personal as you did.' Kitty said.

Scarlet grinned her lopsided grin. 'And we didn't get a salute or a smile from Mr Movie Star himself.' She winked at Kitty. 'You know I reckon he blew her a kiss as well, but she didn't want to tell us that part - it's probably why she threw up when she landed. I know I would.'

Dunne blinked at Scarlet, trying to work out if there was some hidden meaning to her words, but eventually realised that he had to take them literally and turned back to Gwen. 'This was in France, I take it?'

Gwen shook her head. 'No, it was yesterday.'

'Yesterday? But...' He swallowed and his voice cracked slightly. 'They're here?'

'Yes.'

'My word...' He looked down at the model. 'I'd better get this correct then, otherwise we'll be getting complaints; I always do when I get something wrong. You know how aviation spotters are - everything has to be exactly right.'

Gwen laughed. 'Is that a not so subtle jab at me, John?'

'Perish the thought!' He looked at her sideways and grinned. 'Actually aviation spotters are just as likely to get worked up if I get the roundels and rivets in the right places as they are if the design is completely wrong, whereas you didn't care about such minutiae. You only pointed out my mistakes because the aircraft were wrong and wouldn't fly properly, which I never minded one bit, especially because you always pointed out the mistakes the manufacturers had made in the design as well and showed me how it could have been improved. I learnt so much from you and my work improved as a result. Which reminds me... I have an original piece by the master around here somewhere...'

He opened one of the larger drawers at the base of the table and grunted with effort as he lifted a large box out and deposited it in one of the few clear spaces on the deck. It was sealed with string and he cut it open and peeled back the flaps, opening it flat to reveal the almost-finished model within - a white monoplane that was just over a foot long.

'Swan! You kept her!'

'Of course! I would never throw away a Gwen Stone née Hawking original! Apart from the fact it's probably worth a lot to collectors, you never finished her and I always hoped you'd come back and do so one day.'

'Oh, Mr Dunne...'

Gwen picked up the model and turned it round, re-familiarising herself with it and chuckled, shaking her head; it was a very immature design, ineffective, but elegant, based on the lines of a swan she had seen land on the lake on her parents' estate. It would handle like a pig and be absolutely useless as a fighter or a pleasure craft, but would look lovely in an airshow or parade. 'One day I'll finish it for you, but I'll have to make you a proper model or two to go on display as well. Maybe a Misfit aircraft.'

She put the model down, then turned to face Dunne, finding him staring at her, wide-eyed.

'You're in Misfit Squadron?'

Gwen cringed and looked at Kitty and Scarlet. 'Damn, I forgot everything was so hush hush... Am I supposed to keep that a secret as well?'

Kitty shook her head. 'It's only really the base that's secret, but we don't tend to spread it around much; enemy agents and all that.'

Scarlet feigned disappointment. 'Also, unfortunately, we're not going to get bought drinks by handsome men telling them that we're "misfits."'

Gwen raised an eyebrow. 'You didn't do too badly in Selfridges!'

Scarlet nodded and grinned wonkily. 'Ah! But I never told them who we were exactly, did I?'

Gwen laughed, but didn't continue with the banter when she realised that Dunne was just staring at them. 'Mr Dunne? Come on, it's only a squadron! We don't do any more than any of the other squadrons that are fighting for the Kingdom.'

Dunne shook his head. 'You may make light of it, but those of us that are in the know are fully aware of who the Misfits are and the contribution that they've made and are continuing to make to the war effort. We know that without you we would be lost and we thank you.'

Gwen gave him a half smile. 'I've only been in the squadron for a few weeks, these two have been in since the start - it's them and the others who you owe your thanks to, not me.'

It was Kitty's turn to shake her head. 'Don't keep selling yourself short, Gwen! You're one of us and you've made a huge contribution since you arrived, one that goes beyond just the numbers of Fleas you've shot down.'

'Yes! Now we're a squadron again!' Scarlet added enthusiastically. 'Things were a bit shaky for a while there and morale was a bit low because we were a pilot short - it was like a constant shadow hanging over us.'

Gwen blushed and smiled shyly at her fellow Misfits. 'Enough about that, you can tell me how amazing I am later...' She glanced at Dunne, who had been following the conversation intently. 'Mr... uh, John, if you give me a sheet of paper I'll do you a quick sketch of the triplane in return for you telling us all the gossip in the aviation world. Agreed?'

'Agreed! And with pleasure!' Dunne hurriedly set up a clean sheet of paper on a drawing board and, while Gwen began to sketch, he started to fill them in on recent developments.

There was a more-powerful spring in the works, the Phoenix, which would add speed and range to the smaller fighters and which the manufacturers, Rentley-Joyce, hoped to be able to deliver before the end of the summer. They were having problems with it, though, and in the meantime they had developed a better version of the Ozzy, which would be in production soon. A new variant of the Harridan, the Mark IIa, was in production and already going into service and there was a new Spitsteam ready, also designated Mark IIa, but delivery from Supranaval was lagging slightly behind the more efficient Hawking production process.

While the pilots were delighted at prospect of a new spring to add performance to their machines, it was the news coming from across the Atlantic which the old man was most enthusiastic about and that was most interesting to them and Kitty in particular.

'Nicole Tesla's apparently put one of her grandfather's electric engines in an aircraft. It's much lighter than a spring and there's no need to construct around a bulky cylinder, but nobody I've spoken to quite knows how it works and I haven't been able to figure it out myself either. I don't suppose any of you...' He looked at them one by one and sighed when the three pilots shook their heads. 'Oh well, it was too much to hope, I suppose.'

'I went to school with Nicole,' volunteered Kitty. 'She's the one who first got me interested in electricity and in return I got her hooked on aircraft. I can write and ask her about it, although I doubt she'll share the secret; her grandfather learnt his lesson early on and now the whole Tesla clan tend to keep their inventions close to their chest until they've had a chance to patent the hell out of them.'

Dunne beamed at her. 'Really? That would be wonderful!'

Kitty smiled in return. 'I'm not promising anything, John, and it might be a while before she writes back, but I'll let you know what she says.'

'Thank you, my dear!'

'There you go.' Gwen put her pencil down and stepped back from the drawing board allowing the others to crowd around.

Solemnly silent, Scarlet and Kitty surveyed the three drawings Gwen had done, showing Flamme from the front, side and above. They took note of the sheer amount of detail that she had been able to put into them, details that would only be available to someone who had been very, very close to the aircraft. Details which most British aviators wouldn't survive to remember.

Dunne on the other hand overflowed with praise for her quick and exemplary work. He thanked her profusely before looking at the clock on the wall and sighing. 'Well, I suppose you have to come out of hiding and face the music at some point. I apologise in advance in the name of Hamleys for any inconvenience you are about to encounter... I have some vouchers around here somewhere for the tea shoppe in the basement. It's not much in the way of compensation, I know, but...'

The Misfits laughed away his offer.

'No need, John, we'll survive!' Scarlet clapped him on the shoulder and gave him one of her winning grins. 'Come on girls, let's go dazzle them!'

She led the way to the door back into the main room, but as soon as she stepped around the concealing scenery she halted and Gwen almost bumped into the back of her. 'What is it?'

Scarlet's wide grin had rather comically changed to a nervous half-smile as she stared out into the main room. 'I'm kind of scared.'

'Of what?' Gwen poked her head around the scenery and gasped.

The main room was packed with at least twenty times as many people as before and there were quite a few children as well, most of whom had pushed their way to the front and were craning their necks, trying to get a view of them over the Cotswolds hills.

Kitty used her height advantage to peer over the painted wooden board. 'It's like they've never seen pilots before...'

Dunne whispered from behind them. 'They haven't for a while. At least not pilots on active duty in the Royal Aviator Corps who can tell them how the war is going - not many of you lot been getting leave recently and those that do certainly don't end up in here. Just wait until they find out who you all are!' He chuckled, rubbing his hands together gleefully at the prospect.

Gwen shook her head, though. 'Please don't tell them that, John. Just let them think we're ordinary pilots; we should try not to draw too much attention to ourselves and besides,' she eyed the crowd warily, 'we do have plans for the evening and we'd like to be out of here before closing time.'

Dunne checked his pocket watch. 'Well, that gives you five hours.' He snapped the watch closed and grinned. 'It's going to be a close-run thing!'

In the end they were in Hamleys for "only" three hours.

Many of the people who had flocked to the fourth floor weren't particularly keen about aviation, they had just wandered upstairs to see what all the fuss was about and were only really interested in superficial matters, like how fast their aircraft went or how many "kills" the Misfits had - they were disappointed with Scarlet's three, not understanding that even that was a remarkable feat for a scout and especially one whose aircraft was barely even armed, having only two .303 machine guns, then goggled at Gwen's ten before almost shrieking in joy when Kitty admitted to twenty-six. However, they began to wander away again when slightly more technical questions were thrown at the pilots and eventually the crowd shrank back to something approximating its original size, although many of the children remained, watched over by their parents, gobbling up Scarlet's tale of the dog food mission and a couple of other amusing anecdotes that she had stored for a rainy day.

Once the casual admirers had gone, Kitty and Gwen entered into a much more serious discussion with the true enthusiasts and despite their initial trepidation they had a very enjoyable time; Hamleys was *the* place to be to swap opinions, discoveries and experimental results and it was rumoured that the Spitsteam itself had started life during a discussion in that very department. Even though they weren't inventors and didn't have many ideas of their own to share, the people were surprisingly knowledgeable and the views they had on existing machines were interesting and often thought provoking, due to their sometimes innocent, but nonetheless fresh perspective. It was everything that Gwen had told them to expect from a visit to Hamleys and when the Misfits finally did bid Dunne farewell they left with large grins on their faces and even she came away feeling that it had been worth it.

Their smiles and all thoughts of dinner, a show and a night of dancing in one of the famous clubs of London were banished as soon as they returned to The Dorchester, though; there was a message waiting for them from Abby in reception and just the first few words, "I apologise, but", had them groaning, knowing that their plans for fun were going out of the window.

The message went on to say that their presence had been requested at Buckingham Palace that evening by the King himself; he had heard that three of the "famous Misfits", as he had put it, were in the city on leave and had expressed an interest in meeting them.

That interest, of course, was tantamount to a command and Abby had immediately responded that the three pilots would, of course, be delighted to attend the Palace at seven o'clock sharp as requested. She had sent their dress uniforms and the message with Derek in Swift, their fastest aircraft, hoping to catch them before they went out for the night and while Derek returned directly to Badger Base the items had been delivered to the hotel by Royal Guards, causing quite a stir among the guests.

The concierge was far more polite to them than the doorman had been earlier and after he had delivered the message he informed them that their uniforms had been taken up to their rooms and that there were hairdressers and make-up assistants available if they should want them, free of charge.

The pilots thanked him with a smile and told him that it wouldn't be necessary, then took the lift up to their room. They weren't quite sure how they felt about the change in their plans; on the one hand they had been looking forward to blowing off some steam, having a few drinks, a laugh at a variety show and then dancing most of the night away at the Astoria or Covent Garden, but on the other it was what might well be a once-in-a-lifetime opportunity to be presented at court and meet the King. The excitement of that was greatly lessened by the need to wear their dress uniforms, though; they were smart and especially favoured the female form, but were so awfully uncomfortable, especially when compared to their form-fitting flightsuits.

The boxes and bags containing their uniforms were laid out on a sofa in the sitting area, but they pointedly ignored them and went to draw baths - they had two hours before they needed to be at the Palace and weren't going to spend a minute more than necessary in them.

CHAPTER 12

An autocar arrived for them twenty minutes before seven, finding them already waiting in the lobby of The Dorchester. It was an enormous old black steam-powered Rentley-Joyce flying the Royal colours, which they were very happy to see made the doorman, who had turned his nose up at them earlier, blanch.

Their uniforms made getting into the car a difficult prospect, not only because the petticoats wanted to catch on everything that they brushed against, but because the corsets in them made it quite hard to bend at the waist. Eventually, though, they settled in with Gwen sitting with her back to the driver and the other two facing the front opposite her.

Gwen placed her hat on the seat next to her, then lifted herself off the seat and tugged at the base of her tunic, trying to pull it back into place; the whalebone inserts had ridden up quite uncomfortably when she had sat down, making the stiffly-starched high collar of the tunic dig in to her chin. It was also pushing certain parts of her beyond the limits to which they were normally accustomed. Once she had her tunic more or less back in place she fiddled with the double line of brass buttons on her front, buffing them with her cuff and trying to get the RAC crests on them to line up, but completely without success; two of them that had obviously been sewn on badly and while one was pointing to eleven o'clock and wasn't too bad, the other was almost at two o'clock and was very noticeable. She gave up and then turned her attention to her white petticoats, smoothing them down repeatedly to try to get rid of the creases from where they had been folded. They weren't too bad, though, and thankfully there were only a few of them - Scarlet had almost twice as many, although hers were blue to match the rest of her uniform and not a white that would be unforgiving if she got anywhere near a puddle or spilt something down her...

Some awareness pricked at her and she looked up. Instead of enemy fighters she found two pairs of blue eyes staring at her, one set the colour of the ocean and the other the midday sky.

'What?' She frowned at them; they looked absolutely spectacular, while she felt like mutton dressed as lamb, but worse, they seemed to be perfectly relaxed and eminently comfortable.

Scarlet smirked. 'You look like someone put itching powder in your flightsuit. Stop picking at yourself and have some dignity and discipline!'

Gwen snarled at her. 'It's so bloody uncomfortable and then there's... there's... *these!*' She irritably batted at the petticoats that were fluffed up around her legs like a cumulonimbus despite her efforts to smooth them down. 'What idiot designed a dress uniform so impractical? If I was called away to fly in the middle of dinner I wouldn't even be able to get into the cockpit let alone...'

She cut herself off in the middle of her rant when she saw that her two friends were barely containing their laughter. She was tempted to continue; they would probably crack a rib or something if they lost control, which would serve them right, but she didn't and settled for scowling at them. 'I can't help it if I've never worn the damn thing before!'

'Never? But you hide it so well...' Scarlet sniggered.

Kitty was a tad more sympathetic than the Irishwoman and gave Gwen a curious look. 'You've never worn it? How come?'

Gwen shrugged as much as she could. 'I didn't have a graduation ceremony from flight school because I was deployed too quickly and my wings were taken away before I could be invited to dine with anyone important enough to warrant full dress.'

'Really? Well, we had to wear this stuff almost every day in France; we were billeted in a chateau, flying off the lawn, and the Count liked to have guests for dinner and a ball every evening. There were always generals and air marshals and minor royalty wandering around, it got to the point where we were barely ever wearing our day uniforms.'

There was no time for Kitty to elaborate on the delights that they had experienced in France, though, because it was a very short drive to the palace and the car had already arrived. They went through the main gates at the end of The Mall, past a pair of Royal Guards, who presented arms as they went by, then under the archway in the east facade and into the courtyard beyond, where the autocar stopped.

The East Wing with its public façade had been built at the same time as the West Tower, but the two extensions to the original Palace had been separate projects and their architectural styles couldn't have been more different. Most of the official events and entertaining took place in the classically-styled East Wing because of its traditional style and lush interior, befitting the trappings of Royalty, whereas the modern glass and iron West Tower represented the Royal Family's investment in the future of the realm and was reserved largely for the Royal Laboratories.

Many of the best British scientists were hard at work on various projects for the betterment of the realm on the twelve floors of the tower and among the many innovations to come out of it were the gas-powered steam engine, which had changed the face of transport and made Britain once more a world-leader and an electrical generator based on American technology, several of which had been constructed around the country and now supplied free heat and light to the entire Kingdom (a smaller version of which supplied electricity to Badger Base). The Royal Family also worked on personal projects in private laboratories, making their own contribution to the development of the nation and indeed the young Princess Elizabeth, the King's eldest daughter, was a talented engineer in her own right and, despite only being fourteen, had flown an innovative aircraft from the Palace gardens the year before, although her interests weren't as focussed on flight as Gwen's were, but rather on physics as applied to mechanics and motion in general.

The three pilots were handed out of the car by three young Royal Guard officers, resplendent in bright red ceremonial uniforms, and they took a few seconds to settle their hats on their heads for the short walk across the courtyard to the door. Gwen looked at Scarlet's tall hat with its gold-trimmed rim and purple silk band with envy and for the first time ever found herself wishing she were a commissioned officer; the shorter hats that she and Kitty were wearing were not nearly as elegant and the light blue cotton band on them just looked cheap in comparison. Neither did it help Gwen's self-esteem that both Scarlet and Kitty looked absolutely magnificent in their uniforms and that both had several medals pinned to their chests, while her own was conspicuously bare.

The young officers didn't seem to care what rank the pilots held or how often they'd been decorated, or at least they hid their feelings well and when the women were ready they offered carefully rehearsed smiles along with hooked arms to their partners and together the six trouped into the Palace. Gwen was somewhat consoled when they went inside and the Misfits removed their hats, tucking them under their left arms; without the added height, Scarlet once again became shorter than her.

The block heels of their shiny black calf-high boots clicked on the marble floors as they went through large rooms hung with paintings and tapestries, then up a huge staircase with a glass dome overhead through which they could see sky that was almost the colour of their uniforms. This early in summer it was still daylight outside and would be for hours, but the lights were already on in the hallways and staircases, powered by a dozen wind turbines incorporated into Brunel's brilliantly designed tower, which provided electricity to the whole building with enough spare for the mechanisms of the new additions bristling from its highest parts.

Eventually, they came to a pair of huge doors, behind which was the throne room where they would be presented to the King. There they stopped and their escorts gave them a small bow before disappearing, leaving them in the hands of a Herald wearing a uniform which was undoubtedly supposed to be imposing and dignified, but which Gwen thought made him look more like a cinema usher than anything else.

'You are the Misfits, I presume.' The man managed to sneer their squadron name even while keeping a completely impassive face, something that was probably part of his training as an aristocrat.

'You presume correctly, Matey!' Scarlet put her free hand on her hip and peered up at the tall thin man, giving him a wide grin.

Gwen had to hide her laugh with a cough and the back of her hand. Scarlet had expressed her opinion of certain aspects of military discipline and hereditary nobility on many occasions, especially while drunk, and Gwen realised with a start that it would probably be best to keep the Irishwoman as sober as possible that evening.

The man's expression didn't change and he showed impressive control of himself as he looked from Scarlet to Kitty, then to Gwen, before going back to Scarlet, taking in their uniforms and their appearance, obviously working out who each of them were.

'Yes, anyway, welcome to Buckingham Palace. I am the Marshal of the Court. It is my job to make sure that things go smoothly and that people like you, who haven't been here before, know what to do, when to do it and how. To that end...' He cleared his throat and drew himself up slightly, pointedly ignoring Scarlet, who was still staring up at him, as he recited a speech that he had obviously had to give many times before. 'In a few minutes, at precisely seven o'clock, these doors will open and I will precede you as we enter within. As the guests of honour you are the last to arrive and are the sole persons to be presented today. When I announce each of you to the Royal personage you will make your obeisance in turn. You will not speak unless spoken to and your response should be followed by "Your Majesty" in the first instance and by "sir" from there forth; His Majesty does not insist on rigid protocol and his court is kept in a military manner, which I am sure you will find comforting.' The man hesitated at that last as he took the three pilots in, noting their relaxed attitudes and the grin that was still on Scarlet's face; most likely he had never met anybody less military in the military. He struggled on bravely, though. 'When His Majesty has finished with you I will give you a signal. You will take three steps backwards, make a further obeisance, then turn. That is the finality of your presentation and from then on you will be free to move around the room as you wish. Dinner will be served at eight o'clock and you will be escorted to the ballroom by the three Guards who brought you here. As the most junior officers you have been placed very low at table and I suggest you continue to speak only when spoken to; most of your dining partners will be nobility or at the very least hold high rank or esteem in His Majesty's eyes and are worthy of your respect.'

He looked from one of the Misfits to the other and seemed to despair. He sighed and deflated slightly, suddenly seeming almost human. 'Look, Georgie is a forgiving man and has a soft spot for aviators, but not everybody at court appreciates the RAC and the Misfits the way he does. They will use any mistake you make as ammunition against you, so just try not to do anything stupid that will cast a shadow on your squadron or the Aviator Corps, alright? Please?'

Scarlet reached out and patted him on the arm. 'Don't worry, Matey, we know how to behave ourselves... More or less.' She turned to wink at Gwen and Kitty. 'Right, girls?'

The man had by now lost all composure and he groaned, slumping further and putting his hand over his eyes. Unfortunately for him, the doors opened behind him at precisely that moment and he jumped in surprise with a squeak. He hurriedly straightened up and composed himself before turning and leading them forwards.

The throne room was brightly lit and decorated mostly in red and gold, matching the uniforms of the Royal Guards and the Marshal. An enormous, glittering chandelier hung overhead, filled with thousands of brightly burning candles - it seemed that electric bulbs weren't appropriate for this room, although among the candles could be seen a few unlit bulbs, shaped like the candles that surrounded them, likely there for times that the Royal Family weren't present, like when the cleaners came in. The room was crowded with men and women in colourful finery, largely civilians, but the military was well-represented as well - there were a few Naval officers in tail coats the dark blue of the water of the North Sea with glittering gold ceremonial spyglasses at their sides, their white breeches and stockings harking back to the Napoleonic Wars, there were also a few Aviator Corps officers, the women wearing uniforms almost identical to Scarlet's and the men in long jackets over tight riding breeches, but most of the military personnel there were in the Army; with the Kingdom of Britain confined to the British Isles they didn't have very much else to do. They wore swords at their sides and bright uniforms of every colour of the rainbow, as if trying to flee as far from the drab camouflage that they were forced to wear every other day of their lives.

They had only gone a couple of steps into the room before the man came to a stumbling halt and spun around to hiss at them. 'Dammit, he's only bloody gone and changed into uniform again! Hats on!'

He took in their surprised expressions at being told to cover up indoors and sighed, shaking his head. 'Don't ask... Anyway, salute when we halt and give a small bow when I call your name. I'll give the order for when to take your hats off again.'

His face quickly returned to its impassivity, but Gwen thought she noticed a twitch in the corner of his eye. She almost felt sorry for him and wondered how often he'd had troublesome guests to chaperone. He waited impatiently for them to put their hats back on and check each other to make sure that the brim was straight and the precise two fingers above the brow as set down in RAC regulations, then turned away again, leading them on at a pace that was slightly too hurried for dignity.

The guests opened up in front of them, leaving a corridor for them to walk along and giving them a clear view of their destination - a small platform, hung with a small red and gold canopy and holding two golden chairs with red velvet cushions. A woman, Queen Elizabeth, sat delicately in one of the thrones, smiling benignly at them as they approach, but it was the man who was standing at the top of the steps looking down at them that held the gaze of the pilots. This was the King, George VI, who had been Emperor George II until recently; he had renounced his claim on being an Emperor, despite having an empire, and overnight the "British Empire" had become the "Kingdom of Britain". He had also changed his family name, because it had been seen as being "too Prussian". He was wearing an RAC uniform, most likely in their honour, but it was so completely covered by sashes, medals and stars as to be almost unrecognisable as such.

Gwen self-consciously walked behind the Marshal and could feel her body almost twitching as it tried to salute just about everything, an instinct that was drummed into all military personnel during basic training, and she only just managed to resist the impulse by keeping her eyes firmly on the King and reminding herself that, as the senior officer in the room, it was him that should receive the first salute.

The Marshal stepped to the side and stopped in front of the platform and the three Misfits smartly came to a halt in a line behind him. His relief was almost palpable when the pilots saluted together, passably smartly.

'Your Majesty, may I present Aviator Lieutenant Flynn.' Scarlet gave a small bow, not much more than a nod of her head. 'Aviator Sergeant Wright.' It was Kitty's turn to nod. 'Aviator Sergeant Hawking.'

Gwen almost forgot to bow as she had to fight against a new impulse; the urge to correct the man and tell him to use her married name, but she decided that it wasn't the time and managed to nod after a barely perceptible hesitation.

'Hats off.'

The whispered command had them removing their hats and tucking them back under their arms. Gwen found that she was almost relieved - hats were never usually worn indoors and it had felt decidedly strange to have been doing so.

'Welcome, brave pilots!' The King descended the three steps from the dais, grinning widely. 'I apologise for not returning your salute, but as you can see, I am not covered.' He looked from one of them to the other and they smiled back at him uncertainly, not quite sure if they were supposed to answer. They felt even less comfortable when the King's friendly grin suddenly became a frown and he turned to address a nearby RAC officer.

'Sir Douglas, why are these two dressed so poorly?'

There were gasps from a few of the civilians courtiers around the room as the King rather rudely pointed at Gwen and Kitty, however his ire was directed mostly at the RAC officer, who Gwen recognised with a start as Sir Douglas Pewtall, Commander of the Royal Aviator

Corps; she had met him a couple of times in Hamleys when she was younger.

'Poorly, Your Majesty?'

'Yes! These poor pilots have short hats and brass buttons! Why have they been forced to come before me like this?'

The man blinked, not quite understanding. 'That is their uniform, sir. They do not hold commissioned rank, therefore they do not merit...'

'Do not merit? Do not merit?!?' The King's voice rose in pitch as he became almost incredulous. 'These are Misfits! Of course they merit my commission! Don't you agree?'

'Of course, Your Majesty, but we have proper ways of...'

'Pish and tosh! It's only my name on a bit of paper after all, don't make me burn the one *you* have!' The King's words were strong, but there was a glint of humour in his eyes and a smile on his face which removed the force from them. He turned to address the room at large. 'Give these worthy aviators my commission and for pity's sake find them some decent clothes to wear!'

There was applause and not a bit of laughter at his pronouncement, while Kitty and Gwen glanced at each other in amazement; just like that they had been made officers.

The Marshal waved to a servant who had been lurking nearby and whispered in his ear, then nodded at the King.

'Good!' The King turned back to the three pilots and he surveyed them one by one before wandering over to stand before Kitty. '*Aerial Officer* Wright.' He paused to give the commander a stern look and the man chuckled and waved his hand permissively in response. 'You pilot Hawk, do you not?'

'Yes, Your Majesty.'

'Twin airscrew, am I correct?'

'Yes, sir.'

'I'm told that she is one of the fastest aircraft in the world, yet she fights fiercely as well and together you have defended these shores as if they were your own. You do your nation proud, Aerial Officer, and both I and my Kingdom owe you a debt of gratitude which I fear we will never be able to repay.'

Kitty nodded solemnly in the face of his praise. 'Thank you, sir, but it is nothing more than my duty; the fight against tyranny is one that concerns all of us.'

Her response drew polite applause from the audience and the King smiled and waited for it to subside before holding his hand out to the side. 'For continuing gallantry and for the many stirring stories I have heard of your bravery in the face of overwhelming odds, I present you with the Distinguished Aviation Cross.' A servant placed a medal in his hand, an incredibly ornate silver cross on a purple ribbon, and he pinned it to her chest. 'Congratulations, Aerial Officer Wright.'

The King stuck his hand out and Kitty took it, receiving a very hearty shake. Gwen smiled when she saw that the usually unflappable American was indeed quite flapped and had a red glow to her pale cheeks.

The King stepped to the side and stood in front of Scarlet, who peered up at him as he towered over her by almost a foot.

'Aviator Lieutenant Flynn, pilot of Hummingbird, source of so much of the vital information that my armies so desperately need and, so I am told, intrepid photographer of canine sustenance.'

Scarlet laughed, delighted that he had heard of her exploits and showing that, unlike her companions, she was completely at ease in such august company. 'I also do weddings, Your Majesty.'

The King laughed with her, equally delighted with her response. 'I apologise that I cannot promote you also; I'm afraid I don't get as much say in the higher ranks as I insist on having with new recipients of my signature.'

'That's quite alright, sir, I already get paid too much for the fun I'm having.'

The King scowled at her. 'Is that so? Well, maybe I should ask my commander about whether I can hand out demotions...'

'I... uh...' Scarlet stuttered, for once left at a loss for words, but when the King's expression returned to his usual wide smile she laughed. 'That was a good one, sir, to be sure!'

He laughed with her and again held his hand out to the servant hovering nearby. 'Well, Lieutenant, you already have one of these, so they're only letting me put a crosspiece on it - for extreme bravery and continuously putting yourself in the way of harm for the sake of others, I award you your second Distinguished Aviation Cross. Congratulations, Aviator Lieutenant Flynn.'

While the audience applauded he pinned a small star to the purple ribbon of the silver cross that Scarlet already had on her chest, then shook her hand just as heartily as he had Kitty's, almost lifting the smaller woman off the ground with every pump.

He gave her a last smile and a wink that made her laugh before moving to stand in front of Gwen, who felt her cheeks start to burn as all eyes turned to her. 'Aerial Officer Hawking...'

'Stone, Your Majesty, it's Stone.'

The King blinked. 'You're *not* Gwenevere Hawking?'

'I am, sir, but I'm, I mean I *was* married.'

The man searched her eyes briefly, then nodded his understanding before continuing in a much quieter voice than he had used with the other Misfits. 'Aerial Officer Stone. I understand that you, how do they put it in RAC regulations... ah yes, that you are guilty of "interfering" with one of my flying machines, an offence for which you have yet to be sentenced. Is that correct?'

Gwen went an even deeper shade of red, but forced herself to look the King in the eye, determined to receive whatever reprimand was coming with dignity. 'Yes, sir.'

'Hmmm...' The King stroked his short beard thoughtfully while he contemplated her, apparently wanting to prolong her suffering. 'Well... I am of a mind to pardon you... But only on one condition.'

'Name it, sir, please! Anything!' Gwen leapt at the chance to clear the shameful stain from her record; in spite of the fact that her disgrace had been either ignored by her fellow Misfits or in many cases waved away as fully justified, the threat of grounding and imprisonment was still hanging over her.

'That you regale me with the story of how you shot down two Fleas in an aircraft that your parents designed, *with* your help I might add, but that you *still* saw fit to improve upon.'

'With pleasure, sir!' Gwen almost sagged in relief, catching herself just in time when she remembered that she was supposed to be standing at attention.

'Excellent! Well, it looks like we're going to have some decent conversation around the dinner table for once!' The King clapped and rubbed his hands together in glee before continuing. 'Now, I understand that despite not having been with the Misfits for very long, you have made a great impact, both on the effectiveness of the Squadron and on enemy numbers. That is a *remarkable* achievement considering that the Misfits were already being held to an incredibly high standard by their commander. Jolly good show, madam!'

'Thank you, sir.'

'I also read the report of your encounter with Gruber and his Barons. Tell me, what was that like?'

Gwen winced at the sudden memory and took a deep breath before answering. 'Terrifying, sir.'

There was some muttering from the audience at that and Gwen cringed; the overwhelming majority of people still had the opinion that war was something "glorious" and at least the civilians had probably been expecting her to express the desire to have another crack at Gruber or something equally bloodthirsty.

Invariably, it was only the people who had never seen war up close that thought that way and thankfully the King wasn't one of them; he had served in the Great War and seen its misery and horror up close and he gave her a shrewd look before nodding. 'I think I would have been terrified as well. Hopefully next time you'll meet him on more of an even playing field and the outcome will be somewhat different.'

Gwen returned his nod. 'I certainly hope so, sir.'

The King held his hand out to the servant. 'Aerial Officer Stone, for your devotion to duty and the bravery you have shown in the face of extreme danger I award you with the Distinguished Aviation Medal. Congratulations, Aerial Officer.'

He pinned the medal to her chest, then shook her hand like he had the others, before stepping back and mounting the dais from where he led the applause, smiling at each of the three pilots in turn.

The Marshal came and stood in front of them. He bowed to the King and they copied him, then walked backwards as he had instructed him.

Three steps and the crowd closed around them, hiding the royal couple from view and finally they could relax a little bit as people returned to their conversations.

Gwen lifted the medal on her chest and craned her neck to look down at it. It was different from the one that the King had awarded to Kitty and Scarlet - the ribbon was RAC blue with thin diagonal white stripes and the medal itself was a golden oval with the face of the King on it. In the ranking of medals it was below theirs, but not by much and she was immensely proud to have received it, despite feeling that she hadn't really earned it.

'First of many, I hope, *Aerial Officer Stone*.'

Gwen looked up to see Scarlet watching her. 'Actually, I'd rather the war ended before I had the chance to win any more of them.'

Scarlet nodded. 'I know what you mean. But the way I see it is that it's better for us to do these ridiculously brave things and get medals for them, than somebody else, who's not as well equipped,' she grinned, 'or as insanely talented, try and do them and get medals awarded posthumously.'

Gwen shrugged. 'I suppose.' She was going to say more, but stopped when she noticed that Kitty was looking rather unhappy. 'Kitty? What's the matter?'

'We've been promoted. We're officers now.'

Scarlet laughed. 'That's usually seen as a good thing!'

The American nodded sadly. 'I know, but it means that Gwen and I will get separate rooms. I was just getting used to having a roommate.'

Gwen reached out to rub her arm. 'There's no reason we can't keep sharing. I'm fairly sure Abby won't mind if we ask her.'

'And I've been thinking about asking whether you two minded if someone else moved in with you.'

Neither Gwen nor Kitty needed to think about it and they nodded together, Kitty's expression immediately brightening. 'We'd love that!'

'Great! I'll move my stuff in when we get back. Of course, as the senior officer in the billet I get choice of which bunk I want and you'll have to bring me breakfast in bed...'

Kitty rolled her eyes and pulled Gwen around so that their backs were to Scarlet before speaking in a stage whisper. 'I wonder if the King will demote me if I hit a senior officer with a pillow.'

'I don't know. Shall we find out together?'

They turned on Scarlet, glaring at her as fiercely as they could, but Gwen immediately pulled back in shock; her parents were standing right behind the diminutive woman.

They were dressed all in white, like their flightsuits; it had become almost expected of them when they appeared in public. She had to admit they did look quite dashing, though, and it certainly made them stand out in a crowd.

'Mum! Dad! You're here? You were watching?' She frowned as something occurred to her. 'Did you have something to do with my promotion? I thought it was funny when the Marshal announced me as Hawking...'

Her father held up his hands. 'Slow down, Gwenevere! I swear we had nothing to do with your promotion or your medal and as for the Marshal's mistake, it's only because he's a friend of ours and knew you were coming. He just assumed that you had reverted to your name after Richard...' He trailed off sighing.

Her mother took over from him as he faltered. 'The promotion and the medals were all the King's idea, darling. He likes his military pageantry, which is why you wore your hats and saluted him rather than curtseying like the rest of us have to - he has every young and upcoming military man and woman presented the same way.'

'So, we're not the first?' Scarlet's face fell, comically. 'And I thought I was special...'

Gwen gave the Irishwoman a scathing look, receiving a poked-out tongue in reply.

'Ahem! If you've quite finished?'

The pilots turned to find the Marshal standing a couple of paces away, watching them with a thoroughly disapproving expression on his face.

Scarlet was unrepentant, though and frowned at the Hawkings. 'Did he actually *say* ahem? I didn't think people did that, I thought it was just a noise, like clearing your throat.' She demonstrated, coughing a few times, trying to say "ahem" at the same time. 'I can't do it...' She shook her head in mock disappointment.

The Marshal looked at her for a few seconds in something that approached horror, but quickly recovered. He held out two rolled up pieces of paper, sealed with red wax and imprinted with the royal seal, one to Kitty and one to Gwen.

'Here are your commissions and if you would follow me, dressmakers are waiting to fit your uniforms.'

Kitty squealed in delight as she took the scroll from him, but Gwen was slightly less enthusiastic. 'We really are being displayed like prize horses, aren't we?'

Her mother laughed. 'Of course, darling, but that's just part of life at court. You'll get used to it if you come enough times.'

'I'm not sure I really want to.' Gwen turned to Scarlet. 'Are you going to be alright on your own for a while?'

'Of course! I'm pretty sure I saw champagne around here somewhere...'

Gwen shared a worried look with Kitty, but before they could comment or warn her parents to keep the Irishwoman away from drink they were ushered away by the impatient Marshal.

Just under an hour later, feeling more self-conscious than ever, Gwen was escorted by the same young Guardsman as before into the dining room where there was another surprise in store for her - the seating arrangements had been changed at the King's request and the three Misfits had been placed immediately around the Royal Family, along with her parents and Sir Douglas.

A very uncomfortable couple of hours followed, during which she was never quite sure what to say, how to say it or when. On the other hand she marvelled at how well Scarlet handled the situation, often having the King and Queen Elizabeth in stitches and often managing to draw Princess Elizabeth into the conversation to give her expert opinion on aviation matters. Kitty also coped very well, managing to join in the conversation quite naturally, although as an American she probably didn't feel the same cultural awe that Gwen did towards the Royals.

In spite of the incredible food and the remarkable wines, the night couldn't end soon enough for Gwen, although it wasn't so much because she didn't know how to act around the King and his family, it was the presence of her own family that really spoiled the occasion for her; there was too much unsaid between them that it was just a constant pressure on her and she was reminded of that every time she caught a flash of white out of the corner of her eye. She was relieved, therefore, when the Royal Family retired around midnight and the Marshal appeared to inform them that they could leave whenever they felt inclined and that the car was waiting for them, which was essentially his way of throwing them out politely so that the important people could have their important discussions.

None of them was quite sure what the protocol was or whether they should say goodbye to anyone, like their commanding officer, but now that the King wasn't there the other guests were much less interested in them and completely ignored them as they stood up from the table, so they settled for just saying goodbye to the Hawkings, then left, escorted once more by the Guardsmen, their time in the Palace over.

CHAPTER 13

The Misfits were woken by a knocking at the door the next morning at around nine. They had been planning to have a lie in before going down to the restaurant for a hearty breakfast, but the insistence of the knocking put paid to that.

Gwen slipped on a robe and padded across the room to open the door, revealing a moderately impatient doorman, who handed her a note without a word then bent down to pick up various packages from the floor which he deposited on the coffee table in the middle of the room. He bowed his way out again quickly and she shut the door after him before breaking the seal on the note with a yawn.

'What is it?' Scarlet came wandering out of her bedroom. It was just as well that the man had already left because she hadn't bothered to put on a robe and was only wearing an extremely skimpy nightie.

Gwen scanned the note rapidly. 'It's from the commander, Sir Douglas Pewtall... He's sent officer's day uniforms for Kitty and me!'

Kitty squealed in delight and rushed past Gwen to open the packages, but Gwen kept reading. 'The commander also asks whether Aviator Lieutenant Flynn would care to dine with him the next time she is in London.' She turned to grin at Scarlet. 'It seems you made quite an impression last night and not only on the King!'

Scarlet grinned and tossed her hair as she flounced back to her room. 'Of course I did!' she called over her shoulder.

The Misfits spent the day in London, taking in the sights and doing a bit of shopping.

They all enjoyed themselves, but it was Scarlet who had the most fun, laughing at Kitty and Gwen, who were wearing their new officer's uniforms and top hats and couldn't stop peering around to see if anyone was looking at them.

They had lunch in a lovely restaurant near Trafalgar Square after spending a couple of hours in the National Gallery so that Kitty could say that she had at least done something cultural in her next letter home, then at five in the evening they returned to The Dorchester to clean up and get ready for their night out, intending to do the things that they had planned for the previous evening.

However, it seemed that the fates had no intention of letting them enjoy themselves.

Sirens started to blare only five minutes before they were due to leave their room. They were closely followed by the chatter of guns and the Misfits rushed to the windows to look out over the airfield, seeing the flashes from the muzzles of the anti-aircraft guns stationed around its perimeter as they fired at some unseen threat overhead. Seconds later there was the unmistakable crump of bombs exploding, far away, but close enough to be well within the confines of London.

Their eyes were drawn to the hangar at the end of the runway where they had left their aircraft as Spitsteams of the Royal Guards streamed out of it, already accelerating for takeoff as they came through the doors. Sensibly, they weren't red, but instead wore the same camouflage as the Spitsteams of regular squadrons with the addition of a thick gold band running from front to back half-way along the wing, just inside the roundels, to distinguish them from the others. Their formation was slightly ragged as they took off, which was only to be expected with the unusual method that they were employing, but within moments they had formed up in three wings of four and as soon as they cleared the airfield perimeter they turned sharply to fly past The Dorchester, almost close enough to touch.

Kitty looked to Scarlet and Gwen. 'What should we do? Do you think we should get into the air and help?'

Scarlet just shook her head. 'By the time we get up the Fleas will be long gone. Go and pack; we're not going to be having any fun tonight.'

The Irishwoman was right and less than an hour later the call came for them to return to Badger Base; Misfit Squadron had been put back on active duty.

They packed hurriedly and checked out, then rushed to the airfield, where they were expected. They changed into their flightsuits and went through their pre-flight checks as quickly as they could, but even so it was almost dark by the time they were in the air and it became a race against the sun to see if they could get home before it was too dark to see the airfield.

They lost and had to circle the base for half an hour, waiting until a nearby raid had gone by before the electric lights lining the airfield could be switched on to guide them in.

As soon as their aircraft were safely in the hangar they reported to Abby in the mess, which was far quieter than they had ever seen it and she filled them in on what had been happening.

In only two days of operations unchecked by the Misfits, the Fleas, and the Crimson Barons in particular, had undone most of the advances made by the RAC over the previous weeks. They had intensified their offensive against RAC bases and had even bombed many of the flying clubs and mansions that the squadrons had moved to, most of which were marked on pre-war maps. As a result, many of the temporary airfields were now closed and Badger Base was the only official RAC base in the south of England still open for air operations. It was just as well the Mark IIa Harridans had entered into service because they at least were able to somewhat stem the tide against the MU's and HH's, but the Barons were running amok, just like the Misfits before them, and the sixteen of them had reportedly accounted for almost 80 RAC aircraft.

Then, when the British had been placed firmly on the back foot, the enemy had become much bolder and added new targets. The attempted bombing of the London docklands and East End had been only one of several attacks on the cities as the Prussians attempted to demoralise the ordinary civilians, just as they were doing their air force.

It had been no surprise, therefore, when Abby was informed by HQ that the squadron was back on an operational footing, effective immediately, and ordered to recall her pilots and cancel all leave. Only a couple of the pilots were even remotely upset by the news - Monty, because he'd planned to hike the surrounding Downs in search of rare birds, and Mac, because he'd been hoping to nip back up to Scotland in Swordfish to replenish his supply of whisky, which was running dangerously low - but their disappointment was almost completely nullified by the prospect of flying again.

Prussian morale was at an all-time high - captured pilots invariably laughed in the face of captivity, claiming that they would be freed in days when the invasion came and Prussian propaganda came over with the bombers and leaflets were dropped on the cities along with the bombs. They proclaimed that the Misfits were cowards and had gone into hiding, that the population were helpless against the might of Die Fliegertruppe, and that the British King should call for the immediate and unconditional surrender of the entire Kingdom of Britain before too many civilians were killed in the legitimate raids on those military targets which were using the populace as a human shield.

Instead of being cowed, the British public responded to the raids and the propaganda in typical British fashion and were outraged, refusing to give an inch. Even though they had no real idea of who the Misfits were, they began a campaign in support of them. Overnight the squadron became a household name and during the following days the government began to release select details of Misfit Squadron's exploits, not naming the pilots (except for Abby, who was set up as a figurehead) but rather giving the names of the aircraft, which began almost to take on personalities in their own right.

This newfound fame did nothing to change life for the pilots, though, beyond giving them something to laugh about when tales of their exploits, treated with a vast amount of artistic license, began to appear in the newspapers.

The Misfits had gone back onto active duty the morning after the three women had returned from London, but with a single limitation - they were only to engage the Barons and leave the regular Fleas to the other RAC squadrons. They weren't exactly pleased by the order; while they were certainly hoping to get a crack at the Barons, they were forced to ignore the other aircraft, which continued to bomb cities and shoot down their fellow RAC pilots.

As the days passed the tactic began to wear down not only the nerves of the Misfits, but also their reserves of springs; in order to be on hand to respond whenever the Barons appeared, they were forced to go on far longer patrols than usual, using the dual spring capabilities of the aircraft to stay in the air sometime hours at a time and they were going through their stockpile of springs very rapidly and with the turn in the RAC's fortunes, replacements were not particularly forthcoming. They had very little to show for it either because whenever they responded to a sighting of the Barons, the red aircraft invariably broke off and dived away as soon as they were in sight, obviously under instructions not to engage them. The Misfits had orders to pursue the Barons until they were out of British airspace, then loiter along the coast until radar confirmed that Gruber and his troupe weren't swinging back around, but even then they weren't allowed to go after the other Fleas, instead they were ordered to land and rewind, ready to be back in the air for when the Barons returned later.

The one bright light in the darkness was that construction of Bruce's new aircraft had continued apace in Gwen's absence and was well on its way to completion by her return - because the Misfits had been grounded, the entire staff of fitters had been able to work on it and while most of them went about sorting through spare parts or fabricating anything that was missing, Bruce's team of fitters did the actual assembly. Even so, it wasn't quite finished when the squadron was put back into service and once again they were an aircraft short. However, one afternoon, less than a week after Bandicoot's destruction, the aircraft was finished and ready for testing, which Bruce carried out with vigour and not a little impatience, declaring it fit for service after only an hour of aerobatics and manoeuvres above the Kent Downs, a safe distance away from the airfield.

The new craft still didn't have a name, though, and Bruce refused to give it one, insisting that Gwen should have the honour of both that and assigning its colours, although he did make one request: that she use "no bloody pink, please."

After a few hours careful consideration, Gwen had a quiet word with Bruce's fitters and the next morning, when the squadron was pushed out, they were brought back to full strength by a shiny black aircraft named Devil with a white stripe across its belly beneath the cockpit and a dark brown nose.

Fortunately, the squadron's frustration didn't last very long; when RAC command saw the Barons' continuing refusal to engage they gave the Misfits permission to go after the other aircraft in an attempt to lure the elite Prussians back into the fight.

Two glorious days of air combat followed and the Misfits shot down as many Fleas as the Barons had in the same time, but with half as many pilots. It seemed to everyone on the British side that the Barons would have to stop running away and engage them, otherwise they risked the destruction of the morale of their forces by being seen to run in the face of smaller forces.

The response, when it came, was highly disappointing, but at the same time almost impossible to believe; the very next day the Barons turned up escorting bombers engaged in raids on the factories of Manchester, Leeds and Liverpool. According to radar they had come from the direction of Denmark or Norway, but they shouldn't have had the range to fly so far, even with dual springs, let alone have enough tension left to engage the fighters that scrambled to meet them like they did. Unfortunately, that put the Baron's beyond the Misfits' reach; they were just too far away, unless, of course, the squadron moved north, which Whitehall considered ordering them to do until Abby pointed out to them that there was nothing stopping the Barons from just going back to their previous base of operations as soon as the Misfits showed up.

In the end, the Misfits were left where they were and quickly settled back into the rhythm they had established before the Barons had appeared, flying multiple sorties each day against large bombing formations, which was exhausting and dangerous, but not nearly as much as spending hours on end in the cockpit chasing after red ghosts.

With a return to more normal duties, the pilots were able to relax slightly and Abby thought it was high time that they threw a party for the entire squadron, both to celebrate Kitty and Gwen's promotion and as a christening for Devil. In order to accommodate everyone and have enough room left over for the new aircraft, she decided to hold it in the hangar and as soon as the pilots were released for the day, preparations began: the aircraft were pushed to the sides, all except for Dreadnought, which was just pushed back as far as it could go and Devil, which was put in pride of place right in front of the doors so that everybody had to walk past it when they entered and could get a good look at Gwen's design; bars were set up along both sides, both to have drinks within easy reach and to prevent drunken airmen from getting too close to the aircraft; tables were brought in from the messes to hold the food which would be served buffet-style; lastly, a small stage was built for musicians under Dreadnought's nose and the rest of the space was dedicated as a dance floor.

In less than two hours everything was ready and Abby sent messengers to each mess to say that the party would start at eight o'clock, just after sunset.

Despite one of the reasons for the party being the celebration of the recent promotions, the wing commander had announced that, in true Misfit fashion, rank was to be completely set aside for the night, which meant that no saluting was permitted and there were also to be no "sirs" or "madams" or deference of any kind allowed. She also said that, since nobody on the base really had any other clothing apart from their uniforms, any modifications that people wanted to make to them for the night were perfectly acceptable, which included makeup and non-regulation hairdos.

Scarlet had moved in with Kitty and Gwen as soon as they'd gotten back from London and the three of them had gotten dressed together. The Irishwoman had a few silk scarves that she used to protect her neck on missions (she had very delicate skin) and they had each taken one - red for her, pink for Gwen and white for Kitty - and tied them around their waists, disguising their uniforms somewhat and adding a welcome touch of colour that they hoped would make them stand out in a sea of plain blue. It didn't take them long to get ready and at eight o'clock they were in the hangar, along with everybody else in the base not on duty, standing in front of the small stage and looking up at Abby.

The wing commander had given a short speech, welcoming everybody and introducing the aircraft that they had all seen, as well as congratulated Kitty and Gwen on their promotion. She went on to remind everyone that anyone caught giving an order, saluting, or calling anybody sir or madam would be given kitchen duty the next day and have to wash up the plates while the cooks rested from the effort they had made. Owen had interrupted her, asking her whether that was an order and she had answered yes without thinking, then realised what she had done and sworn up a storm, which had everybody laughing. She was pardoned her mistake by a very democratic vote, but warned not to do it again and made to down a pint of beer in punishment.

It was an unusual and fun night and Gwen and Kitty were very much the centre of attention. They received request after request for dances, which they felt that they couldn't refuse, and didn't have any time to themselves, barely being able to snatch a drink in between sets. At one point, Jimmy surprised Gwen by dancing a very energetic jitterbug which had the two of them occupying the centre of the dance floor and being cheered on by everyone else. He tried to hold onto her for a second dance, which happened to be a slow number, but Mad Mac bodily picked him up and deposited the boy to one side saying it was his turn. Jimmy wasn't very disappointed though, because his antics had caught the eye of many of the younger airwomen and they were literally queueing up to dance with him for the rest of the night. The rest of the pilots were also popular targets for dances; the men and women of the base were seizing the opportunity to get to know their heroes with both hands and not letting it escape.

Bruce also received a lot of attention and he spent much of the night standing next to his new aircraft, either gazing at her in admiration or answering questions. The one question that he was asked over and over was about the machine's name and he gave the same answer every time. 'Devil? Nothing to do with the bible, cobber! No, we're talking *Tasmanian* Devil! One of the fiercest creatures you'll ever meet. The perfect name for her!'

Unfortunately, they had operations in the morning so Abby was forced to end the party early and at midnight she gave the band - a group of airmen and women who could play instruments and had volunteered to form a jazz band for the night - instructions for one last slow dance. A rendition of "We'll Meet Again" had the entire squadron singing along and almost in tears, but it was a perfect end to a perfect night and everybody went to bed feeling that they were part of something truly special.

CHAPTER 14

The days turned into weeks and the Misfits were again worked hard, flying at least three sorties a day and sometimes up to six or seven as summer reached its height and daylight lasted longer.

Every single one of the pilots of A and B flights added more kills to their personal tallies - Abby bagged another fourteen, but she wasn't the most successful; it was Bruce who put Devil's cannon to good use and took that honour, outshooting his commander for the first time ever and getting fifteen, both making Gwen's more than creditable six seem almost humble.

However, no matter how many Prussians the Misfits shot down, there were always more to take their place and it never seemed like they were making any headway against the horde that was coming from across the channel. That in itself was disheartening enough, but there was also news every day of mounting civilian casualties from the bombing raids on the cities. The two things combined to make some of the pilots think that perhaps they weren't doing all that they could and they began to take unnecessary risks in the hopes of making more kills. It worked quite spectacularly a few times, but it was bound to catch up with them sooner or later and there were a couple of very near misses - Lady Penelope came back from one mission with gaping holes in both her fuselage and canopy and glass in her cheek and Monty had half of his bottom wing blown off when he broke away from Bruce and dived into a group of eight MU9's who were fighting a single Spitsteam. They both made it back to base safely enough, but their machines were out of commission for days, which just made matters worse in the long run and had each pilot blaming themselves even more. In the end Abby was forced to threaten the next person who did anything stupid with being grounded to put an end to it.

The summer continued to be perfect, every day bright and clear and lovely, but that did absolutely nothing to lift their spirits, in fact it had the opposite effect because it meant that the Fleas had perfect visibility of their targets and the destruction was much higher than it might have been. However, September dawned misty and grey and flight operations were called off as the Prussians stayed at home, giving the beleaguered British forces a well-needed day of rest.

With no flying to be done, rather than feeling relaxed the pilots felt restless and they hung around the mess, drinking tea and talking in hushed tones. Every so often someone would stand up and go to the windows and look up at the clouds and a silence would fall as everybody watched them, waiting for the pronouncement on the weather. It was always the same, though - a brief shake of the head that brought a groan from the audience.

Finally, Abby had had enough. 'Right then you lot, I want everybody in flight gear, minus helmets. Parade in front of the main hangar in ten minutes.'

Owen frowned at her and opened his mouth to state the obvious, that they were grounded, but she cut him off before he could say anything. 'Come on, chop chop, no arguments! Go! Now! Last one on parade has to run a lap of the airfield in their flightsuit.'

The pilots were fairly sure that Abby would never carry out her threat, but there was a general rush for the door anyway; she had been in a particularly vindictive mood and not her usual laid-back self since Lady Penelope and Monty had put themselves out of action and had punished every infraction, no matter how slight and they didn't want to test her (she had made Bruce serve as a waiter during dinner one night for making too many sarcastic comments during a briefing and had banned Mac from drinking for a whole week when he overslept one morning after a particularly heavy night).

In less than ten minutes the pilots were lined up in front of the hangar in rank order at parade rest.

Abby had been watching from the windows of the mess and wandered over to them only after everybody else was there, deliberately making herself the last one so that she didn't have to carry out her threat if anybody had been late.

She came to a halt in front of them and scowled. 'Atten.... Shun!'

She barely managed to keep a straight face as eleven pilots, who hadn't been under proper discipline for months, came to attention in a manner that would have given a parade sergeant a fit.

She took a deep breath, then raised her voice to bellow at them. 'Right then, you sorry lot! It has come to my attention that certain basic training has been neglected recently and this just won't do in my Squadron!'

The volume she was using was completely unnecessarily at the distance she was from them, but she kept her voice raised nonetheless, maintaining her angry glare as she stared at them one by one. 'And I'm not talking about the decidedly shoddy way in which you just came to attention, you sorry excuse for a bunch of soldiers!'

There were titters from the audience which had slowly been gathering behind her as she began to walk back and forth in front of the pilots, imitating a drill sergeant's strut as best she could in her tight flightsuit as she inspected them, stopping every so often to bawl at them. 'Stand straight, Squadron Leader MacShane! You need a haircut, Aviator Lieutenant Fletcher! Get that stupid grin off your face, Aviator Lieutenant Walker! Try not to be so damn *Welsh*, Squadron Leader Llewellyn!' Many of the pilots, the ones who had known her for longest or that were more experienced (or more jaded), had realised what she was doing and were now desperately trying to stay serious as they played along with her, thrusting their chins high into the air and standing with their backs as rigid as possible, but some of the others, especially the younger pilots, looked genuinely surprised and nervous, not having cottoned on to the joke, which just made her own fight to keep a straight face that much more difficult.

Her pretend inspection done, she returned to her place in front of the pilots and deflated, shaking her head with a sigh. She tried hard to actually seem genuinely upset and reinforced that impression by lowering her voice so that the watching men and women couldn't hear her. 'I'm disappointed in you all, very disappointed. Discipline is far too lax and the way you've been acting recently is a complete disgrace. This squadron needs to buck its ideas up and start working together fast, so, as a team-building exercise you're all going to go for that little run around the airfield while I time you.'

Even the more experienced pilots gave her a look of genuine shock at that and it gratified her no end to see that she could still unsettle them, even after more than a year together.

She lifted her right arm and pointedly looked down at the chronograph on her sleeve. 'Go on, off you go!'

The pilots shifted uneasily and she watched as they reacted in various ways. Some were just staring at her, waiting for the rest to make a move. Others were dying to argue, but the fact that they were supposed to be at attention had invoked what little discipline they had and they were holding their tongues. She almost smiled when, predictably, as one of the youngest and the one who had most been under RAC discipline, Gwen was the first to cave in - she gave Kitty a look and a shrug of resignation and they both made to start running, but immediately stopped when they saw that none of the others were moving from their places.

Abby tried to hold on to her serious expression, but failed dismally and after only a few seconds a snigger escaped her, snot threatening to bubble out of her nose. 'You should see your faces!'

Her laughter only increased when the pilots scowled, but before any of them could recriminate with her for the dirty trick she raised her voice again and called out over their heads. 'Sergeant Potter! Bring that gear out here!'

Her chief fitter came out of the darkness of the hangar along with the chief fitters from every other crew, bringing with them the glidewings from the aircraft.

By now the pilots had completely broken discipline and turned to see what was happening behind them, but she didn't reprimand them or bring them back to attention; the charade had served its purpose, setting the mood for the morning and gathered the audience that she wanted.

She waved at the pilots to gather around and spoke to them in a more normal voice, although she made sure that it would carry to most of the watchers as well. 'Regulations state that glidewings should be tested on a monthly basis and to my knowledge we have not been doing that. We are going to rectify that situation this morning and have a bit of fun while we do it. I hope none of you are afraid of heights?'

There was laughter at that from both the pilots and the gathered men and women.

'So, ladies and gentlemen, what we are going to do is make sure they work by jumping off the top of the hangar.' Abby pointed to the building behind them, the roof of which was about a hundred feet off the ground.

She looked around the group, searching each of them for signs of fear or doubt, and smiled when she found nothing except excitement and anticipation - exactly what she had expected from her Misfits. 'To make things a bit more interesting we're going to have a little wager - whoever lands the closest to the mess wins the grand prize!'

The grins widened considerably at the thought of a competition; pilots were often the most egotistical of people and loved the chance to show their superiority over others in any way possible.

'And what, pray tell, is the grand prize?' It was Lady Penelope who asked the question that was on all of their minds and there was an eager, almost greedy look in her eyes that was completely at odds with her normal laid-back attitude.

'The winner of the First Misfit Squadron Glidewing Challenge will receive a trophy engraved with their name and a week's free drinks. So I really hope that Mac doesn't win, otherwise I might go bankrupt.'

When the laughter at that had died down, Abby continued. 'The rules are as follows. Each pilot will get only one attempt. He or she cannot use any means of propulsion other than their own legs.'

'Dammit.' Bruce swore, obviously having been planning some kind of cheat.

Abby thumbed her nose at him to more laughter. 'And the winner will be judged by popular consent. Which means that everybody here decides.' She jerked her thumb over her shoulder at the crowd, which now included nearly all of the base personnel. The ones that weren't on duty anyway. 'So I would recommend you be nice. But any attempts to buy votes will be frowned upon and bear in mind that the free drinks are individual and non-transferable, so you can't use them as bribes!'

'Dammit!' Bruce swore again, bringing even more laughter.

Abby grinned, loving the chance to keep morale as high as possible. 'Right! Well, we're going to do this in order of superiority, so I get to have first crack! It also means that it's my legs that'll get broken if this is as stupid an idea as it seems.'

Gwen watched the wing commander slip on her glidewing and strap it onto her back with help from her fitter before going to the side of the hangar, where there were handrails up to the roof of the building for maintenance purposes. She climbed rapidly, quickly reaching the roof, then disappeared.

Everybody craned their necks, trying to see what was happening, but for long seconds there was no sign of her.

There was a shout, a continuous "aaah" that rose steadily in volume, then suddenly the wing commander appeared on top of the hangar. Her glidewings were fully extended and as she reached the end of the roof she dived forwards as if into a swimming pool.

The entire crowd of watchers held their breath as she plummeted, dropping almost fifty feet before her wings caught enough air to lift her and she pulled up. A few people in the crowd gasped, thinking that she was still going to hit the ground, but she didn't, managing to level off with five feet to spare - a decent margin as far as a pilot, especially one of her calibre, was concerned. She skimmed across the ground, keeping the same height, and made it more than half way across the airstrip before she lost so much speed that she had to pull up and put her feet down.

Her effort was greeted with thunderous applause and Jimmy, who had been armed with a bucket of white paint, ran to mark where she had landed with her initials.

Abby tugged on the lever to retract the wings and they heard the whir of springs as the huge, bat-like wings were swiftly and powerfully folded back into the surprisingly small package on her back.

She turned and began to walk back, grinning widely. When she was within easy earshot she called out. 'Owen! Your turn, up you go!'

Owen made a show of reluctance. 'I'm not sure this is a good idea; I mean, you almost nosedived into the ground and, you must admit, you were rather undignified about the whole thing, all that "aarghing"... It might be bad for discipline.'

The wing commander came to a halt in front of him. 'What discipline?' She grinned, then reached out and grabbed his arms, spinning him in place and giving him a good kick in the arse to get him moving. 'Go on! Get up there!'

Owen continued to pretend not to want to do it, trudging to his fitter and accepting his glidewings, but then when it came time to climb the ladder he ran up it with enthusiasm and leapt onto the roof.

He disappeared out of sight, but not nearly as long as Abby had, appearing again after only a few seconds, his legs and arms pumping and his body tilted forward as he fought against the drag of his extended wings.

'Geronimoooo...oooh, fu....!' He leapt out, dropping like a stone, his greater weight counting against him and he struggled to pull up, only just managing in time and swearing profusely as his toes dragged in the grass. He had overcooked it, though, tilting himself too far up and rising a good twenty feet into the air. He fought desperately with the controls and was able to level himself out again, but it was too late; he had used up too much of his airspeed and all he could do was glide a short distance before landing well short of Abby's mark.

He retracted his wings and stomped back to them, angry with himself. He was still greeted with applause, though, and slapped on the shoulders by many of the men as he passed, which improved his mood quite a lot.

Abby gave him a smile and shook her head. 'Squadron Leader your Ladyship Penny Bagshot! You're up!'

One by one the pilots took their turns. There were no other near-mishaps like Owen's, but none of them could quite beat Abby's mark and it looked more and more likely that the squadron's best pilot was going to win. Nobody cared, though, and Bruce and Mad Mac even came up with their own "competition" instead, namely to see which of the two could give the most bloodcurdling yell as they leapt from the roof.

Abby's record stood, therefore, until it came to Scarlet's turn.

The tiny woman looked smaller yet when she appeared at the edge of the roof high above them and her dive was elegant, serenity itself. The crowed oohed almost as one as she pulled up easily and glided gracefully along the ground at more than twice head height. She easily surpassed Abby's mark and was three-quarters of the way across the runway before she dived, swooping down to gain speed, then pulled herself vertical to almost hover in the air, spinning to face them and retracting her wings even as she settled softly to the ground.

Everybody was so stunned by the beauty of what she had done that it was a good few seconds before the applause started and when it did it was far louder and more enthusiastic than it had been for anyone else. She gave them a small bow, then gestured to Jimmy, who had completely forgotten that he had to mark her landing place and had been staring at her in wonder with his mouth gaping.

It was the general consensus of the crowd that nobody would be able to beat Scarlet's mark, but Kitty's effort was very nearly as good and Gwen remembered that the American had spoken about the times that she and the younger members of the family had played with gliders while they had been growing up, flying similar things to the glidewings off specially constructed towers and into the lake on the Wright Estate. She wasn't quite as dignified about it as Scarlet had been, though, and she fought for every inch, skidding to a halt on her belly in an effort to gain just a little bit more distance, but even so she came up several yards short of the Irishwoman.

Somewhat disappointed, but still smiling, Kitty made her long walk back and all eyes turned to Gwen, who was the last to go.

Without a word, she walked over to Sergeant Jenkins, who helped her to put her glidewings to her back, then bent forward to whisper in her ear while he tightened the straps. 'You can do it, ma'am. Show them what the pilot of Wasp can do.'

She gave him a smile and a nod, then went to the ladder up to the top of the hangar.

Glidewings were surprisingly light and incredibly resilient, constructed with Duralumin, the same as the skin of the aircraft, but much thinner, over a frame composed of mildly flexible steel tubes that were only slightly larger than fishing rods. They were delicately balanced and all a pilot had to do to control his direction was tilt his upper body from the waist, the design so brilliant that it felt like they were part of the pilot. Their opening and closing was controlled by a lever on the left side of the thick strap that came around the waist and had four positions, which determined how many of the four panels on each side were opened by the internal springs - the first setting opened only one panel and its purpose was to provide control and allow a pilot to stop his tumbling, the second panel came out to slow him down by giving him enough lift to start to pull up before deploying a third panel to give better gliding distance, then finally opening the wings fully to settle to a gentle landing, as had been perfectly demonstrated by Scarlet (but not by most of the other pilots).

Gwen had been watching closely as the other pilots had taken their turns and had noted that every one of them had logically chosen to fully extend the wings before jumping, wanting the maximum lift possible, which allowed them to pull up before hitting the ground. However, the drag also stopped them from getting as much speed from their runs as they could and she wondered if that were the best tactic to employ under these highly unusual circumstances.

With nothing to lose she chuckled to herself and decided that she would try something different.

After all, what was the worst that could happen?

She walked towards the back of the hangar along the flat metal roof. It was painted green and lightly corrugated for strength, providing a good grip for her flight boots.

She wanted a good run up, but not so long as to be tired when she got to the edge and decided that ten yards was more than enough. Once in place she faced the airfield and pulled the lever, testing the mechanism. She opened the wings wide, then retracted them again, watching carefully to make sure that they moved at the same rate - if one opened quicker than the other then the lift they provided would be momentarily uneven and send her out of control.

Satisfied, she took a last deep breath, then burst into motion, sprinting as hard as she could, her eyes focussed firmly on the mess building across the airfield. It was slightly blurry through the mist and despite the fact that she knew it couldn't possibly have moved, it looked much further away than it should have.

The crowd below gasped when they saw her appear without wings, but she didn't hear them; she was too focussed on what she was doing.

She leapt out, head first and simultaneously pulled the lever to its second position.

Because she hadn't been fighting against wind resistance on her run up her speed was far higher than anything the other pilots had been able to manage and she had just enough lift already to prevent the same almost vertical plunge that every other pilot had taken. Also, opening only to the second position meant that she could control her direction without as much drag slowing her down so she built speed quickly, flying, rather than falling along a forty-five degree flight path. Once she judged she had enough speed she opened the wings to their third position and ever so slowly pulled up from the dive, then, when she was almost level she snapped the wings open fully.

Now that she was committed to the glide, she finally had time to take in her surroundings and with some shock she saw that she was already passing the first white marks on the airfield, but was still more than twenty feet in the air. She realised that she could afford to push her nose down, so to speak, and keep her airspeed up by slowly sacrificing height; it was far more efficient to glide that way.

She closed her eyes and focussed on the feeling of the air across the wings as she played with her pitch. It was a very delicate balance that she was looking for; she wanted to keep enough speed for the wings to act efficiently, but at the same time not dive so much that she was losing height unnecessarily. She found the place where the glidewings seemed happiest and smiled; they were so intuitive for anyone with even the slightest understanding of flight and such a pleasure to fly. Instinctively knowing that she still had plenty of height to spare, she enjoyed the sensation for a few moments more before reluctantly opened her eyes to check her surroundings.

The wall of the mess was only thirty feet away and approaching *very* rapidly.

She squealed in alarm and immediately dipped towards the ground, losing as much altitude as she could as quickly as possible, before gradually pulling up again, desperately trying to bleed away as much speed as she could while not regaining too much height, slowly tilting herself further and further backwards until finally she managed to reach a vertical position, completely arresting her forward motion. She hung in the air for a heartbeat, then dropped, falling rather heavily to the ground, her nose just inches away from the door to the officer's mess.

Not quite believing exactly how successful her flight had been, she stared at the door for long seconds, then grinned and started to turn, but cringed as her still-extended wings scraped green paint from the walls with a loud squeal. She hastily flicked the lever to retract them, but the damage was done - there was a six inch long white scar of exposed stone in the otherwise perfect green of the mess hall.

The door opened to reveal one of the waiters, come to investigate the noise. He looked at her, then at the crowd of people over her shoulder, then just tutted and rolled his eyes before closing the door again.

Gwen blushed and turned to make her way back to the other pilots, but found a wave of cheering people running towards her. She barely had time to shrug out of the glidewings before she was grabbed from all sides and lifted up into the air, borne aloft by twenty or more hands. They jumped up and down, chanting both her name and the name of her aircraft, as if they were one and the same, which she supposed they almost were in the eyes of people who didn't know her personally and she idly wondered how many of the men and women on the airbase actually believed the embellishments made by the British press of her, or rather of *Wasp's* exploits.

Eventually, she was deposited carefully to the ground in front of Abby and the other pilots.

The wing commander held her hands up for silence and an expectant hush fell over the airfield. 'I declare Aerial Officer Stone the winner of the First Misfit Squadron Glidewing Challenge!' There were cheers and Abby let them go on for a while before again holding up her hands. When silence had fallen she was handed something by an airwoman who Gwen didn't recognise, but who was liberally covered in fresh wood chips - she had evidently been working while the competition had been going on.

Abby held the object up over her head. 'The trophy for our glorious victor!'

The trophy turned out to be a replica of an early model propeller - a nose cone with two propeller blades. It was fully four feet long and the whole thing was lovingly carved from a single piece of dark wood.

'Step forwards, Aerial Officer Stone.'

Gwen went to stand in front of Abby and held out her hands to receive the trophy, but Abby shook her head with a grin before raising her voice once more. 'So that the glory of your victory will live on in the minds of all who witnessed it, you will spend the rest of the day crowned as the champion of the glidewing, while you enjoy your spoils!' She turned the trophy to reveal that the nosecone was hollow, lined with felt and had a chin strap.

Gwen stared at it in not a little horror. 'Now wait a minute!'

The hands that had only a short while ago borne her aloft in celebration now kept her in place as she tried to get away and she had no choice but to face Abby as the trophy was lifted up and placed firmly on her head.

Gwen reached up, intending to remove it, but was stopped when a full pint of Best Bitter was placed in her hand and chants of "drink!" began.

She looked around at the men and women surrounding her, seeing pilots, fitters, airmen and women. Seeing her friends and colleagues. Seeing the squadron that had made her one of their own so quickly. She realised that she could take a little light humiliation if it was the price to pay for the smiles that each and every one of them wore, the grim faces of before banished.

She raised the glass to them. 'The Misfits!'

CHAPTER 15

It had only been a single day's respite, but it had done wonders for the mood of the squadron.

The pilots had done the rounds of the entire base, carrying Gwen with them in her "throne", one of the armchairs from the officer's mess. They had made sure that everybody saw her, spreading smiles and laughter wherever they went and there was a much different feeling on the base the next morning when operations started just after dawn with a clear blue sky and the prospect of more than a dozen hours of flying ahead of them.

The squadron was ready for takeoff and were just waiting for Scarlet in Hummingbird to be pushed into the hangar before taxiing out. She had had another dangerous mission to take care of - she had been woken in the middle of the night by Abby and all but dragged out of bed when surprise orders had come through from Whitehall.

Gwen had been frightened for her - she had been woken as well when Abby had come in, then again when Scarlet had returned to get her flightsuit and the look on the Irishwoman's face when she had muttered something about "ports" before hurrying back out had had her concerned, prevented her from returning to sleep; anything that made the Irishwoman, who daily went across the channel on missions that even the bravest of pilots would shy at, look *that* scared would have to be dangerous indeed.

She was understandably glad to see her safely back, but as the aircraft got closer she was able to make out extensive damage to its tail unit and saw that part of the overhead rotor was missing. Scarlet herself was slumped in the cockpit, her eyes closed and looking paler than ever and Gwen frowned, worried, but realised that the woman couldn't have been injured, otherwise there would have been medical orderlies swarming all over her. She was extremely relieved when Scarlet's eyes opened to meet hers and the Irishwoman smiled faintly, but Gwen lost sight of her as Hummingbird was swung around into position for rewinding and couldn't assess her any better. She desperately wanted to find out what had happened and whether her friend was alright, but she had no choice except to forget her concerns as the order for the fitters to push out the aircraft came and she had to concentrate on the sortie.

The Misfits intercepted a small bomber group with its escort over Dover. There were maybe forty aircraft in total and both A and B flights dropped on them from above, taking down almost a dozen of them in the first pass. The enemy immediately dropped their bombs and dived, turning on their wings and heading back the way they had come in a panic. The Misfits harassed them for as long as they could, but the RAC in its entirety were under orders not to pursue too far out to sea, so they were forced to let the remainder of the bombers go, but they were satisfied with knowing that several tonnes of bombs wouldn't be falling on their targets that morning.

With no other raids within their range they were sent back home and immediately on landing Gwen went in search of Scarlet with Abby. They assumed that they would find her in the mess and were correct, but the door opened before they got even half-way across the airfield and the Irishwoman came out.

Gwen rushed to meet her. 'Scarlet! Are you alright?'

'I'm fine.' She nodded, but barely looked at Gwen, her dark blue eyes immediately going to Abby. 'We need to talk. Everybody needs to hear this.'

The wing commander nodded, then turned to look at the pilots who were coming out of the hangar in dribs and drabs behind them. 'Gwen, make sure everybody comes to the bar as quick as they can, please.'

The wing commander took Scarlet by the arm and disappeared into the mess, leaving Gwen frowning after them.

Gwen waited outside until the last of the pilots, Owen, had made his way across the runway, then accompanied him into the mess. She found the other members of the squadron already sitting in armchairs in a circle on the far side of the room, gathered around Scarlet, who was pacing up and down, clutching a mug of tea in one hand and chewing on the nails of the other, something which Gwen had never seen her do before. She wandered over to the group with Owen and both of them were handed mugs of tea before Abby waved at them to take a seat.

Gwen went to sit down in the armchair that Kitty had saved for her, but paused and looked around the room. Apart from the pilots there was nobody else there, no other officers, which wasn't unusual for that time of day, but also none of the staff that worked in the mess. It looked like whatever Scarlet was going to tell them was for their ears only.

Abby waited until the two latecomers sat down, then spoke quietly. 'What you're about to hear is not common knowledge and it is not likely to become so, at least not until it doesn't matter anymore. Do not speak about this outside of this room, not to your fitters, not to your friends and for god's sake Mac, keep a hold on yourself when you're drunk next.'

There weren't many laughs at her joke and those that came were very subdued as the pilots saw the serious expression on their commander's face.

'Scarlet?' Abby motioned for the restless Irishwoman to take the floor, then sat down.

Gwen had already been quite worried, but she went completely cold when she saw the expression on Abby's face and how white her friend still was.

The Irishwoman spoke quietly, not meeting their eyes. 'I was sent out this morning to recce occupied ports.'

There were gasps at this news because it spoke of a desperation that none of them knew Whitehall possessed; Scarlet was sent on dangerous missions to scout enemy territory all the time, but the places she tended to scout were things like isolated bases and factories in areas with plenty of trees and hills that she could hide among. A port was a whole different matter; not only would she be exposed with no cover, but they were heavily defended with anti-aircraft guns. It was a miracle she had gotten back at all, let alone with so little damage to her machine.

Chalky frowned. 'But we already have enough pictures of the French and Belgian ports from high-level reconnaissance aircraft, god knows I've taken enough of them myself! Why do they need more?'

Abby answered him. 'Whitehall have been interrogating the pilots that have been shot down. As you can imagine, they haven't been giving us much in the way of useful intelligence, but one thing that they all agree on is that they don't expect to be in captivity for long.'

This news was greeted with silence and the blood drained from the faces of not a few of the pilots as if they were under high G's.

Wendy put what they were all thinking into a single, dreadful word. 'Invasion.'

Abby nodded, but all eyes turned back to Scarlet when she resumed speaking. 'Whitehall have known that an invasion has been coming for a while, they just didn't know when, but the enemy pilots seemed fairly sure it was coming soon. They assumed that it was just Prussian propaganda to raise the morale of their own side, but then they spotted a few things on the photos that people like Chalky have been taking. They didn't tell me what they saw exactly, but you can imagine. Unfortunately, while those reconnaissance photos could tell them things like how much shipping is in the ports they couldn't tell them how close the Prussians were to actually mounting the invasion.'

She perched on the arm of Abby's armchair and took a deep breath. 'I only managed to recce Dunkirk and Calais before I sustained too much damage and had to head for home.' She turned to smile weakly at Abby. 'By the way, I was chased by a couple of MU10's and managed to shoot one of them down off Dover - I should have some good photos of that.'

Abby laughed. 'I'll get confirmation. Maybe someone spotted the wreckage.'

'Thanks. *Someone* in this squadron has to get a few kills...'

There were a few chuckles at that, but once again the pilots fell silent when the smile disappeared from the Irishwoman's face once more. 'What I saw...' She coughed and took a big gulp of her tea. 'Sorry. What I saw was...' Her voice failed her again and she closed her eyes and took a shuddering breath. 'I couldn't see how many men there were, but there were thousands upon thousands of tents and row upon row of tanks, guns and vehicles under camouflage netting, so many that it's easy to see why their pilots are so confident they're not going to be prisoners for long.' She opened her eyes and looked at them. 'They're not coming quite yet, but they're definitely ready and when they get here there'll be no stopping them.'

Over the next few days, the Misfits flew one interception mission after another and the story was always the same - they would surprise the bombers, shoot down the ones that they could in two or three passes, but then have to let them go as the enemy invariable jettisoned their bombloads and fled. They were fast approaching the level of frustration that they had been feeling before the glidewing competition, but on the 11th September, before anyone could do anything stupid, the pilots were pleasantly surprised when, instead of being sent up for their usual patrol at dawn, they were called into the briefing hall by Abby.

The pilots wandered into the hall at the appointed time, laughing and joking and bringing with them toast and tea left over from breakfast, as lapse in discipline as ever, but they quickly fell silent when they realised that Abby wasn't alone; she was accompanied by an officer who Gwen recognised as Group Captain Dorothy Campbell, the base commander from her old squadron, but she had obviously been promoted because there was a single thick line of gold braid denoting a sky commodore on her cuffs. The pilots made their way quickly to the front and formed something that approximated a straight line, standing at ease and awkwardly holding the remnants of their breakfasts, unsure of how to behave in the face of this invasion of their territory.

Abby grinned at them. 'While it's nice to see that you haven't completely forgotten about discipline and respect for your betters it would be nice if you showed *me* some every so often.'

Owen turned to frown at his wife. 'Did she say betters?'

Wendy shook her head as she took a loud bite out of her toast then spoke with her mouth full. 'I'm hoping it was something about butter; this toast is dry. But I don't know, I wasn't listening, I was mesmerised by all the gold on that woman's arm... it's so shiny!'

The squadron's lamentable show of discipline completely broke down as the pilots tried to keep straight faces and most failed dismally. Thankfully, the visiting officer had known what she was getting into when she had journeyed to the base that morning (most visitors did and if they didn't, they soon found out) and she just grinned at them and looked sideways at Abby.

The wing commander shook her head in exasperation. 'Sit down and shut up, Misfits. Behave nicely or the nice little officer won't let you go on the lovely mission she's brought for you.'

There was scattered laughter but the pilots did what they were told and sat down, looking at the commodore expectantly, eager to hear anything that would break the monotony of the sorties that they had been flying recently.

'Good morning, my name is Dorothy Campbell and I was appointed to twelve group two weeks ago. As you probably know, we've been taking a bit of a beating from bombers escorted by the Crimson Barons and frankly we're miffed with the situation and would like to put a stop to it, but to do that we need your help.'

'About bloody time!' Mac called out, drawing vigorous nods of agreement from the rest of the Misfits, including Abby and the commodore herself.

'It is, and that's what I've been telling them since the day I was promoted, but they were reluctant to do anything until Abby and I presented them with a plan which they liked.'

'Hang on a second...' Owen interrupted. 'You have a plan and it's already been approved?' He raised an eyebrow at Abby. 'Just how long have you been working on this and why didn't you tell us about it?'

'For about a week and because it's classified. If I'd told you I would have had to kill you.'

Owen crossed his eyes and poked his tongue out at her in reply, drawing more laughs. The Misfits had very quickly returned to their usual high spirits with the prospect of going up against their most dangerous opponents.

Campbell took over, putting the briefing more or less back on track. 'The Barons have become rather comfortable of late and have been flying two missions per day, one in the morning at ten and one in the afternoon at four. Regular as clockwork.'

'Oh, how lovely!' called out Lady Penelope. 'Bomb a few cities after breakfast, be back in time for elevenses, then do it again after lunch and home for afternoon tea and a nap!'

'Indeed.' Campbell nodded. 'They've become rather complacent and you are going to use that against them this very afternoon.'

At precisely four o'clock that afternoon the eight Misfits of A and B flights arrived on their assigned station at thirty five thousand feet over the Lincolnshire countryside. They were all equipped with dual springs, but it had been a long flight, climbing to their maximum ceiling before throttling back to save tension, and they had almost expended the entirety of the first one. The only reason this plan was going to work was because the Barons had gotten into a routine; if they'd had to wait around for them to turn up for more than an hour or so they wouldn't have enough time left in their springs to engage.

At that height it was cold and the air was thin, but the Misfits were well-prepared. Every aircraft in the RAC was fitted with a compartment underneath the seat which could hold a combination heater-breathing apparatus with hoses that attached to flightsuits and masks. Most flights didn't require the apparatus to be carried, instead it was replaced with a simple oxygen supply device, but today's flight up into the rarefied air at high altitude had necessitated its installation. The Misfits had custom-built ones and were consequently all snug and warm with the fluid in their G suits being gently heated, making them feel as if they were surrounded by hot water bottles.

Bloodhound was the only aircraft from C flight that had been called upon to join them and Owen was above them at almost forty-five thousand feet, keeping an eye on the enemy bombers that were about to cross the coast below them. He was accompanied by Wendy, who had threatened to stop servicing the guns of the squadron if Abby didn't let her go along. The wing commander had compromised, not allowing her to bring Dreadnought, but giving her permission to accompany the engineers working the radar in the back of her husband's aircraft. Neither Scarlet nor Chalky Isaacs had accompanied them, though; Vulture had been called upon to do another flyover of the French ports to make sure that the invasion fleet weren't going anyway and Hummingbird was still out of commission. Scarlet's request to accompany Wendy in Bloodhound had been denied; there just wasn't room even for her diminutive form.

The plan that the commodore had outlined was eminently simple - the Misfits would loiter as high up as they could, out of sight of the usual afternoon raid, which would be met by the usual RAC forces. Once the presence of the Barons had been confirmed and they had made their way sufficiently inland, committing to their escort duties, then the Misfits would swoop, ignoring the bombers and engaging the red-painted enemy. If something happened, if for example the target for the day's bombing was not far enough inland for the Barons to not be able to just turn and run, then the Misfits were ordered to remain out of sight and would try again the next day, repeating as many times as they needed in order to get a clear shot at the enemy aces. Every single one of the Misfits was of course hoping that conditions would conspire to allow them to attack that day, though; they were impatient to get another crack at their arch-rivals.

Luck or the fates were with them that day, though, and the raid headed inland towards Sheffield.

The Misfits shadowed them, keeping between them and the sun to minimise the possibility of being seen.

Even with their lenses at maximum magnification the pilots couldn't make out whether any of the enemy aircraft were red or not, so there were some tense moments as they waited for confirmation that their targets were there and every radio was tuned in to the local control frequency, waiting for the intercepting squadrons to give the code and for the commodore in the control room to signal the attack.

The neatly organised black dots far below were met by a lesser amount of smaller ones and a few of them broke formation, spoiling the neatness of the tableau.

The hoped-for report that there were sixteen "Robins" escorting the bombers immediately came from the leader of the RAC squadron.

Eight thick thermal gloves tightened around eight control sticks in eight aircraft as the Misfits tensed, waiting for the command to dive.

A minute passed, then two, until finally Mac's familiar growl came over the squadron frequency. 'What the hell is she waiting for? They're almost over the factories...'

'Be patient Mac, we discussed this - today isn't about a fair fight, we want the Barons committed, tired and low on ammo and we want them as far inland as possible, which means giving the boys and girls down below their crack at them first. If that means a few more bombs are dropped on our factories than is strictly necessary, then so be it; that is a sacrifice that Whitehall are willing to make in the short-term for long-term gains.'

Mac grumbled; like all of them he didn't like it one bit, but he was smart enough to see the twisted logic behind it.

Thankfully, the familiar voice of the commodore came over the radio shortly after, calling the RAC squadrons and identifying herself as "Nest", a code name that was never used, giving the Misfits their go signal.

'Badger leader to all Badgers. Jettison springs and let's go. Happy hunting.'

A sharp pull of a lever was all it took to send eight flat cylinders tumbling away, then the eight aircraft dived together, keeping the sun behind them, aiming well short of the enemy formation so as to be able to pull up and be level when they did their first pass, not wanting to dive below them and have to claw their way back up, making themselves vulnerable.

The enemy formation were at fifteen thousand feet, twenty thousand feet below them. It was a long way down, more than enough distance for the aircraft to reach the maximum speed that their airframes would tolerate. Air brakes deployed from the wings of the faster aircraft as the pilots fought to keep their machines down to the speed of the slowest of them, the two biplanes of Bruce and Monty, wanting to arrive together for the largest punch. Even so they were dropping out of the sky at almost five hundred miles an hour, which was nothing for B flight, whose machines were capable of far more, but disconcerting for the members of A flight, whose machines were not built for such speeds and complained vocally with creaks and whines that their pilots had never heard come from them before.

Such haste was necessary, though, because the Barons would undoubtedly flee as soon as the Misfits were spotted.

They were within a mile or so before they were seen and the bombers started to open fire with their waist and tail guns even as they scattered in panic, but they weren't the targets and the Misfits just ignored them, passing them by.

The enemy fighters had been drawn away by the RAC and taken low. They were going slowly as they gained altitude, clawing their way back up to the bombers that they were supposed to be protecting.

Fifteen red *Blutsauger* fighters, led by a single red triplane, in three finger-four formations.

They were late seeing the Misfits; the sun at the British pilot's backs, usually the friend of the Fleas, worked against them that day, hiding the death that was screaming down on them and by the time they reacted, turning and dipping their wings, pushing their noses down as hard as they could to gain speed, it was already too late.

Eight Misfit fighters, arranged in a neat line and arriving at exactly the same time, opened fire simultaneously with more than fifty guns.

Four of the red monoplanes disintegrated, the Barons losing in an instant as many aircraft as they had during the entirety of the war up to that point.

The Misfits pulled up, streaking back into the sky, G forces, pushing them down into their seats, their shouts and screams not only expressing their triumph, but helping to keep them conscious as not even their suits could keep the blood from draining from their heads.

The speed bled from them as they headed almost directly upwards, but before they could slow too much, Abby took them round, describing a U shape in the air that brought them back to face the enemy squadron.

However, rather than turn to face the British as the Misfits had expected, the Prussians had seized the opportunity given them by the Misfits having to decelerate enough to turn and had beaten a hasty retreat. Even now they were several miles from them and streaking in a shallow dive towards the coast.

Abby swore; there was no way that they would be able to catch them, even with their height advantage.

But there was something else they could do.

'All Badgers, this is Badger leader. Targets at twelve o'clock. Engage in pairs.'

With the Barons gone, the forty enemy bombers which had survived the initial RAC attack were alone, a long way from the sea and the Misfits had a field day.

The bombers dived, frantically trying to copy the Barons' escape, but they were far too slow and the Misfits caught up to them in less than a minute.

With almost a hundred mile per hour advantage in speed over the heavy steam-powered aircraft, the Misfits weaved and turned, swarming around them like mosquitoes around cattle, the return fire from the enemy gunners as effective as the swishes of a cow's tail.

Abby ordered them to break off the pursuit after ten minutes when the bombers reached the coastline, something that the pilots were happy to do, seeing as the only thing they would have been able to throw at them were insults; despite carrying far more ammunition than Harridans and Spitsteams, every single one of them had managed to expend all of their ammunition, the last aircraft to do so, Wasp and Hawk, having run out only moments before.

The Misfits turned for home, leaving the wreckage of twenty-three bombers and four red fighters strewn across the countryside. Fully half of the aircraft that had invaded British soil that afternoon would not be leaving it.

CHAPTER 16

As soon as they landed, Abby got the pilots together and told them that, instead of drinking themselves insensate that night, they would throw another huge party the next day after operations were finished, so that the entire squadron could share in their success. The Misfits never needed much of an excuse to have a party, but this time they had several; not only did they have their victory over the Barons to celebrate, but two birthdays as well - the 12th was Kitty's birthday and the 15th was Gwen's. The pilots readily agreed, but still trooped off to the mess; just because they were saving themselves for the party didn't mean that they had to have a dry night.

The next day there were no raids reported over the Midlands, perhaps because the Fleas were afraid that the Misfits would be waiting for them again, but there were also fewer raids in the South as well and there was some hope that the Prussians were so shocked at their loss and the demonstration that the Barons weren't invincible that they were reluctant to continue their attacks. Some pilots even wondered if the defeat would be enough to dissuade them from invading altogether, but those people were either told by the more logical pilots (Abby and Owen) that it undoubtedly wouldn't, or to shut up and not jinx it by the more superstitious ones (Mac and Chalky). Whatever was going on with the Prussians, the Misfits and the RAC in general were extremely grateful for the respite and prayed that it would continue.

As soon as the decision to have a party had been made, Abby had gone to the radio room to invite Sky Commodore Campbell, as well as Gwen's parents and a couple of the local squadrons who had been flying with them over the summer. In spite of the short notice they all accepted eagerly (a Misfit party was not to be missed) and started turning up just before dark the day of the party, the Hawkings arriving in their dual Harridan, the commodore in her personal Spitsteam and the RAC pilots ferried in by a couple of troop carriers.

Instead of using the hangar again, the briefing hall was restored to its original purpose as a ballroom for the night. It was bedecked with streamers and balloons and Kitty, who had been working in one of the empty workshop on a few pet projects whenever she had time off, wheeled out an device that continuously threw harmless multicoloured arcs of electricity into the air to spark and weave through the web-like structure overhead, giving the room a shimmering glow that was magical and otherworldly. The same men and women that had played the night that they had christened Devil and celebrated Kitty and Gwen's promotion insisted on setting up on the stage and repeating their performance. They had so enjoyed themselves that they had formed a proper band and had been practising, naming themselves the "Individualists". On prominent display in each of the four corner of the room were parts of the four Baron aircraft that had been shot down. They had arrived that morning in a wagon, accompanied by the remains of the four pilots and whatever serial numbers or inscriptions could be salvaged to identify the aircraft that they had flown. Abby had already sent a message to the Barons through official channels and those items would be sent to them at the earliest opportunity, as per their agreement. Unsurprisingly, the red trophies attracted a lot of attention, especially at the start of the evening before the drink started to flow, but as the night went on the people drifted away from them, gravitating towards the dance floor, wanting to forget the war for however long they could.

As before, the Misfits were popular dance partners, especially with the pilots from the other squadrons, who didn't want to let the opportunity to get close to these "mythical creatures" as one inebriated Aviator Lieutenant put it and Gwen found herself with a full dance card in no time at all.

The band took a break at around ten and everybody flocked to the long bars that lined both sides of the room and set about emptying the Misfits' alcohol reserves, only just replenished after the previous big party, as much as possible before they went back to dancing.

Gwen asked one of the waiters to pour her a pint of Best and while she was waiting she turned to look around and found herself face to face with a very drunk Jimmy.

'Gwen!'

She smiled at him. 'Jimmy. Are you having fun?'

'Boy, am I!' He nodded, swaying gently, a big grin plastered over his sweaty face. Gwen had seen him on the dance floor - he had been dancing up a storm, proving more and more dangerous to the people round him as the night went on and he consumed more beer. 'I wanted to apologise.'

Gwen frowned at him. 'For what?'

He reached out to pat her on the arm in what was probably meant to be a consoling manner, but which would most likely leave a bruise. 'It's not going to happen between us, I'm afraid. Sorry. You see, I'm with Julianne...' He turned and pointed to a young woman in a corporal's uniform. He hesitated, squinting, then pointed at a different woman. 'Julianne.'

This one was slightly older, about Gwen's age and height with Aviator Sergeant's stripes on her uniform along with the twin helix of the medical corps.

Jimmy smiled at her and waved. She noticed him waving and waved back, a big smile on her flushed face.

Jimmy turned back to Gwen. 'Anyway, I'm sorry. I know we would have been good together, but... but...' He blinked as he lost track of what he was saying. 'I hope we can still be friends.'

Gwen reached out to put her hand on his shoulder, as much to keep him from falling over, as he tottered unsteadily, as to comfort him. 'I understand, Jimmy, and of course we can be friends.' She sighed dramatically. 'I guess it just wasn't meant to be.'

Jimmy gave her an exaggerated shrug, then leaned in to peck her on the cheek. 'Thank you.'

He turned and staggered away, heading to the wrong woman, hesitated, wobbled, looked around, spotted Julianne, adjusted course, then stumbled the last few steps to land in her arms.

Gwen winced as the pair nearly fell over, then grinned and shook her head. She turned back to the bar to pick up her drink and immediately swallowed half of it; she was very thirsty after having danced so much and was not nearly drunk enough to fully appreciate the absurdity of Jimmy's apology.

'Happy birthday, Gwenevere.'

She almost choked on the drink as her father's voice sounded right in her ear.

'Dad! You startled me!' Gwen put her drink back on the bar before reaching out to fold her mother and father into a hug. 'I'm glad you could come.'

'We wouldn't have missed it for the world, darling.' Her mother beamed at her.

'Why didn't you come and say hello before?'

'You were having too much fun, we didn't want to interrupt.'

They smiled at her and Gwen pulled back, frowning, looking from one to the other; there was something wrong with their smiles, something preventing them from being entirely genuine. 'What's wrong?'

Her father quickly shook his head, waving away her concerns. 'It's nothing. Just war stuff.'

'Yes, and not to be discussed tonight; tonight is about you and your friends and the marvellous things you're doing.'

Sheridan nodded enthusiastically. 'The whole country is talking about what you did yesterday. It's in all of the newspapers and the KBC Global Service is busy shouting to the whole world that Britain is fighting back.'

'Really? That was quick.'

'Whitehall had journalists in vans ready to be taken to crash sights so that they could write their stories and take photos; they weren't going to let an opportunity like this pass them by!'

'And what if it hadn't gone so well?'

Sheridan shrugged. 'Then there would have been no story and it would have been just another day at war.'

Gwen looked at him. She had known that a victory like this would be used to bolster the morale of the British, especially with how Misfit Squadron had been built up in the eyes of the public over the past few weeks, but she hadn't expected Whitehall's propaganda machine to swing into action so efficiently; the way they had treated the day's events really wasn't "British" - it was more Prussian-like in its efficiency and callousness. The more she thought about it, the better she felt, though; it wasn't as if Whitehall were making things up and the public had a right to know what the Misfits had done. And besides, if it gave the Prussians pause then so much the better.

She shrugged. 'It's just as well we got a few of them, then.'

'Anyway, enough about that, we're here to celebrate more important things,' her mother said, reaching not very delicately under her skirts and pulling a small brown paper package out of one of the many pockets on her thigh - she was wearing one of her own creations, a flightsuit in white leather with built-in corset that had skirts which detached for flying. 'Happy birthday, darling.'

Gwen took the gift with a smile and untied the string holding the package together to reveal a highly-polished dark brown wooden box just over four inches square and two inches deep. Embedded behind a glass pane on the lid was a top view blueprint of an aircraft that she knew only too well - Bumblebee, the first aircraft she'd designed and built herself - picked out with incredibly thin gold wire.

'No... It can't be...'

The box was a one-off, a personalised presentation piece made to order for just one thing and Gwen opened the lid, knowing exactly what she was going to find, but not quite able to believe it.

Inside, nestled on a cushion of purple velvet was a brass aviation chronograph, designed to attach to the sleeve of her flightsuit. It was the most sophisticated one that Gwen had ever seen, with not only a timepiece, but also an altimeter and a barometer, as well as a couple of other indicators that she didn't recognise at first glance and would have to read the accompanying instructions to find out exactly what they measured. It looked remarkably delicate, but she knew that it was one of the most robust chronographs that had ever been made, designed specifically for use by pilots.

Normal chronographs, like the one she already had, were readily available to all and were manufactured in varying qualities to suit the depth of one's pocket, but ones such as these were special. Hand-crafted, incredibly rare and unbelievably accurate, only a few people in the world had the skill and the patience to make such items and only one of them lived in the Kingdom of Britain.

'Bloody hell...' Gwen cursed under her breath. 'It's a Frobisher! How on Earth did you get a hold of this? And how the hell did you *afford* it?'

Wilfred Frobisher only made one such chronograph each year and understandably his work was incredibly expensive and sought-after.

Her father shrugged. 'We've been on the waiting list for one of his chronographs since you started building your first aircraft. Even so, we thought we'd have to wait a good many years before we finally got one for you, but apparently Frobisher is a friend of John Dunne and when he heard what you'd been doing recently he got in touch and told us that he wanted us to have the next one, as long as it was intended for you. He even gave us a discount!'

She pulled the chronograph out of the box. It was light, so much lighter than her old one, and the back was engraved. She turned it back and forth, trying to read it in the dim light and felt tears prickling in the corners of her eyes when she finally managed.

For Gwen.
Pilot, mechanic, daughter.
With our love and immense pride.

'Thank you so much! It's magnificent! I... I don't know what to say!' Gwen hugged her parents again, this time one by one, but then the three of them looked up as there was frantic movement in the room behind them - the band, who had been drinking like there was no tomorrow, desperately trying to catch up with their colleagues, were hurrying back onto the stage.

To Gwen it looked like they were just keen to start playing again and most of the rest of the people seemed to think the same, because they streamed on to dance floor eager to continue having fun, but her mother knew better and she grinned gleefully up at her husband. 'Here we go. Pay up, Sherry; you lose!'

'Not yet you haven't, Harry. Not until we actually see...'

He was interrupted by the band, who started to play the national anthem as soon as they were settled.

As Elgar's stirring march filled the room, her father grumbled and handed her mother a golden sovereign, while every airman and woman in the room immediately came to attention. Most of them were frowning in puzzlement, looking at the band, wondering what they were doing, but understanding quickly spread when the doors swung open to admit King George VI, dressed in his RAC uniform, accompanied by Princess Elizabeth as well as a few other dignitaries and a contingent of Royal Guards.

The King made his way through the crowd as they opened up before him, nodding at the men and women, giving each of them a smile and pausing to shake hands with a few. When he reached the centre of the dance floor he stopped and turned in a slow circle to gaze around the room, his busy eyes taking in the red trophies spotlighted in each corner and his smile widening as he watched some of Kitty's electrical arcs fizzling overhead.

As the last triumphal note of the national anthem faded, his eyes came down and absolute silence fell.

'Fine work yesterday. Fine work indeed! Frankly I'd give the whole darned lot of you medals and promotions if I could, but Sir Douglas already told me that I can't, so unfortunately I'm going to have to make do with this.' He raised his voice. 'Wing Commander Lennox! Front and centre, if you please!'

Abby made her way through the crowd to stand at attention in front of him. The Marshal that the Misfits had seen at the palace stepped forward and handed the King a sword before bending to place a red velvet cushion at Abby's feet.

'Kneel, Wing Commander.'

A gasp echoed through the room at the King's words, but it quickly faded once more as everybody present all but held their breath, not wanting to make a sound, not wanting to miss or do anything to spoil such a momentous occasion, one that usually took place with the palace walls and that the vast majority of them were not likely to witness ever again.

As Abby settled on the cushion, the King lifted the sword to his side, describing an elegant circle. The blade flashed as it reached its height, bisecting one of the electrical arcs and sending rainbows flaring briefly around the room, before settling gently onto the woman's shoulder.

'For services rendered in the defence of the Kingdom of Britain, for continued gallantry and bravery in the face of overwhelming odds and for making this squadron into something that has *far* exceeded any hopes or expectations that I or my ministers had of it, I confer upon you the rank of Knight of the Order of Darwin.'

The King lifted the sword over Abby's head, lowered it to briefly touch her other shoulder then turned it with a flourish to hand it back to the Marshal, who gave him what looked like a folded cloth.

'Stand.' The Marshal leaned in to whisper to Abby and while she struggled to her feet, slightly awestruck, he whipped the cushion away.

Abby watched as the King carefully unfolded the cloth, revealing it to be a brown silk sash, attached to which was a large gold oval-shaped medallion with the tree of life engraved on it, picked out in bright silver iron. He stepped forward and Abby bowed her head as he looped it over her and settled it in place with the medallion on her chest.

'Congratulations, Dame Lennox.'

The King held out his hand and Abby grinned and shook it as deafening applause filled the hall.

The Order of Darwin was the lowest of the chivalric orders of the Kingdom of Britain, but nobody cared; it was enough for them that one of their own was receiving recognition for what the squadron had been doing.

The King stepped back and gave Abby a small bow, which she returned before retreating at the Marshal's order to rejoin the crowd, where her fellow pilots were gathered, waiting to inspect the sash and thump her on the back.

However, the King hadn't finished and he held his hands up for silence. 'Where's my favourite Aviation Lieutenant? Scarlet! Step forward!'

Scarlet pushed her way through the pilots and strutted over to the King, who stood grinning, waiting for her.

She came to a halt in front of him and jerked her thumb over her shoulder at Abby. 'If you're going to give me one of those things can you at least make it a decent colour? I suggest red.'

The King laughed; as everybody knew, red was the colour of the highest order that could be bestowed - the Imperial Order of Victoria.

'While I'm certain that one day you will earn "one of those things" and who knows, it might indeed be red, especially if you continue carrying out missions like your latest one, that's not why I've called for you.'

He glanced sideways at where the dignitaries that had accompanied him were standing, among them Commander of the Royal Aviator Corps Sir Douglas Pewtall, who apparently knew what was coming and turned as red as the sash that Scarlet had requested.

'Sir Douglas can't stop speaking about you and I don't want him moping all the way home because I might have to order my guards to throw him out of the aircraft. Will you put him out of his misery and grant him a dance? Please?

Scarlet looked at the poor man out of the corner of her eye before smiling at the King. 'It would be my pleasure, sir.'

She gave him a bow then flounced over to Sir Douglas and grabbed his arm.

The King gave a laugh. 'One last thing before we get back to the festivities. Dame Lennox, my daughter has requested a tour of your hangar, may I suggest Aerial Officers Stone and Wright accompany her? If, that is, they can be persuaded to leave their own birthday party for a short time?'

Abby nodded. 'I'm sure my officers would be delighted, sir.'

'Excellent!' The King turned to the band. 'Music, please! And make it something slow so that Sir Douglas can feel that it's been worth his embarrassment!'

Laughter greeted the King's pronouncement and as he made his way off the floor the music began, the space that he had occupied almost instantly filled with dancers.

Abby motioned to Kitty and Gwen. 'Do you two mind missing some of the party and showing Princess Elizabeth around?'

Kitty shook her head and gave her a wry smile. 'Actually, I'd quite enjoy a breath of fresh air and a rest; my feet hurt.'

Gwen also shook her head. 'And I'd quite enjoy the chance to speak to her; she might have some fresh ideas that we can use.'

Abby nodded. 'That's what I was thinking and it's just as well the King requested that our best aircraft designer show her around. Why don't you go see whether she wants a drink and a dance first?'

The Princess didn't want to dance, but she did want a drink and five minutes later the three women made their way across the airstrip towards the hangar, escorted by a pair of Royal Guards and carrying pint glasses in their hands, although the Princess' drink was not nearly as alcoholic as theirs was.

Gwen opened the small door in the side of the building and Kitty went through the blackout curtains first so that she could turn on the lights.

At her request, the two pilots gave the Princess, who insisted on them calling her Liz, a quick tour and rundown of all the aircraft first, explaining to her the difference in function between A and B flight and the purpose of each of C flight's machines. Kitty then took her for a closer look at Hawk and the Princess listened carefully as Kitty explained how her twin-tailed design gave her a large area of control surfaces meaning that Hawk could turn almost as quickly as anything that the Prussians could put in the air, but that the aircraft's true advantage was in her acceleration and sheer speed which allowed her to gain distance and height from any danger so that she could turn safely before going back into the fight. The aircraft's unique twin-boomed design also allowed for the installation of guns in its nose, directly underneath the cockpit in order to very accurately concentrate firepower in a small area. Until recently Kitty had had four of her eight 0.5 inch machine guns there, but Wendy had found the time to swap two of them for 0.79 inch cannon, which meant that she could now rip through even the thickest armour, something she'd demonstrated just the day before by taking down five enemy bombers.

The Princess exclaimed at the amount of firepower available to Kitty, sparking, quite literally, a conversation about the weapon that Kitty was trying to develop, similar to the arc thrower that was providing so much entertainment at the party and that she hoped would one day replace conventional machine guns.

As the discussion progressed, Gwen was quickly completely lost; her mind was much more mechanically orientated; her realm was the application of physics as it applied to flight, not something so ethereal as electricity.

Despite her young age, the Princess was a good diplomat, highly trained in the social graces and she very quickly noticed that Gwen was being left out. She brought the conversation to a close as soon as she could, promising to send Kitty her notes on similar lines of research that she was pursuing, then turned her attention to Gwen and her aircraft.

Wasp was a very conventionally-designed machine, not much different to a Spitsteam or a Harridan or any other single-spring monoplane aircraft, so the tour didn't take very long, but then Gwen asked the Princess if she would like to sit in the cockpit and her eyes lit up at the suggestion. After handing her empty glass to one of her guards she clambered over the wing and climbed agilely into the cockpit, quickly taking in the layout and commenting on how it differed from the aircraft that she had designed. She ran her finger over the frame that Gwen had attached to hold her husband's photo and was obviously going to ask about it, but saw Gwen's look and decided against it, instead she asked about the modifications that had made to Wasp's original design, which started a discussion between the three of them of the merits of varying thicknesses of wings and the trade that had to be made between lift and drag, especially in multiple-winged aircraft like the A flight biplanes or Gruber's triplane, Flamme, the model of which had caused a sensation in Hamleys when it had been unveiled and which the Princess had gone to see.

The conversation could have gone on all night, and indeed the three of them would have been more than happy for it to have done so, but again the Princess showed diplomacy and suggested that they went back to the party, not wanting to keep them from the fun for too long. However, as they walked her back to the briefing room she invited the two of them to join her at the Palace whenever they had a chance, saying that she would love to continue their conversations as well as return the favour and show them her own workshops in the Brunel Tower. The two aviators readily accepted and bade her farewell at the doors, shaking her hand and receiving her thanks, both for the tour and for doing so much for the war effort. They stammered, not knowing how to answer, but she saved them the embarrassment of trying by nodding and disappearing into the briefing hall with her guards, leaving them alone in the night.

The two aviators looked at each other, speechless for long moments before Kitty squealed and grabbed Gwen by the shoulders. 'We just spent an hour talking about aircraft with a real live princess!'

She started jumping up and down and Gwen laughed and joined her, then when the American finally got tired, she folded her into a hug. 'Happy birthday, Kitty. Thank you for making me feel so welcome when I got here - I wasn't in a very good place and you really helped me.'

'You're more than welcome.'

They fell silent and just stood there in the darkness, listening to the music coming from the hall and the laughter of the people.

Gwen found that she was very comfortable in the woman's arms. She hadn't been held by anybody, been hardly touched by anybody, except for dance partners, since Richard had died and she hadn't realised how much she'd missed simple physical contact with another human being until that moment.

She pulled back, suddenly feeling quite confused for some reason. 'I... I think I need a drink.'

Kitty didn't seem to have noticed Gwen's discomfort and her smile widened. 'And a dance! Let's dance!' Without waiting for an answer, the American grabbed Gwen by the hand and pulled her through the doors and into the noise within.

Kitty and Gwen stumbled down the forest path to the barracks a couple of hours later, just after midnight. Despite the briefing hall being right next to their destination it took them an inordinately long time, both because neither of them seemed capable of walking in a straight line and also because at one point they had started humming one of the tunes the band had been playing and had begun dancing, only stopping when their laughter made them so out of breath that they couldn't continue.

They eventually made it to the right building and tiptoed along the corridor, trying not to disturb the older more boring pilots, most of whom had retired much earlier to rest before the next day's flying. They didn't do a very good job of staying quiet, though and bounced off the walls at regular intervals, drawing a few muttered comments and swearwords from the people they disturbed.

Their room, when they finally reached it, was dark and quiet, empty; Scarlet had hit it off like a house on fire with the commander and they had spent the entire evening together to the annoyance of the many men and some women who had requested dances with her. They were still in the briefing hall, still drinking and laughing together.

Most of the other guests had gone long ago.

The King had left shortly after the Princess had gone back to the party. His incredibly fast two-seater aircraft, piloted by the Princess herself, had been waved off by almost all of the men and women on the base; King George was well loved by all of his people and especially the military, who saw how much he did for them and how much he appreciated them.

Gwen's parents had taken off at the same time in order for the airfield lights to be on as little as possible. They had made their farewells to Gwen and the pilots, most of whom were still rather awestruck of them in spite of their insisting on just being considered as the parents of one of their number, and promised to come back to visit, bringing the prototype of the next model of Harridan with them for their inspection.

The pilots from the other squadrons had left soon after; they, like the Misfits, were flying the next day and had to make their way by road back to their airfields - a long and torturous journey, especially in the dark.

Despite so many people leaving, the party had continued just as enthusiastically and had still been in full swing when Gwen and Kitty had left.

Kitty put the light on and staggered backwards as she threw her arm up to protect her eyes, bumping into Gwen, who grabbed her and only just managed to stop them both from falling over.

Once they were on balance again, the American twisted around in Gwen's arms to face her then bent forwards to kiss her full on the mouth, holding it for long seconds, before finally pulling back. She reached up to caress Gwen's cheek with a smile before stumbling away to fall face first onto her bed and immediately starting to snore.

Gwen stared at her in shock, suddenly feeling quite sober. When she finally managed to pull herself together she removed the American's shoes and covered her with a blanket, then stood for some time, gazing down at her, trying to work out exactly what was going through a head that was already spinning with drink.

CHAPTER 17

The next morning, nobody came to wake the Misfits at dawn. In fact it was past nine o'clock before the first of them wandered out of their rooms in search of answers and when they found Abby gone, the word spread and everyone got dressed to go to the mess.

The wing commander wasn't there, but most of the pilots stayed to have breakfast. Owen, on the other hand, wanted to know what was going on and went to look for her. He found her in operations, having a heated argument on the telephone and backed out quickly to return to the safety of the mess.

Gwen and Kitty ate alone because Scarlet, who had finally made it to the barracks in the small hours of the morning, had decided to forgo breakfast and was still in bed. Gwen said nothing to Kitty about the kiss from the night before and the American woman didn't mention it either. She was just her usual cheerful self and, unlike Gwen, didn't seem to be feeling any ill-effects for the quantity of alcohol she had consumed. So Gwen put the incident and her confused feelings about it out of her mind and instead they spoke about their time with the Princess and had fun debating whether anything had happened between their roommate and Sir Douglas.

It was looking to be a pleasant morning, apart from the pounding in Gwen's head, but then Abby stormed in fifteen minutes later with a face like thunder. 'Briefing hall in half an hour; we've got work to do.' She looked around the room, making sure that they had all heard her, then stormed back out again.

Conversation was much more subdued after that and when they left to go to the briefing many of the pilots requested a vial of Chalky's alchemical hangover cure to take with them, a stock of which was kept behind the bar. It was a rough treatment which served to clear a head for a few hours but left the pilot feeling worse afterwards and was only supposed to be used in emergencies, for when there was no alternative before an important or dangerous mission, but they had a feeling they were going to need it.

'Bomber escort? During the day? They'll be sitting ducks! What bloody idiot came up with that bright idea?'

Abby sighed. 'The bloody idiot who pays your wages, Mac - King George, the sixth of his name.'

Mac may have been mad, but that news gave even him pause. It didn't keep him quiet for long though. 'Hasn't anyone told him that's not the best way to use us? Or the bombers? He could even have asked us last night - I would have happily filled him in.'

'While I would have paid money to see that, I'm sure people have told him anyway, but I happen to agree with him on this occasion.'

A hush fell over the briefing room as the pilots stared at her, not quite believing what they were hearing.

Abby met their eyes one by one, looking around the group that was gathered in a loose semicircle around her. 'As too many people have said recently, desperate times require desperate measures and thanks to Scarlet we know exactly how desperate the situation is. The most important job on the table right now is not preventing their bombers doing damage to our cities and factories, it is preventing their army coming and taking *everything* away from us and Whitehall have been planning this strike on the invasion fleet since Scarlet's recce. So, yes, I believe that the best way to use us, for this mission and this mission only, is as bomber escort. And as for doing this during the day - Whitehall want to make sure we destroy the most important targets in a single huge raid and to do that best we need to see them. They're also gambling that the Fleas are still going to be reeling from our mission and won't be able to mount an effective defence. It's a risk, but one that they are willing to take, because possible gains are huge.'

Abby ignored the grumbling disagreement from the pilots and turned to the large scale map of the French coast pinned to one of the boards behind her. 'Bomber command are putting as many aircraft in the air as they can and are sending a bomber group to each of the five ports where we can see the largest concentration of enemy forces. They have to be very careful what they bomb because of the civilians in the cities, though, so they'll be mostly targeting the shipping in the harbours and the stockpiles and warehouses closest to the water. We will be covering the groups that are heading for Ostend and Dunkirk. We of course will be dissuading the Fleas from intercepting. If the enemy break off you are not to pursue, you are to remain with our boys and girls and see them safe. In the very unlikely event that enemy aircraft do not appear, once our bombers have turned for home we are to strafe any targets of opportunity we find, ammunition and spring tension permitting. Understood?'

Once again she looked at the members of A and B flights one by one, receiving nods from all of them, some more reluctantly than others. She gave them a grim nod in return then continued. 'C flight. Hummingbird is not needed for this mission, but the rest of you have jobs to do. Owen, you'll be above and behind the group; I want to know where the fighters are coming from before they get to us so that A and B flights can move to intercept. Chalky, you're to take Vulture up top; HQ want to know what effect we've had, so after we've done you're going to fly a route along the coast and take pictures of all five ports. And Wendy, Dreadnought will be accompanying the bomber group attacking Dunkirk. You'll be fully loaded, but your priority is the fighters who get through us to the bombers; see if you can't dissuade them from getting too close, I'll leave it up to you how you do that. Questions?'

Owen's face was contorted in fury, but his tone was deathly calm. 'Was the decision to make Dreadnought the enemy's primary target yours, or does that stupidity come from London as well?'

Wendy put her hand on her husband's arm. 'Owen, please.'

Abby gave him a cold look in return. 'Owen, Wendy is a big girl. She knows how to handle Dreadnought and she knows what the stakes are today. As do we all. Yes, she will be a target, a very big and extremely juicy one, but she also has a sting, much more than any of the other bombers do and if she can draw them to her we might have a chance at protecting the rest of them.'

Owen shrugged off his wife's hand and took a step closer to Abby, his hands curling into fists and voice almost a growl. 'I want to know whose decision it was.'

Abby walked forward to meet him. She stared him in the eyes and didn't back down, but while his attitude was purely aggressive hers was matter of fact and her voice was clear and without any anger when she answered. 'Mine. I was tasked with using this squadron in the best way

I could in order to accomplish this mission and that is what I am doing. We are soldiers, Owen, it is our job to lay down our lives to protect others and people in this squadron already have.'

Owen stared her in the eyes for long seconds and the pilots held their breath, wondering if he would really hit her and what it would do to the squadron if he did, but then he deflated with a sigh. 'You're right, of course. I'm sorry.'

Abby reached out and squeezed his shoulder. 'For what it's worth, I wish there was some other way to do this, but there isn't, I'm sorry.'

'I know, dammit, I know.' He walked back to Wendy and took her in his arms.

The other pilots watched them, shifting uncomfortably as the awkward silence went on.

'When?'

Abby tore her eyes from the embracing couple with difficulty and looked at Gwen. 'We takeoff at twelve twenty.'

Gwen looked up at the clock over the stage behind Abby - it was a little before eleven. She nodded. 'Plenty of time for another cup of tea, then. *If* you get on with the damn briefing, ma'am.'

There was a short silence, which was broken after a few seconds by sniggers from both Bruce and Mac, then suddenly all of the pilots were laughing as the tension drained from them.

Abby nodded gratefully at Gwen, but didn't join in.

The Misfits rendezvoused with the first bomber wing that they had been assigned to just north of Canterbury at twenty-five thousand feet and they headed east-southeast together, crossing the English coast near Deal. The white cliffs shone brilliantly in the bright sunshine, but their beauty and majesty went completely unnoticed when the pilots and aircrew caught sight of the French coastline, many of them for the first time, as it appeared out of the haze thirty miles away. It wasn't the land itself, or the fact that everything they could see across the water was in the hands of the enemy that gave them pause or took their breath away, rather it was the hundreds of destroyers, battleships and troop ships as well as thousands of smaller vessels gathered at various points along the coastline. This was the fleet that would carry the unstoppable Prussian army to their country, the threat that it was their job to try to destroy that day. Once and for all.

'Bloody hell, there's millions of the bastards!'

The comment, coming from one of the RAC bombers, had the Misfits laughing, but Abby sobered them up very quickly with only three words - 'Eyes up, Badgers.'

The pilots of A and B flights lifted their gaze from the ports and immediately spotted what Abby was calling their attention to.

The trouble with assembling such large a force of bombers was that many of them had had to be in the air for more than an hour, giving plenty of opportunity for the Prussians' own radar system to spot them and plenty of time for them to scramble forces to intercept.

It seemed that the Fleas weren't nearly as demoralised as Whitehall had hoped and had put what looked like every fighter they owned in the sky to meet them.

There were three distinct groups of Fleas, each comprising more than fifty fighters, spread out along the French and Belgian coast, heading for the British aircraft, and Misfit Squadron would have to face one of them on their own - the RAC fighters from other squadrons, around a hundred of them, had been split between the other bomber groups, leaving the Misfits, with their longer range, to cover the two groups of bombers that were going the furthest and attacking the more important targets.

'Well, at least we don't need Chalky to tell us where they are.' Mac's sardonic comment in his broad Scottish accent came over the radio. It brought some laughter, but it was far more nervous than before as the pilots contemplated the task ahead of them.

'Yes, thank you, *Badger Six*.' Abby's subtle admonishment brought them effectively back to radio discipline. 'A and B flights, go to full throttle and take up stations. Prepare to jettison springs on my mark. You know the plan, people, stick to it or you'll be buying the drinks for the next month.'

Abby had several plans in place for all eventualities. The plan in the case that the enemy was waiting for them was that they would accelerate ahead of the bombers, A flight climbing to two thousand feet above them and B flight a thousand feet above that, so that they could engage the fighters before they could get to the bombers. They planned to do a single pass, diving on the fighters, then pull around to do another. A flight would then stay with the enemy, trying to get them to engage in a turn fight, while B flight would try to pick off anyone that went for the bombers. The wing commander was fully aware that even the best thought-out plans in war usually didn't survive the first shots being fired, but she had every confidence in her pilots and in the leaders of the pairs that they would break into and knew that they would fight to the best of their abilities.

As the Misfits increased speed and started to climb, leaving the bombers behind, Abby's soft voice came over the radio. 'Happy hunting, Dreadnought.'

Surprisingly, it seemed that the Fleas had orders to ignore the British fighters and go straight for the bombers, because the Misfits were met with barely any resistance to their first attack. None of the enemy had tried to match their altitude and any evasive manoeuvres that they had taken were perfunctory at best and didn't deviate them much from their course to the bombers. These were almost suicidal tactics and the Misfits were able to take down six of the enemy fighters in their first pass, however, it did mean that, when they came back for their second crack at them, the Fleas were fast approaching the bombers and there was only just time to catch up with them and knock three more out of the sky before they were in among the heavier machines.

Three of the British bombers slid out of the formation as they took lethal damage, leaking black smoke from stricken hydrogen engines or simply turning over and diving as incapacitated pilots relinquished control on the machines, but they gave almost as good as they got and another two fighters fell out of the sky.

As Owen had predicted, the Fleas were moths around Dreadnought's flame and for a while they were burned and went spinning away just like insects. Enemy pilot after enemy pilot tried his luck and were blasted out of the sky by the weight of metal coming from the big machine's cannons, just one shell of which was sufficient to rip apart the fragile Muhlenberg MU9's and Hock-Hund HH190's that attacked her.

The heavier fighters, like the MU10's, fared much better, though; they were able to take much more punishment than their smaller cousins and a couple of them managed to penetrate the shield of iron that Dreadnought was able to throw around herself. The first stitched a line of large holes across her wing, which the big aircraft barely noticed, but the second, following immediately behind his wingmate, was luckier. He hit the same wing at a slightly different angle and his heavy cannon blasted holes in the armour plating around two of the large aircraft's six engines, which instantly flared into flame as the hydrogen ignited.

Dreadnought's gunners got their revenge, immediately knocking both of the fighters out of the sky, but she was hurt and Wendy had to fight desperately to maintain control as the steam tank of one of the two engines burst, taking a large chunk of her wing and the entire engine with it, the hot vapour threatening to spin the huge aircraft like a top as it was released under immense pressure. The steam dissipated almost immediately, but her problems didn't end there and she had to continue wrestling the controls, trying to correct for the suddenly uneven thrust, while her flight engineer and chief fitter, Roberta, desperately flicked switches in an attempt to extinguish the flames and stop them from making their way up the feed lines to the main hydrogen tanks in the fuselage and destroying the aircraft. Dreadnought creaked and groaned in protest as her airframe twisted under the pressure and entire pieces of Duralumin tore from the stricken wing, exposing the frame underneath, as the wind ripped at the damage, threatening to send the aircraft tumbling from the sky.

Gwen followed Abby as they weaved an unpredictable path through the British bombers, pursuing the nimble enemy fighters. It was second nature to her now; she had gotten to know her wingmate's style so well over so many hours of flying with her that just seeing the situation around them was enough to know what the wing commander was going to do, when she was going to turn and which enemy she was going to attempt to destroy next. Because she didn't have to concentrate so much on staying on Abby's wing any more, she had plenty of time to look around and watch for anything that her leader might not have seen, which meant that she caught the flash when Dreadnought's engines burst into flame. She gasped, unable to keep her eyes from the gigantic aircraft as it lurched and dipped, weaving drunkenly and threatening to tip over before Wendy regained some semblance of control.

She watched, unable to tear her gaze from the sight, as Dreadnought started to lose altitude, drifting down from its position just above the British bombers, and her lack of concentration almost killed her; a looming shape in front of her was the only warning she had of an impending collision with a double-aitch that was turning in front of her.

Her finger automatically pressed the button to activate her guns even as she yanked back on the stick and she was rewarded with the sight of the enemy fighter spinning away with half its wing missing.

Her inattention had meant that she had lost Abby, though, and she weaved through the bombers and fighters, searching for her.

Everywhere she turned there were aircraft going down. Below her she could see the remains of at least fifteen RAC bombers, easier to spot because of the black smoke that invariably poured from them. The fighters were much harder to see and she couldn't afford the time to switch lenses and look for them, but if there weren't more than eight or nine then the Misfits weren't doing their job very well.

She continued to twist and turn, taking whatever shots she could, destroying at least two Fleas and possibly a third, while keeping an eye out for the rest of her squadron, looking to rejoin with Abby. At one point Swift and Hawk zoomed past about half a mile away on the tail of a pair of MU10's, but she saw no sign of any of the other Misfits; it was just a mess of bombers and enemy fighters, spread out across the sky.

The shapes of the bombers changed as their bay doors opened and seconds later streams of iron arrow shapes fell from them. Gwen had been so busy that she hadn't noticed that they had been approaching the French coast and was taken so much by surprise that she had to bank sharply to avoid crossing through one of the deadly curtains spewing from a bomber.

The bomb doors closed again and, their mission carried out, the remaining RAC bombers turned and began a gentle dive, accelerating hard back to the safety of the distant island, which was not much more than an indistinct green shape through the haze of smoke hanging in the air. Their course took them almost directly underneath the second wave of British bombers the Misfits had been tasked with protecting, following up ten miles behind, on a slightly different heading that took them to Belgium.

As the bombers turned for home, Gwen found herself in a patch of empty sky and was finally able to find the other Misfits - they were three or four miles away and a good four or five thousand feet lower, fighting a desperate action against almost two dozen Fleas around the stricken Dreadnought, who had managed to deliver her payload even though she was hurt and was being harassed as she attempting to turn towards home. The Misfits had abandoned the bombers to protect one of their own, which was perfectly understandable, but against their orders. It was just as well that most of the Fleas had been concentrating on Dreadnought anyway, otherwise casualties amongst the RAC bombers might have been even higher.

'Badger Leader, this is Badger Two.'

'Go ahead, Two.' Abby's voice was strained and her annoyance showed. 'Where the hell are you, Gwen?'

'Above you, a few miles away. Sorry, Leader, got sidetracked. Shall I come down to you?'

'Negative, Two. Stay high and go help the second wave. Once Badger Ten is clear we'll come to you.'

'Roger, Leader. Two out.'

Reluctantly, Gwen turned away from her friends and put the fight to save Dreadnought out of her mind as best as she could as she raced towards the incoming bombers who were already under attack.

She had a minute or so before she caught up with the second wave and Gwen used the time to check Wasp. She had plenty of tension left in the spring, the spare had seen to that, and the handy little indicator Wendy had designed showed that she had used up a little under three-quarters of her ammunition. Satisfied that she could still fight she gave the aircraft itself a quick visual inspection and was shocked to see a gaping hole in her left wing, a hit that she hadn't even noticed getting. It had missed her leftmost machine gun and the volatile ammunition supplying it by inches, but she would probably never know whether it had come from friend or foe.

With just a little bit more time to spare, she rolled her shoulders and turned her neck back and forth, trying to release some of the tension that always seemed to build up on missions, then took a deep breath before scanning the sky once more, wagging Wasp's tail to look behind her to make sure that nobody was sneaking up on her and that there were no other enemies to worry about apart from the groups around the bombers and Dreadnought.

She used her final seconds of peace to smile at Richard's photograph, then fixed her gaze back on the battle taking place in front of her.

There were ten or twelve enemy fighters, mostly MU9's, engaging the bombers and Gwen pounced on them, not thinking twice about facing such high odds, just as she hadn't when the eight Misfits had dived into more than fifty Fleas only a few short minutes ago, or when they had dived on twice their number of elite Barons over the Midlands.

The first Flea fell to her before they even knew they were there, an easy deflection shot as he turned and climbed after a run at the bombers blew his entire right wing off and he went spinning. She adjusted to fire at his wingman, but he turned upside down in a panic and dived away almost vertically. She let him go, knowing that he would be out of the fight for a long time, if he even bothered trying to climb back up to it at all.

She spotted her next target swinging round one of the big bombers and was ready for him as he came out the other side. Her first burst went wide and she cursed, but corrected instantly and gave him another second's burst of her guns. This time she was rewarded by the sight of half of the MU9's tailplane spinning away and the enemy pilot immediately pushed his nose down sharply, which must have made his eyes almost pop, and dived away. Once again she let him go; he was no longer a threat, and turned her attention to his wingman. He was smarter than the average Flea, though, and had veered away from her as soon as he had become aware of the threat and there were just too many bombers around him for her to get a clear shot. Going after him would mean flying in a straight line for too long, so she ignored him and turned, looking around for the next target.

Dull thuds shook Wasp, almost knocking the stick from her hand as a long line of holes magically appeared on her undamaged right wing next to the cockpit and pieces of her flaps flew away. She instantly kicked her rudder hard to yaw sharply away from the line of fire, simultaneously pulling back on her stick and flipping into a barrel roll to take her over a bomber and into the relative safety of its far side while she craned her neck, searching for her attacker.

She found not one, but three enemy aircraft on her six, an HH190 and two MU9's, all blazing away with their guns as they tried to follow her desperate manoeuvre and she whispered an apology as the bomber she had used for cover took the majority of their shots and began to drop from the formation, leaving a cloud of white mist in its place as one of its steam tanks burst.

They chased her through the bombers, staying side by side and taking slightly different paths as she went over, under and around the RAC aircraft, but no matter what she did, she couldn't shake them and they were a constant presence in her rearview mirror. One of them she could out turn and get behind, but she couldn't do that with three, nor could she hope to outrun them; Wasp was fast, but she had been primarily designed for agility and the Prussian machines were faster, not by much, but enough to overhaul her in a race. She had two options then - turn and hope that the Flea whose path she turned into missed his shot, or dive, abandoning the bombers but possibly taking the three enemy fighters beyond where they could do any harm. Neither option was particularly attractive but she had to make a decision soon; they weren't going to keep missing for long and she was fast running out of bombers to put between her and them.

The choice was no choice at all really and she knew she was going to have to risk the turn; she couldn't abandon the bombers, no matter the danger to herself. She smiled at the photo on her instrument panel, then prepared to turn into the path of the HH; RAC pilots tended to believe the double-aitch pilots weren't as good as the MU ones in dogfights.

In the end, she didn't have to test that theory as a third option presented itself unexpectedly.

'Need a hand, Badger Two?'

'Not really, Badger Eight, but if you've made the effort to come all the way to Belgium you might as well do *something*. Just try not to miss and hit me, please.'

Kitty's laugh filled Gwen's ears as two aircraft, one red, white and blue and the other brown, streaked across her rear and two of the Prussians following her suddenly became a lot less airworthy than they had been previously.

Gwen could just picture the huge grin that must have been plastered over the American's face and she smiled in return as she pulled back on her stick, moving out of the path of the last of the Fleas. She lost sight of it behind a bomber, but when she saw it next it was diving full throttle towards the coast, only a couple of miles ahead.

'Badger Leader to all Badgers. Rendezvous at two thousand feet above the bomber group.'

As Gwen pulled up she scanned the sky around them. Aside for a few fleeing Fleas there were only British aircraft to be seen and, as she watched, the bay doors swung open and the bombers sent their explosive gifts tumbling away to the port of Ostend far below.

Hardly any aircraft from the second wave had been prevented from carrying out their mission and consequently far more bombs were dropped on Ostend than had been dropped on Dunkirk and as the Misfits turned for home with their countrymen they shared in the jubilation of the bomber crews as ship after ship and barge after barge was torn apart.

The pilots had very mixed feelings about the day's mission when they landed; they were understandably jubilant at having shot down so many enemy fighters (the provisional count was in excess of thirty and likely to be closer to forty) and they were pleased with the success of the raid on Ostend, but they were also distressed by the loss of so many bombers in the first raid on Dunkirk and there was no word yet on the fate of Dreadnought - they had lost sight of her after they had seen off their attackers and climbed to help the second raid.

Abby informed them that they had been released for the day and the pilots hurriedly changed out of their flight gear, then congregated in the mess where they sat together, nursing drinks and swapping stories of their individual dogfights, but in a much more subdued manner than usual as they waited for news of their colleague.

Thankfully, it wasn't long before a call came on the radio that Dreadnought had made it as far as the RAC base at Hawkinge, near Folkestone. Her undercarriage had been damaged and she had been forced to make an extremely rough crash-landing. Wendy herself was fine, just a few scratches and bruised ribs from where her control yoke had dug into her stomach on landing, but she had lost two of her crew and Dreadnought was going to need a lot of work before it was airworthy again. The fitters at Hawkinge, which had been so damaged by Prussian bombing that they had no repair facilities, were working with Wendy and her crew, trying to get the giant aircraft safely dismantled and packed up for transport to Badger Base without causing further damage. They had been given permission to stay with the aircraft until it was done and before he could even ask, Abby told Owen that he could take one of the base's transport aircraft to join his wife. He all but leapt from his seat and ran out of the mess to get into the air immediately.

More news trickled in over the course of the afternoon.

The first thing that they found out, just after lunch, was that none of the other bomber groups had fared nearly as well as the two that the Misfits had escorted; they had hardly shot down any enemy fighters and had lost most of their bombers, many before they managed to drop their payloads. Most of the British fighters had made it home, though, mainly because the Fleas had been so single-minded in their persecution of the bomber wings that they hadn't had ammunition or time left for them.

In mid afternoon Vulture returned from its mission. A Royal Guard Spitsteam had been standing by and it whisked the films away to Whitehall to be developed so the Misfits never got a chance to see them, but Chalky soon joined them in the mess.

He downed almost a whole pint of beer while the other pilots watched, then told them what he'd been able to see through the optical arrays that his aircraft was equipped with in addition to the cameras. 'We did a good job on Ostend - I counted almost a hundred barges sinking or sunk and there were fires in many of the warehouses. Dunkirk was almost as thoroughly roughed up and we've probably got Dreadnought to thank for that.'

The pilots smiled happily; so far the news was good - those numbers were higher than the ones that had been projected for the two ports that they had been assigned to.

However, the smiles faded when Chalky's face turned grim. 'As for the other three ports... Damage was completely insignificant, there was barely any damage to the stockpiles that I could see and the invasion fleets were almost untouched.'

Abby nodded, matching his expression. 'That was what we were expecting; we got word that most of the bombers were destroyed before they got to their targets.' She turned to the assembled pilots. 'We did our best and we all came home. Get plenty of rest and don't drink too much, please, because I'm sure the Prussians will have an answer for us soon.'

CHAPTER 18

The Misfits were woken for a dawn patrol the next day, but there was no sign of the enemy on radar and they were soon released back to standby on the ground. There was so little business in fact that Abby sought and was given permission to contact the Barons and arrange for the return of their bodies and the pieces of their downed aircraft.

Scarlet flew the mission in Hummingbird, just as she had for each of the pilots that the Misfits had shot down and recovered. Boxes which attached to her aircraft in place of a second spring had been created specially for the task and all she had to do was hover a few inches above the ground, pull the spring-release lever, then fly away again. As always, the Prussian air defences had been expecting her and didn't fire a single shot at her as she zoomed in, dropped the box off at the assigned coordinates a couple of miles from the shore, then zoomed away again.

On her return, Scarlet reported that there had been no soldiers at the rendezvous, just a contingent of pilots led by Gruber himself, who saluted her as she left before moving forward to retrieve the box.

Abby nodded grimly at the news; the Barons were back in France.

As the day wore on, the only incidents were an intrusion by a single fast-moving aircraft, which flew reconnaissance just off the coast and a couple of small raids, one on Portsmouth and the other on the Isle of Wight, both of which were handled by regular RAC squadrons and which didn't warrant scrambling the Misfits.

It was nothing compared to what had come over in the previous weeks and the Misfits went to bed with the distinct feeling that something big was about to happen.

The next day, the 15th of September was Gwen's birthday and it dawned bright and cloudless and the forecasts promised that it would continue that way for the rest of the day. It was perfect bombing weather and somehow the Misfits knew that the Prussians wouldn't let this chance pass them by, especially with the Barons back in the area; this late in the English summer such days were likely to be few and far between. It seemed that Whitehall was under the same impression and the Misfits weren't called upon to go out on their dawn patrol, but were instead put straight on standby.

For a while, though, it looked like everybody was going to be wrong, that the Prussians weren't planning something that day in retaliation for the raid on their ports; the skies were completely clear and there was nothing on radar. The Misfits had laid out their deckchairs and were relaxing, enjoying what would possibly be the last of the sunshine for the year, but then at eleven the call came through to scramble as all hell broke loose around the south of England.

The pilots struggled out of the deckchairs, Mac and Bruce just rolling to one side and falling to the floor in a manoeuvre they had practised over the summer (mostly when drunk and to the vast amusement of the other Misfits) and raced across the grass towards the hangar, where the fitters were already pushing out A and B flight's aircraft.

In less than two minutes they were airborne and climbing hard for Folkestone.

'Sapper, this is Badger Leader, over.'

'Badger Leader, Sapper here. Go ahead.'

'Badger Squadron is airborne and awaiting instructions, over.'

'Badger Leader, head east south east and make angels twenty-five. Enemy raid incoming, one hundred plus aircraft, over.'

'Roger, Sapper, Badger leader, out.' Abby switched to the squadron channel. 'Badger Leader to all Badgers. You heard the man. Adjusting course and climbing to angels twenty-five.'

'Bloody hell, looks like we're going to have some fun today!' Mac sounded positively gleeful at the prospect of so much business and Bruce was quick to join in.

'Was yesterday a holiday in Prussia or something? Why take Saturday off, then come on a Sunday? Blimmin' bastards, I was looking forward to a nice roast!'

'Yeah, and about twenty pints!' Mac laughed.

The pilots joined in the laughter as the two pilots carried on with their banter. Abby always let them have their little conversations at such moments where radio discipline wasn't important; it relieved the tension and kept the pilots' minds sharp trying to keep up with them. However, even the two irrepressible pilots knew when they had to shut up and they did so immediately when Sapper called again from the control room at Biggin Hill.

'Badger Leader, Sapper here, over.'

'Badger Leader here, go ahead, Sapper.'

'Badger Leader, be advised - raid is now two hundred and fifty plus. Repeat two hundred and fifty plus, over.'

'Thank you, Sapper. Badger Leader out.'

The radio clicked off and the Misfits flew on in stunned silence, climbing towards the sun and their station.

The enemy raid approaching England had taken off from multiple airfields in both France and Belgium, but they had joined up over Northern France to come across the channel in one huge mass of aircraft.

The RAC had scrambled several squadrons to meet them and there were more than a dozen Spitsteams and Harridans already up and over Canterbury at twenty-five thousand feet when the Misfits reached their station, but most of the British fighters were still trying to climb up to the raid. There wasn't time to wait for them, though, as the enemy were already there.

Prussian bombers formed a huge column that seemed to go on forever, a black line in the sky that pointed straight to London, a dagger held to the heart of the Kingdom of Britain. Over and around them swarmed Prussian fighters, dozens upon dozens of nimble MU's and HH's, ready to defend their comrades.

The British seemed pitifully few, insignificant even, in the face of such might, but they didn't care; they had a job to do and they had people who were depending on them. They engaged without hesitation, diving into the mass of aircraft, guns blazing.

The battle raged over miles and miles of the Kent countryside as the unstoppable force of the Prussian bombers continued its advance, shrugging off any losses it suffered. The Prussian fighters soon had to turn back because they had reached the limits of their range, but their job was done - the bombers were at the gates of London.

More and more RAC squadrons joined the fight, but they barely made a dent in the raid before the bombs began falling onto the city below and the factories and docklands along the winding river started to burn.

The British harassed the bombers all the way back to the coast, but the Misfits were forced to break off over Kent because they were low on tension. They had gotten a good haul, shooting down more than twenty enemy aircraft between them and on a normal day they would have been satisfied, but they had had to let so many Fleas go, many of which were still in sight from Badger Base when they landed, that it left a sour taste in their mouths.

The Misfits barely had time to grab a quick lunch before another call came through to scramble less than an hour later. This time, though, there was an addition to their orders - they were to equip secondary springs so that they could pursue the bombers for longer; Whitehall wanted the Prussians' ability to bomb London if not destroyed then at least severely diminished.

The change in orders meant that it took them slightly more time to get off the ground because the fitters had to rush to install the springs and they were slower climbing to their station, but even then they had plenty of time to spare because it was taking the Fleas far longer to gather their forces for this second raid.

Chalky had been flying a circuit high over the south coast in Vulture, watching the Prussian bombers going home and it was he who had first warned Whitehall of the next raid building up. It was also him that was sent out over the channel to visually verify what the British radar systems were detecting, but what the operators couldn't quite believe. He confirmed what they were seeing - almost twice as many aircraft were gathering for the second raid as had come over in the first.

The Misfits soon received the expected call from Sapper, informing them that the raid was estimated at more than four hundred and fifty aircraft.

This time they didn't make any jokes.

As soon as they had realised the full extent of the enemy raid, Whitehall had ordered more British aircraft into the air and the Harridans and Spitsteams of the other RAC squadrons flew up to join the Misfits as they headed towards the south coast. An endless stream of aircraft appeared and formed up around them and it seemed that there was no room in the sky for any more, but still they kept coming until there must have been over two hundred of them.

Not surprisingly, Mac was the first to comment, but he was also the last, because he summed up what they were all thinking so succinctly that there was no need to say anything else.

'Bloody marvellous! Bloody, *bloody* marvellous!'

Gwen gazed at the aircraft around the Misfits, bobbing up and down as they were gently buffeted by the air currents and gasped when she saw a flight of sixteen Spitsteams a mile off her left wing with gold stripes on their wings - the Spitsteams of the Royal Guard. All of them. They were supposed to be the last defence of the Royal Family, kept in reserve in case all else failed - if they were here then that meant that every aircraft that the RAC could throw into the air *had* been thrown into the air.

It was a stirring sight, but it was also a sobering one; while it might seem that there were a lot of British aircraft, especially compared to what was usually in the air, two hundred or two hundred and fifty was not a large number if you considered that they were all that was standing between the Kingdom of Britain and utter defeat at the hands of the Prussian army waiting just over twenty miles away. If the RAC lost today's battle they would lose control of the air over the British Isles, which meant that the invasion fleet would be free to come without fear of death falling on them from above, which in turn meant that the war would inevitably be lost; there was no way the British army, already broken and defeated once in France, could possibly withstand the hugely powerful Prussian force that had known victory after victory.

It seemed that it wasn't just Gwen who realised how desperately important the coming battle was and when the radio crackled to life it wasn't Sapper they heard, delivering the expected instructions, it was a different voice that spoke, one that was instantly recognisable to the men and women of the RAC from his numerous radio addresses to the besieged nation and needed no introduction.

'Hello, brave pilots of the RAC. I am speaking to you from the eleven group control room at Uxbridge, where I will remain throughout this fateful day so that I can be as close to you as possible during this most difficult of times.'

The King knew that he wasn't obeying radio protocol and he paused for a few seconds to let this information sink in before going on. 'I could easily make a long-winded speech saying that England expects every man and woman to do his duty, or that this will be your finest hour, but I won't; I will save those platitudes for the people and for after the day's work is done because you already know what is at stake and you are well equipped to face the threat that is coming. What I will say, though, is that the thoughts and the hopes of an entire nation are with you. Take our strength, make it your own and come home victorious. Good speed and happy hunting. Out.'

There was a few seconds of respectful silence after the King had finished to allow the pilots to savour the moment, but then Sapper took over again and gave instructions that split the British forces; this time the Prussians had formed three columns, the two largest of which, designated raids one and two, were easily the same size as the morning's raid had been. The smallest, raid three, comprising only fifty bombers or so, was lagging slightly behind.

The Misfits were predictably assigned to the raid that would arrive first, which was also the largest one, and they and around a hundred other fighters manoeuvred to meet it. The Royal Guards led a hundred more to deal with raid two and the rest of the fighters, most of which were still climbing to get to station were given the task of intercepting raid three when it arrived.

The enemy came closer and closer and soon they were able to make out individual machines at maximum magnification. Hands tightened on sticks, last checks were done and nerves were steeled. Some wag, one of the women from the other squadrons briefly came over the radio to give the old joke. 'For what we are about to receive...' but apart from that the British flew on in silence, completely concentrated on the job ahead.

'Er, Leader, this is Three.'

'Go ahead, Three.'

Badger Three was Bruce in Devil and Gwen glanced across Abby's rear to look at him and was surprised to see a frown on his face; normally he had a huge grin plastered on his face before going in to action and he habitually spent most of the dogfights laughing his head off.

'Um. Aren't we going to drop the spares?'

With a start Gwen realised that she had completely forgotten that they were still carrying two springs.

'Negative, Badger Three. Weren't you listening in the briefing, Bruce? I know it was a bit hurried, but even so...'

'Um, I might have dozed off a bit, Leader, sorry.'

222

There were chuckles from most of the pilots at that, but Abby gave a very audible sigh. 'We're using the springs until they're finished, at which point you have my permission to jettison. Got it, Three?'

'I think so, Leader.'

'Good, because we don't exactly have time to go through it again. Happy hunting, Badgers.'

There was no time at all in fact and Abby finished talking just in time to dive onto the enemy formation.

Like so many times before, the plan was to use speed and surprise to blast through escort and make their first pass together at the bombers, then A flight would engage the fighters and try to draw them away while B flight would continue to attack the bombers.

The fight began and as always Gwen stuck to Abby's wing, firing whenever the opportunity to do so presented itself. It was chaotic, far more than the morning's fight had been because, while there were similar numbers of enemy aircraft in the raid they were attacking, there were far more British aircraft and every pilot had to look twice to make sure that they weren't firing at a friend. Gwen felt strange, though, as if she were in a dream, and she struggled to wake herself up and concentrate, blinking and working her jaw, knowing that she couldn't afford any distraction. No matter what she did, the feeling wouldn't go away and eventually she realised that it wasn't her, it was Wasp - Wasp felt sluggish; the fact that the second spring was still attached was making the aircraft react slower to Gwen's every command and it seemed almost as if she were moving through water.

The Misfits had had a lot of invaluable experience of flying with dual springs during the long patrols when they had been trying to engage the Barons, but they had never entered a dogfight with the second one still attached. It was extremely strange, throwing the balance of the aircraft out subtly and making it manoeuvre much slower. However, even though the playing field was suddenly more even, the difference in quality of the Misfit pilots still shone through and they started to make an impact on the Flea forces, but, no matter how many aircraft the Misfits and the RAC shot down, they never seemed to make a dent in the enemy numbers and the bombers continued their inexorable advance on London.

After only five minutes of hard fighting Abby's voice crackled over their personal frequency. 'Badger Two, this is Leader. I'm dropping my spring. How are you doing on tension?'

Gwen flicked her eyes to the indicator. 'One quarter left, Leader.'

'Bloody hell, Two, I'm going to have to set you loose on the rest of the squadron's aircraft when we have a chance to breathe.'

Gwen grinned. 'With pleasure, Leader.'

Abby laughed, then Gwen's radio clicked as the woman switched over to the squadron frequency. 'All right, listen up Badgers. The enemy fighters are going to break off soon and when they do we're going to break into individuals. Take as many of the bombers down as you can and head home only when you have to.'

'Badger Leader this is Badger Nine.'

Gwen frowned when Owen came over the radio. Usually during missions the Welshman was calm and unflappable, one of the reasons why Abby had made him her second in command and given him permission to call the shots in the air if he saw something different to her, but there was a strain in his voice that sent a shiver through not a few of the pilots; they knew him well and could tell that bad news was coming.

'Go ahead, Badger Nine.'

'Raid three... They're heading directly for Badger Base.'

The entire squadron had the same reaction, but Lady Penelope beat them all to it. 'That's impossible!'

Abby swore. 'When we landed after the first raid there were bombers in sight, one of them must have seen us.'

'What do we do, Leader?' asked Kitty, almost in a panic. 'Are we going to break off and defend the base? Scarlet's there, and the others... They can't withstand a raid by fifty bombers!'

'Negative, Eight. We have a job to do and we're going to stick with it. Badger Base isn't important in the grand scheme of things. If its destruction is the price we have to pay to make sure that the Fleas can't bring this kind of force back ever again, then so be it.'

'But our people...'

'They have been warned, Eight, and the raiders are being intercepted. Now get your mind back on the job!'

'Roger, Leader.'

There was silence for long seconds as their thoughts went to Badger Base and the friends and colleagues that were facing the bombs of as big a raid as any that had been sent to London and other British cities over the last few days. They continued to fight during that time and it was a testament to their ability that they had been able to carry out an entire conversation while still flying rings around the Prussians.

Gwen watched Abby blast apart a double-aitch then looked around for the next fighter that her leader would target, but didn't see one. 'Leader, the fighters are leaving.'

'I see it, Two. All Badgers, let the fighters go and stay with the bombers. Split up and happy hunting.'

Gwen immediately broke away from Abby, already honing in on one of the bombers. She gave it a two-second burst and saw one of the engines flare, but had to pull up and over it. She left it behind, forgetting about it; there were too many targets in the sky to waste time circling around one and she would just have to trust that somebody else would finish off the job she started.

There was a slight stutter as her spare spring ran out of tension, but it was barely noticeable as the main one kicked in automatically and she smiled wickedly as she picked out her next target. It was less than half a mile away and well within range, but she didn't open fire, instead she headed straight for it. In less than two seconds she was so close that she could see the face of the gunner in the glass bubble in the big aircraft's side. He was young, blonde-haired, good-looking, but his face was contorted in a mask of fury and hatred as he swung his dual cannons towards her, already depressing the triggers and sending twin lines of fire searching for her.

His face disappeared from view as she brought her nose up sharply, simultaneously pulling the lever by her right buttock which released the spring.

Despite the fact that she had perfect targets lined up in front of her, she couldn't resist banking to see the results of her mischief and quickly spotted three objects spinning to the ground - the tail of an aircraft, the wings and cockpit of the same aircraft and the thick disk of the spring that had neatly separated one from the other.

She laughed in glee and swung back to continue the destruction.

It was almost precisely two-thirty in the afternoon, according to the synchronised chronometers of the Misfits, when the bombers arrived over London and opened their bay doors.

The city below them was already wreathed in smoke; fires from the earlier raid were still raging, the civilian firefighting brigades stretched too thin and unable to effectively combat so many of them, despite the ingeniously efficient clockwork engines that they were equipped with. It was impossible for the bombers to see their targets, but they didn't care, they released their loads, sending them tumbling indiscriminately into the city below, before turning and heading for home.

The British fighters had no choice but to ignore the explosions that started to bloom below as they followed the bombers, continuing to harass them. The Spitsteams and Harridans didn't have the luxury of spare springs or increased ammo supplies courtesy of Wendy, though, and it wasn't long before the Misfits were the only British aircraft left. They followed the bombers as they headed back the way they came, shooting down one after the other, leaving a trail of wrecked Prussian machinery behind them. They were beginning to tire now, though; they had been fighting solidly for almost an hour. Arms were becoming heavy on sticks and heads were pounding from the strain of fighting against extreme G forces that their aircraft could withstand far better than they could.

They lost two pilots during that return journey as concentration wavered and nerves frayed.

Bruce lost almost half of his left lower wing when he lingered too long behind a bomber that was reluctant to go down, giving the tail gunners time to bring him into their sights. The last the Misfits saw of him he was spinning towards the ground, swearing as he fought to regain control of Devil.

Mad Mac had been ceaselessly zooming at top speed in and out of the formation in Swordfish, diving and swooping, always seeming to come perilously close to a collision, making more than one bomber pilot swerve or dive in panic. Somewhere over the Kent Downs, just out of sight of Badger Base, he finally misjudged and clipped the cockpit of a Hoffman with the tip of his wing. Swordfish was instantly ripped apart and fell, dropping swiftly out of sight and into the sparse cloud that had been building during the afternoon.

It was almost a relief when the coast came into sight because it meant that the Misfits would finally be able to break off and head for home. Even better, there was a squadron of fighters fast approaching from the east who would be able to take some of the pressure off them and draw some of the fire from the bombers.

Any thoughts that help was coming were immediately shattered by Owen, though.

'Badger Leader, this is Badger Nine.'

'Go ahead, Nine.' The tiredness and strain made Abby's voice barely audible in the squadron's ears.

'Enemy aircraft approaching from the east.'

The hesitation before the wing commander replied was a clear indication of how tired she was. 'Say again, please, Nine.'

'Enemy aircraft, repeat, *enemy* aircraft, approaching from the east.'

'Where did they come from, Owen?'

'They were with raid three, Leader. They turned back when the bombers crossed the coast. Pilots who met raid three are reporting that there were red aircraft escorting them.'

Abby swore on the open channel.

There were no laughs from the other pilots at her slip; they were all too tired and too chilled by the prospect of facing the Barons when they were so far from their best and missing members.

'Recommend you break off and head for Hawkinge, Leader. Badger Base is inoperable.'

If the news of the incoming enemy aces wasn't enough, the news of their base was a hammer blow to them. However, while it would have demoralised many pilots it had the opposite effect on the Misfits.

'Let's get the bastards, Abby, I've got tons of ammo left.'

The bloodthirsty growl was so incongruous, coming from the amiable Monty, that it took Gwen a second to realise it had been him, but then every other pilot joined in, clamouring for action, and she found herself calling out along with them.

'MISFITS! SHUT UP!'

The radio instantly fell silent as Abby's shout all but deafened them.

There were long seconds of quiet, at least on the radio, during which another two enemy bombers fell from the sky.

'Reform flights and break off to the north, maximum climb.'

There was no argument from any of the Misfits as they separated from the bomber formation; Abby's decision made perfect sense. The bombers were a high priority because destroying them would destroy the Prussians' ability to attack Britain, but the Barons were far more important - if they could be defeated again, then the enemy's morale would take a significant beating; one defeat could be explained away, especially because they had been taken by surprise, but a second defeat, on more even terms, wouldn't be as easy to justify.

The Misfits were exhausted, but it was entirely possible that the Barons were equally tired; they had had further to fly before fighting. It was also quite possible that they had lost members as well, but that proved to be a false hope as the two forces drew closer and the Misfits were able to make out that they were facing a full complement of sixteen red aircraft - they were outnumbered almost three to one.

'It's not too late to run, Misfits.' Abby's weary voice expressed what had crossed the minds of all of them at some point since the Barons had first been spotted.

'Bugger that, Abby.'

Gwen was shocked to find that it was she herself who had answered. She didn't know why she'd spoken; the words had just forced their way out, but she realised that she'd wholeheartedly meant what she'd said.

There was a shocked silence as the other pilots assimilated her words and Gwen blushed when she looked out at the colourful machines grouped around her and saw that every single face was turned towards her.

The laughter started softly with a couple of chuckles from Kitty and Lady Penelope, but they swiftly spread and grew until all six of them were roaring with laughter as they sped towards the deadliest fight of their lives.

CHAPTER 19

The two forces had been at roughly the same altitude when the Misfits had spotted the Barons, but the British machines were able to out climb the Prussians and, when they finally came together, the Misfits had a distinct height advantage, which they put to good use, diving twice on the Prussians, knocking two of the Blutsaugers out of the sky. Two more, undamaged but panicked, dived away, racing for the coast and the thick clouds creeping over the Channel from France.

'Let them go,' said Abby gleefully. 'We need someone to survive and let the rest of the Fleas know what happened to the Barons today anyway.'

Abby might have been pleased with how the fight had been progressing and the odds were suddenly more even, but the Misfits had spent their advantage and were going to have to get their hands dirty in a turn fight, unless they wanted to take their small victory and run. None of them wanted to do that, though, and they all knew that if the result of the battle wasn't decisive then the Prussians would just keep coming back.

'A flight, we're going to mix it up, B flight just do what you do best.'

Abby's orders sent three of the Misfits turning to meet the Barons, while the other three climbed away. On the face of things it seemed like suicide, as the members of A flight now faced the twelve remaining enemy aircraft, but there was at least some wisdom in her decision; the Prussians were unable to fully concentrate their forces on the three incredibly nimble aircraft, both because they got in each other's way, making it almost impossible to get a clear shot without having to worry about hitting one of their own comrades and also because now they had to keep an eye on B flight, lurking overhead and waiting for any opportunity to pounce.

Gwen, Abby and Monty put the experience they had garnered in months of almost continuous flying to full use, carrying out complex manoeuvres that had become second nature to them and using tricks and tactic that they had practised in fight after fight to confuse and confound their enemies. They never flew a predictable path, never fixed on a single target, instead constantly banked and turned, while taking opportunistic shots - just as they had done so many times before when they had been equally, or more, outnumbered.

In the past couple of months, while the Misfits had been fighting for their lives and their country, the Barons had mostly been putting on displays to raise the morale of the Prussian people and army. They lacked the hard-earned combat instincts of the British pilots and it showed. Abby made short work of two fighters, two red monoplanes that had been lining up for a shot on Gwen and in return Gwen shot down the fighter that had been pursuing Abby. Monty managed to take down another that had swerved out of the way of one of his comrades, straight into his sights and B flight destroyed two more that had been trying to gain some distance from the main fight in order to turn and get a clear shot.

In less than a minute, the odds had gone from impossible to completely even.

The fight didn't go the Misfits' way for long, though.

In his tiredness, Monty spent a split second too long savouring his kill and three of the remaining six Barons took the opportunity they were handed and honed in on him. A stream of lead blew the struts from one side of Ballerina, weakening her structure, and the top wing of the biplane all but ripped itself from the aircraft, sending it into an uncontrollable flat spin.

Gruber had been far from idle and, while the rest of his squadron had kept A flight occupied, he had been watching for an opportunity to take B flight down a peg. He had designed and constructed his triplane (emulating the iconic aircraft flown by one of his heroes in the First Great War) specifically for fights like this one and he knew how to best use the incredible firepower and agility that he had in his hands. He also knew his opponents very well and was amused to see that their tactics hadn't evolved in the two months since the two squadrons had last faced each other in France.

His first chance came when Swift swooped down on a loose Baron - Derek was so concentrated on his target that he didn't see the triplane turning towards him and metal from Gruber's twelve machine guns shredded his tail, rendering him incapable not only of destroying the Baron he'd been focussed on, but also of returning to the fight.

The next target was Lady Penelope and he used the same tactic as before, watching as the triangular shape of Cheetah dropped onto one of his comrades, predicting her path easily, then sending lines of fire streaming out in front of her. She flew right through them and never pulled up, her aircraft's control surfaces completely destroyed and her aircraft falling apart around her.

Gruber grinned, more than satisfied with how the fight was going, and turned his attention to Abby. A quick call to his squadron had them turning to engage the other Misfits, leaving him alone with her - it was time to have some fun.

Abby knew that, with her squadron whittled down, Gruber would be coming for her soon; they had faced off enough times for her to know how his mind worked - he wouldn't want to risk another pilot getting the glory of shooting her down.

She was eager for the confrontation; the other Barons were faceless pilots, above average and talented, certainly, but nonetheless simply there to provide a squadron for Gruber to lead and terrorise the RAC with - it was the erstwhile movie star who was the linchpin of the Crimson Barons, without him they would simply cease to exist as a threat and it was her duty, one that the King himself had personally given her, to eliminate that threat.

She just wondered how long it would take him to get around to her. All she knew was that it would be soon, because the longer the fight went on, the more of his pilots would get shot down and he risked being left alone with multiple enemies.

She had her answer when a thick stream of bright tracers flicked past just over her right wing.

She dived away from the bullets, pushing her nose down so hard that her vision turned red and her eyeball seemed to swell in her skull, almost instantly, though, she did a quick roll, then pulled the stick into her stomach, pulling hard G's and draining the blood away just as quickly. More bullets flew past, but they went under her wing, missing her by even more than the first burst had and she laughed; Gruber must have been desperate to have even taken the shot.

As she approached, then passed the vertical, her speed rose and the G's increased, but she kept the stick in her lap and forced her neck to turn, looking for Gruber over her shoulder.

He had followed her into the dive, trying to cut her off, but his shots had cost him; the incredible weight of metal his guns could throw easily ripped apart any target that he hit, but the recoil from them was just as incredible and it had slowed him and he was only just going through the vertical as Dragonfly's nose approached the horizon.

His face was craned up to glare back at her and she lifted her left hand from where it had been helping her right to keep the stick fully back, grunting at the supreme effort that it took and gave him the two-fingered salute.

She grinned in satisfaction when she saw Gruber's face contort in rage; an angry pilot was one who made mistakes and she would need every advantage that she could claw for herself to win against the Prussian - she was the better pilot, there was no doubt about that, but Flamme was the better machine; the Prussians had far more resources than the blockaded British and they had given the man everything that he had asked for and more, including the latest technology and the best materials. His machine had a tighter turning circle than Dragonfly and he was already gaining on her, which meant that if she wanted to be victorious she was going to have to fall back on the manoeuvres she had used against Gwen when they had tested Wasp - she had never told her new pilot, but those dogfights had been practice for this, a fight that she knew she would have one day and which might well play a large part in deciding the fate of Kingdom of Britain and the outcome of the Second Great War.

The weight came off of her as she centred her stick, but it was only for an instant before she was brought up hard against her straps as she kicked the rudder and simultaneously jerked the stick to the side, hurled Dragonfly into a twisting barrel roll that swapped sky for ground and back again in an instant. She looked for the triplane, expecting to find it in front of her, but it wasn't there, instead, another stream of metal flew past her cockpit, much closer this time.

She threw Dragonfly into one move after another, using every trick that she knew, taking herself and her machine to the limit and beyond, but it was no good, she just couldn't shake him. She did manage to prevent him from taking another shot at her, though, but that wasn't going to be enough; she was down to only a quarter tension and would have to break off soon, exposing herself to attack, if the fight didn't end quickly.

In the end it didn't come to that.

Her tiredness caught up with her and when she went to pull the stick back to put Dragonfly into another high-G manoeuvre her hand slipped, the strained muscles of her fingers finally giving out.

It was only a momentary loss of control, but that was all that it took.

Multiple overlapping impacts shook Dragonfly's entire being and Abby cried out as the aircraft lurched to the side, beginning a long looping spin. A quick glance to her left showed her why - almost half of her wing was missing and the loss of lift on one side had caused the imbalance.

She fought the stick, bringing the aircraft back under control with some difficulty, knowing all the time that she was dead.

Gruber had won.

Gwen hadn't bothered to count the number of bombers she'd shot down, or even make sure of the kills, but she savoured each and every one of the red aircraft she destroyed; these were the pilots who had killed so many of her colleagues over France, who had given the Prussians the confidence to think that they could come to the British Isles and bomb what they wanted and she paid them back at more than a thousand rounds per minute.

She didn't think she'd ever been so tired, not even during the long route marches during basic training carrying almost half her bodyweight on her back, not even during the long weeks of flying nearly ten hours a day, but she refused to give in to the exhaustion, blinking sweat out of her eyes and easing cramped muscles whenever she had the chance and using her anger at the destruction of her fellow Misfits to fuel her.

The Blutsauger that she had shot off Abby's tail was joined by another as she took down one of the Barons that had destroyed Ballerina, leaving just five, but her jubilation at the kill was short lived and she was left cold when first Derek and then Penelope were taken down by the red triplane, Flamme.

She directed her fury at the man who might have killed her friends, but as she was turning to engage him the remaining four red monoplanes converged on her and she had to throw Wasp into frantic evasive manoeuvres.

With odds of four on one the Barons could afford to play it slow and while two of them engaged Gwen up close the other two got some distance and climbed, obviously intending to use the tactics that the Misfits had on them.

However, they had completely forgotten about the lone fighter remaining from B flight.

Kitty had been loitering overhead in the sun, watching the battle unfold, anxiously waiting for a chance to intervene that had never come. She had watched her fellows dive to their death and realised that a similar fate was waiting for her if she tried to do the same thing.

Now, though, with Gruber engaged, she could act almost with impunity.

She dived on the two Barons that were clawing for height, using her air brakes in order to give her more time on her targets, but, even so, she was going well in excess of four hundred miles per hour when they got in range.

A short burst from more than five hundred yards swatted the first aircraft from the sky, the tight grouping of guns underneath her nose permitting accuracy at such distances. She adjusted her aim to the second Baron, then opened fire at much closer range. A single loud shot came from each of the two cannon beneath her nose and her machine guns lasted a heartbeat more, but then silence fell. The second aircraft lurched, struck hard, and started a slow turn towards home, but Kitty barely saw it; she was too busy cursing the fact that she was out of ammunition.

Gwen saw the two fighters meet their ends and smiled as Kitty's colourful aircraft flashed past, but that smile disappeared when Kitty's voice sounded in her ears. It was totally devoid of the energy and enthusiasm that it usually had, instead it was dull with exhaustion and tinged with anger. 'I'm out of ammunition and down to one tenth tension. Sorry, Gwen, I have to head for home.'

'Don't worry, Kitty. Go. And remember you need to land at Hawkinge.'

Kitty swore, before laughing nervously. 'Thanks, I'd forgotten! See you there.'

There was a long pause, during which Gwen rolled out of a steep turn and onto her opposite wing, coming up behind one of the two remaining fighters.

'Gwen.'

'Yes, Kitty.'

'Give them hell.'

'Roger that.'

Gwen depressed her firing button and tracers leapt out towards the enemy aircraft, tearing it to shreds. It spun away and she looked for the last one, finding it almost a mile away and diving hard towards the clouds and safety.

'Oh no you don't.'

She swung Wasp to follow, but before she could dive her eyes were drawn inexorably to the last two machines sharing the sky with her, slightly below her less than a mile away and she watched in horror as they were joined momentarily by a delicate line of fire, which sent large chunks of yellow wing spinning lazily away.

Gwen didn't hesitate, she abandoned the fleeing Baron and turned towards the fight, pushing her throttle to the stop and praying that she wouldn't be too late.

Gruber savoured the moment, watching the hated enemy who had caused him so much shame, Abigail "Abby" Lennox, the "Abbess", struggling for control of her gaily-painted aircraft.

The aircraft that would soon be spread across the countryside below.

Countryside that would very soon belong to the Prussian Empire.

He had been promised land in England and a title to go with it and he amused himself with the thought of requesting the piece of land where his greatest enemy had fallen. Perhaps he would use bits of her aircraft to decorate his gardens and lift a monument to his prowess on the spot.

All tiredness was instantly banished from his body as adrenaline coursed through it and his hands curled eagerly around the yoke, his thumb sliding onto the red button embedded in the black leather, but before he could open fire, a flash of pink in the corner of his eye had him frantically thrusting the stick forwards, roaring in rage at being denied his kill.

The red triplane dived away just as she opened fire and she cursed as her shots flew harmlessly over the cockpit, even as she rejoiced at having saved Abby. She tried to adjust her aim, but it was impossible as Flamme turned sharply and passed underneath her.

She banked, passing within yards of the stricken Dragonfly, turning sharply to follow Gruber. He was obviously trying to get behind her, but there was no way she was going to let him and she pulled the stick back into her lap, putting firm pressure on the rudder to keep her from spiralling from the sky.

Gwen's vision narrowed, her eyes glued to her enemy, her world reduced to just her and Gruber as the two aircraft wheeled around each other on two sides of a tight circle. She had no need to look at her instruments, no need to search for the trimmer or the throttle; every minute adjustment she needed to do came naturally to her, the hours spent in the cockpit making her relationship with Wasp less that of a pilot and her machine and more akin to a symbiosis.

She matched Gruber's every attempt to influence the turn and saw his mouth drop open and his eyes widen when he realised that the two machines were almost completely evenly-matched. She had to laugh; the expression was exactly the one that he used every time on the big screen when he was about to be shot down by the good guy, or had just had his advances refused by the heroine.

She saw his eyes go to his instrument panel and knew exactly what he was looking at - home for him was across a strip of water that looked so narrow from this height, but was miles and miles wide and had already swallowed many pilots, both British and Prussian. - he needed a fair amount of tension to make that trip safely, especially if he had to do it at top speed. Safety for her, on the other hand, was any field she could find, or, failing that, an open cockpit and an easy jump - she could afford to use every single last Newton per yard of tension in her spring.

His eyes flicked to the clouds and she smiled grimly at the confirmation that he was running low on tension. She could almost see the calculations taking place in his head as he worked out how much more time he could afford to spend trying to outsmart his opponent, whether it was worth staying and hoping that she made a mistake, or whether he should immediately make a break for it and run for home, keeping any spare tension he had in case something unexpected happened.

Gwen wondered whether the Prussian was one to take a risk or if he would play it safe. Everything Abby had told her about the man pointed towards him not putting his own life at risk unnecessarily, but he might still surprise her...

He didn't.

Almost as soon as Gwen had finished the thought, Gruber reversed his rudder and stood Flamme on its nose, streaking straight for the clouds that had been slowly thickening below them as the minutes had gone by. She had been expecting the move and followed him immediately, plummeting out of the sky with him less than a hundred feet behind.

Gruber had seen her react and obviously knew that he wasn't far enough away from her to dive in a straight line - that would be tantamount to handing her his life - so he went into a defensive spiral, making it incredibly hard for her to target him. The G forces must have been immense, but the man kept it up, spinning and lurching from side to side unpredictably, preventing Gwen from getting her sights on him.

With every passing second they were getting closer and closer to the cloud cover and finally she realised she couldn't wait for a clean shot, she had no choice but to take a chance.

She pressed her thumb on the firing button and kept it there, praying that her ammunition wouldn't run out before she hit him.

For a couple of seconds Flamme seemed to wheel around the deadly stream of metal, going around and under it as Gwen gave her rudder small touches to try to follow him, but then, unbelievably almost, the aircraft passed through it.

Bullets from Gwen's cannon ripped through all three of Gruber's wings on his left side, opening huge holes in the metal covering them and drastically reducing their capacity to create lift. Flamme's spiral intensified, going from a brilliantly controlled manoeuvre to an out of control tumble in an instant before turning into a deadly flat spin and Gwen saw Gruber's head bang against the side of his cockpit as the G forces on the aircraft grew to a level that it was impossible for a human body to withstand.

'Come on, get out, get out...'

Gwen found herself almost pleading with the man and realised that after everything she still didn't want to watch him die. All of the other Fleas she had shot down had been faceless men, complete unknowns, and she had almost been able to imagine that she was just destroying their machines, but Gruber was different; he was too well-known to her. He had been a friend, a hero, a gallant enemy, a role model. Someone to aspire to being. Someone to fall in love with.

Yes, she hated the leader of the Crimson Barons because he'd killed many of her countrymen in the past months and possibly some of her friends that day, but she still found it hard to see Hans Gruber as her enemy.

'Jump, damn you, jump!'

The clouds were coming up fast and Gwen glanced nervously at her altimeter. The dogfight had started at around twenty-five thousand feet and they now were less than six thousand feet above the ground - they had fallen more than three miles in a very short time and Gruber was running out of air to fly in.

She watched Gruber as he strained against the G forces and was amazed to see that, instead of reaching up to release his canopy, he was struggling with his controls. She could hardly believe that he was even conscious, yet, unbelievably, he was succeeding and Flamme's spin was starting to slow.

Five thousand feet.

The red triplane plunged into the clouds. They were fairly sparse still and Gwen had no trouble following it, circling around it, throttle all the way back and air brakes out. She watched as Gruber almost brought the spin under control, but then lost it again as his damaged wings rebelled.

Four thousand feet.

Three thousand feet and the aircraft burst from the clouds, the green fields of Kent coming into stark focus, so close below them. They were only a couple of miles from the coastline and Gwen took a split second to glance around to get her bearings, finding the fortress of Dover to one side and the shipping at Folkestone to the other - they were only a few miles from Hawkinge.

Two thousand feet.

Gwen pursed her lips; Gruber was now at the very limit of the altitude at which he could safely jump, but still he was fighting with his controls.

One thousand feet.

Flamme came level, lurched, then came level again, slipping and sliding around the sky until Gruber managed to trim her to some semblance of normality, scarcely two hundred feet above the ground.

Gwen fell in beside him and looked across the gap between them. If his fans could see him now they would barely be able to recognise him - blood was streaming from Gruber's nose and there was a smear of blood on the glass where his head had hit the canopy, his face was swollen and his eyes were red and filled with burst blood vessels from the extreme G forces.

He was being kept very busy by his aircraft; trimming wheels would never be enough to counteract the damage it had taken, so it took him a while to notice she was there, but eventually he turned his head towards her and smiled, his famous movie star smile somewhat spoiled by the blood on his teeth and lips.

Gwen returned the smile, then gave him a loose salute. He gave her a nod in return, not able to take his hands off of his controls, then looked back to the front to continue his struggle with Flamme as Gwen throttled back to pull Wasp in behind him.

EPILOGUE

'You let him go?!?'

A stunned silence filled the conference room in Buckingham Palace as all eyes turned from Abby, who had just finished giving a detailed report of the battle with the Barons, to Gwen.

She nodded. 'Yes, sir. I escorted him as far as the coast and then turned back.'

'You... you...'

Sir Douglas sputtered, lost for words, but Scarlet neatly removed the need for him to find them, leaning over from her seat next to him and laying her hand on his arm. 'Don't be such a bore, Dougy dear, you know what she did was the right thing, the decent thing, dare I say it the *British* thing to do. Isn't that right, Your Maj?'

King George had been following the conversation gravely from his place at the head of the table, stroking his beard with a frown, but he grinned at Scarlet's question and winked at her. 'Indubitably, my dear Scarlet. Indubitably.'

There had been a pleasant surprise waiting for Gwen when she landed at Hawkinge after escorting Gruber a short way out to sea, a bright spark of hope in the darkest day in the squadron's history - as she taxied towards the standby point, she spotted not only a squadron of Spitsteams parked there, but also several Misfit aircraft. They were definitely worse for wear, but they were there, which meant the pilots were alive.

She parked Wasp on the end of the line of aircraft next to a battered Spitsteam and switched off, then reached out to take the photo off the instrument panel. 'Sorry, darling.' She put the picture in her pocket, then pulled back her canopy, taking a moment to savour the warm late-summer breeze on her face before climbing out to greet her friends, who were crowding around, looking up at her in expectation.

Not only was Kitty there, but so were Abby, Derek, Scarlet and Wendy and they crowded around her as she slid to the ground on tired legs, bombarding her with questions - they had seen her fly by with Gruber, seemingly in formation with him, and were dying to know what had happened.

She told them, but skipped many of the details because she was desperate to find out what had happened to everyone else in the squadron.

Scarlet had been at Badger base when the air raid warning had come. She had gotten Hummingbird off the ground just before the bombs had started to fall and assured them that the people on the base had had plenty of time to get into the underground shelters the base was equipped with. She had hid in the trees a few miles away and then after the raid had gone she had done a flyby to check out the damage. She reported that the hangar had taken several direct hits, the airstrip was a mess and several of the other buildings were in flames, but that the airmen and women were already making repairs. The barracks buildings were almost completely untouched, as were Wendy's workshop in the woods and the barracks hall and to everybody's relief she also reported that the mess and the beer supply were intact.

Abby had struggled with Dragonfly the whole way, but managed to land safely - "a piece of cake" she told a sceptical Gwen with a shrug - and her aircraft would only require minor repairs.

Swift's tail had all but gone, but somehow Derek had managed to land her safely and, like Dragonfly, the aircraft would fly again soon.

Ballerina's top wing had been completely ripped off, knocking off about a foot of vertical stabiliser and the rudder in passing, but Monty had still managed to find Hawkinge and crash land on the grass. The aircraft had been badly damaged, but was probably salvageable and had been put with Dreadnought, which was disassembled and sitting in a hangar next to the airstrip. Monty had broken his left arm in the rough landing and was in the medical building having it set and plastered as they spoke.

They had news of the other pilots as well - Owen had tracked each Misfit as they had been forced from the fight and Abby had already been to Hawkinge's communications shed to speak to him. He was still up in the sky with Chalky, watching what was left of the Prussian raids as they crossed back over the channel.

Bruce had crash landed Devil in a field near Rochester and was waiting there for fitters from Badger Base to pick him up.

Mac had managed to get out of Swordfish and had used his glidewings to get all the way to the outskirts of Maidstone where he had walked into a pub, ordered a pint, then promptly been arrested because they couldn't understand his thick Scottish accent and thought he was a Prussian.

There was no sign of Penelope, though, and it was a nervous hour, spent hanging around the communications shed and pestering the operators, before they got a phone call from a hospital in Folkestone telling them that she was there, in critical condition but alive.

Cheetah had come apart around her and, still strapped to her seat, she had been thrown from the cockpit as it had disintegrated around her, unconscious from a blow to the head, with two machine gun rounds in her left thigh and a jagged piece of shrapnel sticking completely through her left forearm. She had regained some semblance of consciousness only a few thousand feet above the ground, after having tumbling head over heels for a couple of miles and barely managed to gain enough awareness of what was going on to struggle out of her straps and deploy her glidewings before hitting the ground hard, breaking her other leg. Thankfully, she had come down close to a village and everybody had been in the streets watching the fight taking place overhead. They had put her in the back of the local policeman's car and rushed her to the hospital. Her tight G suit had apparently saved her life, keeping pressure on her wounds and stopping her from bleeding too much before they were able to transfuse her.

When the news about Penelope came in, the Misfits were finally able to relax and when Owen and Chalky landed half an hour later they found them in the bar, released from duty and making a heavy dent in the RAC base's supplies.

Because of the cloud cover rolling in from the continent there had been no further raids that day, except for one much smaller one on the Spitsteam factory at Southampton which had been beaten off by regular RAC fighters. There were no enemy raids in the offing the next day either and no sorties to fly, which was just as well because the squadron only had two functioning fighters left to put in the air - Wasp, with minor damage, and a completely untouched Hawk.

There were fairly strong rumours flying around that they were going to be supplied with stock Spitsteams or Harridans, but when reconnaissance flights over France and Belgium showed the invasion forces packing up and streaming away from their coastal stations, heading east and south, that idea was apparently discarded and word came in the afternoon that Misfit Squadron were officially grounded until their machines could be repaired. Shortly after that another message arrived, but this one summoned them to Buckingham Palace the next day for an audience with the King.

They travelled up to London by train in the morning and were reunited with Mac and Bruce at The Dorchester. The two men had gotten to the city the night before and after check in had proceeded directly to a nearby pub, where they had attracted a lot of attention to themselves and had been bought dozens of drinks by civilians eager to hear their stories. They had apparently returned to the hotel around midnight and promptly vomited copiously on the steps. When she arrived, Abby was quietly taken to one side by the manager and told that any favours that were owed to her had been fully cashed in and that after their stay the Misfits were to be relegated to the ranks of paying customers.

The Misfits spent a couple of hours relaxing in the two suites that Abby had still managed to get the hotel to part with for the night, before putting on their dress uniforms and making their way down to where two enormous black Rentley-Joyce autocars were waiting to take them to Buckingham Palace.

The meeting at the Palace was very different from the dinner to which the three junior Misfits had been invited; it took place in a conference room and because it involved matters of the utmost military import the only people present were the Misfits, the heads of the armed forces, the cabinet ministers and the King himself.

After Scarlet had so adeptly calmed Sir Douglas' indignation and forestalled all thoughts of punishment for Gwen's chivalric, but perhaps misguided actions, the atmosphere became rather more relaxed and the King quickly brought the meeting to a close and led them into the salon next door where a buffet was waiting for them along with Princess Elizabeth and a few dozen courtiers.

The Misfits were immediately drawn into conversation and the ministers especially were curious about the pilots that had become such heroes to the nation in such a short time.

Despite having the King's approval of her decision to let Gruber go, Gwen was avoided by the people who had been in the meeting and instead was approached by a couple of the courtiers. The two men turned out to be Mr Rentley and Mr Joyce, the spring and autocar manufacturers, and she ended up getting more information from them about advances in spring technology than they did from her about the Misfits and their activities.

In a short break in the conversation, while the three of them got refreshments from the buffet, Gwen noticed Kitty leaving the room with Princess Elizabeth. They were probably going to visit her workshop, most likely to continue the discussion they had started about electricity and electrical weapons the night of the party. Gwen knew she should have felt slightly hurt that the two were going off without her, after all the invitation to the Royal Laboratories had been for both of them, but she found that she wasn't at all; not only did the Princess's interests more closely align with the American's, but Gwen had been avoiding any chance of being alone with Kitty. She had yet to speak with the young woman about the night of the party and still didn't quite know what exactly she was going to say, especially since she had removed the attachment for her husband's photo from her instrument panel and decided to move on with her life.

That was a worry for another day, though, because right then the King was walking towards her, his eyes fixed firmly on her and she couldn't afford to be distracted in the face of her monarch.

'I have something for you, Aerial Officer.' The King held out his hand and the Marshal of the Court, standing by at the ready as always, handed him a tightly rolled piece of paper tied with a red ribbon and sealed with red wax. 'Your pardon, as promised.'

'Thank you, sir.' Gwen took it from him and a huge weight she hadn't even been aware she was carrying was lifted from her shoulders.

'I predict great things for you, Gwen, and you don't need something silly like that hanging over your head; there are too many people in this world who would set more store by that conviction than they would your countless merits and achievements. So, with the permission of Sir Douglas and the blessing of sky commodore Campbell as the accusing officer, I have had the incident expunged from your records The commodore sends her apologies by the way and asked me to tell you that she hated the fact that she had no choice in the matter. She is glad that you have landed firmly on your feet, though, as are we all!'

King George gave her a wink, then beckoned for Abby to join them.

'Damn good showing, Dame Lennox, damn good.' The King pronounced.

Abby gave him a small bow. 'Thank you, sir.'

'I want Misfit Squadron back in the air as soon as possible. If there is anything you need, name it and I will make sure you get it.'

Abby inclined her head at Gwen. 'I already have exactly what I need, sir.'

'Good, good!' The King gave them each a smile and a nod before moving off to fulfil his duty to make sure that everybody in his presence had at least a modicum of his time.

The pilots watched him go, then Abby turned to Gwen. 'Looks like you're going to be working on our aircraft a lot sooner than I thought and with your expertise next time we'll *really* show the Barons what for!'

Gwen smiled. 'I can't wait.'

ABOUT THE AUTHOR

Simon Brading's interest in aviation began when he was very young and at thirteen he joined the RAF section of the Combined Cadet Forces of Dulwich College with the aim of becoming a pilot. However, when he was 18, had reached the rank of Flight Sergeant in the CCF and was trying to get into a University Air Squadron, he was told that his eyesight wasn't good enough to be a pilot, so he had to move onto plan B... something else.

He tried his hand at many things before it occurred to him that he might have a few stories to tell. He never lost his interest in flight, though, and hopes to add a PPL to his very basic and probably extremely expired glider license.

www.simonbrading.co.uk

For news of special offers, upcoming releases, exclusive content, competitions and events, please follow me on social media.

Instagram - @sibrading
Facebook - Simon Brading Author
Tiktok - @SimonBradingAuthor

In addition, souvenirs and merchandise, including T-shirts, badges, stickers and more, are available from the Misfit Squadron store on REDBUBBLE at -
https://www.redbubble.com/people/misfitsquadron/shop

ALSO BY SIMON BRADING

The "Displacers" series - a young adult time travel adventure series for all ages.
The Pirate's Heir
The Secret of the Ancients
The Whitechapel Plot
The Price of Greed
The Time for Vengeance

The "Misfit Squadron" Series - a Steampunk series set in an alternate World War 2.
The Battle Over Britain
The Russian Resistance
A Misfit Midwinter
The Lion and the Baron
The Maltese Defence
Tales from the Second Great War
The Siege of Gibraltar
The King's Mission
The Home Front
Taking to the Skies
The Invasion of Britain

The "Twin Ambitions" series - ballet books for children ages 7 and up.
Fight to Dance
Back to Basics

The "Ni Hon - The Two Books" Series - a young adult series set in a dystopian future Japan.
The Black Book

Others
Public Enemy
Empath
The Lifeboat at the End of the Universe

Printed in Dunstable, United Kingdom